A SYMPHONY OF RIVALS

A NOVEL

ROMA CALATAYUD-STOCKS

CALUMET EDITIONS
Minneapolis

Praise for *A Song in My Heart*

"Calatayud-Stocks' debut is a historical novel set to music. The story is compelling that this novel deserves to find a larger audience. The author intends this to be the first in a trilogy, and she has created enough momentum to build on. An auspicious debut."

KIRKUS REVIEWS

"Ms Calatayud-Stocks' writing style is a "You Are There" approach that is intensely personalized. The author's unique approach to telling this story is demonstrated by her composing and recording music that exemplifies the moods of different story segments as they unfold. In all, this was a highly unusual and well-done project that marries the written word with the musical words. We rated it five hearts (5 Stars)."

HEARTLAND REVIEWS – Bob Spear

"An extraordinary fusion of music and literature. Through her novel, Calatayud-Stocks establishes herself as a first-rate storyteller, showcasing her equal talents for both writing and music through the story of Alejandra Stanford. Calatayud-Stocks deftly interweaves the themes of music, art, romance, passion, and history. *A Song in My Heart*, which is the first book in a trilogy, leaves readers anxious for the next installment, *A Symphony of Rivals*, which will resume the story in Berlin, Germany in 1933."

BOOK REVIEWER LIST

"*A Song In My Heart* is a delightful reading. I enjoyed it immensely. The novel flows softly and rhythmically. Roma did a wonderful job in researching the history of music, the classic composers, Schumann, Bach, Liszt and Debussy. We love and suffer dawns and sunsets, war and peace, but it is always MUSIC in the novel that offers a safe port. Alejandra Stanford, the main character in the novel, shows us the sweetness of life but at the same time the strength, the power of seduction, the firmness of a decision. I will be awaiting *A Symphony of Rivals*."

ANA LUISA FAJER FLORES,
Consul General of Mexico in St. Paul, Minnesota

**CALUMET
EDITIONS**
Minneapolis

FIRST EDITION July 2018
A Symphony of Rivals
Copyright © 2018 by Roma Calatayud-Stocks

This is a work of fiction. All of the characters, names, incidents, organizations, and dialogue are either the products of the author's imagination or are used fictiously.

Printed in the United States of America.
10 9 8 7 6 5 4 3 2 1

ISBN: 978-0-9987319-3-3

Cover design by Gary Lindberg and John Currie
Book Design by Gary Lindberg

To Beatrice, Thomas, Anissa and Chris

"Music is the one incorporeal entrance into the higher world of knowledge which comprehends mankind but which mankind cannot comprehend."

Ludwig van Beethoven

Also by Roma Calatayud-Stocks

A Song In My Heart

A SYMPHONY OF RIVALS

A NOVEL

ROMA CALATAYUD-STOCKS

AUTHOR'S NOTE

The musical selections chosen throughout the narrative highlight the characters' emotional and creative expressions. A comprehensive list of the music and the composers are available in the Appendix. If you wish to listen to the compositions which correspond to the chapter titles in the book, visit www.RomaStocks.com/music/.

PART
ONE

RONDO ALLA TURCA

February 19, 1933

Alejandra Morrison leaned against her husband, Richard, in the back seat of a black Mercedes-Benz as the chauffeur drove through the Unter den Linden, the main boulevard in central Berlin. It was her first time visiting a country shrouded in stories told by her German-born grandmother, who spoke longingly of ancestors that lived in beautiful towns from Bavaria to the Baltic. For Alejandra, Germany was the land of Bach, Beethoven, and Brahms—composers whose music commanded a constant beat in her daily awareness. She was finally there to realize a long-standing dream, considered by many of her family to be a nearly impossible feat for a woman. Their skepticism made her all the more determined to succeed. With growing expectation, she looked forward to the next seven days of her trip, hoping to extend it longer if luck were on her side.

She caught her breath at the sight of the grandly lit Staatsoper, the premier opera house where renowned conductors had made their mark. And a favorite opera was featured—Mozart's *The Magic Flute*. But as they passed other buildings, she noticed with distaste that the classical architecture was obstructed by flags that hung from rooftops, row upon row of them, bearing black swastikas on a red and white field, contrasting against the falling snow.

She recalled a recent newspaper editorial that stated that the equilateral cross at the center of the flag, an ancient Asian symbol to signify prosperity and noble existence, had been taken as the symbol of the *Nationalsozialistische Deutsche Arbeiterpartei*—the Nazis. In conversations with Richard,

Alejandra questioned how the new National Socialist government would differ from the former Weimar Republic. What was at the core of its ideology, and what would that mean for its citizens? After the horrors of the Great War and the severe depredation of the recent depression, would the Nazis bring an era of prosperity and security, as they claimed? Or was their formidable presence an ominous sign of worse things to come? Richard believed the latter, which was why he had been reluctant to visit Berlin. They had argued about it on numerous occasions. Alejandra had grown up exposed to differing political views, since her father had often engaged her in discussions of international affairs, but politics made her uncomfortable; it was a messy business, beyond the control of most citizens. From a young age, Alejandra had learned the profound effects that governmental policies had on people's lives, and this was of great concern to her. But she also hoped that the political affairs of a foreign country would not affect her plans.

As they approached the Adlon Hotel in Pariser Platz, she saw the city's most recognizable landmark—the two-hundred-year-old Brandenburg Gate—beautifully illuminated. The driver stopped in front of the hotel, which was flanked by lush, potted evergreens. He got out and opened the door for Alejandra. "*Vielen dank*," she said.

The old chauffeur assisted her as she stepped out onto the sidewalk. With great charm, he released her in front of the warm lights of the hotel entrance and said, "*Sie sprechen gutes Deutsch, Frau Morrison.*" She replied, "*Danke. Ich mussen* üben." Richard had warned her about conversing with strangers and hotel personnel, but she disagreed and was pleased that the language she had learned from her grandmother had stayed with her so well.

Against a chilly breeze, Alejandra covered her neck with a beige cashmere scarf and buttoned her camel-wool coat. Richard arrived at her side after paying the driver. A young bellboy greeted them and proceeded to assist with their luggage. Holding Richard's arm, Alejandra adjusted her hat and entered the hotel through its art deco doors. In the busy lobby, she noticed the décor—glass chandeliers fashioned with spring leaves and vines in the style of Tiffany lamps, orange and green floral wallpaper, and ochre-painted furniture with intricate geometric carvings. To her delight, she heard music playing in the distance. It was instantly recognizable to her as Mozart's "Rondo Alla Turca."

"Darling, I need a drink. You'll find me where the music is," Alejandra said. Richard slipped out of his long gray overcoat, folded it over his arm, and took off his fedora, revealing his wavy, light brown hair. Wearing pressed black slacks, a white shirt, a tweed sport coat, and derby shoes, he looked to Alejandra like the perfect gentleman. He kissed her and over his shoulder, as he headed to reception, said, "Now don't get kidnapped. You're way too pretty."

She laughed and walked away down a marble floored hallway. She liked the sound of her heels creating counterpoint against the lively melody emanating nearby. Then she came upon a smoke-filled salon, appointed with mural ceilings, fluted white columns, moldings, and a stone fireplace. She halted in the French doorway, pulled off her gloves, and placed them inside her handbag. Next to the musicians, she spotted an empty table where she sat down. A loud disturbance drew her attention. On the other side of where the trio was playing, several men, dressed in brown shirts, were yelling heatedly and nearly drowning out the music. Among them, a jagged-looking man with a gaunt face, narrow eyes, and a pencil mustache, dressed in a black uniform with a swastika armband, stood up upon seeing her. He then shouted to the musicians, "*Judenrein*, play the Horst Wessel song or I'll shut you for the night." Alejandra was appalled by his rudeness and thought his agitated gestures must be those of a madman. He turned toward her with a penetrating stare. She held his gaze defiantly for a few seconds, then, making sure he had registered her look of disgust, she looked away. Was this a common occurrence? And if not, where was the management to eject the crude men from the room? To her relief, another guest, an older man, asked the same Nazi officer to settle down, but he refused and continued to harass the trio.

In an attempt to ignore the jeering, she concentrated on the accomplished violinist who, like his fellow musicians, a pianist and a cellist, was dressed in an elegant gray suit and continued to perform with dignity. His playing flooded her with emotion. The extraordinary music was the reason for her visit, to interview for an intensive program in conducting and to visit the city's major conservatories. And in two days she would travel to Bonn, the birthplace of her beloved Beethoven. Since childhood, Beethoven's music had been at the center of her training, and by the age of twelve she could play all his thirty-two piano sonatas. The following year, she attended her first live concert and was so inspired by the symphonic music and the director, Emil Oberhoffer, standing on the podium, that she envisioned herself becoming a conductor. It was only later that she became aware of all the obstacles, being a woman in a field dominated by men.

Just then, the musicians finished playing Mozart's piece, and Alejandra congratulated their performance and requested a Schumann composition. The violinist smiled, tipping his head to her. Then she momentarily turned her gaze to the same Nazi officer who rose to his feet and started to walk toward her. With his determined gait and his dark eyes fixed upon her, she felt threatened by him and considered walking away, but stood her ground. She would stay for the musicians. With her head held high, she straightened her back and folded her hands on the table, ignoring his approach.

PIANO TRIO IN D MINOR, OP. 11

Richard came into the salon and noticed the uniformed man opposite Alejandra. He hurried there, moments before the man spoke to his wife. "Excuse me, have we met?" The stranger, caught off guard by Richard's sudden appearance, replied sternly, "Nein." He gave Alejandra a quick glance, turned to the musicians with a scornful look, and returned to his table. Richard placed his belongings on an empty chair and sat next to Alejandra, who was pulling her gloves back on. "We're leaving? Is it because of him?" She nodded and said, "But I want to stay until the musicians finish this piece. I'll explain later." Richard frowned at the rowdy Brownshirts.

For the remainder of the performance, Richard watched Alejandra listen to Clara Schumann's Piano Trio in D Minor, op. 11. Her natural beauty and graceful poise would catch the eye of any man. It was something that could make him feel proud and worried at the same time. Richard had met Alejandra as an adolescent, and from first sight he knew they would get married, although it would take years for her to accept his proposal. Alejandra was determined to finish her studies at the conservatory. Early on, he realized she was never one to be impressed by frivolities. She was a woman of keen intellect, integrity, and high aspirations.

When the music ended, Richard joined his wife in vigorous applause as did other guests in the salon, drowning out the rowdies. Alejandra said to the pianist, "*Das war wunderbah, vielen dank.*"

"*Wir freuen uns,*" the musician said.

At that point, Richard noticed the Nazi officer lighting a cigar and intensely observing them. He sensed the man wanted to provoke a confrontation and whispered in Alejandra's ear, "It's best to ignore him unless he becomes belligerent. From a distance, one might think he's Hitler's twin brother."

"I thought the same thing with those chilling eyes and slicked back undercut," she said. "But the man's looks are the least of my concerns." She related how the Nazi official and Brownshirts had slighted the musicians when she first came into the salon.

"I'm not surprised," he said. "I'm afraid that what you witnessed is just the tip of the iceberg. I'd have said something to that bigot. And if he does it again, I will."

"Yes, I wanted to," she said.

Richard continued. "I've been reading that the National Socialist Workers Party and their members don't have the best reputation, and that Hitler's policies may not be that much better."

"Oh, for the sake of the people, I hope you're wrong," she said. "I'm sure most of them don't share their views. Let's just go."

Richard, aware of the Nazi's eyes following them, led Alejandra out of the salon.

Ten minutes later, he was in their hotel room, on the first floor, seated in an upholstered armchair below a large window with open paisley draperies, reading *The London Times*. The suite, with wooden floors, a poster bed on the right, a fireplace on the left, and a desk on the side, was spacious but cold. Richard had ordered room service, and Alejandra was at the door when he glimpsed the attendant, a young man, who greeted them. He placed a tray on the desk containing a tea service and then started a fire.

Alejandra thanked the man and gave him a tip. He left the room. She poured herself a cup of English tea, and with the cup in her hand she walked to Richard. From there she could see the Brandenburg Gate. "Are you sure you don't want tea? It might help you to relax."

"No," he replied. "I'm just tired, and I haven't been sleeping."

"Oh? Insomnia again? I hope you'll have a better night," she said. "We have a big day tomorrow, and I'm so looking forward to seeing Hannah and Ben, and of course going to Bonn."

He sighed, thinking he had no interest in going to Bonn or anywhere but back home. "I know you are, but there's something about the attitude in this town that ruins it for me."

"We must remember why we're here. This city and country have incredible history and culture. It's part of my heritage, and I want to enjoy the time we have."

He placed the newspaper on the desk and got up from the chair, putting his hands on her shoulders. "You're right. I promise to behave myself and make the best of it. I know how much this trip means to you."

"I'd appreciate that, Richard, and hope you'll even begin to like it."

He chuckled. "That might be too much to ask."

N ear midnight, a sound of shattering glass woke Richard. He assumed it was the result of a gunshot since he heard more bangs in the distance. Alejandra, who was next to the window, also woke up. "Ah! My arm. What's happening?" A gust of cold wind entered through the opening. In the dark, Richard sprang out of bed, pulling Alejandra down to the floor. "It sounds like fighting out there. Are you hurt?"

"Yes," she replied. He felt her shivering.

The street echoed with shouting. "*Holen Sie sich in das Auto!*" The voice of another man screamed, "*Ubergeben Sie Ihre Waffen jetzt!*"

"I don't think it's safe to get up now. What are they saying?" Richard asked.

"They're being told to get in the car and to hand over their weapons," Alejandra replied.

The sound of gunshots ceased, and after hearing car doors shut, Richard got up and walked to the window, cutting the soles of his feet on glass fragments. "Damn!" he said. He guardedly looked into the street as the nondescript vehicles pulled away. "It must have been those crazy Brownshirts, but who knows?" He turned on the bedside light, accidentally knocking a fruit bowl and its contents to the floor. Alejandra's forearm was bleeding profusely. He grabbed a linen napkin from the tray and wrapped it tightly around her wound. He was grateful that the shards of glass had missed her body except for a triangular piece that had lacerated her lower right arm and a few smaller pieces that grazed her hand.

"This will need stitches immediately." With his feet bleeding, he slid into his loafers, picked up the newspaper from the desk, using it to brush away debris from the chair, and helped Alejandra into it. The blood had ruined her nightgown. "Please, get me clean clothes and my shoes," she said.

As he walked to the closet, he saw apples and oranges scattered amidst broken glass. He muttered, "Damn, I knew we shouldn't have come." He returned from the closet with a rose-colored dress and her saddle shoes, handing them to her. "I'm so sorry about this."

"I'm sure it's nothing serious," she said. "And your feet?"

"Just superficial cuts."

While she changed her clothes, Richard took off his pajamas and put on a pair of corduroy pants and a gray pullover and wiped his bloodied feet. When he finished putting on socks and shoes, someone knocked on their door. "Who's there?" he asked.

"*Der Intendant.* Is everyone all right?"

Richard walked to the door and cautiously opened it an inch until he confirmed it was the manager. "My wife needs medical care. Where's the nearest hospital? What the hell is going on?"

"My sincerest apologies, sir! Drunken policemen got into a scuffle and started shooting off their guns. We have a doctor on staff. Please come with me."

"Just a minute," Richard said, shutting the door.

He walked back to Alejandra, who was in the chair with regained composure but with a complexion paler than usual, such that when she tried to get up, feeling faint, she nearly collapsed. He eased her back on the seat. "What's wrong?"

"I'm not sure," she replied softly. "I just need a moment."

He waited as she stretched her neck in both directions and undid her chignon, letting her auburn hair fall loosely to her back. Then, slowly, she rose to her feet and walked with Richard to the door. He took her coat from a wrought iron stand, and as he draped it over her shoulders, she briefly touched the bullet hole in the wall with her index finger. "Thank God we're all right."

Richard, who was doing his best to control his temper, said, "But maybe not next time."

Soon after, they were in the brightly lit infirmary of the hotel, waiting for the doctor. With only a twin bed set against the wall and a small upper window, the room's sterile accommodations contrasted poorly with the rest of the hotel's opulent décor. As Alejandra sat on the bed, Richard remarked that while she maintained her usual serenity as though nothing had happened, he was filled with apprehension, recalling that two years before she had almost died of a rare illness.

"You mustn't think about that. It was probably the accident that affected me. But I'm physically fine, and there has been no sign of any recurrence, so please don't worry," she said.

"It was no accident but the negligence of drunks. But you can under-

8

stand why I've become rather protective of you since your illness, especially since you hate to show weakness and rarely express your emotions. Would you like to talk about what just happened?"

"No, and if I don't express as much as you'd like me to it's because I don't want to worry you unnecessarily," she said. "I admit it was frightening, but it's over. The only thing I'm worried about is the injury to my arm."

"A man does like to be needed, you know."

"I assure you... I do need you." She extended her left hand to his.

Just then the doctor entered the room. "Frau Morrison, how are you feeling?"

"I've been better."

Richard looked at the blond-haired, blue-eyed man, who seemed to be of similar age... in his mid-thirties. His name, Hanz Hedwig Schultz, was stitched above the pocket of his white coat. Dr. Schultz proceeded to check Alejandra's pulse and other vital signs. Then he unwrapped the blood-soaked napkin from her arm and tossed it into a wastebasket. He then peered closely at the wound for a few seconds before he walked to a glass cabinet and took a syringe, iodine, needle, and bandages, and placed them on a table covered with a white cloth. "I'm sorry for what must have been a traumatic experience." He pulled up a chair from the side of the room. "It was," she said.

"Would you like a sedative before we proceed?" She shook her head, no. He cleaned her wound with alcohol and stitched the cut with a fine needle. Alejandra grimaced and bit her lip. Haltingly, she said, "It's more painful than I thought."

"It won't be much longer," the physician said. "And you're fortunate it wasn't much deeper, or it might have cut the tendon."

"That's a relief," she said, sighing.

When Dr. Schultz finished, he carefully bandaged her arm and asked, "Would you like something for the pain and to help you sleep?"

"That won't be necessary," she said.

"I'd like to see you on Monday to remove the stiches," the doctor said.

"We won't be here on Monday," Richard said. "So, if possible on Sunday."

"Anything you need, call me. I'm sure the rest of your trip will go better," Dr. Schultz said.

"I know it will. Thank you, doctor," she said as they left the infirmary.

It was well past midnight when they returned to their new accommodations. The manager had switched their belongings to a more spacious suite on the same floor. Richard removed her coat and tossed it onto a chair. "Can I get you anything?"

"A bath might be calming," she said, stepping into the washroom and turning on the lights.

"Would my lady like me to draw the bath for her?"

"If you wish, my lord. That would be very kind. It's good to see you more relaxed."

He turned on the faucets, and she took a blue flask of lavender oil from a shelf and sprinkled several drops into the water.

"That's terribly strong," he said, turning to her as she breathed in its fragrant aroma.

"I like it. It's better than the medicinal smell I've brought back from the infirmary."

He then helped her to undress.

"Oh my, I never knew you could be such a good valet," she said.

"I'd do anything for you. Be careful with that arm."

"I'm not that feeble," she said, sliding into the hot water. "Would you like to join me?"

"I might get other ideas." He gathered Alejandra's clothes, placing them on a shelf below a stack of towels. "Your arm will be sore for some time."

She stretched out her arm, wiggling her fingers. "You see, they're in perfect working condition, and I'm so thankful for that."

He took her hand and kissed it. "Indeed. I don't know what you'd do if you couldn't play your precious piano. That might be the only thing to push you over the edge."

"I think I'd rather forget what happened, so if you don't mind, let's talk about something else. We should call the children tomorrow. I've been thinking about them all day. I miss them."

Richard sat on a bench opposite the bathtub and with a bit of sarcasm said, "How is it so easy for you to wash away the unpleasantness of the last hours?"

"One of us has to keep things calm. What good would it do to rehash that?"

"I guess. But will you even mention what happened tonight?" he asked.

"I don't think so. Our kids are too young. I'd rather tell them about Amalfi. For who can forget that ancient town by the sea? Those idyllic images are still vivid in my mind."

"Oh? And what images might those be?"

"Sun-drenched days and moonlit nights. Not those that you're thinking." She laughed.

"Always the artist. You sound too poetic for someone who just nearly got shot."

"That's the point. We were there only yesterday."

"Yes, celebrating our tenth wedding anniversary, and now we're in this frigid cold."

"Darling, please, I'm certain tomorrow will be a splendid day," Alejandra said.

Richard felt aroused as she rested her head on a towel atop the bathtub, her body tilted toward him. Her breasts surfaced slightly above the water like lilies on a pond, and her left leg was bent at an angle. But it was her optimism that was perhaps her most appealing character trait. She always knew just what to say to bring him out of his gloominess. "Seeing that you're in better spirits, I'll leave you alone to enjoy. A drink will help me to relax." He rose to his feet and left.

In the bedroom, from atop the dresser, he took the bottle and poured himself a glass of whiskey. While he drank the smoky liquor, he thought about the events of the evening. It was not as easy for him to just let go. First the vile Nazi officer, then the violent episode in the room, and the day after tomorrow they were expected to go on a long trip. And if all that wasn't enough, there were her plans to audition for a conducting program, which he strongly opposed. In the morning, he would tell her they would not be going to Bonn as planned. As a physician himself, he worried her wound could get infected, and he sure as hell did not want any more unpleasant situations, or to run into other unsavory characters. No optimism in the world could abate their presence and malice. She would be greatly disappointed.

VARIATIONS ON A THEME OF PAGANINI

Hannah Adelman, a dark-haired woman with an olive complexion, brown eyes, and a petite figure had just finished putting on her burgundy, floral-patterned dress. She scanned the bedroom of her rented home for her suede shoes, which she soon spotted below a nightstand next to a silver-plated cufflink laying on the floor. She put on the shoes, picked up the cufflink, and placed it inside her jewelry box on the dresser. Then, she took her favorite gold bracelet, clamping it around her wrist. It was a gift from her father who gave it to her on the day of her Bat Mitzvah. As one of a kind, the flex-fit 14k Mendes & Sons bracelet had a little inscription—*To my daughter with love.*

For generations, the gold and silversmith business, established in New York by her father's family, had been successful, but the collapse of the American stock market in 1929 had substantially contracted the trade. As the Depression continued to intensify, Hannah, who was well versed in art history and had the expert eye of an art connoisseur, turned to art dealing to maintain the family's economic status. While not wealthy herself, she had grown up in upper-middle-class comfort. Known as quick witted, action oriented, and with excellent social skills, Hannah embraced her new role, acquainting herself with the profession, art gallery owners, and with many once wealthy art collectors who were selling their art at exceptional prices. After four years of robust buying and selling of Dutch masterpieces and often traveling to the art capitals of Europe, she had managed to specialize in Rembrandts. Portraits by the Dutch master represented the largest share in American owned collections.

Hannah was in Berlin with her husband, Benjamin, who was training to be a conductor at the Stern Conservatory. She was also there to attend several auctions. Since the 1920s, Berlin had been the epicenter of a vibrant international market trade known as Reichshauptstadt, with several high-caliber galleries and auction houses. The next day, she would attend an auction hoping to acquire a baroque masterpiece for one of her most loyal customers who had prospered in real estate investments despite the economic downturn.

From a side table, she took one of the art catalogs, and as she paged through it for several potential buys, Ben, wearing a brown suit, came into the room. Adjusting his tie before a full-length mirror, he asked, "Anything worthwhile?"

"Can my client afford it? That might be the better question," she said. Then, from the jewelry box, she retrieved a cufflink. "Is this what you were looking for earlier?"

"Yes!" he said, taking it from her hand. "This time, I thought I had lost it for good." Ben took it and placed it inside the pocket of his pants.

Hannah thought Ben was usually distracted by trivial matters, but when it came to his profession, he was a perfectionist. They had met at the Institute of Musical Art, later known as Juilliard, on her first day of class. What impressed her the most on that day was his willingness to assist new students. She discovered he was one of the few men she had met who showed interest in advancing women's musical careers, especially hers. He founded the Regatta Quartet, and two of the musicians were female, including herself. But they often clashed over matters about the interpretation of the music, so for that and other reasons she had quit the music profession.

The telephone rang.

"I'll get it," he said, walking away.

Hannah overheard the conversation from the bedroom, and she became concerned by Ben's apprehension, apparent as he spoke on the phone. She stepped out into the hallway when he finished the call. "Alejandra was injured," he said.

"How is that possible? They just got here last night."

"The window in their room was shattered by a gunshot while they were sleeping. Fortunately, the bullet missed Alejandra, but her arm was cut."

"Oh, my goodness. Is it serious? And who would do that?"

"Does that surprise you, when there are so many radicals roaming around? It isn't too serious, although she needed stitches," Ben said.

"She was so excited about coming here. I hope it doesn't change her plans," Hannah said. "I'm eager to see her this afternoon. It's been almost two years since we last met."

Hannah and Alejandra had been friends since they met on a cruise ship in 1920, both just out of high school. The year after, they studied together at Juilliard, and Alejandra lived with Hannah's family for a semester. Through the years, they had developed a close relationship, more like sisters, despite the fact that they lived more than thirteen hundred miles apart in the United States.

At four o'clock in the afternoon, Hannah and Ben arrived at the Adlon Hotel's art deco-appointed restaurant where several people waited for the hostess, and she quickly spotted her friends at a corner table by the entrance. Alejandra wore a beige skirt and white blouse, with a black wool cardigan, and Richard wore brown pants and a blue V-neck sweater.

"It's so good to see you!" Hannah said, embracing Alejandra. "How do you feel?"

"Better. I'm thrilled to see you both," Alejandra said.

Hannah gave her coat to Ben who went to the cloakroom. Then she joined them at the table and said, "I still can't believe what happened to you last night."

"This is not how I imagined my first day in Berlin. But it could have been worse."

"It must have been terrifying, and you're so calm about it," Hannah said.

"You know my wife is always the perfect lady, no dramatic outbursts," Richard said.

The waiter brought platters of bite-size sandwiches, a variety of pastries, and a pot of black tea, along with saucers and cups. Alejandra poured the tea.

"I'd be crying and screaming," Hannah said, as she stirred sugar and cream into her cup. "Oh, and that strudel looks to die for. I hope you don't mind if I start. I'm starving." She cut a piece of the pastry and put it on her plate.

Ben joined them, sitting down. "Thank goodness last night's episode wasn't more serious." He lowered his voice and removed his round glasses. "I have to admit nothing comes as a shock anymore. We knew things might be a little strained when we arrived last fall, but since Hitler and his government took power two weeks ago, there seems to be an increase in random violence against civilians."

"Why don't you leave?" Richard said. "I've been here one day, and I already hate it."

"It's not like that everywhere, and our local friends are just as outraged and believe the situation is temporary," Ben said. "I'd like to finish my training. That aspect has been terrific."

"Richard, you can't associate everyone with the government. The staff and the doctor have been superb," Alejandra said. "Ben, I'm excited to hear about my audition."

Richard interrupted. "Yes. That's true, but I'm just repulsed by last night's experience. It's not about the people but those running the country. I can't wait to leave."

"We need to make the best of it," Alejandra insisted.

Ben turned to Alejandra. "To answer your question, the director received your application. Your interview with him, and the tour of the conservatory, is on Friday. He'll give you an overview of the course in conducting. What will you be performing?"

"Liszt's Second Hungarian Rhapsody, Rachmaninov's Prelude in G minor, and another piece of his choice. I plan to practice at the conservatory on Thursday," Alejandra said.

Richard sighed.

"It's important to me! If not now, when?" Alejandra said.

"Ále, I think you should also do Brahms' Variations on a Theme of Paganini that will show off your technical abilities," Hannah suggested. "Isn't that the one you played for the audition at Juilliard?"

"Yes, it's a very emotional piece," Alejandra said. "Perhaps it will bring me luck."

"You might need it. Auditioning for the program is very competitive," Ben added. "With the injury, can you even perform?"

"It will be sore, but it didn't affect any tendons," Alejandra said. "That would have been a disaster if I couldn't audition for the program. I've been waiting for this chance for ten years."

"Yes. I can still remember the day you told me you were getting married instead of continuing with your studies," Hannah said. "So, you see, here is a second opportunity."

"Has the last ten years with me been bad?" Richard asked.

"Darling, of course not. I'm happy with my choice, but that doesn't mean I have to stop dreaming of other things," Alejandra said, patting his hand.

"How about a concert tonight? There's one at the synagogue," Hannah said. "The architecture itself is worth seeing as it resembles the Alhambra with its stunning Moorish design. Einstein performed there in the past. They say he enjoys playing for relaxation, as I do now."

"Although, I don't think he'll ever perform there again. Rumors are that he has left Germany for good. Many brilliant minds like him are also moving away," Ben said.

"You see. I'm not the only one who feels that way," Richard said.

Alejandra turned to Hannah. "I'd love to go there, although perhaps another night. But when did you decide to stop playing professionally? I always envisioned you in an orchestra. You have a gift. It's a shame."

"I quit last summer. I'm also busy with the business," Hannah said.

"I hope someday she'll change her mind," Ben said.

"Absolutely not!" Hannah exclaimed. "There's nothing that could make me ever want to play professionally again."

"Did I touch on a sore point?" Alejandra asked.

"Yes! Ask Ben," Hannah said.

"I prefer not to discuss it. I can't win," Ben said.

Richard smirked. "Did you ever think you could?"

"Are you going to Bonn tomorrow?" Hannah asked.

"Regrettably, not," Alejandra replied.

An uncomfortable silence fell between the couples until Hannah broke the ice, saying, "Then you must come to the auction. I'm hoping to acquire a Rembrandt. And there will also be works by Picasso, Beckmann, and Dada."

"Dada?" Richard remarked. "What kind of name is that, and how about Mama?"

Hannah laughed. "It's an avant-garde movement. Artists were protesting against nationalism, materialism, irrationalism, you name it, all contributing to the foolish Great War."

"It was a foolish war where millions died," Richard said. "All because of the assassination of one man and his wife."

"It was a little more complicated than that, Richard," Alejandra said. "And you know, I'm not keen on discussing politics. And what about the art?"

"It's a bit shocking, with obscenity and odd humor. You probably wouldn't like it," Hannah replied.

"Where's the line between staying true to art versus creating art to make political statements at the cost of aesthetics?" Alejandra asked.

"That's a good question, but we can't escape it. Many artists use it as a tool to advocate their views, and many patrons themselves use it to their benefit," Hannah replied.

"I'm always concerned about mixing art with politics," Alejandra said. "I've never seen it lead to any good."

"I get your point, but art is always political at some level. But if I may switch subjects, how was Italy?" Ben asked.

"Fantastic," Richard replied. "Now *that's* the place for unpolluted art."

"Well, yes and no. Have you forgotten Pompeii's exhibit where it was forbidden for women to enter the gallery?" Alejandra remarked.

With a grin, Richard said, "How could I forget? I'd much prefer to see erotic art than art about human tragedy."

"Forbidden exhibition, ha?" Ben said. "I need more details."

"Well, before you men discuss your erotic fantasies, Hannah and I will go up to the room. I have a gift for you from Naples," Alejandra said, getting up from her chair. "I'll see you tomorrow. Ben, I want to hear your impressions about conducting."

"I feel that with your excellent ear and analytical skills, you'll impress the director, and you'd be outstanding as a conductor," Ben said. "I still remember our days with the Regatta Quartet. You are someone who puts everything into her art."

"Thank you for that unwavering confidence in me," Alejandra said, placing her left hand on Richard's shoulder. "God knows what I'd give to be in that profession, but as a wife and a mother it would be a challenge for everyone, but it's possible. Don't you agree, darling?"

Richard cleared his throat, looking up at her. "I admit, it's not something of interest to me for obvious reasons. But even if such a goal seems like a long shot, you'll audition for the program. Perhaps then, if you're accepted, I may reconsider."

"You'll come around, won't you?" Hannah asked Richard.

"What chance do I have with you and Ben on her side?"

"That's the idea," Hannah said, rising to her feet. "Ben, I'll see you in the lobby in thirty minutes, and don't forget my coat."

Hannah linked her arm to Alejandra's as they walked out of the restaurant.

A few moments later, they entered the suite in the hotel room. "Oh, what a lovely place. I suppose they're trying to make it up to you," Hannah said.

"It's pretty much like the other room, only a bit larger but without the great view of the gate," Alejandra said, giving Hannah a wrapped box from atop the nightstand.

"What's going on with you and Richard? I noticed a little tension."

They both sat on the bed. "Same old argument about my professional aspirations. We've been at odds with that since we got married. Once, Richard even went as far as saying he wished he'd married a more submissive wife, and that I should be content with my life as it is. I know he didn't mean it because he wholeheartedly apologized later."

"He's just afraid of losing you," Hannah said. "He knows that if you became a conductor, you'd need to travel. And then what? Leave him behind? It's still a man's world."

"I'd never leave my family on a permanent basis. I love them," Alejandra said. "But I do understand that's what's troubling Richard. I've always known the long path confronted by other women. I'm not alone in the struggle to claim a place in the profession."

"You know how difficult it has been for women musicians since the beginning of time."

"It's not like I'm the first one ever to aspire to be a conductor," Alejandra said. "There's a list of accomplished women in the field, including my mentor Anna Schoen-René, who was the first female conductor in my hometown in the late 1800s. Caroline Nichols founded The Fadette Lady Orchestra, and Rugh Haroldson the Los Angeles Women's Orchestra. Mari Gruner was a conductor of the Ludwig Morelli Orchestra in Vienna, and Ethel Smyth in England. And so on."

"You don't need to convince me," Hannah said, "although I'm astounded in this day and age there's still such a battle when you consider that women have a long tradition of being participants in musical life as dancers, choral and opera singers, copyists, and composers. Many women are still not accepted into membership in many orchestras. And when they are, the vicious competition and pressure are the reasons why I lost interest in pursuing a musical career."

"For me, going into this profession overrides any impediment I may confront," Alejandra said. "I love music as much as you probably love art and art dealing."

"Let me ask you something else," Hannah continued. "Most women would be satisfied to have what you have. So like me, others may ask, what's driving you?"

"Music isn't merely entertainment for me. It's what I turn to for comfort and how I best express my emotions. It's part of who I am and central to my vocation and future. I know it's not common or acceptable for women to have professional ambitions of this nature, particularly if they're married and with children. But I can't see my life complete unless I'm standing at the podium, conducting. Is it too much to want it all?"

Hannah paused. "I guess not, but you know others are not as fortunate as you are."

"What do you mean?"

"Well for starters, you have three children, and I can't even have one. I'm sometimes a little envious of you that way."

Alejandra placed her hand over Hannah's. "You will! I feel that fortune comes and goes, and we each experience it in different ways throughout our lives."

"And what if you get accepted into the program? How will you manage to be without your children for so long?" Hannah asked.

"I'd miss them terribly. We spoke earlier with them, and it was wonderful to hear each of their voices. But right now may be the best time for me to pursue this training. They're not infants or adolescents. I also find reassurance knowing they're close to my mother who offered to move to the house in my absence. She'll have assistance with running the house. But, let's not get ahead, and I have other hurdles to jump, like getting accepted into the program."

"Well, whatever happens, it would be great to have you," Hannah said.

"You know that I'd never have considered staying here if it wasn't for that fact, and I'm grateful for that," Alejandra said. "Enough of this serious conversation. Open your gift."

Hannah unwrapped and opened a small box that revealed a hand-carved shell cameo necklace on a sterling silver chain. "It's gorgeous, Ále. Thank you. I'll always cherish it. How did you know I wanted something like this?"

"I know you liked mine, and it's a similar design. I wanted both of us to have one."

Hannah hugged her. "Just what I need, a talisman. That's how people used them in ancient times. She held the cameo to her chest. "Perhaps it'll bring me what I most want. I wonder, if I'm ever so lucky to have one, what the child would look like."

"Your baby will be a perfect mix of you and Ben," Alejandra said. "You'll see."

"Well, then, may both our wishes come true," Hannah said.

GRANDJANY'S CADENZA

February 22, 1933

Anton Everhardt, wearing a brown bathrobe, drew open the damask patterned drapes in his bedroom. The eastern sunlight, pouring in, highlighted an impeccably furnished space with an oak bed, a brown damask-upholstered armchair, a carved chest of drawers, and two nightstands.

He had been listening to the radio for the last ten minutes, but when the music was interrupted by a broadcast of political speech, he shut it off. He realized it was past nine o'clock, and he was late for a meeting. Before rushing off to take a shower, he left the door open for the chambermaid to do her chores. "Guten Morgen, Fraulein Helga," Anton said to a woman in her seventies. She greeted him and placed a tray on the nightstand that contained the day's newspaper, a coffee pot, cup, and silverware. Anton was fond of the woman who had been in his service for the last twelve years and who was like the mother he never had. Then he left.

Twenty minutes later, dressed in a charcoal-toned striped suit, he returned to the bedroom. Helga had left clean clothes on top of the made-up bed. Before a mirror, above the chest of drawers, he combed his wet hair in a side-swept style. He noticed he had trimmed his beard too closely, showing a scar on his chin, a mark he preferred to hide because it reminded him of a tragedy that haunted him to this day.

He served himself a cup of coffee and picked up the newspaper, reading the headline: "Herman Göring appoints 55,000 members of the German Socialist Workers' Party's storm troopers as auxiliary policemen."

He shook his head, recalling that as a member of the class of 1917 he had enlisted for military service in May of 1916. After three months of training, he fought in the Great War with the German Army against the French in the battle of Verdun. Even to this day, he had nightmares about it—dead and mutilated men everywhere. He, and for that matter many of his countrymen, could not imagine fighting in another senseless war. Anton loathed war and did not like Hitler's policies. Disgusted at the news, he tossed the paper into the trash bin.

He sipped his coffee and put the cup back on the tray, turning his gaze to a seventeenth-century portrait that hung on the wall next to a dresser, which depicted the image of Aristotle with a bust of Homer. He had owned it for years and agonized over parting with the masterpiece. As a fond admirer of the epic poet, he remembered his discovery of *The Iliad* and *The Odyssey* as a boy during a tumultuous period in his life. Homer's poems and Aristotle's philosophical teachings had provided him with hope and escape. And in his youth he had read the classical humanistic traditions embodied in the writings of German figures such as Lessing, Herder, Schiller, Goethe, and Kant. He had aspired to live by those principles of justice, charity, and truth. But at thirty-seven years of age, he had failed miserably by yielding to what he knew was his greatest weakness—unfettered greed. He knew that his wealth had come at the price of his conscience.

He contemplated the Rembrandt portrait, thinking that by giving up his most cherished work of art he was also, symbolically, giving up on his once idealistic and unattainable aspirations.

He removed the painting from the wall and placed it on the bed. From a corner of the floor, he took a white drop cloth, unfolded it, and wrapped the gilded-framed canvas. He held the precious cargo close to his chest as he walked out of the bedroom.

The Steinhoff Auktionshaus, located on the ground floor of a nineteenth-century building in the west of Berlin, was a block away from Charlottenburg Palace, which had been occupied by several German monarchs and once housed the "The Eighth Wonder of the World," the Amber Room. As a gesture to gain favor, in a new alliance between Prussia and Russia, Frederick William gifted the treasure room to the Tsar of Russia, Peter the Great, in 1716.

As Anton entered the auction house that day, he was pleased he had also made a Russian alliance with Sacha Korsakov who was a collector of amber artifacts and the curator of jewelry and decorative arts of the Hermitage Museum in St. Petersburg. And while they were not always of the same mind, for Korsakov was a communist who had supported the Bolshevik Revolution and the creation of the Soviet Union in 1922 under Vladimir Lenin, they had things in common—a penchant for fine art, wine, and art dealing. Anton had met Korsakov when he traveled to St. Petersburg, two years prior, on business. Together, they went to Pushkin, twenty-four kilometers from St. Petersburg, where the famed Amber Room now adorned one of the rooms in Catherine's Palace and where Korsakov had introduced Anton to a Russian oligarch and a major collector of fine art. Korsakov was once again in Berlin, and Anton expected to meet with him at the auction to close another lucrative deal and later that evening for dinner.

A few minutes before two o'clock, Anton was in the auction house, standing in line outside the cloakroom. While he waited, he noticed only a few people remained there as most had gone into the gallery. He heard a harpist, a young blond woman, playing Handel's "Grandjany's Cadenza." He thought the peaceful melody created a pleasant ambiance in an otherwise commercial setting, plainly furnished with leather chairs and with little decoration, except for a few scattered ferns. Soon, his thoughts were interrupted when he overheard a conversation in English between a man and two women who were also waiting in line to check their coats.

"Hopefully, Richard won't be too late," one of the women said.

"Who called him?" the second woman asked.

"His mother. But after speaking for a few minutes, he deemed it not serious enough for me to miss the auction," she said. "So despite my initial hesitation in leaving him at the hotel, I'm glad I decided to come. I wasn't expecting to hear such lovely music before the auction."

"I agree. She's quite a skilled musician," the man said. "And how's your arm?"

"Still sore, but the stitches should be out in less than a week."

When they reached the front of the line, they gave their coats to a female clerk. Anton watched the three individuals walk away until he lost sight of them. A few moments later, a friendly middle-aged woman took his coat. "Sir, it's good to see you again. You left your book last time you were here," she said. He thanked her, took the paperback from her hand, and went to the next gallery, illuminated with a pair of oversized crystal chandeliers. The walls, covered in Japanese silk wallpaper, depicted landscape scenes that matched the forest-green carpet. With several hundred people in attendance most of the seats were taken, except for one seat in the back row. To his surprise, the woman he had seen moments earlier in the foyer, the one with auburn hair, wearing a short-sleeve white knit dress, was seated next to the empty chair. He thought she was striking, and a bandaged forearm seemed to enhance her allure. So without any hesitation or permission, he sat next to her, placing the book on the floor below his chair.

Politely but firmly, in good German with an American accent, the woman said, "*Entschuldigen Sie, Herr, ich rette diesen Platz.*"

He glanced at his watch and in English replied, "Pardon me. The auction is about to begin. Is your companion here yet?"

"No, but he soon will be," she replied.

"Madam, please forgive my manners, but if you would allow me to stay until your companion arrives, I'd be most grateful," he said. "I have my eye on a painting."

Before the woman could object further, the auctioneer, a slender man in his fifties, dressed in a black suit and scholarly looking, appeared on stage. "Welcome to Steinhoff Auktionshaus. Our first painting is *Girl before a Mirror* by Pablo Picasso. It's the portrait of the artist's French mistress Marie-Thérèse Walter." The auctioneer gestured toward the painting, which was displayed on an easel on the stage.

Just then Anton heard a couple in front of him whispering in French, and while he wasn't fluent in that language, he could understand a few words. They were discussing Picasso's cubism. Then the bejeweled woman began bidding as did other potential buyers, including his friend Korsakov, who was in the front row. Finally, the Picasso was sold to a man seated in the back of the gallery. Anton felt irritated, since he had wanted his friend, Korsakov, to take the cubist painting back to St. Petersburg. His collector there would be extremely upset.

As the auction continued, Anton decided to stay. For the next half hour, other modern paintings were brought up for auction until the auctioneer announced a fifteen-minute intermission. The woman next to him was about to leave when he asked her, "Are you American?"

"Yes."

"Pardon my curiosity, but what happened to your arm?"

She remained silent as she turned her gaze toward the stage and seemed to have changed her mind about leaving. "It's a complicated story."

"I don't mind," he said, turning toward her with increased interest.

She paused, relaxing her shoulders. "It happened two nights ago after arriving in your charming city," she said. "Although, nothing was charming about it."

"Now you must tell me more," he said.

"You're German, I assume, by your accent? And very inquisitive. You remind me of friends back home. And you might even have some insight into the situation." She laughed and proceeded with her account.

"I'm very disappointed with some of my fellow countrymen. I'm afraid that of late there's been a lot of that sort of thing," he said in a whisper, too close for her comfort, he noticed, since she immediately pulled back. "I hope you'll not judge us all by your experience."

"Certainly not," she said. "Unfortunate things happen everywhere, although it was disturbing to be sure, and it did change our plans for today. I should be in Bonn."

"What brings you to Germany?"

She smiled. "Music and friends. That's my friend Hannah and her husband on stage talking to the auctioneer. She's an art dealer."

"Yes, I've heard about her, perhaps you can introduce us later. And what's your name?"

"Alejandra Stanford Morrison."

"It's a pleasure to make your acquaintance. And what about your companion?" he asked. "I don't see a wedding ring on your finger."

"You're too familiar for my taste. Are you always this impolite?" she asked. "My husband had business matters to attend to, but I expect him at any moment."

"You must know we Germans are sometimes more direct than other nationalities."

"And you are?" she asked.

But before he could answer her question, they were interrupted by the woman who had been playing the harp earlier, requesting his presence elsewhere. "Excuse me," he said and left.

"Wait," Alejandra said, taking the paperback from the floor. "Your book."

"I'll be back momentarily," he said, rushing away and thinking he wanted an excuse to talk to her later. On second thought, he would come up with a plan to see her again in a more formal setting. He felt a strong attraction toward her.

PIANO TRIO IN A MINOR

With a few minutes left of intermission, Alejandra glanced back at the entrance just as Richard entered through a pair of paneled doors. She waved, and he walked to her location, sitting down. "I'm so glad you're finally here. How's your mother?" She placed the book on her lap.

"It's her finances, but nothing she can't resolve by selling her house. She's decided to move to Newport with my sister. We can talk about it later. How's the auction?"

"Hannah seems delighted." Alejandra glanced around the room, hoping to locate the stranger with brown hair and blue-gray eyes so that she could return his book, but he was nowhere in sight.

"Looks like the auction is about to resume," Richard said. "I hope the second half goes quickly. I find them rather dull."

"I know, but I'm happy that you're here with me."

When the selling resumed, the auctioneer listed twenty antique objects as part of a lot. Not particularly interested in that, Alejandra took the book and read the title: *Mozart's Journey to Prague and a Selection of Poems* by Eduard Mörike. She wondered how such an ill-mannered man could be drawn to poetry. Although, despite the man's boorishness, he had an enigmatic presence. But there was something about him that bothered her sensibilities. Thankfully, she would return the book, and it would be the end of that unnerving acquaintance.

She examined the cover—an illustration of Wolfgang Amadeus Mozart seated before a harpsichord in a palatial eighteenth-century salon. Curious about the topic of the novella, she leafed through the pages, instantly smelling a scent of bergamot, which she presumed came from the man's cologne. Then she found a passage underlined with black ink:

> *"To an Aeolian harp—leaning against the ivy-covered wall of this old terrace, mysterious instrument of a muse, born in the air, oh begin to sing. Begin to utter your melodious lament! How sweetly you besiege my heart! And into the strings you murmur, drawn my sorrow's euphonious music, waxing in the movement of my heart's desire..."*

She decided to read from the beginning of the book, and found, on the first page, a handwritten dedication: *"Bis wir uns wieder treffen."* Feeling mortified that she had breached the man's privacy, she instantly shut the book, but the words in the dedication stayed with her—until we meet again.

Then, as she often did, she began to daydream about living in Prague, Vienna, Budapest, or any other place where she may have been a student of Beethoven or Mozart. For when it came to music, she was at heart a complete romantic. Her thoughts were interrupted by the auctioneer as he presented the last work to go on auction—*Aristotle with a Bust of Homer* by Rembrandt. She turned her gaze to the painting, noting the figures bathed in a luminous light against a dark contrast, typical of all Rembrandts. Other painters rarely replicated the artist's talent for bringing out the essence of a person in a portrait. He was her favorite baroque painter.

"The Dutch Master created this perfectly preserved painting in 1653, and it once adorned the palace of the Sicilian nobleman Don Antonio Ruffo in Amsterdam," the auctioneer said. "We begin bidding at 300,000 francs."

Several patrons bid on the painting, including Hannah. The auction continued until the painting reached 590,000 francs. But with no other bids, the auctioneer finally acknowledged Hannah's last offer, pounding the gavel loudly on the podium: "590,000 going once ... twice ... it's yours, madam. Thank you all for coming, and please join us for a reception in the atrium."

As the chattering crowd began to disperse toward the exit, Alejandra barely heard Richard saying, "I'm glad that's over."

"You don't want to stay?" she asked.

"I'd prefer to return to the hotel, if you don't mind. I'm expecting a call from our real estate associate who'll put mother's house on the market."

"I'm sure Hannah will understand." They made their way out of the gallery and joined the Adelmans in the foyer. A woman played a harp glissando in the corner. "Congratulations on your purchase," Alejandra said. "Was that the painting you were hoping for?"

"No. It was another Rembrandt, but this one is far better," Hannah replied. "It wasn't even in the catalog. I must send my client a telegram with the good news. He'll be ecstatic."

"Clearly, he isn't affected by the depression," Richard said sarcastically. "I hope you have the certificate of authenticity. There are a lot of fakes out there."

"Richard," Ben asked, laughing, "since when do you know so much about art?"

"My apologies," Richard said. "I seem to be a bit preoccupied and don't know anything about art, but I recently read an article about that in *The New York Times*."

"It's true," Hannah said. "A good third of former Rembrandts in American collections have now been deemed to have been painted by his students. It was a common practice in those days for paintings to be made by students and signed by the master."

"To think he died impoverished is ironic," Ben said. "I suppose he painted for posterity."

Then the auctioneer approached Hannah, giving her a sealed envelope. Alejandra gave him the book. "Sir, this was left behind by a patron."

He laughed. "It's not the first time, nor do I suspect the last time that he forgets his books." He walked away.

Hannah ripped open the envelope and read the invitation. "How would you all like to attend an authentic German dinner? The owner of the auction house has invited us to a private soiree. It sounds entertaining, and I wouldn't mind meeting him."

Richard sighed. "Why don't you and Ben go? I'm not in the best disposition."

"He extended the invitation to you both," Hannah said. "Won't you reconsider?"

"We only have a few days together so why not?" Alejandra said. "What time?"

"Six o'clock. Come on Richard! You won't regret it," Hannah added.

"I know it will make Ále happy, so we'll meet you at the hotel at half past five."

"Perfect, I have a telegram to send. We'll see you soon," Hannah said, leaving with Ben.

"I appreciate it," Alejandra said. "I'm sure we'll have fun."

"One can never be sure, but hopefully, you're right," Richard said, taking his wife's hand. "I know I've been difficult, but it's because I want you all to myself."

That evening, after driving to the Tiergarten district, a forested neighborhood surrounding the park, Alejandra and her companions were waiting outside a Gothic Revival style residence with one-story bay windows, towering black iron doors, and pedestal cherubs. Ben pressed the doorbell, and soon a bald man of short stature, wearing black pants, a white shirt, and a light grey jacket opened the door. With a British inflection, he said, "Good evening. We've been expecting you. I'm Wellington. Please come in."

After taking their coats, the butler led them to a drawing room with dark wooden floors, cream painted walls, and mahogany furniture upholstered in monochromatic neutrals of gray and white. On one side, next to another bay window, rested a walnut grand piano. A glass vase with a bouquet of fuchsia bleeding-heart flowers placed atop the piano stood out as the only colorful decoration of its kind. It caught Alejandra's eye because fuchsia was her favorite color. It was also the color of unrequited love. Unrequited love wasn't something she had ever experienced in her life, but heartbreak had inspired several compositions of her most cherished composer.

As they waited for the dinner host, Alejandra joined Hannah, who was admiring a decorative sculpture on the cocktail table—a Nautilus shell cup with a silver rim and the gilt figure of Neptune. "This exquisite work is considered one of the first chambers of art and wonder, a popular object of the sixteen hundreds," Hannah said. "Curiosity cabinets were filled with all kinds of odd objects made of natural materials."

"One could say all art and humankind also hold chambers of art and wonder," Alejandra said playfully. "Even your butterfly dress is a wonder of sorts. It looks beautiful on you."

"You like it? It's by Elsa Schiaparelli, inspired by Dali," Hannah said. "It's bold, but at least it draws attention away from my horrid curly hair."

"Wavy hair is fashionable these days. And I like your hair. So it's me who's not in fashion with my plain, straight hair."

"You might not follow *Vogue's* fashion, but you're always classically elegant," Hannah said. "That silk gown is gorgeous on you."

"It's a relic, but I love the indigo-blue tone. It still shows like new." Alejandra discreetly adjusted the beaded clip on her shoulder-length hair that was parted on the side, delineating the contour of her oval face and high cheekbones.

"Although our husbands don't seem to care much about fashion with their ordinary black suits," Hannah said.

"That's all right by me," Alejandra said.

"They're both endowed with other magnificent wonders," Hannah said, whispering in Alejandra's ear. "I mean their minds of course."

They both laughed.

Wellington returned with a martini tray, and Hannah, Richard, and Ben each took a glass. "Anything else for you, madam?" Wellington asked.

"Not right now," Alejandra replied. She was looking inside a leaded glass étagère that showcased a collection of Amati, Klotz, and Guarneri violins. There were nine in all, but there was one Stradivarius displayed apart from the rest on its own shelf. "How remarkable. Is he a musician?"

Just then she heard the deep voice of another man who had walked into the room wearing a double-breasted navy-blue suit with broad sweeping lapels, a gold geometric-design tie, and a matching pocket square.

"Welcome, and please forgive my delay. I'm Anton Everhardt. A pleasure to meet you both." He extended his hand to Hannah and Ben.

"These are our friends, Alejandra and Richard Morrison."

Anton greeted the couple. "Lovely to see you again, Mrs. Morrison."

Astounded that the stranger she had met earlier was the owner of the auction house, Alejandra realized this was no coincidence. He apparently had invited them on purpose. His apparent eagerness further increased her discomfort about him.

"We briefly met at the auction," she said to Richard, who was looking at Anton with suspicion. Richard, of similar height at six foot two, shook his hand.

"I'm pleased you all came," Anton said.

"Is this a tradition to entertain your buyers?" Hannah asked.

"Only those I want to know better. I'm delighted you're now the new owner of one of my most prized Rembrandts," Anton replied.

"I *wish* it was mine. It's for a client who's collected Rembrandts for twenty years," Hannah said. "It must have been difficult to part with."

"Yes. Each painting takes on its own persona. It's almost like losing a relative," Anton said. He pointed to the tufted sofas with tapered legs. "Please." He sat on one of the wing chairs.

Alejandra and the rest of the group took their seats on the sofa. "I can relate to that," she said. "I could never let go of my mother's portraitures. As an only child growing up, they were my constant companions."

"You still have the Beethoven portrait?" Hannah asked.

"Yes, I'll never part with it. I think I was five when I first saw it, and it influenced me on many levels," Alejandra said.

"Indeed. Alejandra's mother, Lydia Stanford, is an excellent painter," Hannah said. "Her portraits sold quite well back home. We started our business by selling those paintings. And how long have you owned your auction house?"

"Seventeen years," Anton replied. "I started with musical instruments, but after meeting new upcoming artists, such as Miró, Klee, Picasso, and others, I decided to switch to paintings as they were more affordable, although recently I've been acquiring Renaissance works of art."

"Are you a collector? I'd have expected to see walls full of art," Hannah said.

"No. I keep very few. I don't want that kind of attachment," Anton replied.

"It can be an addictive endeavor," Hannah said. "I've been collecting fine jewelry of historical significance for some time."

"And Benjamin, what do you do?"

"I'm a violinist," he replied. "Formerly, a musician with the American Opera Company until it went bankrupt in 1930. Currently, I'm studying conducting."

"And you, Mrs. Morrison? If I recall correctly, you mentioned your visit had something to do with music," Anton said.

"A wife and a mother," Alejandra said.

"Ále! Don't be so modest," Hannah said. "And a pianist and an aspiring conductor."

Embarrassed by her friend's remarks, Alejandra said, "Perhaps someday."

"Someday? That's all you've wanted since I've known you," Hannah insisted, putting her on the spot. "Isn't that why you're here?"

Anton leaned forward in his chair. "A conductor? Really? I might have thought it inconceivable for a woman to be one just a decade ago. But only three years ago, Antonia Brico was the guest conductor of our own Berlin Philharmonic."

His remark troubled her sensitivity about the subject. "Inconceivable!" she exclaimed.

"Certainly rare. Pardon me if I sounded doubtful. And Richard, what do you do?"

"I'm a surgeon."

"Oh. Like to do experiments?" Anton quipped.

"More like improving a patient's health, but you wouldn't understand."

"Richard, I'm sure Anton meant no harm," Hannah said.

"I meant no disrespect," Anton said.

Then Wellington interrupted. "Sir, Mr. Korsakov has arrived, and dinner is ready."

"Please, show him in," Anton said. "A friend of mine will be joining us. I think you'll find him to be charming. Hannah, he happens to be interested in jewelry and decorative arts."

"Really?" Hannah said. "How interesting."

Just then, Sacha Korsakov came into the room, grinning. His face was round with thick eyebrows that met and a dark complexion. "Anton, sorry for my delay. You Germans have quite the collection of Islamic art, and your comrades wouldn't let me go."

Anton stood up, patting his friend on the back. "He was at The Kaiser-Friedrich Museum, and you're just in time for dinner. Let me introduce you to Hannah and Ben Adelman and Alejandra and Richard Morrison."

As he shook hands with everyone, Alejandra noticed that his suit, slightly tight on his broad-shouldered frame, had a hammer and sickle red star pin on its lapel, something that struck her as odd considering local politics.

"Weren't you at the auction today?" Hannah asked.

"Yes. Although, I wasn't as fortunate as you. The Picasso that I wanted went to another bidder," Korsakov said.

"Yes, I'm sorry about that. I wanted you to have it," Anton said. "The buyer came from nowhere, and I'd never seen him before. I'll make it up to you and your collector."

Anton led the group to the dining room, which was softly lit by a Gothic iron and glass chandelier. The table was set with an embroidered tablecloth, geometric porcelain dinnerware, silver-plated utensils, and German Roemer glasses filled with wine. The two couples sat across from each other with Anton at one end, next to the female guests, and Sacha at the other.

Lifting his glass, Anton said, "For the pleasure of your company and for prosperous times ahead." Everyone followed suit.

After taking a sip of wine, Alejandra said, "What a sweet taste. Is it German?"

"From the banks of the Mosel, one of the most scenic valleys in Germany," Anton said. "We've been making wine for two thousand years. Vineyards planted on its steep slopes produce a singular style of Riesling."

"Oh? My grandmother was born not far from there," Alejandra said.

"Where exactly?" Anton asked.

"Bingen. I'd like to go there someday."

"A lot of points of interest there. And how is your visit to Berlin? How long will you stay?" Anton asked.

"Stimulating. The training has been superb," Ben said. "We'll be here for another six months or so."

"We're renting a house a few miles away, owned by Ben's relatives, Joshua and Sarah Oldenburg," Hannah said. "They'll be staying at their country house outside Vienna until fall."

"We leave on Sunday, and so far I haven't been impressed," Richard said.

"I can understand why. Alejandra told me about the unfortunate incident at your hotel."

"Yes. Because of it, I guess I've been out of sorts since," Richard said.

"Please. Can we not discuss this anymore?" Alejandra said. "I'm looking forward to enjoying the rest of our time here. Maybe Ben could share his experiences at the conservatory."

"As you'll learn on Friday, the program covers theoretical training, composition, orchestral scores, and baton technique. But there are also opportunities to attend rehearsals with other European orchestras."

"And why did you choose Germany over England or France?" Richard asked.

"It would have been fine to study in either country, but with its musical legacy and methodic instruction, Germany seemed the best fit. It's often referred to as *the mother country of music*. It was also practical, considering we had a place to stay."

"I assume there's emphasis on the Austrian-German repertoire," Alejandra said.

"Yes, and we're going to Vienna for rehearsals with the Vienna Philharmonic," Ben said.

"Perhaps Tchaikovsky and Stravinsky should be in the repertoire," Sacha exclaimed.

"They are, but I'd like to hear more of Rossini and Puccini," Ben said. "I'd like to specialize in opera."

"Pardon us. This is what happens when you get musicians together. All we want to talk about is music," Alejandra said.

"I think I can speak for both Sacha and I that we share your enthusiasm," Anton said. "Alejandra is an aspiring conductor. So I'm curious... what inspired you to want to be one?"

"It probably started with Beethoven's portrait, and later after attending my first live concert. It was also at the encouragement of Anna Schoen-René. Are you familiar with her?"

"She's German and taught bel canto at Juilliard," Ben interrupted. "Didn't she also live in Minneapolis?"

"Yes," Alejandra replied. "She was one of Minnesota's musical pioneers along with other German-born conductors such as Emil Oberhoffer and Bruno Walter."

"Walter is very active here in Berlin and Leipzig," Anton said. "But how did they end up in Minneapolis as opposed to Chicago or New York? I've heard it's nearly as cold as Siberia."

"Sometimes it feels like it," said Richard. "And Berlin is not that much better."

Hannah laughed. "That's the same question I asked Ále, years ago."

"We have one of the best orchestras in the country and a large German population," Alejandra said. "The landscape is similar to that of northern Germany with its marshland along the coastline, although in Minnesota we have an abundance of lakes, but it was the farmland that brought immigrants there, including my father's family."

Richard turned to Anton. "So long as we're on the topic of Germany, what are your thoughts on your newly minted chancellor?"

Alejandra looked at her husband somewhat aghast for bringing up the subject of politics in polite conversation. His behavior was out of character, and she wasn't sure of the reason.

Then Wellington came into the room and served the first course—cabbage soup in porcelain bowls. When he left, Anton replied, "Pardon me for what I'm about to say, but I loathe politics. It's all *Kuhscheiße*!"

"And what does that mean?" Richard asked.

"Mildly put, nonsense," Alejandra answered.

Anton said, "I think you call it bullshit. It's all self-aggrandizement. I'm troubled by politicians whose pernicious speech pits one group of people against another. Hindenburg may be the president, but Hitler as chancellor is pulling the strings. And I'm afraid that if Hindenburg dies, Hitler will take complete control."

"I thought Hitler was all about nationalism and improving your economy," Sacha said.

"His party claims that the emphasis is on rebuilding our economy, which is dismal," Anton said. "Inflation is out of control, and they blame, justly, the deal we got with the Treaty of Versailles. Germany was utterly humiliated. But my gut tells me there may be something more sinister happening behind the scenes." Anton took another drink of his wine. "To find meaningful discourse nowadays, one must turn to our history. Goethe underscored in his writings the need for mutual harmonious existence and restraint. Currently, we seem to be devoid of leaders of good moral standing."

Hannah asked, "Isn't that a bit cynical? There must be a few good men. After all, here we are having a nice meal together as individuals possibly representing capitalism, communism, and fascism."

"I'm no fascist, I assure you!" Anton said. "I'm a capitalist like the rest of you."

"Well, I'm a proud communist," added Sacha. "I raised a few eyebrows today at the museum by wearing this pin."

"You're lucky they didn't jail you on the spot," Anton said. "Hitler hates communists."

"Is anybody speaking out against fascism in Berlin?" Richard asked.

"I know there's a large percentage of people opposed to it, but many are not speaking publicly for obvious reasons," Anton replied. "The era of the Weimar Republic is sadly gone. It was a period of intellectual prominence. Berlin was a mecca for scientists and artists alike. And now, we have a government that has tapped into the economic dissatisfaction of the nation, and it's stifling the expression of ideas and dissent and taking us back to the dark ages in a kind of intellectual oblivion I've never seen before."

"You've confirmed my concerns," Richard said. "James Madison once said that due to the weak nature of man, governments needed to exist. And that if men were angels, no government would be necessary. He thought the most virtuous of men deserved to be elected to public office. But obviously that may not always apply."

Anton laughed as if ridiculing the statement. "Who are these moral men elected to office? They are all hopelessly flawed."

Alejandra noticed some strain building between Richard and Anton and was about to interrupt the conversation when Richard said, "There have been plenty of them, and there's a place for government. But it's up to each of us to follow our moral code, to question things, and to refrain from following word for word rantings of imperfect leaders."

"So, what can you tell me about the recently elected American president?" Anton asked. "Is he a man to be trusted or just another megalomaniac?"

"Franklin Roosevelt, I believe, is a man of honor," Richard replied. "Amidst our deep depression, he won over the majority of Americans with his optimism and a pledge to create work opportunities and a New Deal for the American people."

"And what about Stalin?" Ben asked Sacha.

"He's feared. I don't condone his policies either," Sacha said.

"We must make them accountable," Ben said. "The greatest threat to society is that it's not necessarily the wisest men who get elected, but those who can fire up the masses with empty promises and massive propaganda."

Richard faced Anton. "Or have brutal tactics. So, what happens if a demon is in charge of a government?"

There was a moment of silence as everyone turned to Anton and awaited his response. Wellington, having already collected the soup dishes, brought plates of buttered trout, spätzle, and green beans.

When the butler left the room, Anton responded, "In time, we'll know the answer to your question. But if I'm honest, what I know about Hitler's irrational creed is a bad omen. We need only to look at history to know that men who lacked education possessed a streak of paranoia, and combined with absolute power they were utterly vicious."

"That's what I thought," Richard said. "But what's at the core of his ideology?"

"It's too odious to discuss now and not appropriate for our lovely dinner," Anton said.

"Then let me ask you something else," Richard continued. "Do you foresee any immediate policy changes that could affect the well-being of the people coming here?"

"Not at the moment," Anton replied. "Under the Weimar Republic, the Olympics were proposed, and they will take place in Berlin three years from now, so I believe the current government will want to maintain a good face internationally."

Alejandra said, "I've always thought that to find angels on earth, we must turn to the arts. Humanity is at its best when creating music and art. It may be a romantic view of the world, but it is worthy of my devotion, and that's why we're all here."

"Let's leave politics to the politicians. It's because of art that I have a job," Sacha said. "And thanks to Catherine the Great who outsmarted Frederick II of Prussia. She bought a collection intended for him with over two hundred paintings by Dutch and Flemish masters."

"It was indeed an auspicious takeover that propelled the Hermitage collection," Hannah said. "How marvelous you work there. Someday I hope to visit. I've read that by the time she had died, she owned more than four thousand paintings."

"And sparkling gems, coins, and medals. Something all Russians can now see," Sacha added. "I'd love to show you around the museum if you ever visit my country."

"That would be great," Hannah said. "But for tonight, perhaps Ále might be inclined to play for us. After all, you do need to practice for the audition."

"Oh. You enjoy putting me on the spot, don't you? I'll play if you and Ben accompany me like old times," Alejandra said.

"What instrument do you play?" Sacha asked Hannah.

"Violoncello," she replied.

"Well, you're in luck because Anton owns one. You still do?"

Anton nodded.

It was evident to Alejandra that Sacha had taken an interest in Hannah, but Ben was not the jealous type. He, in fact, was amused by the flirtatious Russian and said, "Oh, Mr. Korsakov, perhaps you can convince my wife to play again professionally, because I can't."

"Not that again. But, I'll be happy to play with Ále. It's been too long since we did that."

"But first, may I entice you all with a shot of Bavarian honey liqueur?" Anton asked.

"Yes, that sounds awfully tempting," Hannah replied.

"One or more shots of good vodka will suit me best," Sacha said, laughing.

"Or would you like wine from your favorite vineyard?" Anton asked.

"Is there such a thing?" Ben asked.

"It depends on the year and the wine. I recommend Novyi Svet in Crimea," Sacha said.

"I'll have to check into that," Hannah said.

After supper, everyone was back in the drawing room, and Alejandra was browsing through a pile of manuscripts on top of a Bechstein piano when Anton, holding the Stradivarius violin, stood next to her.

"I'd like to join you," Anton said. "Unless, Ben, you'd prefer to play."

"I've played with these ladies many times," he said. "Besides, I'd like to hear you."

"My dear Ben was such a perfectionist and nearly drove us crazy," Hannah said.

"But it made for flawless performances, didn't it?" Ben asked.

"Yes, it certainly did," Alejandra said.

Wellington entered the drawing room holding a violoncello and gave it to Hannah, who took it and sat on a chair next to the piano, making tuning adjustments. Ben assisted Wellington in placing the music stands and brought a chair next to the piano.

"Will you be able to play?" Anton asked Alejandra.

"My arm is a bit sore, so my playing may be a little lacking," she said.

"I doubt that, but I do have a contemporary piece in mind. May I show you?" Anton said.

"How contemporary? A little of Django Reinhardt?" she asked with a smile.

"What? I'd have thought that as a classically trained pianist and aspiring conductor, you would shun modern music," Anton said.

"Nonsense! I love Jazz. It's all music. Talent is talent, and Reinhardt is an exceptional guitarist and composer," Alejandra said.

"You should have seen her back in our student days. We had a hell of a time getting her out of Tin Pan Alley," Hannah said.

Alejandra stepped back from the piano, and as Anton searched through the scores, she turned to Richard, now engaged in conversation with Sacha. The Russian had such a contagious laugh that he had gotten Richard laughing too. Whether it was the drinks or the company, she was pleased that her husband was enjoying himself.

Anton said, "Here it is." He handed the piano and cello parts to the ladies. Alejandra pondered why he had selected that particular composition, considering it required a high level of virtuosity from its players. She sat at the piano and placed the score on the ledge.

Ben was seated beside her to help turn the pages. "This might be the only time I say this, but don't push yourself too hard."

"I'll be all right," Alejandra said, stretching her arm.

From his seat, Richard asked, "And what will you be playing?"

"Ravel's Piano Trio in A Minor," Alejandra said. "It's a lengthy piece and brilliantly orchestrated... one we have fortunately played on several occasions because it's very demanding."

On the count of four, Alejandra signaled the start of the first movement—"Modéré." She felt a strange sensation through her arm, but the discomfort was not enough to disrupt her performance. As the trio performed together, she was happy to be playing alongside Hannah, and surprised by the manner in which Anton played the violin with remarkable natural talent. For the different soft and energetic passages of the composition served to showcase his stunning sentiment and virtuosity. Where had he learned to play with such skill and emotion? It was as though the interplay of melodies, harmonies, and shifting meters of the composition transformed Anton into another person Alejandra could relate to as someone who expressed his emotions through the music. The guarded feelings she initially felt toward Anton began to dissipate. Over the next three movements—Pantoum, Passacaille, and the Finale, they engaged in a musical conversation of playfulness, tenderness, and wonderment.

It was magical playing with other musicians, and as her heart beat with emotion, she could not fathom giving up on her professional ambitions. For the last seventeen years, she had dreamed of conducting. The realization that she was just days away from auditioning at the conservatory heightened her exhilaration. Would she be accepted? Could she imagine herself standing at the podium before an orchestra conducting the symphonies of musical geniuses—music inspired by God? Oh! She hoped so.

When they finished playing the last cadence, after almost thirty minutes, Anton immediately suggested they play another piece, but Richard rose swiftly to his feet. "Pardon me. It's late, and we must go. Thank you for your hospitality, Anton."

"Yes," Hannah replied. "It's been a lovely evening."

"And you play exceptionally well, Hannah," Sacha said. "Now that I know you'll be in Berlin for some time, I'd like to invite you and Ben for dinner next time I'm in town. You might even help me to locate a few pieces of Russian jewelry from private collections in America."

"Certainly," Hannah said.

"You're both excellent musicians. Please excuse me for a moment," Anton said.

"What a perfect ending to our day," Alejandra remarked.

"I suppose we have Richard to thank for not taking you to Beethoven's birthplace. Perhaps you were not meant to go there. We'd have never met Anton," Hannah said.

"You would have, Hannah. You were the main guest, let's not forget that!" Richard said.

"I'm not so sure that's true," Hannah said, turning to Alejandra.

Wellington brought their coats, and Anton returned holding the book he had with him at the auction. He placed a hand on the butler's shoulder. "I don't know what I'd do without this good man who strives so hard to perfect my English." Anton then gave Alejandra the book. "It's one of my favorite novellas. Please, consider it as a farewell souvenir of delightful German poetry and literature on Mozart's trip to premiere *Don Giovanni*."

"Your favorite? You forgot it! More than once I hear." Alejandra laughed.

Anton smiled and shrugged his shoulders.

"Let's see, might you be a modern-day Don Giovanni?" Hannah asked.

"Absolutely not!" Anton said. "But I do love that opera."

"Why?" Alejandra asked.

"The freedom of expression it espouses, even if it came at the protagonist's expense. Interestingly enough, it premiered only a month after your constitution had been written, following word by word the meaning of the first amendment."

"How interesting. Either way, I look forward to reading this book," Alejandra said.

"And we may even run into the opera house for *Die Zauberflöte*," Hannah said.

"That's another brilliant Mozart opera with its references to Freemasonry," Anton said.

"And his emphasis on the age of reason," Alejandra said. "Which is why I like it."

"*The Magic Flute* has incredible range," Ben said. "Perhaps Schinkel's staging from the eighteen hundreds with Egyptian-style architecture will be on display. It's considered the best production ever."

"And when are you going to the opera?" Anton asked.

"On Saturday," Hannah replied.

"A pleasure to meet you. If you're ever in St. Petersburg, please call me," Sacha said.

"Until we meet again," Anton said.

Alejandra took a deep breath and reflected upon Hannah's earlier comments on the serendipity of the day's events—certain fate had stepped in for some mysterious purpose.

"We never know what the future may bring. Perhaps we're all destined to meet again under very different circumstances... or not?" Alejandra smiled as they all departed.

VIOLIN CONCERTO IN E MINOR, OP. 64

Anton returned to the drawing room, thinking about his guests. He was mesmerized by Alejandra's musical endowment and dedication and how she took command of the keyboard while her face radiated contentment. She was obviously raised in privilege; yet, she shared none of the snobberies often found in people born into wealth. He felt a connection to her as from one soul to another. He couldn't put it into words, but only once before had he felt that magical bond through the music. The experience of playing with the two women left him craving for more as if touched by a muse. To savor the memory, he sat on the same chair where only moments before he had played with his new acquaintances, intending to play music again. Then Wellington came into the room with a glass of brandy, as he did every night, placing it on the cocktail table. "Here's your drink, sir. You seem happy tonight. May I get you anything else?"

"It was one of the best evenings I can remember," Anton replied. "Good night."

He took his treasured violin, touching it with melancholy, as he thought for the first time in a long time about his father, Fritz Everhardt. Despite having conflicting emotions and a turbulent relationship with him growing up, he now felt gratitude for passing on the gift of music. Since his father's death, Anton struggled to reconcile his painful past with his current material success—searching to accomplish something meaningful in his life.

He had grown up in poverty and without a mother—she had left his father when Anton was a young boy. Fritz, a frustrated violinist, wanted to be an orchestral musician, even moving his family from Leipzig to Berlin for better opportunities. But he had never achieved those aspirations and made a living by giving lessons and playing in bars and cafes. Known as the "one drink fiddler," Fritz spent his earnings on an all-consuming alcohol addiction. Over the years, Anton experienced his father's bitterness. Anton's childhood and adolescence were filled with memories of humiliation and ridicule, collecting a drunken father from brothels and bars. As a result, Anton swore to never follow in his father's footsteps. He excelled in his academic studies and became an avid reader, mastering all of the Greek classics by the age of fourteen.

Before his fifteenth birthday, he had planned to leave home, but in March of that year his father was beaten to death during a brawl and left to die on a muddy street. The next Sunday morning, the local authorities summoned Anton to identify his father's corpse at the morgue. At times, Anton had wanted his father gone when he became violent, but never dead. With a profound sense of guilt and anger, he had collapsed sobbing and wondered who could have murdered his father. The perpetrator would go free, and justice would not be served.

Later that day, his father's corpse was placed in a simple coffin, and Anton transported it to the cemetery on a motor carriage he had borrowed from his landlord. On the way to the grave site, he was unnerved by a sea of granite tombstones. He would always remember the heaviness of his chest, as if his father's death weighed him down. He had felt unable to breathe and stopped the vehicle, opening a window. The harsh wind slapped his face, leaving a taste of dirt in his mouth. Then, from a distance, he spotted the gravedigger smoking a cigarette like it was just another day. But for Anton, it was like the end of the world.

The gravedigger helped Anton lower Fritz Everhardt into his final resting place. Anton stood silently, feeling overcome by that inevitable fate everyone must confront regardless of position and power and thinking that death was the only equalizer in life. He considered his father's character—a man who was never strong enough to manage his failures. There was no one to give him a solemn rite as if his death was of no consequence and his life had been meaningless. With a shovel in his hand, Anton assisted in covering the coffin with earth. He promised his father that someday he would return to place a proper marker on his grave.

When he returned to his apartment, his mind was a blur. The landlord, a middle-aged man with a scabby pate, was waiting at the bottom of the staircase. While expressing sympathy for Anton's loss, he complained that Anton's father was more than ten weeks behind on the rent. He asked Anton to leave by morning. There was a new renter willing to pay two months in advance to move in the next day. Anton understood and promised to return someday to pay his father's debts. He gave the landlord the keys to the wagon and thanked him for his kindness.

At home, Anton noticed his father's violin on the floor. Filled with grief, he picked it up and played Mendelssohn's Violin Concerto in E Minor, Op. 64, just as his father had done every night before going to sleep. As he played, he realized that contrary to his father's daily habit of taking the violin with him, he had gone without it that morning. The violin was all he had left of his father, and for that, he was most grateful. Tears dripped down his cheeks, and unable to play the music any longer he took the instrument and carefully stored it in the case. Then, for the rest of the evening, he packed and cleaned the small space.

The next morning, Anton left the apartment, taking with him the violin and a single suitcase. For the next week, he roamed the streets of Berlin looking for work and eating whatever food he could scrounge in restaurant trash bins. The nights were cold, and he sought refuge under bridges. Playing the violin on those desolate nights gave him consolation. Like his father, Anton had inherited an innate talent for playing the violin with precision and emotion. He always considered that musical ability to be as much a misfortune as a gift. For his father, the music had been his heaven. But it was also his hell since Fritz never accomplished playing with an orchestra. And for that reason, Anton decided he would never pursue a musical profession.

One evening, before the stores on Das Schaufenster Street closed, Anton found a shop with a large sign on the windowpane that read: "We buy and sell musical instruments." Carrying the violin case, he walked into the brick building. The messy shop reeked of sweat and mildew. A scruffy looking man yelled, "No beggars here. Get out!"

"Sir, I'm no beggar. I'm here to pawn my father's violin. You'll want to see it!"

The man, dumbfounded by his self-assurance, asked, "What do you have there?"

Anton approached the man standing behind a dented counter. He thought the man unworthy of holding the violin, so he gently took it from the case and lovingly placed it on the counter, as if it held his father's ashes.

The man inspected the violin. "Who did you steal it from?"

"I told you… it was my father's. He just died."

"A Stradivarius?" He stared at Anton, surprised. "I'll give you one hundred marks."

Anton laughed. "It's worth a thousand times more." He felt insulted and was not willing to part with it for so little. On further consideration, he would never want to part with it and thought of options. "I've another proposition for you."

"What can an orphan offer me?"

"This shop could use some cleaning and organizing. I'm a hard worker. If you give me room, board, and a job, I'll loan you my violin. You can display it and show it off as your own. A Stradivarius, compared to the ones you have here, will bring in better-paying customers."

"Kid, you've got guts and a good business sense. In all my years, I've never heard such an offer." With a chuckle, a nod, and a wink, he said, "I'm Leo Steinhoff. Come back tomorrow."

"Well, Leo, you'll thank me someday," Anton said.

Never hopeless, he had left the shop confident it would be the last night he would sleep outside and on an empty stomach. He made a promise to work his way up into fortune and never live in poverty again at whatever cost.

Heartened by those memories, Anton returned to the present, thinking he had come a long way from his modest beginnings. He had honored the promise of paying his father's debts and placing an epitaph on his grave. He was grateful for his current life even if it lacked the one thing that had eluded him all his life. As he drank his brandy, savoring it, he thought of the enchanting pianist, Alejandra Morrison, whom he would love to see again, despite her marriage to that pompous Richard. It would be nearly impossible unless fate were on his side. Then he lifted the violin from the table, placing it under his chin, and payed tribute to his father by playing his favorite Mendelssohn composition.

SYMPHONY NO. 5 IN C MINOR, OP. 67

It was Saturday when Alejandra finished eating breakfast at a little café on Pariser Platz, plainly decorated except for a collection of plates and spoons that adorned the walls. She looked out the window, noticing it was sunny—an ideal day to take a walk through the city's most prominent park. She needed time to reflect on what had happened the day before. Nature always had a calming effect and allowed her to put everything into perspective. She pulled out a note that Richard had left on the nightstand and reread it:

> *Ále, my dearest, I'm sorry for leaving so early this morning, but I did not want to wake you. I feel terrible for getting angry with you last night and for all the things I said. I hope you'll forgive me! My behavior was inexcusable. I have something important to do. I should be back by lunch. For our last day in Berlin, I have made plans, which I'm sure you'll enjoy. Love, Richard.*

She would accept his apology, but his harsh words still rang in her mind like some discordant tone that lingers day and night. Even more troubling to her was the unexpected argument they had the previous day after they returned from the conservatory. She had auditioned for the introductory conducting program, performing exceptionally well and completing an extensive interview with the director who, to her great satisfaction, had accepted her application. What should have been a day of joy and celebration turned into an evening of huge disappointment; for when they returned to their hotel, they discussed the offer, and Richard rejected it with unyielding vigor. His opinion was that there was no place for a woman of her stature and class to take on such a "manly" role or to be working professionally. She was a mother and a wife, and that should be enough. Her aspiration of being a conductor had been jettisoned from her future, like ashes scattered to the wind. Recalling his hurtful words, she felt a knot in her throat. Although she felt angry, she was too proud to accept defeat. It was only a temporary setback. As someone who did not dwell on things that were out of her control, she needed time to reflect on her husband's arguments and to find a way to convey to Richard that her desire to be a conductor was as strong as being a wife and a mother.

Upon leaving the café, a short time later, Alejandra was in Tiergarten. It was cold, but nothing out of the ordinary for her. Dressed in a camel-wool coat, scarf, and boots, she took in the snowy landscape and the smell of evergreen needles mixed with burning wood. She recalled that the park had once been the private hunting grounds of King Friedrich Wilhelm. How enticing it must have been to ride a horse through such lush forest, and Alejandra wished she could be riding on her Paso Fino stallion, as she had as a child when living with her maternal grandparents in their sprawling hacienda in Cuernavaca, Mexico. The sense of freedom of galloping on a horse was something she greatly missed. She learned to ride from her mother, Lydia Merino, who had been born into a Mexican family, owners of a successful sugar mill. Independently minded, Alejandra's mother went to study abroad at the Sorbonne in Paris. It was there, in 1900 at the world's fair in France, that Lydia had met Edward, an American architect. One year later, they were married, against Lydia's father's wishes. And in December of 1902, Alejandra was born in Minneapolis, Minnesota.

Alejandra had grown up with the intermingling of American, English, German, Mexican, and Spanish cultures. She always considered that having such a diverse heritage was a privilege. Both her parents were highly educated and not particularly suited to conventional attitudes. Her mother had also been active in the suffrage movement, and Lydia had always emboldened Alejandra's vocational aspirations. Her father supported education for women.

Through their travels abroad, Lydia and Edward highlighted the contributions of all cultures in the fields of architecture, economics, astronomy, science, and the arts in general. They had always encouraged Alejandra's inquisitiveness and seeing the world through a lens of differing perspectives. At the core of her parents' philosophy and values was the belief that reason must always supersede emotion. In most things, this was the approach by which Alejandra measured disagreement and conflict with others. From an early age, she had learned to dominate her feelings and to maintain serenity. But in subsequent years, contrary to her parents' beliefs, she had developed a propensity toward mysticism. This tendency, however, she kept private.

As Alejandra continued on her walk, meandering through tree-lined pathways in the park, she made several stops to admire the statues of notable German artists such as Goethe, Fontane, and Drake, until she came to her desired location—a handsomely landscaped memorial honoring musical giants. With personal devotion, she stared at the life-size marble sculpture of Ludwig van Beethoven. He was the embodiment of a musical genius for Germans and the pride of their culture and country. For Alejandra, the music and life of Beethoven had taken root in her consciousness since she was five years old. First, it was the discovery of music as the sweetest of feelings, as when being kissed for the first time. Her introduction to Beethoven began with her mother's obsession, manifested by painting several portraits of the composer. On her eighth birthday, she had been given dozens of Beethoven's manuscripts upon starting piano lessons. Over the next few years, she had mastered those compositions. In her adolescence, while a student at Juilliard, she wrote an essay on Beethoven—"his revolutionary approach to classical music composition by the use of large orchestras, his prolific works for symphony, choral, and chamber music, his transition from the classical to the romantic periods, and the universal quality of his music." The culmination of her exposure to Beethoven's music happened during a Beethoven festival in Mexico City when she was a nineteen-year-old student at the National Conservatory of Mexico. She heard *Symphony No. 5 in C Minor* performed live by the National Symphonic Orchestra of Mexico and conducted by Julian Carrillo. It was the most fantastic and powerful symphony she had ever heard—a breathtaking sound bearing down on all who listened as if the composer was speaking through his music. It was then that she knew, with absolute conviction, that she could never give up her desire to be a conductor—no matter how impossible it seemed, no matter what anyone said, and no matter how long it took to accomplish it.

High wind, rustling through the oak trees, brought her back to the present. She felt invigorated by the wind's cold caress on her face and by those transcendent experiences and memories from her past. So as she stood before the Beethoven statue, she heard an inner voice extolling her never to give up on her dreams. Perhaps, she thought with a smile, it was Beethoven himself or some other spirit speaking in some mystical fashion from the infinite universe. Wherever that voice came from, it would remain alive in her heart until her last breath. For she knew that no one could ever dominate her spirit or change the course of her destiny.

Two hours had elapsed, and soon Richard would be back at the hotel. She was eager to see him and find out where he had been, but mostly to make peace with the man she loved.

Later in the evening, after attending Mozart's *The Magic Flute* at the Berlin Opera House, Alejandra was mesmerized by the experience of having seen the famed opera in the historic setting where many prominent conductors she admired had left extraordinary legacies. There, she had imagined herself at the podium, conducting. Was that an impossible dream? Perhaps it was, but there was always magic. She smiled to herself.

Alejandra and Richard took a taxi to a Viennese restaurant located near Gendarmenmarkt square, behind the German Cathedral. The old establishment, with its coffered ceilings, wainscot, linen-covered tables, and candle lighting, was the ideal setting for their last dinner in Berlin. As they entered the intimate space, the hostess greeted them and led them to a table in an alcove overlooking an interior courtyard with a small fountain surrounded by potted green plants. Richard pulled out a chair, waited for her to sit down, and took his place across from her. She felt comfortable in her velvet, cherry-red gown and a string of pearls.

"You've been awfully quiet most of the day. Was the opera not to your liking?" he asked.

Alejandra gazed at Richard, who looked handsome in his navy-blue suit, white shirt, and striped green tie that matched his eyes. "Of course I liked it. If you only knew how much. But you haven't told me yet where you went this morning."

"I'm not sure I'm ready to divulge my secret. You'll know soon enough."

"But we leave tomorrow," she said.

"Please enjoy the night. I see you've got your ring back on. I was starting to worry."

"You have nothing to worry about. The little cut on my finger has healed," she said.

The waiter brought a bottle of champagne and crystal flutes. Then he served the sparkling drink and took their order. She asked for the house specialty, *Paprikahenderl* and salad. He ordered old Viennese caraway style pork, stuffed peppers, and plum cake for dessert.

When the waiter left, Alejandra said, "Richard, I've been thinking about what you said yesterday. I felt hurt by your barbed comments, and it was the worst argument we ever had. I regret that, but I do understand your concerns, and it would have been difficult for me to be away from you and the children for so long."

"I said many things I regret and hope you know I didn't mean any of it," he said. "When you were admitted to the conservatory, I could see your face light up, and it was a great honor for it's highly competitive, and only a few women apply."

"It was my main motivation for being here. Back home I discussed with my mother the possibility of staying in Berlin to study. She was supportive and offered to care for the children in my absence. I know how hard it would be for all of you. I've always struggled to balance being a good wife and mother with a musical profession. I'm patient and can wait for the right time for us, even if it takes another decade. But something more profound happened today."

"What?" he asked.

"As I stood before Beethoven's memorial, I felt spiritually compelled to become a conductor for a greater purpose. I don't know why or what the reason may be, but I need you to understand that this career will be an integral part of my life at some point."

Richard sighed. "I love your devotion, but it often conflicts with what I want for us. I was wrong, however, to tell you it was impossible. I'm doing my best to come to terms with it. I recognize you were born with a musical gift. I should be helping, not hindering you. I'd never want to be perceived as the evil husband."

She laughed and caressed his hand. "There will be other opportunities. I'll write the director a letter to explain. But to be clear, it's something I must do sooner rather than later."

"Yes. I've been selfish, but I just want you for me and our children," Richard said. "I dreaded coming here knowing your plans. Somewhere I knew you'd be accepted, but I'm sorry to say I hoped you wouldn't be. I love you too much to let you go that easily."

"You sound a little sentimental. What's wrong?" Alejandra asked.

"Nothing. We're still celebrating our tenth wedding anniversary, are we not? You look especially tempting tonight," he said, staring at her cleavage.

"I know that look of yours," she said.

He smiled. "What look?"

"That starry-eyed one. I don't remember you ever calling me 'tempting.' Why not fetching, sultry, alluring?" Alejandra said, laughing.

"Let's toast to the next forty years," he said.

"That's a long time. Maybe we should revisit our intentions every year," she said.

He raised his eyebrows. "No. I know what I want."

"Well then, here's to as long as life gives us," she said, lifting her flute.

Later, they returned to their hotel to find the suite lit only by the warm glow of burning logs in the fireplace, and there was an unexpected fragrance from a dozen white winter tulips in a vase on her nightstand. A saffron colored silk negligée was spread over a chair. "Darling," she said, "you never cease to amaze me." They tossed their coats on a bench at the foot of the bed.

"This is what I want you to remember from our last day here," he said, "considering how awful our first day was... and that I haven't been the easiest to be around lately." He approached her and unbuttoned the front of her dress, removing it. She smiled as he undressed fully, exposing his muscular body. Then he kissed her shoulders, neck, and lips, biting into them lightly. He removed the rest of her clothes. "What about the negligée?" she murmured. "For some other time," he said.

Richard drew Alejandra to him, carried her to the bed, and placed her on white linens. As he reclined next to her, lightly caressing her limbs with his fingers, she sensed an unusual intensity in him. Despite ten years of marriage, it was the kind of lovemaking she felt when they were first married. That night, she felt his love in every way a man could love a woman and emotionally connected to Richard more than in their recent past. He had finally understood all the various dimensions about her and upon feeling her husband's touch she too succumbed to her sensual cravings, hearing each other's heartbeat as he entered her like she was a deity of pleasure—one he would surrender to for eternity. With her eyes closed, she too delighted in that ardent passion between them. They had entered a new phase in their marriage. She felt completely committed to him. It was a union of mind, body, and soul.

WHAT IS THIS THING CALLED LOVE

Richard woke at dawn feeling anxious. The day before he had made a decision, unknown to Alejandra, which could change their lives. For the next hour, he agonized over whether to follow through or set aside his carefully laid out plan. He was pleased to have satisfied his pledge of taking his wife for a week to the Italian coast for their wedding anniversary. He had agreed to come to Berlin despite his mounting objections. In the last two years, she had worked hard to complete her musical degree to go on to the next level, which she did in addition to having numerous demands on her time as a wife and mother. And at this very challenging moment in their lives, he could finally give her the one thing she had longed for since he had known her—to become a conductor, the odds stacked against her notwithstanding. She was strong willed and thrived on challenge, and it was these traits that he most admired about her, even if at times she used them to confront him in ways no other woman ever could.

He stroked his wife's hair as she slumbered next to him, recalling the rare illness that had nearly ended her life two years before and the violent episode on their first night in Berlin. He finally realized her urgency to execute her goal at this time—for life indeed was unpredictable, as she had said on numerous occasions. So he had to ask himself… what if an opportunity like this never arose again? Could he live with knowing he had crushed her dream? He knew this impasse between them would come to a crisis and might potentially over time erode their relationship and cause resentment. So, perhaps he should be the one to take control of their future. Was she right? Was her desire to become a conductor more than a personal dream and part of a larger plan?

He had to trust Alejandra's intuition and his own feelings on the matter.

Then, as sunlight invaded the room, Alejandra woke up and covered herself with the blanket.

"A little too bright for you?" he asked.

She turned away from the window toward him. "Good morning. How long have you been awake?"

"Since dawn. I'm ready to go home," he said. "There's been a change of plans. We're having breakfast with Hannah and Ben at their house. Ben will pick us up and drive us to the train station from their home."

"Splendid! That will give us more time together."

The Adelman's residence, located at the upper-end district in Charlottenburg, near Savigny-Platz, was a charming residential neighborhood. The streets, with a dusting of snow, were almost desolate at that time of the day. Their apartment, on the first floor of a nineteenth century building, could be reached through an iron gate. When Ben let them in, Hannah was playing the violoncello in the drawing room, furnished with a pair of weathered leather club chairs, a brown sofa, and a Persian Kashan rug, faded by the sun. Modest but inviting, the room was light-filled due to its eastern exposure. Upon seeing Richard and Alejandra, Hannah placed the musical instrument against an upright Brunswick piano and walked to her friends, greeting them. "Good morning and welcome."

"How splendid to hear you play. Is this part of your daily routine?" Alejandra asked.

"It's my therapy. Hopefully, I'm not disturbing the neighbors this early in the day," Hannah said. "We're having breakfast in the sunroom. Please follow me."

"Do I smell freshly baked bread?" Richard asked.

"More like strudel," Hannah replied.

"You all go on," Richard said. "I left something in the car."

"Leave it to Richard to be so mysterious," Alejandra said.

A few minutes later, Richard joined them in the sunroom with its tiled floor, potted plants placed against the windows, and a round wicker table with a marble top and chairs. A daisy embroidered tablecloth, blue porcelain dinnerware, and pansies in a vase added a look of spring to the room. Hannah served coffee, and Alejandra passed platters containing cheese, sausage, potato pancakes, and fruit.

"This looks delicious. You do much German cuisine?" Alejandra asked.

"Sure, why not," Hannah replied.

As they ate their breakfast, they discussed last night's opera and how much they had all enjoyed it. Then they talked more about Hannah's recent art acquisitions, but Richard wandered off with his thoughts and questioned whether he could go through with the plans he had put in motion. He lost track of the conversation until Alejandra said, "You seem distracted. Are you all right?"

"I'm fine," he said. "I'm sorry, what were you saying?" He reached under the table and held Alejandra's hand.

"That it's been a stormy week," Alejandra said.

"To put it mildly," Hannah said.

"So, how did you go from talking about art to a stormy week?" Richard asked.

"We were talking about a Pierre-Auguste Cot commission painting about a couple running for shelter in a rainstorm," Alejandra said.

"Well, I guess we could have been that couple a few days ago," Richard said with a little sarcasm. "So, tell me your plans. Are you returning to New York anytime soon, Hannah?"

"She better not!" Ben exclaimed.

"Not until August. Ben has several opportunities to rehearse with other orchestras around Europe, and I'd love to be part of it, even as a bystander. Wouldn't you?" She asked Alejandra. Richard noticed Alejandra glancing at the landscape outside a manicured garden where a large bronze statue of an animal, reminiscent of something out of a Grimm's tale, stood in front of a row of hedges.

"Yes, it all sounds like a wonderful fairy-tale," Alejandra replied.

"Fairy-tale?" Hannah asked.

"A fairy-tale for me," she said.

"What do you mean? You have your whole life ahead of you," Hannah said.

"There's something about that fairy-tale I'd like to show you," Richard said.

"Now? Can it wait?" Alejandra replied.

He stood. "Not really."

"I know that wayward smile of his," Alejandra said. Then Richard led her to the library and watched her face when she saw her two suitcases set by the window under the light of a fringed floor lamp. "You know I'll miss you terribly." Alejandra's expression of disbelief delighted him since it was evident that his change of heart was completely unexpected.

"What's happening?" she asked.

"It's no fairy-tale," he said. "I went to the conservatory yesterday and made arrangements for you to start your studies tomorrow. Consider it a present for our wedding anniversary. You impressed the director with your talent and commitment. He was pleased that you were staying. So there's nothing more for you to be concerned with except your training."

Alejandra's eyes became watery. "Richard, are you sure?"

He said nothing, thinking that her staying in Berlin would come at a significant emotional cost to him, but he was finally giving her the opportunity of a lifetime. "Yes, I am, and don't worry. Everything is being taken care of. I'll return at the end of the summer, and by then, I might even get to see you in action."

"I'm overwhelmed. Now that it's within my reach I can hardly believe it," she said, placing her hand on the bandaged arm. "This might sound a little strange, but this injury, rather than making me afraid of staying, made me more determined. I accept your generous gift, and I'm shocked, ecstatic, and bewildered."

"It doesn't surprise me. I know you too well to let any obstacles get in the way of what you want," he said.

"But what changed your mind?"

He took her face between his hands. "As I told you last night, I finally understand this is part of what you were born to do. Music was part of you before we came into your life. You could have gone to England to pursue your dream, but instead agreed to marry me. Now it's time for me to make a little sacrifice. I don't want to go through life denying it or have it come between us. I love you too much."

"You know what this means to me after years of imagining? I'll get the chance to walk in the footsteps of my favorite composers and to study alongside the finest conductors. I'll miss you and the children, though, and I'm forever grateful to you and mother."

Richard kissed her hand. "Now, I'm confident nothing will ever come between us. Just come back to me as you are at this very moment."

"Darling, after six months apart, I'll be bursting with excitement," she said, laughing.

"Bursting with excitement, now that's something to look forward to," Richard said. "Let's tell the Adelmans."

As they walked out of the library, Richard, for a brief moment, felt a pang in his stomach. He hoped he had made the right decision, a decision he would no doubt question for some time to come, as it could make or break their future together. He felt uncomfortably aware of all the pitfalls that a long separation could entail. But it was done.

They joined their friends back in the sunroom. Hannah had cleared the table. "It's official," Richard said. "She's staying."

"You all know how much he likes to surprise me with the impossible," Alejandra said.

"Like at Juilliard, we'll be a threesome again," Ben said.

"I hope you won't be as bossy as before," she said.

"Me bossy? Where did you get that idea?" Ben laughed. "I'll put together a folder with lessons and readings I've studied thus far that should help you get up to speed."

"I'd appreciate it. Did you know about this, Hannah?" Alejandra asked.

"No. I'm as stunned as you are, but Ben obviously knew something," Hannah said. "You sneaky pair. See, I told you Richard would come around."

"I'm stunned that he went through with the plan. I wasn't sure until he brought in the suitcases earlier," Ben said.

"I leave knowing you'll be safe with Hannah and Ben, and that gives me peace of mind," Richard said. "But still, be careful, particularly with unsavory characters or Don Giovannis."

"Darling, I assure you, nothing bad will happen. I can handle myself," Alejandra said, squeezing his hand.

"Indeed," Richard said, believing that her character had always been above reproach.

"This separation will only be a brief time in your lives, Richard," Hannah said.

He looked at his wristwatch. "Time to go."

"I'll accompany you to the station," Alejandra said.

"If you do, I might change my mind," he said. "Let me help you with your luggage to the bedroom. Ben showed it to me earlier."

Back in the library, Richard picked up the cases and led Alejandra to her room, which was furnished with a double bed, a nightstand, a chest of drawers, and a rolltop desk adorned with a crystal vase filled with water and white and red roses. She immediately walked to the flowers. "You don't miss anything, do you?"

"I can't break with a ten-year plus tradition," Richard said. "I wish we had time for one more rendezvous." He kissed her passionately. Then he took her dress off and gently pulled her by the hand.

"One moment." Wearing only her slip, she took the letter-sized envelope on the dresser and ripped it open, finding a note and the sheet music of Cole Porter's "What Is This Thing Called Love?" She smiled. "Your favorite song."

As he undressed, he said, "Perhaps you should wait and read the note later. Come to bed my sweet alluring nun."

She laughed. "You're never going to let that go, are you?"

"Never. It's too much fun." It was a moniker he often used to tease her with after he had learned she wanted to be a nun when she was a young girl.

She laughed, taking off her slip. "I love you."

"I love you more," he said. "Now I'll miss the train for sure."

PIANO CONCERTO NO. 1 IN B-FLAT MINOR, OP. 23

At the end of the first day of classes, on February 27, Alejandra had agreed to meet Ben at the conservatory's concert hall, which was located with the Berlin Philharmonic at Bernburger Strasse in Berlin-Kreuzberg. Dressed in a gray suit, she arrived at five, thinking of the hundreds of musicians who had trained there since Julius Stern founded the music school in 1850, including Manuel M. Ponce, a Mexican composer and conductor, and Bruno Walter, a German guest conductor of the Minneapolis Symphony Orchestra. She had met and admired both.

With no one else in the hall and with a sense of awe, she climbed the stage, walked to the podium, and passed the palm of her hand over a score that had been left behind. Earlier in the morning, she had watched the orchestra with Ben at the helm perform Tchaikovsky's Piano Concerto no. 1 in B-Flat Minor, op. 23. Comprised of flutes, oboes, clarinets, bassoons, horns, trumpets, trombones, timpani, and strings, it had become a favorite piano concerto after it first premiered in Boston, on October 25, 1875. On several occasions, she had performed the solo piano part back home, finding it extremely difficult with its hammered octaves, but equally exquisite with its captivating and dramatic melodies. Like her, the pianist who performed the piece that morning was also an aspiring conductor who had decided not to pursue a career as a concert pianist. But as far as she was concerned, she would attend every rehearsal possible, for she knew observing rehearsals and studying scores were the best methods of instruction for aspiring conductors.

With her bandaged arm, she raised her hand in a triangular motion, as if conducting Tchaikovsky. She was glad that the stitches would be taken out the next day.

She glanced up at the wall clock and realized Ben was ten minutes late, so she descended to the ground floor where dozens of empty chairs and music stands occupied most of the space. After taking a seat in the front row, she organized the items in her briefcase, including Italian, French, and German dictionaries as well as folders delineating the intensive course curriculum in conducting. She pulled out the top one, reading it to herself: principles of composition, a study of orchestral scores, instrumentation, conducting styles, composers' biographies, and historical practices. From the latter, she had learned the conducting tradition traced back to ancient Greece. But it was in the early 1800s when the profession prospered as a vital factor of musical performance at the direction of composer-conductors such as Beethoven, Berlioz, Liszt, and Mendelssohn, followed by Bülow, Mahler, and Wagner. In contemporary times, Furtwängler and Toscanini, by their exceptional conducting skills, had elevated the profession to such heights and prestige as had never been seen before in musical history.

Among the names who had made their mark as principal conductor of the Berlin Philharmonic Orchestra, she noted the three most recent conductors whose styles she would study in greater detail: Hans von Bülow (1887–1892), Arthur Nikisch (1895–1922), and the current conductor Wilhelm Furtwängler since 1922. It was Bülow, as a pianist-conductor and enthusiast of Tchaikovsky, who took the composer's work to great acclaim when he toured in the United States in 1875. And for that, Tchaikovsky had dedicated his Piano Concerto no. 1 in B-flat Minor, op. 23 to Bülow. He also brought the Berlin Philharmonic Orchestra into international prominence in the late 1880s due to his capacity to conduct multipart works of music without a score. Bülow's goal as a conductor was to reproduce the work with the utmost integrity and to have hand gestures so inconspicuous that the attention was drawn to the music and not the musical director. He would often say, "You should have the score in your head and not your head in the score."

With relish, she recalled that her class, in the afternoon, had heard two recordings with Arthur Nikisch at the helm. His first recording with the Berlin Philharmonic was from September 20, 1913—Beethoven's *Symphony no. 5 in C Minor*, lasting thirty-three minutes and nine seconds. She would study it in detail, for that symphony would always be close to her heart as it provoked a range of emotions and memories unlike any other. It was also a chosen symphony among most conductors. The second recording they heard and analyzed was Mozart's *The Marriage of Figaro*, K 492, recorded with the London Symphony Orchestra on June 21, 1914, lasting four minutes and seventeen seconds. Immersed in her readings, she didn't notice when Ben arrived into the hall at twenty minutes past five o'clock, startling her.

"Ále, forgive my delay. I was talking to Professor Weber. He told me there are problems with the Berlin Philharmonic that may prevent us from rehearsing with them later in the spring."

"What kind of problems?" she asked.

"Financial problems, but let's discuss it later over dinner if you don't mind. Anton is meeting us at six at Zur Letzten."

"I don't think I'll be joining you. I have too much reading to do, but I'd like to hear about the orchestra," she said.

"Are you sure?" he asked.

"I just need time on my own. You go on. I'll take a cab."

It was bitterly cold that night as she walked through the Brandenburg Gate colonnade after being dropped off by the taxi driver. With a strong wind, she tightened her white scarf around her neck and decided to remain under the protection of the gate, leaning against the mighty structure and placing her hands inside the pockets of her wool coat. But then she felt a shiver down her spine and had a strange sensation as though being sucked into a black whirlpool. Suddenly, she questioned her decision to remain in this foreign land away from her family for such an extended period. It was unusual for her to have self-doubts and apprehension. What had started as a seven-day journey had now extended to six months, and with that reality she felt conflicted. Was it the love for her family and the inability to see them that confused her? She was sure that had Richard stayed she would not be having second thoughts.

She gazed at the architectural details of the gate, thinking of her father who would be explaining the gate's historical and architectural significance if he were there. Since his death, there wasn't a day that she didn't think of him. He had passed away several years prior from complications after a heart attack. They were best of friends, and she missed his advice more than ever. Would he have approved of her staying behind in Berlin? No. Her father, too, while supportive of her general education, was also of the mind that conducting was not a suitable profession for a woman. He would have preferred she became a music teacher, a concert pianist, or anything but a conductor.

Just then a friendly police officer approached her. "*Geht es dir gut?*"

She sighed. "Ja." She was all right but felt out of place in a foreign city. *"Sie sollten nicht zu dieser Stunde allein sein,"* he said. His calm demeanor, almost protective, made her feel safe at that moment.

She agreed with him that she should not be alone at such an hour. She nodded. *"Ich gehe zum Adlon Hotel."*

"Ich werde Sie dort zu Fuß," he said.

She thanked him for offering to walk her to the hotel, but she declined and left the gate.

As she approached the entrance of the hotel, she visualized Richard waiting for her to have dinner together. But that night and for many more nights, she would dine alone. He was now thousands of miles away, crossing the Atlantic. She would have to wait a week or more to hear from him again.

She went to the restaurant, hoping to see a familiar face and was pleased that the friendly hostess recognized her. "Frau Morrison, it's good to see you again. Would you like to be seated at your usual table?"

"Yes, please," she replied.

She led Alejandra to a table with a clear view of the Brandenburg Gate. Only two days before, she and Richard had sat there, enjoying a nightcap. For an instant, she wished to turn the clock back forty-eight hours. But if she could, would she have made a different choice? And without pondering long, the answer was a definite no. She knew musical devotion often came at a high price. Many composers and conductors dedicated everything to their profession, sometimes at the expense of personal relationships. This thought was far from reassuring for she had never loved a man as she did Richard and could not imagine a life without her family. She suffered their separation deeply. She only hoped, in due course, that she could reconcile her love of family with her equal love to have absolute dominion in her creativity as a musician and soon as a conductor.

She placed her belongings next to her and took the note from her handbag, the one Richard had written before he departed.

It read:

Ále, I'm not a man of many words, but know I'll always love you with everything I have. When you think of me now and then, please play for us "What Is This Thing Called love?"

She placed the note against her chest, and those simple words written with such heartfelt love brought a deluge of emotions. Richard had demonstrated not only that he loved her unconditionally, but that he was willing to let her go so that she could realize her dreams. She knew that not only could she not turn back, but she must prove to herself and others that pursuing her studies would be a worthwhile effort.

Then the waiter, tall, young and dark-haired, asked, "May I take your order?" She scanned the menu and replied, "A cup of espresso, a bowl of vegetable soup, and a ham sandwich."

When he left, she reached into her briefcase and pulled out her schedule. In two weeks, she would travel to Leipzig to observe rehearsals of the Leipzig Gewandhaus Orchestra under its current musical director Bruno Walter, who was known to be supportive of women's professional careers. Leipzig had also been home to Felix Mendelssohn, who had been a powerful influence on the musical life of the city as a founder of its conservatory and as conductor of its orchestra. Mendelssohn revolutionized the concert program by starting with an overture, proceeding to a larger scale work, then to a concerto, and ending with a shorter piece. He was known for his dictatorial approach, fast tempos, and exact rhythms. He was also one of the first to use a baton. Curious to learn the differing conducting styles, she wondered who she might model herself after and which conducting approach aligned best with her temperament. While it was too soon to pass judgment at this early stage in her training, she thought that a dictatorial approach would not suit her personality, although it may be necessary at times.

Later at night, in Pariser platz, a family of four walked next to her, and two young boys ran ahead of their parents, pushing and playing with each other. Her children would soon be getting out of school while their mother was on another continent as if she did not have a care in the world. She would make it up to them and write to explain her absence, hoping they were old enough to understand. Overcome with guilt, she wondered what kind of mother would make such a choice.

Searching for some assurance, she raised her eyes to the heavens and saw a dark blue sky sprinkled with bright stars and a half moon, suffused in golden hues. She sighed, thinking Berlin was a city with a history spanning nine hundred years from the twelfth century to a vibrant city in the 1920s, and now the third largest in the world and home to the Third Reich. She took in the icy air and all the sights and sounds around her of passing vehicles and distant laughter. She hoped that Berlin, with the passage of time, would feel like a second home as it once had to her ancestors, and that her conflicting emotions would settle down.

Back at the Adelman's residence, she changed into comfortable apparel and slipped on her feather slippers. In the living room, she looked at the various Judaica decorations, including Hannah's acquisition hanging on the wall—an embroidered tapestry depicting the twelve tribes of Israel. Because of her friendship with Hannah she was well versed in Sephardic traditions. She appreciated the teachings of other religions even though she did not consider herself staunchly religious. With a more spiritual orientation, she preferred to find connections amongst all faiths.

Then she noticed a new painting of Fanny and Felix Mendelssohn sitting together at the piano. For them, music was a family affair. Those two siblings had performed weekly concerts, making their home in the early 1820s the intellectual center of Berlin. Of particular interest to Alejandra had always been the life of Fanny Mendelssohn, who, like many women, also struggled in her role as a mother, wife, and professional musician. Fanny was as gifted a composer as her brother, and she had composed over four hundred pieces, but her music was not as well known. Some of her compositions were published by her brother, Felix, to help her gain recognition. With these thoughts, Alejandra approached the bookcase behind the piano and searched through piles of manuscripts. To her satisfaction, at the bottom of the stack, she found two of Fanny Mendelssohn's manuscripts—Trio, op.11 and the Piano Sonata in G Minor.

Still feeling uncertain by the separation from her family, Alejandra turned to the only preoccupation that always gave her a sense of permanence and purpose—playing music. She sat at the piano and softly touched the white and black keys, each producing a different feeling, low and high. It was like caressing something organic. She decided to play the exquisite piano sonata, building to a crescendo, and felt that the music nourished her spirit. Then, for the next two hours, she played other favorites from memory.

Hannah and Ben, coming into the house, looking desperately grim, interrupted her. Hannah, her eyes full of terror, approached her and said, "The Reichstag is on fire."

"It can't be! I was just there, and from a distance everything seemed normal. How is that possible?" Alejandra asked.

"Some nearby spectators heard it was arson by the communists, but Ben thinks it was the work of the Nazis," Hannah said.

"Why do you say that?" Alejandra asked.

Ben joined them at the piano. "Because no communist could be stupid enough to do something like that. But I'm sure we'll know soon enough."

CONCERTO NO. 4

Alejandra, with her back arched over her desk and wearing a nightgown and robe, reviewed several scores of Bach's Brandenburg Concertos. Bach, who was considered the supreme contrapuntist of all time, created original music packed with dense counterpoint. For the opportunity to perform his music in a historical context, she had accepted an invitation to perform the composer's *Concerto no. 4* the next day with the Leipzig chamber orchestra. As her preferred one of the six concertos, it was scored with a variety of instrumental combinations, giving it a distinct character. All six concertos reflected some of the finest compositions in baroque music. The concert at St. Thomas Church, the composer's final resting place, would commemorate the two hundred and forty-eighth anniversary of his birth.

Fueled by the momentous occasion, she had devoted most of her time in the last week to practice on a 1758 harpsichord. She was proficient on piano, but she found the older keyboard to be more challenging due to its lighter dynamics, narrower keys, and lack of pedals. It was essential for her to preserve the original sound as intended by Bach. And while she was concerned about her performance not being optimal, she was relieved by the fact that the score called for a violin solo, which would highlight Ben's virtuosity.

Alejandra heard a tap on her bedroom door.

"Ále, I'm sorry it's so late. I need to speak with you," Hannah said from the hallway.

"Come in, Hannah, please."

She stepped inside and sat on a chair next to a desk. "Tonight we met with Anton, and he offered to drive us to Leipzig tomorrow. You don't care, do you?"

She had not seen Anton since the dinner at his residence, even though he had invited her with Hannah and Ben to several outings. She wasn't sure why, but she had refused every time.

"If you don't feel comfortable, we'll drive separately. Are you hesitant because he may like you?" Hannah asked.

"Why do you say that?" Alejandra asked.

"Well, I can't be sure, but he often asks about you. I noticed his interest in you since the first day we met him."

"I hope not. I'd like to think his interest has to do more with his fondness for music, and we all have that in common," Alejandra said. "You and Ben enjoy his company, and I wouldn't want to come in the way of that. So I guess I can handle a two-hour drive."

"It will be for more than that. He'll join us throughout the week," Hannah said.

Alejandra paused, thinking she did not want to make it difficult for Hannah and Ben. "Well, then, I guess we can all be good friends."

"He was born in Leipzig, so he'll be an excellent guide," Hannah said. "His cottage is close to the Fürstenhof Hotel where we'll be staying. Until tomorrow, then."

After Hannah left, her thoughts reverted to more encouraging events of the upcoming week—rehearsals with the Leipzig Gewandhaus Orchestra under its conductor Bruno Walter and the concert on Thursday, March 16.

Early next morning, Alejandra, dressed in an ivory wool suit, carried her suitcase into the living room where she saw Anton standing by the bookshelves perusing the literature selection. He was wearing black slacks, a blue shirt, and a leather jacket. "Let me help you. It's so nice to see you again. Ben and Hannah went to do a last-minute errand. They let me in before they left."

"I can manage, but thank you," she said, placing her suitcase by the entrance. "Would you like a cup of coffee?"

"Yes please, one teaspoon of sugar and no cream."

She returned holding two cups and handed one to Anton, who was now sitting down. As she took her seat across from him, she felt uneasy, recalling Hannah's previous comment.

"I was astounded to know you decided to stay. It was my impression you were restless to go home," Anton said. "You know, I looked for you all at the opera. Did you end up going?"

"After being admitted to the program, how could I refuse?" she said. "And yes, we did go. But we left the opera house soon after. It was marvelous."

"So, how has the training been?" he asked.

"It's wonderful, but I miss my husband and children."

"How old are they?"

She sighed. "Lydia Hannah, Richard Edward, and Delia Rose are ages eight, six, and four. I feel overwhelmed with guilt. Thank goodness for my mother. She's very close to them."

"Would you have it any other way?" he asked.

"If I'm perfectly honest, no. Because as much I love them, I'd always wonder 'what if?' I can only hope they'll forgive me and won't forget me."

"I don't think you're someone who could be easily forgotten."

"That's kind of you to say," she said.

Just then, Ben and Hannah returned. "Why don't we pack up the car? We should still be there by noon," Ben said.

"I'd like that, and I wouldn't mind rehearsing the piece one more time," Alejandra said. "I'm not sure I'm ready."

"If you play like you did the last time I saw you, you'll be great," Anton said.

"A harpsichord is much different than a pianoforte, so we shall see," Alejandra said.

W alking to Gewandhaus, Leipzig's concert hall, on Sunday March 12, Alejandra turned to the neo-classical structure with three large arched windows and columns below a series of Greek-style statuettes. At the top of the building, carved in scripted Latin, read the phrase "*Res Severa Verum Gaudium*"—True joy is a serious thing. She smiled, thinking the words perfectly expressed her sentiments at the moment. For the night before, her performance at the harpsichord before several hundred people had not been up to her technical standards. The balance of contrapuntal clarity, tempi, and timbre, may have been lacking. She was mightily relieved that it was over, and she would not be eager to repeat the experience.

As she walked about the courtyard, she glanced at the landscape that was beginning to show signs of spring. She stopped at the Felix Mendelssohn monument, waiting for the musicians to arrive for the public rehearsal.

Anton joined her. "Good morning. I met Ben earlier, and he said I would find you here after Mass."

"It seems I find myself more in need of prayer without my family," she said, smiling.

"What a loss at such a young age. I'm sure you know that at thirty-eight Mendelssohn left an extraordinary musical legacy."

"He was only twenty-six when he became conductor of Gewandhaus. But what brings you here?"

"Last night I wanted to congratulate you on your performance, but you left immediately after the concert," Anton said.

"I'm not sure it was my best, and I wasn't in much of a mood for socializing," she said.

"Perhaps you'll make an exception tonight and join us. I would like to request a favor from you, which is why I'm here."

A growing crowd, gathering around the courtyard, distracted her with their loud voices. She noticed several musicians approaching the music hall and from afar she recognized the conductor. It had been ten years since she had first become acquainted with Bruno Walter in Minneapolis when she had seen him perform at a fundraising concert for German children. He had aged a little, but he still had that distinguished appearance. "I should go. But what favor?"

"Would you be so kind as to accompany my protégé? She's an excellent lieder singer. I want to encourage her talent, and we'd like your assessment on her aptitude to sing opera."

She was inclined to refuse his invitation, trying her best to keep a distance but was interested in hearing his friend whom he considered a candidate for opera singing. After momentary consideration, she replied, "Ben could also give you his assessment."

"True, but I was also hoping you could accompany her at the piano," he said.

"Mendelssohn had a vast repertoire in this genre, and I'm rather fond of the German traditional art song. My grandmother often sang for us, so I accept."

"I appreciate that you'll join us. Hannah has all the details," Anton said.

"See you then," she said, walking away.

HUNGARIAN RHAPSODY NO. 2

Anton waited in the cottage for his guests to arrive, but like a furious fox whose territory was about to be violated, he strode back and forth in the drawing room, feeling distressed. An hour earlier, he had dismissed his long-time housekeeper, Helga, and her husband, the property caretaker. He overheard them discussing their unbending support of the government's alarming response to the Reichstag fire. The Nazi administration had rounded up and imprisoned hundreds of individuals who were considered to be communists, socialists, and the perpetrators of the disaster. Anton, who suspected it was all a setup, was opposed to those policies, which included the suspension of many civil liberties. He felt that he could no longer trust anyone as the atmosphere everywhere had become increasingly paranoid. He must be careful when expressing anti-government sentiments if he wanted to continue to run a successful business.

When the grandfather clock chimed at seven o'clock, he went into the foyer and looked out the window, spotting his first guest—a young woman with white-blond hair. He wasn't sure whether he could trust her either, but she was someone with whom he could ease the tension he was feeling. Impatiently, he opened the door. "Isolde, you're late. Did you memorize the song?"

She slipped off her coat, revealing a long-sleeved violet dress, which fit snugly around her slim figure. "You only gave me a couple of days, but yes," Isolde said. "I'm prepared to sing as you requested. I'd like to be paid in advance though."

He pulled out a wallet from his coat pocket and took a small wad of Swiss francs, which at the moment were more valuable than Reich marks.

She grabbed the money, saying, "Such pretty notes, but why so much?"

"I want you for the next two days. It's been two weeks since you visited me in Berlin."

"I'm busy with another client," she said smugly.

"Cancel it!" he said, putting his hands on her waist and pulling her forcibly to him. "You don't need to work like this. I can support you."

"Not tonight." She turned away coquettishly. "You'll have to wait for tomorrow."

"No, I don't," he said, leading her to his bedroom.

"But don't you have guests coming?" She laughed.

"Not for another hour. There's plenty of time for you to entertain me," Anton said, eyeing Isolde's ample bosom. Then he stroked her firm buttocks, as she unbuttoned his pants.

"Fine. I'm all yours," she said, undressing.

An hour later, Anton greeted his three American friends when they arrived. He led them through a hallway and into the music salon where two crimson-covered Empire sofas, a cocktail table, a wooden cabinet, and an upright piano filled the cramped space. He introduced his guests to Isolde. She shook their hands, and said, "*Vergnügen, Sie zu treffen.*"

"*Es freut mich, Sie kennenzulernen,*" Alejandra said. She continued in German."What a lovely name. Wagner opera inspired?"

"Yes. My mother was a huge fan of his operas. And she often said I too could be an opera singer based on the quality of my infant cries."

"That's one way to look at it. Perhaps we'll agree with your mother," Ben said.

"How were the rehearsals?" Anton asked.

"Bruno Walter will be conducting Mahler at Thursday's concert. He reminded me he was once Mahler's student," Ben said. "But on a darker note, I'm concerned about troubling rumors floating around that may affect him."

"I'd prefer we leave that discussion for later," Anton said. "Please sit down. Can I get you something to drink? No butler at my service tonight."

"A cognac please," Ben said.

"A glass of water for me," Hannah added.

"Likewise," Alejandra said as she sat next to Isolde to continue their conversation.

Anton took a key from a small herringbone box atop a side table and walked to an intricately carved cabinet. He unlocked it, revealing a complete bar set with decanters, glasses, shaker set, slicing knife, strainers, chopping board, and a selection of liquor.

He had barely finished serving drinks when Isolde abruptly stood. "I'm not feeling well, and my throat is bothering me. I'm not sure I can sing tonight."

"Not even one song?" Anton asked.

She shook her head no, as she played nervously with her fingers. "I'm sorry."

"If it's just your nerves you have nothing to worry about," Anton said. "My friends came to hear you sing."

"That's all right, you can sing some other time for us," Alejandra said.

Anton walked to Isolde. "Will you excuse us for a moment?" He then escorted her to another room. Once they were alone in the parlor, Anton said, "You know how I feel about the work that you do. It's degrading and dangerous. Wouldn't you prefer to make a living giving pleasure with your beautiful voice instead of your body? I honestly believe you have a future as a singer, and I wanted my friends to confirm that for you so you would take it seriously. Will you please sing one song for them?"

Stunned, Isolde said, "Is that the reason why you are so insistent? You care about me?"

"Partly, yes," he said, placing his hands on her shoulders.

"What if I make a mistake?" she asked. "I don't think I can ever be an opera singer."

"That's for them to decide. Ben used to work for an opera company. As far as you making a mistake, that won't matter. Of course you will make mistakes. Everybody does."

"But they're Jews," Isolde said. "I don't want to sing for them. Some of my friends say they want to harm us."

Anton sighed. "Isolde. You can't believe everything you hear. Ben and Hannah are Jews, Alejandra is not, and all three are very kind people. They would want you to succeed, and they have been good friends to me. But you should be careful what you say because there's a lot of ignorant people out there. You understand?"

She nodded, tilting her head down like a scolded child.

"Will you sing?"

"I will try."

They returned to the salon, and Isolde walked to the piano. "I was nervous."

"Don't worry, enjoy," Alejandra said. "Even famous opera singers get anxious before performances. I had one last night, and I assure you I was very tense."

Isolde nodded in agreement. "If I sing now, I won't have to think about it," she said, smoothing her dress.

"Let's get on with it, then," Alejandra said as she went to the piano, glancing at the score—"Im Frühling" by Franz Schubert, lyrics by Ernst Schulze. She gave Isolde a few moments to concentrate, but Isolde interrupted. "I'd like to first sing a favorite of mine. It will help me to warm up."

"Certainly," Alejandra said. "And which one is that?"

"'Falling in Love Again' from Blue Angel," Isolde said.

"Yes. It's famous all over the world. Will you do it a cappella?" Alejandra asked.

Isolde nodded, and started to sing it. "*Ich bin von Kopf bis Fuß auf Liebe eingestellt.*"

When Isolde finished, Alejandra said, "Perfect pitch. Perhaps, you could be the next Marlene Dietrich."

"I think Isolde's voice is better than hers," Ben said.

Isolde smiled. "I can now sing Schubert's lieder."

Alejandra played the introduction. Soon after, Isolde began to sing: "*Still sitz' ich an des Hügels Hang, der Himmel ist so klar, das Lüftchen spielt im grünen Tal. Wo ich beim ersten Frühlingsstrahleinst, ach so glücklich war. Wo ich an ihrer Seite ging so traulich und so nah, und tief im dunkeln Felsenquell*"—Quietly I sit on the hill's slope. The sky is so clear; a breeze plays in the green valley. Where I was at spring's first sunbeam once, alas, I was so happy! When I was walking at her side, so intimate and so close, and deep in the dark rocky spring was the beautiful sky, blue and bright.

Isolde finished singing and she curtsied, turning to Alejandra, who said, "That was splendid. Do you have a good teacher?"

"No. But do you think I can sing opera?"

"Yes, but it will take a lot of dedication on your part," Alejandra said. "Years ago, I met one of the finest voice instructors at Juilliard. Her name is Anna Schoen-René, and she learned to sing from Pauline Garcia-Viardot, who was one of the best opera singers in the world. You must find a teacher who's versed in the bel canto singing style. Ben might also have suggestions."

"I agree with Alejandra's assessment. I'm very impressed. However, opera requires intense training, commitment, and stamina. Are you prepared for that?"

"I'm not sure, but I'll consider everything you've said, and thank you for your time. I must go now," Isolde said, and hastily left the room.

"Pardon me," Anton said, walking out with her.

When he returned to the salon, he overheard Hannah say, "What talent, but what strikes me as odd was the heavy makeup and her attire, a bit risqué for such a young girl. She can't be more than twenty."

"She's certainly very beautiful, and it would be a pity if she doesn't take advantage of her powerful voice," Ben said.

"She has the potential to be a great opera singer but needs training," Alejandra added.

Anton interrupted. "Since our musical program was cut short, would you mind if we play together? I'll be the second violin."

"You have extra instruments laying around here too?" Ben asked incredulously.

"I always have violins, but no cello at my disposal."

"I'll pass, but please feel free to play," Ben said.

"Alejandra, would you like to accompany me?"

She paused, still sitting by the piano. "Depends on the music," she said playfully. "May I see the manuscripts?"

"Of course," Anton replied, pushing a folder across the top of the piano toward her. After sorting through a handful of them, she said enthusiastically, "I love this one."

"Which one?" Hannah asked.

"Franz Liszt's Hungarian Rhapsody no. 2," Alejandra replied.

"Oh, but of course, she was enthralled with his music back at Juilliard. She could play all nineteen rhapsodies by heart," Ben said.

Alejandra smiled humbly, putting her hands together. "I think it's the gypsy scale that appeals to me."

"I won't need the score," Anton said, gazing directly at Alejandra as he placed the violin under his chin. In such proximity to her, he looked at the expression on her face as she reverted her attention to the manuscript and motioned her hand after the count of four. Then Anton, as though he was in conversation with her, immersed himself in the composition's melancholic overture known as the *lassan*, followed by the more capricious and spirited modulations of the second part, *friska*. As they played together, Anton found himself smitten with Alejandra, and fantasies about the alluring pianist surfaced in his mind.

When they ended their performance eight minutes later, Hannah applauded vigorously. "Gracious, what a perfect duet you make. You played like you were both in musical ecstasy."

Alejandra said, "It's easy to forget oneself when playing Liszt. I'll have that brandy."

"One coming up," Anton said, as he placed the violin and bow on top of the piano, feeling ecstatic.

"You're a brilliant violinist. Why don't you play for an orchestra? Have you ever considered it?" Ben asked.

"No! I'd never," Anton said, walking to the bar cabinet.

"I hear a touch of bitterness in your reply," Ben remarked.

"You could say that, but obviously, it's not about the music, but more about the profession," Anton replied, giving Alejandra her drink. He sat down on a leopard, animal-print upholstered armchair. "It's difficult to make a good living as a musician. I'm sure you know what happened to our two largest orchestras?"

"Yes, the merging of the two orchestras was a contentious issue for Furtwängler," Ben said. "And now, due to their fiscal struggles, the Berlin Philharmonic has been forced to accept the government's financial support."

Anton cleared his throat. "More like a takeover by Goebbels. I find it most alarming. First out with our civil liberties and free press, and now Hitler and his collaborators are seizing our cultural institutions one by one. Once a government has control over what music gets played, what art gets shown, or who says what, we're at full dictatorship."

"What's also becoming crystal clear is the anti-Semitic fervor every-where," Hannah said. "How is all this going to end? It's frightening."

"That's what I was concerned about exactly," Ben said. "The rumors are that Nazi officials in Leipzig will not permit Walter's concert to take place this Thursday. He's been the Genwandhaus's conductor for four years and has offered to resign."

"I'm truly sorry to hear that. With their destructive policies, they are determined to expel all Jews from artistic employment," Anton said.

Alejandra, who had been listening quietly, said, "When I first came, I had naively trusted that politicians would abstain from corrupting the arts by their radical views. I believed that artists, regardless of their background, would be left alone to do their work. Art is the most sublime expression of our humanity. It has inspired humankind since the beginning of time."

Anton said, "It's the perfect setup. What better way than to thrust their hateful ideology through the prism of culture. By using our rich artistic inheritance, they'll infiltrate every aspect of our society until everyone is forced to submit to their policies either by ignorance or fear. I can't say I'm shocked. I saw it coming."

"How?" Alejandra asked.

"It was all there in *Mein Kampf.* The disgusting diatribe Hitler wrote while in prison now serves as the Nazi playbook," Anton said. "He's a demagogue who knows just how to divide our country."

"It's so unfortunate. Richard told me so, but I had hoped it wasn't true," Alejandra said. "You must have hope that at some point their power will end."

"Yes. Will his policies have an effect on your plans?" Anton asked.

"Regrettably. We're going to wait for a week or two, and then we'll decide whether or not to continue our training in Vienna," Ben said.

"Because of all these changes and the fact that we may leave soon, we're going to Bonn on Friday," Alejandra said. "It may be our only chance to visit Beethoven's birthplace."

"If I remember correctly, that was something you wanted to do since your arrival. The Rhineland is my favorite area of Germany," Anton said.

"It was Beethoven's too," Alejandra said. "Have I said that before?"

"You could never hide your enthusiasm for the composer," Ben said. "We should go since I have an early rehearsal tomorrow."

"And if I may suggest finding a good voice teacher for Isolde," Alejandra said to Anton.

"I'll do my best, and let's hope the concert goes as planned," Anton said.

TRISTESSE

April 3, 1933 – Minneapolis, Minnesota

Late in the evening, Richard entered his home located in an affluent neighborhood surrounding Lake of the Isles, one of the principle four lakes in the city of Minneapolis. The others were Calhoun, Cedar, and Harriet. Since the early twentieth century, many prominent businessmen and professionals had chosen this location to build their stately homes, making it the most desirable residential area with a vibrant cultural scene, wooded landscapes, and not far from the Mississippi River, which ran through the city. With nearly half a million in population, the city had been growing steadily since the turn of the century. But in 1933, as the depression deepened, trade and banking were significantly affected, but not as badly as had been feared. And thanks to a large inheritance from his father, who had been in the lumber business, and his medical practice, Richard remained optimistic about his family's future livelihood.

The foyer, with checkerboard marble floors, Doric columns, and arches, was a pleasant sight after working a long day at the hospital. He loosened his tie, removed his coat, hung it, and proceeded to the library hoping to find a letter from his wife. He had been thinking about her all day and wondered whether her plans had changed since her last letter.

To his amusement, his oldest daughter, Leidy, wearing a yellow cotton dress, socks, and shoes, was on the button-tufted leather chair. Eagerly, she jumped out of the seat, swinging an envelope back and forth in her hand. "A letter from Mommy... open it!" He approached his vintage desk and took the envelope from her hand. "How about, hello, Daddy first," he said.

"Hello, Daddy," the girl said.

From a drawer, he pulled out a letter opener and carefully cut through the top flap, extracting the five-page, hand-written letter. "Maybe I should read it first."

"No, Daddy. I've been waiting all afternoon," his daughter pleaded, as she sat on top of the desk with her legs dangling like a rag doll.

He patted his daughter's hand. "All right," he said, sitting down. He began to read aloud:

My dearest Richard: It has been a week since we last spoke, and your voice still lingers in my ear like a sweet melody. Thank you for sending photographs of the children. I carry them everywhere. Please also thank my mother for keeping me posted on their daily happenings. I just received a letter from her yesterday. I've written to her to express my gratitude, for I could not have pursued my studies without her and your support. Please also tell the children I love them and wish for the day we will be together again.

My heart filled with sadness and joy, for nothing is ever the way we imagine things to be. Like never before, I find myself praying for you and our children; praying that I've made the right choice by being here; praying that people feel more love for one another. I'd never thought praying would give me such comfort and peace of mind. I don't know whether to begin to tell you about my sadness or my joy, but wanting to leave you with a smile, I'll relate the sadness that is sifting through my heart at an ever-growing pace.

Richard paused. "Please, get me a glass of water."

"Why did you stop, Daddy?" Leidy asked, pouting.

"Go on." Then, when she left to fetch his water, he continued to read the rest of the letter.

As you know from our last conversation, we were in keen anticipation to be in Leipzig for Bruno Walter's concert and to participate in the rehearsals. On Thursday, March 17, at eleven in the morning, we, along with groups of enthusiastic people, gathered outside Gewandhaus concert hall to see the orchestra's public rehearsal. Unfortunately, we were all denied admission into the venue. A notice, prominently displayed at the entrance, read that both the rehearsal and the concert were can-

celed. Many individuals, including members of the orchestra, were stunned and troubled by the Nazi's police actions and radical measures, which also ended Walter's tenure as the conductor of the Leipzig orchestra. In a show of kindness, the orchestra's administration and other German people made generous offerings, bringing flowers to Walter, but nothing could ever undo this wrong. This situation was not to be an isolated event, for when we returned to Berlin on Sunday, we were made aware that Josef Goebbels, the propaganda minister, sent out a message that the Bruno Walter Concert series at Philharmonic Hall would also be canceled, forecasting threats of violence unless another conductor took his place. Walter had no choice but to withdraw permanently from that concert and any future musical engagements in his country.

In light of these events and others of similar nature, Ben and Hannah no longer feel safe to remain here. We are finding it extremely tough to ignore the increasingly arbitrary violence, and of course the ever-present threatening gatherings of storm troopers marching around the city with impunity. We have decided to continue with our studies in Vienna. We plan to relocate there by the first week in May. In the meantime, we will continue with our training at the Stern Conservatory until then.

Leidy returned with a glass of water, which Richard drank. She sat once again on his desk, and he resumed reading the letter aloud.

Turning to my source of happiness is, of course, thinking of you and the children. But it is also true that music is my saving grace. I spend most of my time at rehearsals and at the royal library, which holds an immense collection of medieval, Renaissance, baroque, classical, Romantic, and contemporary scores written by every composer known. Studying scores is an arduous task and time consuming, but one that is enormously enjoyable, especially when reviewing the notes as I'm listening to the music performed live. Being here, in a place known as a treasure trove of music, I take every opportunity to attend rehearsals and live concerts; for this is the best source of training for aspiring conductors. And my focus has been to develop skills in the principles of conducting—the capacity to intuit the composer's intention, attain the overview of a score, and then to convey it to the orchestra.

Traveling to Bonn to see all traces of Beethoven's life from birth to death gave me such joy and repose. Words cannot come close to describing it, although I will attempt. Imagine, my darling, seeing his last pianoforte where he composed Symphony no. 9 and Missa Solemnis. What would I have given to touch that one-hundred-year-old keyboard? I could only close my eyes and envision his hands on the pianoforte, creating for the benefit of mankind his exalted symphonies. And what of his manuscripts? To behold the originals of Moonlight Sonata and the Pastoral Symphony. The letters he wrote to his nephew, and everyday objects of his personal use including his ear trumpets—all giving us the measure of his humanity. Despite terrible hardships that he experienced as a young boy, he created such beauty. He was a man of profound wisdom who once said, "Music is the one incorporeal entrance into the higher world of knowledge which comprehends mankind, but which mankind cannot comprehend."

Walking by his humble home reminded me how unimportant it is what we are born into, compared to what we are capable of doing despite our beginnings... what we leave behind, and isn't that what life is all about?

With everything that is happening here, I can't help but wonder what would Beethoven do or say? And I have no answer, except perhaps to know the ideals of the enlightenment appealed to him. And I believe he had found God's light through his music, where there is only love for one another. Guided by his sense of universal peace, Beethoven set Friedrich von Schiller's poem to "Ode to Joy"—his Ninth Symphony Chorale: Freudig, wie ein Held zum Siegen (Joyful as a hero in victory.) *Seid umschlungen, Millionen!* (Be embraced, you Millions!) *Diesen Kuß der ganzen Welt!* (This kiss for the entire world!*) Brüder, über'm Sternenzelt* (Brothers, beyond the stars) *Muß ein lieber Vater wohnen.* (Must a loving father live).

What a different world it would be today if current leaders would not have turned away from earlier German philosophy. Men of wisdom who spoke and practiced noble traditions of tolerance and understanding.

Forgive me if I in any way sound dissatisfied. I'll forever be grateful for this opportunity, despite its sober situations. I worry for the future, and I feel powerless to do anything about it. For the moment, all I can do is focus on my studies. I know there's a greater purpose for why I'm here away from you. I can only trust that God's plan will reveal itself in time.

Tell the children I'm writing a diary of the highlights, so I can later share my experiences in my letters to them. Please kiss them for me and know that I love you all deeply. Alejandra.

He placed the letter on the desk.

"Daddy, why is Mommy worried for the future?"

"It's complicated. Now go on and practice your piano," Richard said.

After his daughter had left the library, he gazed at a family picture on his desk. Taken last summer at their cabin, Alejandra was surrounded by their three children. He could have never predicted then that now she would be on the other side of the Atlantic amid increasing instability. He regretted his decision to allow Alejandra to stay abroad. He worried about her. The political situation was escalating out of control. Then he heard his daughter play "Tristesse" by Chopin, allaying his worries at least for the time being. For he was reminded of an Emerson poem that Alejandra often recited—"Do not go where the path may lead, go instead where there is no path and leave a trail." He knew that her optimistic and idealistic spirit would keep her going forward and that she would return only when her mission was completed. She was someone who thrived on making a difference in the world. He must accept that even if inside he felt increasing trepidation.

MISSA SOLEMNIS

On April 22, 1933, Alejandra arrived home to find Ben sitting on a kitchen chair, severely beaten up. Hannah was cleansing wounds on his face with a white cloth. A tin pan filled with warm water was on the table. "Oh, my goodness, what happened to you?" she asked, dropping her handbag on the kitchen counter.

"After dinner, we were walking on Wilhelmstraße toward the Reich's Chancellery, when a group of Brownshirts, or should I say thugs, gathered there harassing anyone who walked by. An old man refused to respond to them with a Hitler salute, so he was stopped. Two Brownshirts started beating him up. Ben ran to defend the man, but they turned their rage toward Ben, punching him in the face and yelling racial slurs. I showed them our American passports. They finally ceased, and as if their actions were of no consequence, they walked away laughing. We helped the man from the ground and walked with him until we were all out of sight. The poor man was a proud German general who now feared more than ever for the future of his country, he told us. We just got here ten minutes ago."

"Ben, I'm so appalled by this," Alejandra said, placing her hand on his shoulder.

"I'm all right," Ben said.

"The hell you're all right," Hannah said.

"You'll report this to the American embassy, won't you?" Alejandra asked.

"You bet I will. I'm going first thing tomorrow. Although, I doubt the staff can do much except make a formal complaint."

"We're leaving next weekend for Vienna, and there we won't have to deal with this anymore," Ben said. "So, just let it go."

"No! They need to do something about it. How many more people have to suffer this?"

"I spoke with Richard, and he wants me to return home." Alejandra took the dirty tin pan with sullied water to the sink, emptied it, and refilled it with clean water.

"I wouldn't mind going back," Hannah said. "Well? Are you?"

"I would if you do, of course," Alejandra said.

"My body may be aching and my face a mess, but I won't be chased down like some scared cat. I've made arrangements to complete our training in Vienna. We'll finish what we came to accomplish. Hitler doesn't own Europe. And I'm certainly not a quitter because of some setback at the hands of savages. There's still civility elsewhere." He stood up, taking the wet cloth to wipe his neck. "What I need is a shower and to get off these bloody clothes." He left.

"I have to agree. It would be a shame to give it all up after so much effort," Alejandra said. "As Ben said, it's safe in Vienna. Would you like me to go the embassy with you?"

"No. I'm fine. I guess you're both right. I'm just glad we'll be getting out of here soon."

A week later, aboard the train to Vienna, Alejandra unbuttoned her ivory-colored wool coat, folded it neatly, and placed it on a shelf in the compartment. Sitting by the window, she felt a deep sense of loss because her departure had come under the darkest of circumstances. Not only had Ben been assaulted, but he later told her of the creation of a new secret police—Geheime staatspolizei, the Gestapo. The secret police's principle mission was to investigate, hunt, and incarcerate anyone considered a threat to the Nationalist Socialist ideology.

The beloved country of her grandmother was entering a frightening phase under a dictatorship, leaving its people powerless to change its course. Would she ever return to Germany? Oh, she hoped so, but under other leadership.

In a melancholy mood, she relived her experiences of the last two months—a mix of disturbing and inspiring occurrences. Each experience had left haunting and remarkable impressions. Sadness and bliss played in an endless loop in her mind. She could never forget the glass shattering in her hotel room, cutting her arm; and at the other extreme, performing on the piano with the conservatory's orchestra Mozart's Symphony no. 40, or rehearsing alongside other student conductors Mahler's Symphony no. 6. Despite of it all, she was committed to stay and accomplish her goal.

She took off her shoes and lay down on the single bed. Under a wool blanket, she closed her eyes, imagining the city by the Danube. She hummed a melody until, with the murmur and steady motion of the train, she fell asleep and dreamed.

Wearing a garnet-tone velvet gown, she entered a lavishly decorated ballroom in the Habsburg Palace as a chamber orchestra played the "Blue Danube." She glanced about the domed hall, noticing hundreds of people dancing to the waltz. It was the year 1876, and they were celebrating their new Archduke, Austrian-born Ferdinand Maximillian von Habsburg, crowned Emperor of Mexico. Maximillian's impending decree had been cheered by Mexican conservatives but opposed by liberal forces because he had been appointed by Napoleon III, bringing yet another foreign ruler to Mexico after obtaining independence from Spain. Suddenly, the music stopped, and his Royal Highness, along with his wife Carlota, wearing formal attire, descended the palace's grand staircase. What was the imperial couple doing in Vienna when their official residence was the Chapultepec Castle in Mexico City? Baffled, she approached them wanting to warn the emperor of his inevitable fate unless he abdicated the Mexican crown. He was a worthy man living in a foreign place at the wrong time. She wished that Maximillian would replace Hitler. For surely, between the two Austrian-born leaders, Maximillian would be a far better choice to rule Germany. But before she could reach Maximilian, she was suddenly transported to another time and location—the bottom of the steps outside the Reichstag building in 1933. There too, a multitude cheered that Ferdinand Maximillian von Habsburg was the new leader of the Third Reich. Then the ambiance in the street transformed from festive to solemn. A chorus, gathered on the building's landing, sang from Beethoven's Missa Solemnis... "Miserere nobis"—Have mercy on us. From a side entrance of the neo-classical building, in slow motion, one woman, similar to her in appearance and wearing a white veil, and six men carried a black coffin down the steps. "It's Maximillian, he's dead," the woman yelled in despair. The people stood still, overwhelmed with anguish, but the chorus continued to sing… "Have mercy on us…"

With those four words echoing in her ear, Alejandra woke up feeling powerless to change things. What was the meaning of such a surreal dream? Sure, it was all tied to the Austrian, German, and Mexican history that she had known since childhood. She wished for an alternative universe where Archduke Ferdinand Maximillian von Habsburg was Germany's leader in 1933. Or another, where Franz Josef, his brother, had succeeded in reuniting Germany in 1876. Either one would have created a better world than the one ruled today by a fascist government.

Or did the dream reveal something of a more personal nature? Did it foretell of her life and future? Would Alejandra's life trajectory begin as a wistful waltz and end in a tragic requiem?

Just then, at seven o'clock, she heard Hannah speaking outside in the corridor. The train was still moving at high speed.

"Ále, are you ready to join us for breakfast?"

"Come in. I'm not hungry, but a cup of hot chocolate sounds good," Alejandra replied.

Hannah came in and sat across from her friend, pulling down the shade as the bright sunlight, peeking through the window, blinded her. "Were you able to sleep?"

"Yes, I was so tired and had the strangest dream. How's Ben feeling today?"

"Physically still sore. But in a much better mood knowing we'll be in Vienna in an hour. I think he'd rather not talk about it," Hannah said.

"Did you ever hear back from the American embassy?" Alejandra asked.

"Yes, we received a letter saying they would investigate. I gave the secretary our forwarding address. I'm not holding my breath thinking anyone will be held accountable."

"I'm so sad about what's happening," Alejandra said. "With all the rush of the last week, I don't even know about our living arrangements in Vienna."

"The apartment is close to the conservatory in the Alsergrund ninth district in a scenic area at the foothills of Vienna's forest, coincidently near Sigmund Freud's house," Hannah said.

"How convenient. Perhaps he can help me interpret my dream," Alejandra said.

"So what was it about anyway?" Hannah asked.

After Alejandra had related the fantastical, unconscious wishes and partially truthful episodes in her dream, Hannah said, "That might take multiple sessions of psychoanalysis. I'd forgotten about your vivid dreams. You're lucky, or not, to remember them. I've got a few nightmares of my own to decipher. Perhaps we both need a session with Vienna's favorite psychiatrist." They laughed.

14

SYMPHONY NO. 6 IN A MINOR

May 13, 1933 – Vienna, Austria

Hannah, wearing a light green brocade dress, glanced at Ben's reflection in the mirror. She thought his image was that of a man past forty with a receding and graying hairline, although he was only thirty-six years old. He was about to achieve his professional ambitions in a highly competitive profession. In only a few hours he finally would debut as a guest conductor with one of the most prestigious symphony orchestras in the world. It was unfortunate that neither his father nor mother had lived to see this accomplishment.

His parents had worked hard to educate him. His father was an electrical engineer and his mother a seamstress. His family had emigrated to New York from Poland at the turn of the century, and like other immigrants, they had experienced discrimination and hardship. His father had been killed fighting in the Great War, and his mother succumbed a few years later to cancer. Hannah concluded perhaps it was for the best they did not live to see this day when a cancer of the soul was spreading against their Jewish brethren. Although persecution was nothing new, what was happening now seemed to be much more dangerous than ever before. *But,* she thought, *come on, this is not a day to be gloomy.*

As she sprayed on perfume, she noticed Ben pacing back and forth in the bedroom, looking sharp in his new tuxedo, but a nervous wreck, muttering to himself.

"Benjamin, stop fretting. You look smashing with that baton in your hand," she said.

"I don't care if I look smashing or not. I just want everything to go perfectly. I don't want to look awkward on stage."

"Since when do you care what other people think of you? I've seen you rehearse many times, and your manners are confident and as inconspicuous as any conductor I've seen."

"I suppose you're right. At least my beat and rhythm pattern is unmistakable," Ben said.

She laughed. "You mean musicians don't have to wait until the baton reaches a button on your waistcoat like Furtwängler?"

"I like your sense of humor," Ben said. "But on that topic, I might add that Furtwängler might have peculiar arm motions when conducting, yet he's a brilliant conductor who has an unparalleled level of communication with his musicians and knows the music as if he had composed it himself. I recall seeing him eight years ago when he conducted Brahms' First Symphony for his debut with the New York Philharmonic. He garnered marvelous reviews."

"And what of his politics today? Do you respect that too?" she asked.

Ben paused. "I need to be fair, and I don't know the essence of the man, but I know that he has attempted to separate art from politics. After the whole incident with Bruno Walter, Furtwängler wrote an extensive letter to Goebbels in direct disagreement with their prejudicial policies. He stated that the fight against Jewish artists would not be in the interest of German cultural life. He went as far as saying that Walter, Klemperer, Reinhardt, and other artists like them should be allowed to express their art in Germany."

"It was a good attempt, but unfortunately his efforts may be disregarded," Hannah said. "Well, here in Vienna you'll finally get the chance to realize your ambitions."

"Walter and Furtwängler will be sharing duties with the Vienna Philharmonic. At least, so far in Vienna life seems normal," Ben said. "I'd like to leave soon."

Hannah walked to Ben, placing her hand on his cheek. "We have two hours. I just need to put on my necklace, but I have something for you. She took a pair of silver cufflinks from her jewelry box and gave them to her husband. "Just a little token to bring you luck. They were my father's, and he wanted you to have them on this day."

"That's a good thing because I'm sorry to say I lost the other ones, including the set you gave me. It was very thoughtful of your father to think of me, considering he hated me."

"Now, now. That was a long time ago. Dad is finally coming around. And I'm sure your mother and father are here in spirit. I'm so proud of you."

"Yes. All right, let's go," he said.

She smiled, understanding that at this moment, Ben had no time for sentimentality. Then she clipped on her necklace and went into the drawing room where Alejandra, at the piano, was making notes on a score. "Will you be coming with us?"

"No. I'll meet you there," she said, putting down the pencil on the ledge. "How do you feel, maestro?"

Hannah, looking at Ben, said, "I don't think I've ever seen him this nervous."

Ben placed his elbow on top of the piano. "I'm not as anxious as I may seem. To tell you the truth, it's a bit anti-climactic. I have rehearsed this work more times than needed, but it's the beginning of something very promising. To debut with the Vienna Philharmonic is a fulfillment of the highest order for any conductor."

"Yes, it is. I'm sure Mahler would be pleased with your dedication," Alejandra said.

"But not with what's going on today in the world," Ben said solemnly. "This is why I chose this piece, to give voice to what's happening. As a proud Austrian Jew, Mahler premiered it in Germany, and it seemed the ideal music."

"Yes, that may be true, Ben. Although, I don't want to hear any sadness!" Alejandra said. "You'll be fantastic. Remember the reason why we've chosen this profession, to keep the music of our idols alive and to bring pleasure to our audiences."

"Sometimes it's easy to forget that," Ben said. "Thanks for the morale booster."

"It's me who's thankful. I've learned so much from you, and I'm looking forward to seeing you on stage and to follow your every move. And may I say also that you and Hannah mean the world to me."

"As you do," Hannah said. "Now don't be late."

VALS DEL SOL

Alone in the apartment, Alejandra walked to the window, framed with linen pleated drapery in beige and sage green, and glanced out into the hills. With a magnificent view from the third floor, she considered taking her afternoon walk, but it was windy, and it had started to rain. She decided to finish a waltz arrangement. She was playing the piece when someone knocked on the door. Not expecting a visitor, she was tempted to ignore it, but thinking it could be important, she opened the door. To her surprise, Anton stood there dressed in black pants, a white shirt, and a striped jacket. With a grim expression and sunken eyes, he said, "I'm so glad to see you."

"We weren't expecting you. Please come in. And if I may say, you don't look well." She led him to the living room. He slumped into the overstuffed chair with torn upholstery. Barely audible, he uttered, "That was a beautiful melody. I'd never heard it before."

"It's something I wrote many years ago," she said. "Can I get you something to drink?"

"No. Just sit with me. Does it have a name?" he asked.

"'Vals del Sol.'"

"What does it mean?"

"'The Sun Waltz,'" she replied.

"That's what I need," he said. "More sun in my life and the company of friends."

"Tonight is Ben's debut as conductor," she said.

He leaned forward. "That's one of the reasons I'm here. And you never said goodbye."

She was caught off guard by Anton's comment. "I wanted to, but with what happened to Ben and having to leave on such short notice, it was difficult."

"I'm disgusted with what Ben went through. I find it increasingly hard to be in Berlin these days," he said.

"I've never asked you before. Do you have a family?"

"No, I almost married once," Anton said. "She was a harpist, but things didn't work out. We stayed friends for a while, and Josephine used to play at some of my social functions."

"Was she at your auction?"

He took a moment to remember. "Yes, of course, she was playing that day," he said. "But of late, she and other friends… I don't know anymore. They're like strangers."

"Why?" she asked.

He let out a big sigh and leaned back in the chair again, dropping his arms down, as if he had lost all muscle tone. "A day after the despicable book burning episode, two days ago, I met with Josephine who I thought shared my views. I expressed my disgust about what was happening in our nation. She was in complete silence, and I wanted to say wake up. These are the works of Freud, Heine, Mann, Marx, and dozens of other German, French, and American authors. Even Hemingway's and H.G Wells' books were burned. I went to Opernplatz that night and saw and heard for myself the whole revolting spectacle, the bonfires, bands playing in celebration, and incendiary speeches. Similar displays happened in cities across the country. I felt we were all entering Dante's inferno."

"I truly empathize with you. Have you considered leaving?"

"That's certainly an option for wealthy Germans. But would you leave your country because of a corrupt government? Surely, sooner rather than later, people will realize we're on a very dangerous path. We must expel this government from power."

"You think it can happen… now?"

He looked away for a moment. "One can only hope."

"It saddens me too," Alejandra said.

He sighed. Then from the cocktail table, he picked up the Mozart book, which he had given her back in February. "I don't want to spoil the time we have together. Perhaps, a little diversion from my troubles might do me some good. Looks like you have been reading it."

"I have," she said. "I love the poetry, which is why I keep it handy."

"Do you have a favorite poem? Because I do." Then after finding his desired page, he said, "The poem before me perfectly reflects how I feel these days. May I read it to you?"

She glimpsed at her wristwatch. "I'm afraid that if we stay here longer, we'll be late for Ben's concert. We should go, but I'll read it on my own later."

He folded the corner of the page and placed the book back on the table. "Of course."

Alejandra took her beige cardigan, draping it over her shoulder. She picked up her clutch handbag and keys from the side table. She noticed Anton watching her every move, which made her uncomfortable. "I think we need a pleasant distraction. I'm sure the music will be splendid."

Arriving at Wiener Konzerthaus, Alejandra scanned the venue's burgundy and gold décor with marble columns. The entire hall was a sea of red with its plush, crimson-toned seats. Despite a full house, Alejandra saw Hannah waving in the front row, prompting her to hurry. The concert was about to begin.

"What took you so long?" Hannah asked.

"Anton arrived at the house shortly after you both left. He was very gloomy, and now he's somewhere in the back row," Alejandra said.

"Tell me later," Hannah said, as they took their seats.

The orchestra had changed its approach from having a principal conductor to allowing guest conductors. Alejandra had known for years the Vienna Philharmonic did not accept women to permanent membership. But she was intrigued to hear their unique sound, which was known to be distinct from other orchestras due to their instruments that were tuned to slightly altered pitches. She had heard Bruno Walter speak about the manner of vibrato, the blend of woodwinds with the strings, the brass, and the percussion, contributing to the overall sonority of the orchestra.

Just then, Benjamin Adelman appeared on stage, and the audience applauded. With his usual confident bearing, he bowed and gave Hannah a discreet smile. Then he stepped up to the podium and took his position in front of the orchestra. Lifting his baton, he marked the first beat of Symphony no. 6 in A Minor, by Gustav Mahler. Almost immediately, Alejandra was captivated by the swelling sound resonating in the hall. The motif and melody of the first movement of the march, known as "Alma Theme," was steady and crisp. It was the first time she heard a symphony as a back-seat conductor, having memorized the score. As the symphony unfolded, a dramatic change in feeling was evident. Mahler had composed it differently in character from his previous five symphonies. But was the ending *a crisis in faith,* as some other conductor had alluded to? Or did Mahler, unconsciously, foretell the tragic events to come, not only in his personal life, but also for his people twenty-seven years later, as Ben had said?

Throughout Ben's direction, Alejandra considered his beat pattern to be exact yet subtle. And while she had seen him conduct on many occasions, he was exceptional tonight. For he possessed many of the attributes assigned to the finest conductors… "a good ear, a sense of order and organizational skills to sort through thousands of notes in a score, intelligence, physical vigor, and magnetism," but not staunch ambition. It was no wonder why conductors rose to such mythical status.

While this bothered Alejandra's sensibilities, she reassured herself that her desire to be a conductor was never about control, power, or even ultimate prestige. Conducting for her was about connecting musically with the composer, understanding his or her emotions and ethos through music. It was about conveying a composer's genius to an appreciative audience, one moment at a time, one phrase at a time, and one symphony at a time.

OVER THE WAVES

May 20, 1933

Aboard the boat *MS Ana*, Alejandra rested her hands on the railing as she contemplated the Danube and a magnificent sunset. With her hair blowing in the wind, she enjoyed the fresh air and thought about an auspicious plan she was eager to put into action—a musical discovery termed *Vienna con Brio*. Vienna with spirit would trail in the footsteps of Beethoven, Haydn, Mozart, and Schubert, who were the masters of the Viennese school doctrine of the classical period, an era of unprecedented creativity when instrumental music, fashioned in various forms—solo, duo, sonata, trio, quartet, concerto, and the symphony—was done for the first time.

In the next weeks, she planned to see and experience the humble dwellings, royal palaces, and inspirational locations where those composers had lived, composed, performed, and were laid to rest. From this musical treasure, she would select the music for a concert program—perhaps her conducting debut. She savored the idea of at last fulfilling her long-time professional ambition.

Anton joined her. "Dinner is being served."

She scanned the area, noticing only a few people scattered around the sundeck. "I lost track of time. I'll be down in a moment. It's a beautiful sunset. I never tire of seeing one."

"Then I shall stay with you," he said.

He was only a few feet away, but she could hear his breathing and feel his gaze as he turned his entire body toward her. "There's something I've been wanting to say for some time."

While she had kept a distance, she was now sure of his increased interest in her, one that went beyond friendship. Fearful of an unwanted revelation, she took a step away from the railing. "Let's not keep Ben and Hannah waiting."

"Yes," he said, sounding disappointed. "But at least, let me say you look lovely tonight."

"With this old dress?"

"It's not the dress, but the eyes, the smile, and everything else."

"Your praises embarrass me. You know that, don't you?"

"I don't say anything that isn't true," he said.

She shook her head. "So perhaps you shouldn't. Let's go."

A few moments later, with Anton by her side, Alejandra came into the interior dining room of the cruiser where Ben and Hannah and dozens of other guests were seated, enjoying Verdi's "Drinking Song," from *La Traviata*. Tables covered in yellow tablecloths, candle lighting, and waiters serving a pre-set menu of Viennese dishes containing veal liver dumplings, Wiener schnitzel, salad, Sachertorte, and red wine, made the space festive and noisy.

Alejandra and Anton sat across from the Adelmans.

"I thought you had abandoned us," Ben said.

"The sunset was too gorgeous to ignore," Alejandra said.

"And the surroundings too," Anton said. "It's been ages since I've taken this cruise, and the scenery is certainly a welcome change." He sipped his wine.

"Since we arrived here, I feel things are looking up," Hannah said.

"I feel it too," Alejandra said. "I don't know what it is about waltzes, but they put me in the best of moods."

"Did you know her name comes from a waltz?" Hannah remarked.

"Your name?" Anton asked. "And what waltz is that?"

"'Alejandra' by Enrique Mora."

"I'd like to hear it," Anton said. "Perhaps, the musicians can play it."

"My fondness for waltzes has to do more with my maternal grandmother than my name. She was the one who introduced me to the piano on my eighth birthday. That was when I heard her play delightful Mexican waltzes."

"She must have made quite the impression, considering your relentless devotion to music," Ben said.

"As a child, I was impressed by her poise and the music."

"Similar story for me. My grandfather introduced me to the violoncello," Hannah said. "He was a fan of Pablo Casals after hearing him play

Strauss's Don Quijote at Carnegie Hall. He bought me a cello for my birthday, and once I became pretty good, at least in his eyes, he bought me a Guarneri. It's the one I use now."

"What about you, Ben? Who was your inspiration?" Alejandra asked.

"My story isn't as memorable as either of yours. My father won a violin at a raffle, brought it home, and it was love at first sight."

"Lucky for you," Anton said, excusing himself to speak with the trio. Moments later, he returned. "They're not familiar with the 'Alejandra Waltz,' but offered to play another by Juven… I didn't quite catch his name."

Upon hearing the next waltz the trio played, Alejandra recognized it. "Over the Waves," or "*Sobre las Olas*," was composed by Juventino Rosas. It was his most famous waltz back in the day of Mexican salon music."

"I recognize the melody," Anton said. "I never knew who'd written it. But it would be delightful to dance to it. Alejandra?"

"I don't think so," she said.

"I had to try," Anton said, as he finished his drink and ordered another.

"It was a pity that Rosas died so young. Although, he left a fine body of work. So, perhaps that's the challenge and opportunity of a conductor to highlight forgotten music."

"I've always thought that our role is also to educate the public," Ben added. "We tend to perform the music of the same composers over and over again."

"Well, now you'll be able to do as you wish. Your debut was fantastic. Let's toast," Hannah said.

"I do feel energized by the experience," Ben said.

"What's next for you?" Anton asked Alejandra.

Ben interrupted. "Ále will be rehearsing for her first conducting solo with the Mozart orchestra in two weeks."

"Oh? How do you feel about it, and how does the training compare here?" Anton asked.

"The Vienna Conservatory is the feeder for all of Vienna's orchestras, so that's a plus right there," Ben said.

"To answer your question, I'm anxious, worried, and happy," she replied. "The basic coursework is the same. Although lately, we've been focusing on gestures and baton technique. Our professor, Max Suitner, is very strict and allows no room for mistakes. Thank goodness Ben is ahead of me because he's turned out to be an ideal model to follow."

"You have an excellent ear, and I'm sure you'll be a famous female conductor," Ben said.

"You're too kind, but I'm not in search of fame. Besides, there's already a renowned woman conductor, Antonia Brico," Alejandra said. "She's forming an orchestra next year."

"Let's be honest, conducting will always be a man's world," Hannah said. "We can only hope it changes in the future. I fear there will continue to be a lack of opportunities for women."

"That may be true, and I confess it can be intimidating, but I won't let it stop me," Alejandra said. "It's not like I'll be the first. There's a long list of other women pioneers in the field as you've heard me mention countless times."

"Which is why I'm checking into the possibility for both Ále and I to conduct a joint concert in either Florence or Prague upon graduation," Ben said. "A new opera festival, the Maggio Musicale Florentino, was founded last month. I'm told they have a fine orchestra, and they are offering summer opportunities for aspiring conductors."

"Choosing between Prague and Florence is a tough one," Alejandra said. "Although I'm inclined to go with the one that benefits us all."

"Let me know if Florence is your next destination as I have some unfinished business there, and I'd love to join you," Anton said.

"Unfinished?" Hannah asked. "Italy would be a dream for me."

"I have a Renaissance art collector who's interested in the works of Medici supported artists," Anton added. "I have offered to make recommendations and to buy on his behalf."

"Well, then it's settled. I'll zero in on Florence," Ben said. "It will probably happen at the end of August."

"Splendid. By then Richard will join us," Alejandra said.

"I didn't know your husband was coming back," Anton said, surprised. "That could change everything. I have three months to conquer." He paused.

"He wouldn't want me going back alone, and I can't wait to see him," Alejandra said. "But what were you saying? Three months to conquer what?"

Anton took another drink. "To conquer this wine."

"I think you've already conquered it tonight," Ben said, laughing.

"I have not... I assure you," Anton said, staring at Alejandra.

With such directness and attentions throughout the evening, Alejandra said with nervous laughter, "In my opinion, it might be best to have better control over one's emotions."

"Oh? But, Ále, that can only last for so long," Anton said. "And, it would be no fun."

A week later, on Saturday, Alejandra woke up to Bach's dynamic violoncello "Suite No. 3," one of the more difficult works, but not in the hands of Hannah who was a virtuoso in her own right. Like most mornings, she was playing, and it was something that Alejandra greatly enjoyed about living with her friends. For soon Ben was also playing the violin, accompanying his wife as though inspired by Aphrodite, the Greek goddess of love and beauty. How gratifying it would be to share that passion with the person you love. She thought of Richard and wished he was there lying beside her, and that they too could be like Hannah and Ben, love-making with the melodies of Bach, Beethoven, or Debussy.

That morning, however, she could not have asked for a more perfect prelude to the start of her carefully planned *Vienna con Brio* discovery. Her heart swelled with emotion thinking about a time when Vienna had been the capital of the musical world and a cauldron of creativity; a time when classical music was at a pinnacle of its existence, the eighteenth and nineteenth centuries. It was also an essential part of court life as numerous members of the aristocracy maintained private orchestras. With no radios or recordings available, live music was the leading type of entertainment. If she could have, she yearned to live in that period when music was as vital as the air the composers breathed, bringing spiritual enrichment to their daily lives. Yet Vienna, at the turn of the twentieth century and after the Great War, despite the fall of the Habsburg dynasty, was vibrant and an exemplary city where gifted artists and scientists thrived, and where utopian ideas of education for all, freedom of expression, and social planning prevailed.

It was a bright spring morning, and with the smell of hyacinth in the air Alejandra's walk reached an old apartment building at the ramparts of the city. As she climbed the stairs to the fourth floor her heart beat faster, for in moments she would be entering Pasqualatihaus, the living quarters of Ludwig van Beethoven from 1804 to 1814. When Alejandra stepped into the sparsely furnished abode, she was met at the door by a young woman with dark hair and eyes and a high-pitched voice. She was sitting behind a desk and collected the entrance fee. She gave Alejandra a brochure explaining the history of the house. *"Guten Morgen,"* she said. Alejandra greeted her, and she noticed an elderly group of people who were inside their thoughts, looking through several glass cases that contained objects once touched by the hands of Beethoven—letters, manuscripts, dinnerware, silverware, clothing, and a top hat.

With a sense of reverence, Alejandra walked about the room, floors creaking, knowing that it was in this small and humble residence where Beethoven composed his Fourth, Fifth, and Seventh symphonies at a period in his life when he had begun to experience deafness. She thought he must have been chosen by God in order to create those symphonies with such an ironic disability. It was also during that period when he fell in love with Therese von Malfatti for whom he composed "Für Therese," as a prelude to a marriage proposal—one that never happened since she went on to marry another man. However, by a simple twist of fate and a copyist's error, the bagatelle would be forever known to the world as "Für Elise," an ironic end to unrequited love. But his devotion to music would give him solace and strength. Beethoven became isolated and tormented but remained filled with intense love, expressing, in his music, the fullest range of musical and human emotion. It was this legacy that she revered the most, how so much suffering had led to so much magnificence.

Alejandra had envisioned Beethoven's home, described by several biographers as messy with scattered sheet music, inkwell spilled over tables, and dirty clothes and dishes scattered about the floor. But what did that matter in the end? She preferred to conjure images of the benevolent man that he was, hunched over piano keys attempting to hear the sound of the music he heard in his head, music he went on to compose on two pianofortes housed there. And, like faithful old friends, they witnessed his everyday life, his sorrows and his joys, accompanying Beethoven until his death.

As she waited for the other visitors to leave, hoping to experience the place alone, she gazed at the Vienna woodland thinking of the many times Beethoven would have walked upon those sylvan pathways to take in the spring or fall colors, rain or shine. Dressed in a black suit and a top hat, he would have looked like any mortal gentleman of the nineteenth century, but his music would become immortal. Then, as she thought of going to her next stop, a favorite theater of Viennese society, she spotted a familiar looking man walking through a narrow street below her view. The tall man wore no top hat but had on a brown fedora. No, it can't be him. Could it? Perhaps her mind was playing tricks on her.

Not long after, she was walking through tree-lined streets and following perhaps the same footsteps as Beethoven had on numerous times toward *Theater an der Wien*. When she arrived at the historical theater, she pushed open a black door and stepped inside. Like other operatic and concert venues, appointed with the customary décor in tones of red and gold, the theater had four tiered balconies. The one-hundred-and-thirty-one-year-old building had been a center of musical performance where many works of note had premiered. It was at this location where Mozart staged his opera *The Magic Flute*, and hundreds heard, for the first time, Beethoven's opera *Fidelio*, as well as his Second, Third, Fifth, and Sixth symphonies. She was about to sit down in the front row to make some notes when a custodian, who was mopping the floor, asked, "*Darf ich Ihnen helfen?*"

Smiling wistfully, she replied, "Can you bring me back to December 22, 1808?"

"Pardon me?"

"It's the date when Beethoven premiered, perhaps, the world's greatest symphony."

The custodian, with worn-out clothes and wrinkled face and hands, leaned the mop against the wall and approached her. "That's why I work here. I saw the premiere of *The Merry Widow*, he said animatedly.

"The era of Viennese operetta," she added, sensing the man wanted to go on talking about his experiences.

In such proximity to him, she noticed his brown eyes revealed wisdom and sincerity. On a whim she invited him to lunch. "I'm going to Frauenhuber Café, Beethoven's favorite restaurant. It's only a five-minute walk. Would you like to join me?"

He stared at her, a little befuddled, and then said, "No visitor has ever invited me there, so I gladly accept. My lunch break starts in ten minutes."

"Then I'm glad to be the first. I shall enjoy hearing about your most memorable performance. What's your name?"

"Leopold," he replied. "Let me get my coat. I'll be back shortly."

While waiting for Leopold's return, she looked around the theater once again, but this time she turned her attention toward one of the boxes on the upper tier, recalling that it was from there that Francis II, the Austrian emperor, would have perhaps witnessed the public premiere of Beethoven's Third Symphony, "Eroica." It was a symphony that Beethoven had dedicated to Napoleon Bonaparte, who had ironically forced Francis II to dissolve the Holy

Roman Empire. Initially, Beethoven's democratic ideals and anti-monarchy views supported Napoleon's revolution for liberty and equality. Later, however, Bonaparte too proclaimed himself emperor. For that shameful reversal, Beethoven scratched Bonaparte's name from the Third Symphony manuscript and dedicated it instead to a benefactor and member of the aristocracy, a prince who had lived in now the oldest palace of the city, her next stop.

Leopold returned, wearing an elegant black overcoat, slightly too large for his frame. With pride, he straightened himself, clutching the lapels. "I'm still waiting for its owner to claim it. It's been a year since someone left it in the cloakroom. For a day, I can be that gentleman who can go to any theater or concert he likes."

"You wear it well. Shall we?" Alejandra said. "But what do you mean?"

"I long for a time when operas were performed for the public at large and not just for the privileged few," Leopold said.

"I agree. But let me say that you're a gentleman with or without the coat," Alejandra said.

"Very kind of you to say that," Leopold said.

"I can tell we're going to have a very good discussion on the subject." She took a final look around the theater, and they left.

Two hours later, after having lunch, she was thinking about her conversation with Leopold, who expressed a unique perspective on accessibility in the arts. She would discuss it later with Hannah as they had agreed to meet at the famous Baroque Palace and the former home of Joseph František Maximilian, the seventh Prince Lobkowicz, who had been Beethoven's most significant benefactor.

Upon arriving there, she reviewed her notes. The palace had been the center of influence and power in the city of Vienna from the late 1700s to the early 1800s, but it was now refitted as a governmental office, presently serving as the Czech embassy. Inside, visitors saw a large portrait of Princess Wilhelmina Lobkowicz, a young woman dressed in a white, embroidered silk gown. Alejandra proceeded to the formal entrance where she expected to find Hannah, but instead she spotted the same man she had seen earlier from the window in Beethoven's museum. He was speaking to a middle-aged woman who wore a navy-blue suit.

"Anton, what in the world are you doing here? Have you been following me? I thought I saw you earlier near Pasqualatihaus," Alejandra said, annoyed.

"I was in town for a meeting in that area, and then I went to your apartment where Hannah told me of your plans to be here, but she had urgent matters to attend to and asked me to take her place. I was just asking Madame Vlasak if you'd arrived."

Not pleased nor disappointed, Alejandra said, "Nothing serious with Hannah, I hope."

"No. She had documents to send to a dealer."

"I'm glad there's nothing of concern," Alejandra said, turning to the receptionist, Madame Vlasak. "Good afternoon."

"Your friend is requesting to see Eroica Hall without an appointment. I won't be able to show you around the palace, but you may see the hall if you'd like," the woman said. "I have a little time to spare before a meeting. We can go now."

"We appreciate it," Alejandra said. "You've been here before, Anton?"

"You might find it hard to believe, but I haven't," he replied.

In Eroica Hall, the Czech woman pointed out the gold-leaf ceiling and mural paintings, arched windows, and other architectural details. As they walked through the room, set for a concert performance, Alejandra thought that the guide resembled the noblewoman whose portrait she had just seen at the entrance. Both were beautiful. "Pardon my curiosity, but the portrait of Princess Wilhelmina made quite the impression on me. Can you tell me more about her? And if I may add, you resemble her a lot."

"I've been told that, but an older version," the guide said. "She's the daughter of Moric, ninth Prince Lobkowicz, and she established the religious order "The Sisters of God's Love" for unmarried and widowed noblewomen in Nelahozeves Castle, in Prague. Are you familiar with the family's history?"

"A little about their patronage of music," Alejandra said. "But tell us more."

The Czechoslovakian woman said, "Of great significance is that a Spanish duchess, by the name of Pernštejn, had a daughter, Polyxena of Lobkowicz. Her heirs, who would become major patrons of the arts, and the seventh Prince Lobkowicz, were Beethoven's benefactors and friends. In 1804, Beethoven premiered the 'Eroica' Symphony privately at this very hall. The family owns the original manuscript."

"It must have been difficult for Beethoven to navigate between his ideals and reliance on the financial support of highborn friends," Alejandra said.

"It was also here where Beethoven performed in competition with his biggest rival at the time. Isn't that true?" Anton asked.

"Yes, indeed. It's hard to believe someone thought he could actually challenge Beethoven to a musical duel," Alejandra said.

"Yes. I guess it was very humiliating for Daniel Steibelt, who left Vienna after the duel," the guide said.

"Not only did Beethoven outperform Steibelt technically, but from that musical improvisation, Beethoven went on to compose the 'Eroica' Symphony," Alejandra said. "How marvelous it must be for you to wander about the palace and discuss this history."

"I cherish working here," she said. "Today, as you can see, the palace is used by diplomats with a few rooms open to the public. Stay here for as long as you like. I must go now."

When she left, Alejandra said to Anton, "Can you imagine being a guest of the seventh Prince Lobkowitz and attending his private concerts? How wonderful!"

"What's most remarkable is the prince's legacy, for he was the one who convinced Beethoven to remain in Vienna," Anton said. "I've been doing a little reading on my own. The two men met in their early twenties and formed a partnership of monumental significance, culminating in some of the greatest musical works ever written. But I'm sure you know that."

"That's why Beethoven, in gratitude, dedicated both his third and fifth symphonies to him," Alejandra said. "This was perhaps one of the best examples of altruistic patronage and creativity co-existing in perfect harmony."

"Do you think that kind of friendship will ever be possible between us? Can you see yourself ever dedicating one of your works to me?" Anton asked.

"No." She laughed nervously at her own vehemence. "I think for that to happen we would have to have a very special bond, and I don't think we could ever be there."

"Only because you don't want to, but maybe someday you'll feel differently," he said. "So what's next on your Vienna con Brio tour?"

"What? Hannah told you that too?"

He nodded.

"Well, I was thinking of following the steps of Haydn," she said.

"Or we could go down the street to one of the best patisseries in town. I've heard their plum jam turnover is out of this world," Anton said. "And you can tell me all about your visit to Beethoven's museum."

"Oh, you tempt me so. I think a cup of hot chocolate sounds good just about now," Alejandra said. "I did meet an older gentleman at the Theater an der Wien, and he was interesting with all kinds of stories that I'd like your take on."

"That's a start of a great friendship," Anton said.

Soon after, they were at a quaint pastry shop filled with display cases and shelving racks with an assortment of bonbons and other confectionaries, tartlets, and cakes. The smell of freshly brewed coffee was in the air. And the space, with paneled walls and glass chandeliers, was crowded. Alejandra, who sat at a table for two, thought Anton had lost weight, for both his gray sweater and black slacks hung loosely on him. He joined her, holding two beautifully packaged ballotins of chocolates by Neuhaus. "Best chocolates in the world. One for you, and one for the Adelmans."

"Thank you. Hannah will love these, and so will I," Alejandra said.

Then the waitress, a young woman with braids and peach colored ribbons in her hair, brought their cups of hot chocolate and two plates with the plum jam turnovers.

Alejandra took a sip of her drink. "Ah, it's delicious. So you said earlier you were here for a meeting?"

"Yes. I'm considering several paintings from the Vienna Secession."

"I don't know anything about that," she said.

"Klimt led the movement to form a new society. But, I'd rather talk about your lunch with an older gentleman."

"His name is Leopold, and he has worked at Theater an der Wien since the early 1900s. He complained that individuals of limited resources did not have easy access to concerts since it has become the domain of the rich. He's right. Music of this genre should reach the widest audience possible."

"How to approach it is a matter of practical and economic considerations," Anton said. "For the best entity to provide public concerts could be the city or state government. But there's a risk. No question that the linking of power with the arts is rooted in civilizations from the earliest onset of humankind. Art has always been used as an instrument to enhance the physical and mythical status of royalty as we just witnessed at the palace."

"And also in the service of religion," Alejandra said. "I suppose that art has also served as a catalyst for change or as a response to challenging events."

"It's true. However, it is one thing to be a patron of the arts to foster creativity or to commission new works," Anton said. "But it is quite another for a government, especially a corrupt one, to use works of art to promote a political ideology."

"We must resist being drawn into the politics of others," Alejandra said. "But I see your point. For my part, I'm determined to devote my energy to preserve the purity of art."

"It may be difficult under a fascist ruler," Anton said. "You must know you won't be able to please everyone. There will be critics on all sides. What would you do if you were ever invited to be a guest conductor for one of our orchestras under the auspices of Goebbels?"

She laughed. "What kind of question is that?"

"We're talking about the merging of arts and politics, and you're saying you must preserve the purity of the art. But what if you were asked to do work for current leaders whose policies you disagree with or their conduct is counter to your morality?"

Alejandra replied, "I don't think I'd ever be in that position, considering I'm new at this. There are several arguments for and against doing so. I'll give it serious consideration, although, fortunately, I'll never have to worry about it."

"It's not always easy to separate art from politics. Don't you agree?" he said.

"Yes. But for now, I'm more concerned with Leopold's complaint. I feel that art and music should be accessible to everyone, no matter what. So let's leave it at that."

"All right," Anton said. "But do you remember my Russian friend, Sacha, who was ecstatic when the Hermitage, thanks to the Bolshevik Revolution, became a public entity. That's a communist ideal. So are you for communism, then?"

"It has its advantages, and it sounds good in theory, but perhaps not for everyday life," Alejandra said. "I'd prefer the right to have freedom to make choices despite one's circumstances. I never thought I'd be discussing this topic with you. But in today's world it seems politics are taking over."

"To say the least," he said.

"It's almost five, and I think it's time to go home. When does your train leave?"

"At ten. Perhaps we can have dinner together later on?" he suggested.

"No. I have a lot of studying to do for my first solo rehearsal this week," she said, standing. "But it was nice that you joined me this afternoon. I hope you have a safe trip."

"Until we meet again," he said.

Then they parted ways.

SYMPHONY NO. 40 IN G MINOR

On the following day, Alejandra was in the dining room writing a letter to her family when Hannah approached her, holding an invitation. "How would you like to attend a Viennese ball?"

"Who's hosting and where?"

"The American embassy at Schönbrunn Palace."

"That's a bit odd. How did we get on their list?"

"I gave the Berlin embassy our forwarding address. Perhaps that had something to do with it," Hannah replied.

"The invitation is probably just for the two of you then."

"No. Your name is also on the letter. It came in the mail yesterday."

"May I see it?"

Hannah handed her the envelope. Then she looked at the handwriting in black ink addressed to Mr. and Mrs. Benjamin Adelman and Mrs. Alejandra Stanford Morrison. She noticed the embassy's seal on both the envelope and invitation. She read:

Gilchrist Baker Stockton,
Envoy Extraordinary and Minister Plenipotentiary
Requests the honor of your company to celebrate the 157th
Anniversary of the American Independence and to a Viennese Ball
Saturday, July 8, 1933 - At seven o'clock
Schönbrunn Palace - Schönbrunner Schlossstrasse 47
1130 Vienna, Austria –
Black Tie (Optional Tour of the Palace at 5:00 P.M.)

"Perhaps your dream was a premonition after all? And it's a sign you must attend."

Alejandra laughed. "Or not. It could be risky. I'm not superstitious, but if I do choose to go, I'll definitely not be wearing a red gown. I wouldn't want to replicate the role in that dream."

"Then you'll come?"

She considered the alternatives. "Why not? As the old proverb says, when in Rome do as the Romans do. And from what I know, Viennese balls are as much a part of the country's culture as anything else."

"I'll write a formal response accepting their invitation," Hannah said. "But I'd like to talk to you about something else."

"So serious," Alejandra said as Hannah sat across from her.

"Anton is returning to Vienna next weekend. How do you feel about that?"

She paused. "If I'm honest, I didn't care much for him in the beginning, but he's becoming a friend who shares our love of music, and he's fond of you and Ben."

"Yes. We have a lot in common, but I think it's obvious he may be falling in love with you. We've discussed this before, hoping it wasn't the case, but now I'm sure," Hannah said.

"Has he said something to you to that effect? He hasn't mentioned it to me. And I obviously wouldn't want him to."

"Forgive me if I sound blunt, but you must have noticed his continued courtesies toward you. He was so eager yesterday to meet you at the palace. He invited himself. How do you feel?"

"I have recently noticed changes in his attitude toward me. I don't deny it, and it makes me feel very uncomfortable. However, I also think that he's lonely and closed off from his friends with what's happening in his country. We're his escape. If he ever said anything of that nature I'd remind him that I'm married and not interested in any way, shape, or form. I can't believe you even asked me such a question."

"I didn't mean to upset you. I just wanted to be sure you were aware," Hannah said.

"I appreciate your candidness," Alejandra said. "Obviously, I can't control how he feels, but you don't have to be concerned for there will only be a handful of times more that I'll see him. I'll be very careful to avoid any misunderstandings, now more than ever."

"You're right. He'll just have to learn to be good friends. I just don't know if he can," Hannah said.

Alejandra reflected briefly on the conversation, and she was concerned about hurting Anton's feelings but aware of the potential problem and how best to resolve it. An honest discussion about it was necessary, and she hoped to address the issue at the soonest opportunity.

On June 25, she was kneeling in a pew in the third row inside Saint Stephen's Cathedral. Having just received Communion, Alejandra watched the rest of the faithful walk to the altar to receive the Eucharist. Seated next to her were Anton, Ben, and Hannah, all dressed in their Sunday best. They had decided to accompany her to Mass that morning, as it was also common for Alejandra to attend services at the synagogue. For even if they practiced different faiths, they all believed in a greater power, except for Anton, who was an atheist; yet he was there.

She listened to the choir who sang God's praises just as Haydn had done many times as a young boy. It was said his career had started there in that church filled with paintings, stained glass windows, an ornate nave, and statues of the church fathers serving as structural support for an intricately designed Gothic pulpit.

The priest's sermon had cited biblical passages asking the devotees to maintain their faith despite personal adversity. In her life, Alejandra had thought about such moments, including her father's death. In the present, she was in constant conflict with herself about balancing the demands of a family with that of her aspirations, which often led to a profound guilt—one she appeased by the belief in having a mission to fulfill. But then she thought of Beethoven, who discovered he could not hear the church bells ring at this very church. She could now only imagine the agony and struggle he must have felt at losing his hearing. From that point on, it had been said, he had segregated himself from everything except his music. In the end, Beethoven overcame everything, and despite being deaf, he composed his most revered choral symphony, "Ode to Joy," considered his greatest gift to mankind. And to Alejandra, this impossible act of creativity by a man burdened with such an impairment is where faith truly existed. So when Mass finally ended, she felt inspired by those recollections and more at peace with herself. She made the sign of the cross and walked out of the cathedral with her companions.

Outside in the courtyard, they gathered in a circle amongst the multitude of people. Hannah asked Alejandra, "Did you confess all your sins?"

"I'm sure she has none to confess," Anton said playfully.

Alejandra laughed. "I assure you I do, but that's between the Lord and me. But I am curious, knowing you're not a believer, what prompted you to attend Mass?"

"Being with you all was an incentive, and I enjoy the music. But also, it was here where Mozart was married and also venerated at his death," Anton replied.

"Can art inspire even a hardened atheist?" Ben asked.

"I do find churches calming even if I'm not devoutly religious," Alejandra said. "That was the whole aim of the Catholic Church, to create churches so beautiful that you'd think you were in heaven."

"Not beautiful enough to convert me," Anton replied. "As a young man, my father was a fan of Martin Luther, and not even the monk's progressive ideas on religion could save my father. I suppose prayer, for some, serves to fight off temptation."

"That certainly was the case for Luther for a time. He also forced the Catholic Church to reform but also wrote some very offensive things," Ben said. "But that's another discussion altogether that may not end well."

"It's true that inspired thought can come from broken men. Aren't we all?" Anton asked.

"Do you think you could ever be a man of faith?" Hannah asked.

"No. I think it's safer to be an atheist than a fanatic these days," Anton said. "I haven't always found the Catholic Church to be honest in its endeavors."

"A man without faith can't always be trusted," Ben said.

"And a man with faith can?" Anton questioned. "I didn't expect you to be conservative on this matter. Faith may move people to do great things, but also awful things. Just take a look at the Crusades and other irrational wars fought throughout history in the name of God."

"An argument of the times, but don't let it get out of hand," Hannah said.

"No religion is perfect, but you must separate religion and God," Alejandra said. "Maybe we can settle this with a compromise."

"How do you compromise between believing or not?" Anton asked.

"By reason, if only my own. There's no proof of God's existence, but they call it faith for a reason. We should rely on our morality and let that be our guide while leaving the matter of a belief or not to our personal preference without condemning one another."

"I see the sermon inspired you," Hannah said.

"Regardless, faith can't be imposed," Alejandra added.

"I don't want to make an argument about it, but it is men who create enemies by their illogical interpretations of a particular text or event, not God," Ben said. "Unfortunately, people insert their religion to execute political agendas. And for many today, Jews are the scapegoats, and it's easy to blame us for things that happened millennia ago."

"So true what you say, which is why I don't believe in a God who would choose one group of people over another," Anton said.

"I do believe in a God of all humanity," Alejandra said. "But let's end this discussion. I don't think we'll ever agree."

"Sorry if I offended you, Anton. There are just certain topics that get to me," Ben said.

"Nothing to be sorry about," Anton said, patting Ben on the shoulder.

"Well, that's why politics and religion are not the best topics for conversation," Hannah said. "So, we must not let it get out of hand if we're to stay friends." She laughed.

"But, you must admit those subjects are definitely interesting," Ben said. "And relevant to our times. They're all intertwined."

"Agreed. Let's get on with going to the museum where we will find common ground," Alejandra said.

Later that morning, she was inside the Baroque Marble Hall of the Upper Belvedere Palace. It was one of Vienna's old baroque strongholds, built in the 1700s and adorned with Palladian arched windows, sculpture sconces, and murals, and was the summer home of Prince Eugene of Savoy. Alejandra had wandered off on her own, and among dozens of other visitors she was admiring a ceiling fresco by Carlo Innocenzo Carlone, which depicted Prince Eugene as Apollo. She thought the gods of Greek mythology all had some human quality, making it possible for anyone to find similar attributes within themselves. As an idealistic adolescent, she had been interested in Athena, the goddess of reason, but at present and as someone far from home and separated from her family by choice, she at times yearned to be more like Hestia, the goddess of family and domestic life. Why couldn't she be satisfied with being that person?

Then, suddenly, from behind, Anton asked, "Are you trying to lose us?"

"Yes," she said, laughing. It was now clear that Anton's reason for being there, like attending church, was to be with her. So far, he had been a gentleman, and she couldn't fault him for being a friend. Perhaps that was possible, for she did enjoy his company as someone who shared her interests.

He pointed to the center of the ceiling fresco. "Fascinating juxtaposition of the real and the mythical, don't you think?"

"The illusion of light and the visual details of the painting are impressive," she said.

"And how about Apollo surrounded by his muses? And of the nine muses which would you choose to be?" he asked.

"I'm not sure where you're going with that. Earlier, I was thinking about the goddesses, but the muses... I'm not sure. I suppose you'd like to be Apollo with his muses."

Anton said, "Yes, but I only want one Polyhymnia, your equal? The muse of songs to the gods. Isn't music the way to your heart?"

She shook her head, for his remarks were inappropriate. He knew her weak spot, and she now needed to thwart his advances. "Anton, I'm sure that if my husband were here, we wouldn't be having this discussion. Let's not make it personal and stay on the topic of the art, all right? I enjoy your company as a friend, and that's all."

"Then, I'll say something of more interest to you. It appears Prince Eugene of Savoy chose this illustrative depiction of himself, as he was a conqueror in every aspect. He was French and rejected for military service in his country, so he turned his alliance to the Habsburgs. Ironically, Prince Eugene became one of the most successful military commanders in Europe and also a major patron of the arts."

"I do find it fascinating that underestimated individuals like him are the ones who often achieve the greatest feats," Alejandra said.

"Then perhaps I'll have a chance," Anton said.

"A chance for what?" she asked.

Just then Ben joined them. "Hannah and I have been walking about the gardens. The view of Vienna from there is breathtaking. You've seen it?"

"Yes. And where's Hannah?" Alejandra asked.

"She's waiting for us at the Österreichische Galerie on the other side of the palace."

Several minutes later they reached the contemporary gallery of the palace, filled with people, where Hannah was standing before Klimt's oil on canvas painting titled *Kuss*.

"I'm glad you're finally here," Hannah said. "This is the painting I wanted you to see."

"It's gorgeous. The shimmering effect surrounding the couple is fantastic," Alejandra said.

"And the application of gold leaf and silver plating is unique," Hannah said. "Have you ever owned any of Klimt's work?"

Anton replied, "I have not, but coincidently one of my collectors has been on the hunt for the *Beethoven Frieze*. Are any of you acquainted with it?"

"I've heard it's a bit eccentric," Hannah said.

"The description alone could be a lecture," Anton said. "While *The Kiss* may be Klimt's most famous painting, he had other works of note. He was known for being an independent artist, and he often felt derided for his work."

"He presided over the Viennese avant-garde and secession movements," Hannah said.

"Isn't that who you were talking about at the patisserie last week?" Alejandra asked.

Anton nodded and said, "I might also add that one of my collectors was present when Klimt and some twenty other artists put together an exhibition at the turn of the century, uniting architecture, painting, music, and sculpture. The show centered on Max Klinger's sculpture of Beethoven. Klimt showcased the controversial *Beethoven Frieze.*"

"Why is it controversial?" Alejandra asked.

"It features three panels depicting images of mythological characters, gorgons, and deities symbolizing men's virtues and foibles. At the center of the work is Wagner's analysis of Beethoven's Ninth, showing the salvation of humanity as a chorus sings 'Ode to Joy.'"

"It could be an opera," Ben remarked.

"I'm curious to see it," Alejandra said. "It sounds whimsical. You've seen it, I presume?"

"Yes, it's witty and bold. Nothing like the frescoes we just saw in Marble Hall," Anton said. "It's currently in a private collection."

"Without seeing it, I appreciate the symbolism of saving mankind through music," Alejandra said.

"If only it were true," Ben said pensively.

"No more philosophy, Benjamin. I'm tapped out for the day," Hannah said. "Let's see the rest of the works and later enjoy simple pleasures."

"You know what it means when Hannah uses my full name. So, my dear, what might those pleasures be?" Ben asked.

"You men seem to think of only one thing. I was thinking about something to eat."

They all laughed.

"I wish I could join you, but I have a train to catch. I'll be back next weekend," Anton said.

"Ben and I are going to Salzburg on Friday."

"And what are your plans, Alejandra?" Anton asked.

"I have a rehearsal on Thursday, and I'll be enjoying more of Vienna's musical legacy."

"There are several hidden gems I could show you," Anton said.

"I'm sure, but we can leave that for another weekend when Hannah and Ben are back."

"Sure. Until we meet again." Anton bowed to the ladies and shook Ben's hand.

"Have a good trip," Hannah said before he left the gallery.

On Thursday of the following week, at two o'clock, Alejandra was standing on stage at the Stern Conservatory before the podium to begin her first rehearsal as a student conductor. Unlike the rest of the thirty-seven musicians who were casually dressed, she wore a two-piece gray suit and white blouse with her hair in a bun and had no makeup. Feeling more nervous than anticipated, she turned her gaze toward the instructor, Max, an older man with sagging skin and stooped posture, who was seated in the front row. Ben was acting as concertmaster.

The size of the orchestra was small compared to others of the day. And while it was the standard size of the classical period of Mozart, there was emphasis on the string section. For this exercise, she would conduct the first movement of Mozart's Symphony no. 40 in G minor, a symphony that Mozart wrote during a very creative period in his life. For he also went on to compose symphonies 39 and 41. She had been preparing for this moment for several months and had studied the score in detail, memorizing it. She had practiced several times with Ben who was a perfectionist—a trait she very much appreciated. The first movement, written in sonata form, had three sections—exposition, development, and recapitulation.

"Good afternoon," she said in clear, crisp voice. The musicians turned to her and readied their instruments. Her heart was beating hard when she marked the downbeat with her baton. The orchestra played through several measures, but she immediately recognized her tempo was too fast. Out of nervousness, she wanted to laugh and stopped. The musicians looked at each other. She felt embarrassed. Her teacher, unexpectedly reassuring, said, "Take your time and try again. Stay focused on the music." Then Ben added, "It happens to the best of us."

She thought about Mozart who was known for walking out when orchestras performed inadequately. Or he might have been amused, considering his light-heartedness and fondness for the work of women, including his talented sister, Maria Anna Walburga Ignatia Mozart, who was five years his senior. Or he might have joined her at the podium and modeled how to conduct his work. That latter notion relaxed her somewhat even though the musicians were all staring at her, waiting for her next move. Some, perhaps, were waiting for her to make another mistake. She stood still for a few seconds glancing at their faces, knowing that if she failed again, it would confirm their pre-conceived notions about female conductors. So she quickly steadied her nerves and resolved to be the best she could be, not as a woman, but simply as a musician and a conductor. But then suddenly, as she momentarily turned toward the side of the stage, sitting way in the back, she caught a glimpse of Anton. She felt extremely irritated he was there. Was he following her?

"Excuse me for a moment," she said to the musicians and walked to Anton, who was wearing black pants, a beige shirt, and a familiar leather jacket. "I need a word with you!" She led him to a closet room on the hall, filled with musical instruments. "What are you doing here? I don't have time to discuss this with you now, but I want you to leave!"

"I have no explanation other than to say I wanted to support you in some way, knowing how important today was for you. I thought it was a public rehearsal."

Feeling extremely upset, she took a deep breath. "All right. But don't ever do anything like that again. I have to go now."

After he left, she returned to her post at the podium, holding a baton. Now more than ever she needed to convince the musicians she was in command and knew the score perfectly as well as the composer's intention. "Please forgive the interruption. It won't happen again." Then she turned to the score, and after she marked the downbeat on her second try, the right tempo, dynamics, and balance were all there. She heard the strings and woodwinds swell in unison during the symphony's opening movement with its powerful melody and sharp contrasts, even though one of the flutists was a bit behind the tempo, which was noticeable considering the composition called for only eight woodwinds. She would talk to him in private after the first run; for stopping too many times during rehearsal was frowned upon by musicians. So despite that, for the next eight-plus minutes, she felt in harmony with the orchestra. And for the first time since she had begun her training, all her previous doubts and mixed emotions about her professional aspirations dissipated. The decision to remain in Europe to pursue her studies had been the correct one, and all the training in both Berlin and Vienna had not been in vain. It would be hard work that would challenge her in every possible way.

The next day, Alejandra was working on another waltz arrangement for piano and strings. Recently, she had shied away from composing new music, intimidated by all the complex symphonic scores she had been studying for the rehearsals. Yet, the process of arranging music for small ensembles and chamber orchestras was a creative exercise that provided relaxation and also allowed her to experiment with the development of the musical motif by accentuating various tonalities at lower and higher pitches.

Suddenly, interrupted by the sound of torrential rain outside her window, she realized it was time for dinner. But, without an appetite, she resumed her task at hand, preferring to work on the quartet arrangement than to work on preparing a meal. In truth, she was more comfortable in front of the piano than in front of a stove, although she thought it would be a shame to waste all the food she had bought the day before to try out a new recipe. She chided herself for her lack of interest in the art of cooking, and so, despite her initial hesitation, she went into the kitchen determined to make the best dumplings and fish soup she had ever tasted.

Taking an apron from behind the door, she wrapped it around her waist, covering a lime-green floral cotton dress. She could count only a few times when she had cooked a full meal by herself. Back home, Millie, their long-time housekeeper, did most of the cooking, and in Vienna Hannah did all the cooking, for it was essential to her to follow proper kosher instructions. And that night Hannah and Ben were in Salzburg.

The kitchen was tiny with a counter facing a window. An icebox, next to the stove, was small, so it was full. The walls, painted in gray, matched the tile floors. A wooden table at the center with four chairs occupied most of the space. From a drawer, she took the single page recipe which called for slices of bread, onion, vegetable oil, catfish fillets, tender scallions, egg, zucchini, celery, fresh chives, a pinch of thyme and saffron, pepper, and lemon juice. After collecting all the ingredients, she placed them on the counter next to the sink. Following step-by-step directions for about twenty minutes, she was almost finished. As she was sprinkling the catfish with salt and pepper, she heard the doorbell ring. After rinsing and drying her hands, she opened the door. A young boy with wet hair courteously asked, "Are you Mrs. Morrison?"

"Yes, how may I help you?"

He handed her a damp, paper-wrapped package.

"Thank you," she said as she prepared to close the door.

"I was instructed to wait for your reply."

"By whom?" she asked, noticing the boy's eagerness as he took a step closer to the door.

"A gentleman who's waiting downstairs."

"One moment," she said, stepping back into the apartment.

She placed the package on the entrance table and unwrapped it, revealing a symphonion music box with a card attached to it that read:

Dear Alejandra: Please forgive my intrusion into your private time. I hope this music box will diminish your disapproval of me for showing up without your permission at the rehearsal. I'm also aware that you had expressed a desire to spend the weekend alone. However, I'd like to make it up to you and invite you to Sala Terrena, the former residence of Mozart. Tomorrow night a chamber orchestra will perform several of the composer's sonatas. If you wish to accompany me, please inform the young man. I will then come upstairs to make plans for tomorrow's concert. Sincerely, Anton

"Oh, no," she said under her breath and walked back to the doorway. "You may inform the gentleman that he may come up for a few minutes."

"Yes, madam."

Shortly after, Anton tapped on the door.

"Come in. I'm in the middle of cooking dinner."

He walked in. "It smells awfully good. I'll return later if you prefer," he said.

She felt uneasy, but there was no harm in inviting him to dinner as she could use the occasion to decline his invitation and to return his gift. "Have you eaten?"

"No, I'm starving."

"Would you like to join me?"

"I'd love to. May I get a bottle of wine from the shop down the street? White or red?"

"White will do. I'll leave the door unlocked," she said.

While he was gone, she set the table and noticed the rain had subsided. She was nervous about the unexpected meeting. She would look for an opportunity during the conversation to set boundaries once and for all… for his advances were becoming more prominent and challenging.

A SONG IN MY HEART

A few minutes later, Anton arrived holding a bottle of wine in one hand and his bunched-up raincoat in the other. "What's for dinner?" He placed his garment on a chair in the entry.

"Fish soup," she replied, taking the bottle of wine from his hand. "Please sit down. I'll be back momentarily."

As he waited, he scanned the table set with a white tablecloth, green-rimmed porcelain dishes, silverware, silver-plated salt and pepper shakers, and a loaf of freshly-baked bread on a platter with butter on the side. He couldn't be more pleased than to be with Alejandra in such an intimate setting. He would be honest with his feelings, hoping she would accept his invitation to the concert.

Alejandra came in with two crystal glasses and the bottle of wine, setting them on the table. He poured the wine into the glasses. Later, she brought a large-handled ceramic bowl and sat across from him. She took the soup ladle and served the bouillabaisse into the bowls. "I hope it's good. It's my first time making it."

He took a slice of the bread, spreading butter with his knife, then placed it on a plate underneath the bowl. "You like cooking?"

"No, not really. Is that bad?"

"You can't be good at everything," he said, bringing a spoonful of the soup to his mouth. "It's quite tasty."

"I'm satisfied with quite tasty. Next time I'll strive for delicious. Are you staying at the Grand Hotel Wien?"

"Yes, I like its location. It's only a few steps from the opera house. They're familiar with me, so it made for an easy check-in."

There was a moment of awkward silence between them.

"How are things going back home?"

"The political situation is steadily worsening, but I'm dealing with it as best I can by getting out whenever possible," Anton replied. "And I don't have many places to go where I have friends. In fact, you and the Adelmans may be my only friends whom I can trust." He paused. "I'd like to apologize for yesterday. Although I admit I was curious to see you on the podium, it was inappropriate for me to show up without your approval."

"I was a little miffed. First at the palace and then at the concert hall, I was starting to think you were trailing my every move," she said.

"I can see why you might feel that way, but I assure you that's not the case. I'm not that kind of person. I may be perseverant, stubborn, and even too bold, but I'd never cross the line."

"I'm glad to hear that," she said. "I do understand your need to be with friends. Because that's what we are… good friends, and that's all, as I've said before."

"Of course. Now that all that is out of the way, how did the rehearsal go?" he asked.

She replied more enthusiastically. "At first I was very nervous, as you can imagine. Where to begin? It was with Mozart's Symphony no. 40 in G Minor."

"How about from the moment you marked the downbeat with your baton," he said.

"So you didn't see the first act?" she asked.

"No. I came in just when Ben said, 'It happens to the best of us' or something like that."

"To summarize, in my first attempt my tempo was off, the gestures on my hands too distracting, and I was too focused on the beat as opposed to the intent of the composer. Did I miss anything else?" She laughed. "Then on my second try it was much better, my gestures subtle but precise. There's so much to learn, but even though it was a rehearsal and not perfect, it proved to me I could do it. I loved the experience and felt so fulfilled."

"Perhaps the spirits of Mozart and Haydn were watching over you."

"Yes, especially Haydn, the father of the symphony," she said, smiling. "More soup?"

"Please," he said, refilling the wine glasses. Then he lifted his glass and recited a favorite poem. "Wine comes in at the mouth, and love comes in at the eye. That's all we shall know for the truth. Before we grow old and die, I lift the glass to my mouth, I look at you, and I sigh."

"Oh! You're inspired tonight," she said.

"Alas but it's not my inspiration, it's W.B. Yeats," he said. "It was too much to resist to toast for your accomplishment, and I thought it fit the moment."

"You must resist," she said. "I don't want you to get the wrong impression about me. I may be away for the moment from my family to pursue my training, but my husband and children are always on my mind, and I miss them terribly."

"I see. But I also see an independent woman who has a strong drive to accomplish many things. So, in all seriousness, I have two questions. The first is how do you do it standing before dozens of male musicians?"

She narrowed her eyes. "I'm not sure what you mean by that?"

"I don't agree with what I'm about to say, but I've heard more than once that some musicians express their reticence about female conductors as they may be too distracting."

"I've experienced that, and I don't deny this is a profession dominated by men. But little by little women are getting their foot in the door, as you know. And I won't let anyone deter me from being one of them. If someone shows prejudice against me as a woman, well that's their problem. In fact, on one occasion a couple of years ago I was practicing for a concert, and one of the musicians in the group viciously called me an unsavory name." She paused. "I felt deeply humiliated. It's still difficult to talk about it."

"I'm sorry you had to experience that. How did you deal with it?" Anton asked.

"It won't be the last time," she said. "My response was to put that person in his place by telling him that his insults were of no value to me and that his judgment had nothing to do with who I am. When you're in the public arena, you can't escape it." She paused. "I come from a line of strong women who did not meekly accept their assigned roles. My mother had to confront other types of prejudice but always taught me to conduct myself with dignity. On my fifteenth birthday, she gave me a remarkable book, written in the late 1700s by Mary Wollstonecraft, *A Vindication of the Rights of Women*. I often think of all those brave women and men since the Age of Enlightenment who dedicated their lives to gender equality. At the same time, I don't hold any hard feelings toward anyone with other perspectives. I choose to remain above the fray. My day to day intention is to focus on my studies and to do the best work possible."

Anton asked, "What will you do after you've completed your training? Would you consider traveling as a guest conductor?"

"My current situation aside, I can't see myself leaving my family for extended periods. Richard has been supportive of my endeavors, and I could not be more grateful. It's not an easy time for musicians and conductors. The eighteenth and nineteenth centuries, particularly here in Vienna, would have been better suited for me. I'd have loved to live in that era."

"Because of the patronage system and court orchestras?" he asked.

"And the salons. There was an overall appreciation and emphasis on music as a primary source of entertainment. And, surprisingly, a few women had significant roles, including a composer by the name of Marianna Martines, and piano virtuosos such as Maria Theresa von Paradis and Josepha von Auernhammer. I've been doing a lot of research on that period."

"In Austria, that was the Golden Age under Emperor Joseph II's reign," Anton said. "He was the musical king. His entire governance was based on principles of the Enlightenment."

"Indeed, Beethoven composed a cantata for him," Alejandra said. "The world has changed much since then."

"And not for the better," he said somberly. "I fear that the uncertainty we're now experiencing in Berlin may spread here too."

"I hope not… that would be dreadful," she said. "But if you look at the world after Mozart and Beethoven, there was Schubert, Schumann, Chopin, Tchaikovsky, Rossini, von Weber, the operas of Verdi, and so on. An endless stream of musical creativity."

"I've never seen you speak with such exuberance. Do you see everything through the prism of music?"

"Is there any other way?" she answered.

"I like your optimism," he said. "So, will you accept my invitation to hear the music of Mozart tomorrow?"

"Anton. I appreciate the invitation, but I must decline."

"Why must you decline?" he asked.

"I wouldn't feel comfortable, but tell me about Sala Terrena."

"That's a shame. You'd have loved it with its magnificent Venetian architecture and ceiling frescoes. The Deutsche Ritterorden convent was home to Mozart and Brahms."

"I do plan to go there at some point. Oh, I almost forgot dessert." She got up and laughed. "My goodness, I'm still wearing the apron. Would you like tea or coffee?"

"Coffee," he said as she picked up the bowls and went into the kitchen.

He felt disappointed she would not accompany him to the concert, so he thought of an alternative plan. He was running out of time.

She returned holding a tray and placed it on the table, distributing the coffee cups and plates filled with slices of Linzer torte.

"Did you also prepare this?"

She smiled. "No. I wouldn't even know where to begin."

"Have you gone to Mozart's other home in Alsergrund where he composed *The Magic Flute?*" he asked.

"No."

"Why not go there together. We could discuss his opera buffa. He altered the medium. I'll take comedy over drama any day," Anton said.

"I'd never have guessed that. I thought dramatic art would be more to your liking. Am I to presume that Mozart is your favorite composer?" she asked.

"Absolutely. Mozart's operas, piano concertos in the minor keys, and his compositional style are the best. I know Beethoven is your idol," Anton said.

"Very different personalities and life experiences. I suppose we could talk about who was best, but it's all personal preference. Beethoven's music manifests such range of emotions, from tenderness to absolute heartbreak. His music often brings me back to memories where I experienced such feelings."

"Tenderness?" he asked.

"The tenderness and mystery you hear in the second movement of Beethoven's Seventh Symphony. It begins softly, building to a crescendo of pure joy, reminding me of when I first held my newborn and touched her little fingers. She was someone at the threshold of discovering all sorts of emotions and experiences."

"What kind of heartbreak could you have ever experienced?" he asked.

She closed her eyes momentarily. "When my father died, seeing his body lifeless inside a coffin. No words can explain knowing that a person you love is gone. It's an awful feeling. I still have dreams about him, but they don't frighten me. And you?"

"Too many to count. Like you, I saw my father dead, but being at war was the most wrenching experience," Anton said.

"You want to talk about it?" she asked.

He felt remorse and sadness. "Ending the life of a young French soldier in self-defense. I'm reminded of it every time I see my face." He pointed to a scar on his chin.

"It must have been awful. War makes people do terrible things."

"I hated it. And I can tell you that I'd rather be imprisoned than fight in a war again." Then he said, "It wasn't my intention to dampen your spirits."

"You're not. I appreciate you sharing that with me. And that was a long time ago. If drafted like millions of others, you didn't have much choice, except to go to prison. Richard was about to go, but thankfully the war ended before he was to leave. But many other acquaintances were not as fortunate."

"Your husband is a lucky man," Anton said. "No one should have to die because of war."

"Many artists with promising futures died at war. Thank goodness that Schönberg and Ravel survived. On Sunday I'll be going to Vienna's cemetery where many composers were laid to rest. It might sound a little macabre to go there, but I'd like to honor their memories. So this is why I cannot go with you to Mozart's house."

"Then what about a companion to the cemetery?" He smiled.

"No thanks. You'd be too distracting for the occasion," Alejandra said, standing. "While I tidy up a bit here, why don't you wait in the drawing room? I'll come soon."

Anton made his way there thinking he had never met anyone like Alejandra, and she had captivated him completely. He was in love with her. She had revived in him feelings that had been dormant for years. For despite all his wealth and social position, he had been like a drifting spirit. It was as if he was just going through the motions without feeling until she entered his life, piercing his heart with the sweet sting of love. But she was married and allegedly happily so. He never understood how her husband could have permitted her to stay. If she were his wife, he would never let her go for such a prolonged period. He would be devoted to her.

At the piano, he saw a manuscript on the ledge titled "A Song in My Heart." He had played a few notes when Alejandra returned, holding the music box. "It's lovely. I've never seen anything like it, but I can't accept it."

"Why not? It's one of the first of its kind ever made. Your children would love it. I thought of them when I bought it."

"You did? You thought of my children? How very thoughtful."

"You don't believe me, do you?" he asked.

She laughed. "No, but it was a good try. Although, I admit that my son would be fascinated by the mechanics of it, and my daughters would be equally enchanted by the music. So on behalf of them, I thank you." She placed it atop the piano.

"Is this another of your compositions?" he asked, pointing to "A Song in My Heart."

"Yes. I was finishing a new arrangement just before you came."

"It's ready to be premiered. Why don't we play it together?" Anton said encouragingly. "Do you think Ben would mind if I used his violin?"

"No. That's not his preferred violin. He keeps this one on hand for guests, and he wouldn't mind. Playing together might be an indulgence on my part. It would be the first time I play this piece with another musician."

"Oh, but it's such an innocent indulgence, two musicians playing together. There's no harm in that," he said, taking the violin from its case.

She sat at the piano and handed him the violin part. He took the manuscript and placed it on a music stand that was next to the piano. He took a chair from the corner of the room, and with the violin and bow in hand, sat across from her. He gazed at her intensely, but she quickly turned her eyes to the manuscript. Taking a few seconds, she straightened her back and signaled for them to begin.

Anton yielded to the musical encounter and soon felt transported near the sea where crashing waves melted away with the soaring melody. With every note his bow played on the strings, his thoughts were of caressing Alejandra, as if the outlines of the violin were the curves on her figure. He conjured up sensual images in his mind as he imagined kissing her on those pink and supple lips and making love to her to the rhythm of the music. As far as he was concerned if she was in Vienna and they shared the love of music, he would find every opportunity possible to be with her. And even if it seemed like a long shot, he had two months to conquer her heart.

When they had finished playing, Alejandra said, "You're an exceptional musician."

"Playing with you is what makes me exceptional," Anton said.

"All good friends play together well. It's getting late," she said.

He put the violin and bow back in the case. Once they both reached the door, she handed him his raincoat. "Have a good trip, and be safe."

Anton smiled at her. "Thank you for dinner and such an enjoyable evening. Until we meet again."

VIENNA WALTZ

After taking her evening walk about the neighborhood, Alejandra returned home and found Hannah in the drawing room reading *Eugene Onegin* by Alexander Pushkin, translated from Russian to German. It was a gift from Sacha Korsakov. They had exchanged correspondence since their meeting back in February. "How are you getting along reading in German?"

"I may not be fluent like you, but reading is a lot easier for me. It's quite a story, written in verse, about a dandy and a virtuous woman of Russian aristocracy. You would like it."

"Sure, I'd like that. And how is Sacha these days?" Alejandra asked.

"Good. He invited us to St. Petersburg in the fall, before we go back to New York."

"Are you going?"

"I want to. When am I ever going to have another chance? I almost forgot, a letter from Richard came in. What is this, his tenth? Maybe he'll surprise you and show up for the ball."

"No teasing, please," Alejandra said, taking the letter from the table. She tore it open and read it.

My dearest Ále: No words can entirely express my satisfaction knowing that you are enjoying your time in Vienna, and how pleased I am to hear of the conducting rehearsals with the orchestra. For the first time in my life, I wish I was a musician to share with you this exhilarating journey. I can only imagine, from what seems a universe away, how you must relish every moment.

Your last letter made for a bedtime story. The children were fascinated as you described the picturesque cobblestoned streets, crystal water-ways, castles, and music composed by child prodigies. They miss you, but your mother has done an excellent job in keeping them busy. Del is learning how to swim; Richie has become interested in entomological science; and Leidy has been busy planting perennials in the backyard garden. And for the Fourth of July, we will go to the lakeshore cottage and venture into town to see the fireworks, but it won't be the same in your absence. It is difficult to be without you, especially on holidays.

From my perspective, my practice has increased, and most days I'm busier than ever. Even amidst the rush, I'm always thinking of you. The nights are cold and barren, and I must admit, I yearn for you like a pubescent boy in love for the first time. I can't wait to see you again, to hear your sweet voice, and to feel the touch of your soft skin next to me. Remembering our last time together sparked regret for letting you be so far away from me. But at the same time, I know it was the right choice, or at least I've convinced myself so. I know you're happy!

I'm sorry I won't be there with you at the ball, so please dance one or two pieces, but no more, for I would certainly be jealous thinking about you being in the arms of another man.

I hope you are thinking of me wherever you are. In less than two months, I shall see and hold you again. Give my best regards to Hannah and Ben. Forever yours, Richard.

She brought the letter to her lips, thinking how much she missed him too and wished he could be there with her; for all her wants and desires revolved around him and him alone. She too suffered emotionally, and she yearned for his touch, his kisses, and to be in his arms once again. But she had also learned to live without him—something she had never thought possible.

Saturday, July 8, 1933

Before the Viennese ball, Alejandra donned a long silver-satin dress with a white ruffled hem. She was in the courtyard of Schönbrunn Palace, surrounded by baroque gardens—a natural and man-made landscape filled with a kaleidoscope of flowers. She stopped at the fountain where other people strolled past her. With the sound of water gushing down next to her, she noticed in the distance an arched Romanesque structure, which attested to the Habsburg monarchy and their centuries-old history. The palace itself had been home to emperors and their families from the eighteenth to the early twentieth century. It was here that Ferdinand Maximilian Josef von Habsburg, the Mexican emperor, and his older brother Emperor Franz Josef were born.

She recalled her maternal grandfather, Calixto, had met Maximilian during his brief reign as emperor of Mexico from 1864 to 1867. From her grandfather's stories, she had gathered that the Austrian emperor's alliance and commitment to his adopted country were real and sincere. With noble intentions, Maximiliano, as he was known to the Mexican people, implemented various laws benefiting the poorest of the Mexican people, following the tradition of other Austrian emperors who had supported compulsory education for all citizens. She had seen his portraits and his personal belongings in Chapultepec Castle in Mexico City, making his reign part of Mexican cultural and political history.

Her thoughts were interrupted when Hannah, dressed in a long black and white chiffon dress, met her by the fountain. "The tour is about to begin. We'll finally get to see where Maximilian grew up. I've been interested in his story since my time living in Mexico."

"He was a man of courage who stayed in Mexico despite perilous times," Alejandra said. "I heard so much about him as a child that I feel a particular fondness for his memory. His last words say it all."

"His last words?" Hannah asked. "I've always thought they give some measure of a person's character. What were they?"

"I read yesterday that when he was thirty-four and about to be executed, he said, 'I forgive all and ask all to forgive me. That my blood which is about to be spilled is for the good of this country, Viva Mexico! Viva la Independencia!' My grandfather thought that his life should have been spared, but those were difficult times."

"Maximilian was a real Mexican at heart," Hannah said. "Where's he buried?"

"His body was returned to Austria. He's with the rest of the monarchy in the imperial crypt in Capuchin Church," Alejandra replied.

"I'm sure your grandfather would be pleased by your visit here today," Hannah said, "but we should go."

They went inside the Imperial Apartments—Alejandra, Hannah, and Ben, along with about fifty people, elegantly dressed. Divided into two groups of twenty-five people each, their guide, a red-haired woman of mature age and dressed in an authentic period costume of the eighteenth century, led them up a blue staircase to their first stop—Franz Josef's study. Like the rest of the palace, the room was appointed with velvet drapery, gold leaf wallpaper, and red-upholstered furniture in the Louis XIV style. "Franz Josef was the penultimate Austro-Hungarian emperor. He ruled for more than sixty years and built the Kunsthistorisches Museum in Vienna to house the enormous art collection amassed by the Habsburg dynasty, which lasted more than six hundred and fifty years," the guide said.

Alejandra studied the life-size portraitures of the emperor and his wife, Elizabeth. The room housed several desks with hundreds of documents, outlining the emperor's policies. The guide stated that it had been his intention to unify Germany under the House of Habsburg, as they previously held the German crown from 1452 to 1806.

From there they toured the emperor's bedroom and other rooms including the hall where a six-year-old Wolfgang Amadeus Mozart had performed on the clavichord before Empress Maria Theresa—the first female empress of the Habsburg dynasty and the *mother-in-law of Europe*, who bore sixteen children including Marie Antoinette.

Then Alejandra and the rest of the visitors went into the Gobelin Salon filled with Belgian tapestries, many of which depicted the dynasty's coat of arms—a double-headed eagle. It was no revelation to Alejandra that the room's name came from a Spanish word for tapestry. The guide continued to discuss the Habsburg's power of influence, which linked to the Spanish Crown due to the marriage between Philip the Fair, son of Maximilian I, to Joanna of Castille, daughter of the Spanish Catholic Kings Isabella I and Ferdinand II of Aragon. The powerful connection initiated the rule of the Habsburgs in Spain. Joanna and Philip's son, Charles V, would succeed his grandfather Maximilian I as Holy Roman Emperor in 1519, making Charles V the most powerful emperor of all time.

As a young child, Alejandra often heard that Charles V's immense kingdom was known as the *Empire where the sun never sets*; for he ruled both the Holy Roman and the Spanish Empires, including the colonies in the Americas. Many Austrian Habsburgs traveled to the Spanish court during the Golden Age of Spain when their language and culture was emulated throughout Europe. Alejandra thought of the influence one culture had over other cultures—more than individual nations care to admit.

Toward the end of the tour, she came to the penultimate room—the garden room decadently covered in frescoes depicting statuaries, gardens, and lush landscapes. She was so taken in by the details of the mural that she fell behind the rest of the group, remaining by herself. Soon, however, she heard a familiar voice.

"Is this where you would spend your days?"

She turned around and saw Anton standing only a few feet from her in a black tuxedo.

"I didn't know you were coming. You know I'm getting very suspicious. If this isn't pursuing me, what would you call it?"

He smiled. "Overwhelming interest. But how could I possibly miss the opportunity of attending an embassy ball? Can you blame me for wanting to be here? I also have connections."

"I'm sure you do," she said. "I'd prefer if you didn't have overwhelming interest as you put it. To answer your question, I'd be here on rainy days or nights when I could not be outside."

As he approached, she felt his eyes on her as he glanced at her bare shoulders and modest cleavage. "May I be so bold as to say you look stunning?"

Embarrassed, she placed her hand on her chest, nervously touching her ruby necklace and replied, "I'm going to ignore you said that. How many Viennese balls have you attended?"

"Many. They're a tradition not to be missed that started under Joseph II in the late 1700s. He didn't think balls should be exclusively for nobility," he said. "And the tour... are you enjoying yourself?"

"Very much so. Although I'm surprised only a fraction of the guests came to the tour. I suppose most of the diplomats have probably been here before. Have you?"

"Yes. My first ball was at Hofburg palace," he said.

The guide came into the room and said, "Please, the ceremony is about to begin." She led them down the hallway until they reached the grand ballroom, painted with ceiling frescos and adorned with flowers and garlands amid waterfalls. Crystal chandeliers and arched mirrors gave the entire space a brilliant glow.

Soon after, they were standing in line with Hannah, Ben, and other attendees who were local government officials and American embassy staff. As they waited for the ceremony to begin, a twenty-two-piece orchestra played Haydn's "Austrian Imperial Hymn." When the music ended, a trumpet played from the opposite side of the hall, signaling the beginning of the procession. Dozens of dignitaries from various embassies, dressed in elaborate regalia and military attire, strode into the ballroom. Marine security guards followed, carrying American flags, until everyone reached their assigned places on stage. Then a uniformed young man sang "The Star-Spangled Banner."

Upon conclusion of the performance, the American ambassador, a man of average height but dignified bearing, worked his way up to the stage. He delivered a prepared speech, thanking his guests for their attendance, giving a brief history of American independence and the significance of freedom. He ended by inviting everyone to dinner. The four hundred guests applauded and dispersed into the adjacent gilded dining hall.

Alejandra thought the entire ceremony was carried out with proper pomp and circumstance, and while she was not one to relish such formality, she was pleased to have been able to participate in a celebration of America's independence. She wished Richard, who was patriotic, could have been there with her to enjoy the grand spectacle.

After entering through fourteen-foot-tall doors, she approached one of the dozens of circular tables, all set with silver candelabras, edelweiss and rose centerpieces, Herend porcelain dinnerware, silverware, and crystal glassware. When she reached her table, she noticed Anton had been assigned to sit next to her. He pulled out the chair.

"Another coincidence we're sitting together. Did you arrange this too?"

He nodded.

She sat down and placed the napkin on her lap, glancing at the five-course menu printed on a card: mushroom soup, Bibb lettuce salad, saddle of spring lamb, artichokes St. Germain, and mousse au chocolat, all paired up with several Austrian wines.

The American ambassador then stood, lifted his champagne glass and quoted Walt Whitman. "The genius of the United States is not best or most in its executives or legislatures, nor in its ambassadors or authors or colleges, or churches, or parlors, nor even in its newspapers or inventors, but always most in the common people."

Two hours later, after finishing their dinner, they returned to the palace ballroom where many couples were dancing to Strauss's "Frühlingsstimmen." Alejandra turned to Anton, who was approaching her when suddenly a distinguished brown-haired man spoke first. "Madam, please allow me to introduce myself. I'm Octavio Fuentes Medina, and I work for the Mexican embassy. Will you do me the honor and dance with me?" he asked, extending his hand. She hesitated. "*Es un placer,*" she said, reciprocating the handshake.

"One dance?" he insisted charmingly. "I noticed earlier you were speaking with one of my staff, who informed me you are a professional musician and fluent in Spanish. So I thought we might discuss a musical program we're planning for early fall to commemorate our independence."

"That certainly captures my curiosity," she said.

"Shall we then?"

"May I then have the next dance?" Anton asked, glaring at the man.

"Yes," she said, walking away with Mr. Fuentes. As they danced, Alejandra asked, "*Cual es su trabajo en la embajada?*"

"I'm Chargé d'affaires in the absence of Ing. Javier Sánchez Mejorada, our representative in Germany and Austria."

"Have you been here for long?"

"Since January, and after being in France for three years," the diplomat said. "And what brings you to Vienna?"

"I'm a student at the conservatory," she said.

"And what's your instrument?"

"Piano. Although, at the moment I'm taking a course in conducting," she replied.

"Conducting? Now that's not something you hear often," he said. "Isn't that a bit of a challenge for a woman?"

"I think perceptions about women conductors are the challenge," she said.

"That's true. Then you'd be ideal for the concert. Can I interest you in being one of our musical guests for our celebration in September? We are presenting a program composed of Mexican classical music."

"And who else are you're considering?" she asked.

"Carlos Chávez. He's working on Sinfornía de Antígona, which he hopes to premiere."

"With such a prestigious conductor and composer, it would have been an honor, but I'll be returning home in two months."

"How unfortunate for us. Where's home?" he asked.

"Minnesota."

"How in the world did you end up there?" he asked. "I can't imagine living half a year under such extremely cold conditions."

She laughed. "I was born there."

"But you speak Spanish like a native."

"Thanks to my mother."

The music ended. "May I offer you something to drink?"

"Thank you, yes," she said.

Upon arriving at a refreshment table, he took two glasses of champagne and handed one to Alejandra. "You're obviously familiar with Mexican history?"

"Somewhat. Though I must ask, when did Mexico reestablish relations with Austria?"

"In 1901. And more recently, we're revisiting the life and work of Ferdinand Maximilian von Habsburg, or should I say Maximiliano."

"I'm glad to hear that," she said. "He had many accomplishments."

"He was also a collector of pre-Hispanic documents and works of art," he said. "It's with the luxury of hindsight we can go back to see his contributions."

"Diplomatic work is fascinating to me, although I'm not keen on politics," she said. "That sounds contradictory, I know."

"Accentuating our culture is my favorite undertaking, but addressing political conflicts can be challenging," he said. "You could say that diplomacy is the constructive side of politics."

"Diplomatic negotiations, now that would be appealing on several levels," she said.

"These are not easy times, and it takes courage to stand up for what's right," he said. "In our privileged position, we can advocate for a particular cause or point of view. I have several concerns, but I can't always voice them."

"Oh? So what if your values and beliefs are in conflict with your president? How do you approach that?" she asked.

"In cases like that, you leave your agenda at the door and commit to the policies of your country's leader," he said. "Although at present, I very much agree with my leader and his stance against fascism. I greatly appreciate the local government's decision to ban the Austrian Nazi Party after the violence in Krems. But, if it's a situation where you cannot compromise your principles, then you must resign. Not many individuals would go to such extremes."

"I do hope peace prevails here. I've enjoyed our conversation, but I should return to my friends," she said.

"It has been a pleasure meeting you. If someday you return to Vienna, and I may be of any assistance, please don't hesitate to call me," he said, handing her his card.

"Muchas gracias," she said, placing it inside her clutch bag. "Hasta luego."

Moments later she joined her group. "What was that about?" Hannah asked her.

"He invited me to participate in a musical program, but it will take place after I'm gone."

"For now, the night is young, and you've yet to dance with me," Anton said. "And from observing your movements, you seem quite at ease dancing the waltz."

Alejandra smiled at Hannah.

"That's because we took dancing lessons last week. There was no way we were going to a Viennese ball and dance with two left feet," Hannah said.

"I would have loved to have seen that." Anton laughed. "How about you, Ben?"

Ben rolled his eyes. "Do you think Hannah would let me skip out? Not a chance."

"Let's not waste any more time. From the five hundred waltzes Strauss composed, the orchestra has still yet to play my favorite, so if you don't mind, I'd like to request it."

Soon, the orchestra began playing the "Vienna Waltz," and Anton swept Alejandra to the dance floor. He lightly gripped her right hand and placed his left arm around her waist, his body pressed firmly against hers. "What's that perfume you're wearing? I smell a hint of jasmine."

"Arpège. It's a mix of jasmine, rose, and lilies. You don't miss anything, do you?"

He smiled, glancing at her bosom, then her neck, lips, and finally looking directly into her eyes with such intensity that she was compelled to return his stare for a brief moment, and with that glance came a dose of chemistry coursing through her body that frightened her.

"You're awfully quiet," he whispered, holding her close. "Has the ball met with your expectations?"

She did not reply and fixed her gaze toward a distant point in the ballroom as she listened to the endless medley of waltzes. "Does this waltz ever end?"

"I didn't think one waltz with you would be enough. I hope you don't mind."

She turned silent again thinking of Richard, letting go of Anton's hand. "I'm sorry, but I do mind." She stopped dancing.

"Excuse me. I was caught up in all the excitement. May I get you something?"

"No," she replied, feeling her face flushed as he escorted her back to the table.

When the medley ended, the Adelmans returned. "Are we ready to go?" Alejandra asked.

"Yes, it's been a long day," Hannah said. "Are you all right?"

"It's been an interesting night, but I need fresh air. That's all," Alejandra said.

Ben turned to Anton. "We're calling it a night. When do you go back home?"

"Early tomorrow. But before you go, did you make a decision on Bayreuth?" Anton asked. "I'd like to make plans."

"It's a tough call, and we need to discuss it further. We'll let you know soon," Ben said.

"And you have a good trip," Hannah said.

"It was a pleasure to be with all of you," Anton said. "Until we meet again."

That night, Alejandra, who had changed into her sleeveless pink nightgown, opened the rain-spattered window to let in the cool breeze. She took in the moist night air, thinking about her day so full of surprises. Now more than ever she felt the absence of her husband and longed for his embrace. Turning off her bedside lamp, she went to bed and fell asleep.

From the ceiling, she saw herself out of body, looking down onto the dark room. She rested on the bed, like a frozen corpse. Suddenly, a raven of a man entered the bedroom through the open window. With his long arms, he removed a pair of bird-like black wings from his back, carefully placing them at the foot of the bed. Then he lay next to her, caressing her breasts. His electrifying touch made her flesh come alive. She felt a physical pleasure radiating from her lower extremities slowly up to her lips. He continued kissing her with passion as if absorbing her into himself. Then he carried her to the window and flew into a forest, where he placed her on a quilt of magenta wildflowers. As the stars shone brightly, she saw his angular face and glittering eyes, and he whispered, "I'll never let you go." He made love to her rapturously.

She awoke with a cry in the darkness, and felt conflicted by such a vivid dream, for she couldn't make out the face of the man. Willing it to be Richard, she lapsed into her wishful reverie once again, but images of Anton at the ballroom dominated her thoughts, and she was alarmed. Now fully awake, she turned on her bedside lamp and took Richard's letter from the nightstand's drawer. She read the letter and placed it on her chest, feeling laden with guilt for having such a dream and for suddenly thinking about another man. In the past, she had rationalized that the connection to Anton was simply their mutual affinity toward music, but now it was something more that she must suppress at all costs. She turned off the lights. It was three in the morning, but she could not fall asleep again. Richard's words, "Forever Yours," stayed with her like a ghostly chant.

THE MASTERSINGERS OF NUREMBERG

At the conservatory's library, seated at an empty table, Alejandra was reviewing a medieval musical score when Ben approached her. In a hushed voice, he asked, "Do you have a few minutes? I need to speak with you. It's a delicate matter."

"Of course," she said, putting away the manuscript in a folder. "This is a gem."

"Why don't we go to one of the private rooms."

She nodded and followed Ben through a long corridor, walking by rows of bookshelves and more tables filled with students until they reached a small study alcove with no windows and only a desk and two armless chairs. After closing the door, they sat across from each other, and Ben leaned toward her clasping his hands. "I've got some good news. We'll be conducting together in Florence at the end of August. I just got word from the orchestra's management."

"That's marvelous," she said. "I hope not to disappoint."

"You will not. Once you got through the nerves at the last rehearsal, you were in full command," Ben said. "And you'll have a lot more rehearsals by then."

"You're always so encouraging," she said. "What's the delicate matter?"

"What to do about the two upcoming opera festivals. I feel torn between going to Bayreuth or Salzburg," Ben said.

"Oh? I thought you discarded the idea of going to Bayreuth," she said.

"No question Salzburg would be the safer choice. But as an opera conductor, I cannot dismiss Bayreuth just on political grounds," he said.

"Toscanini refused to conduct at Bayreuth for the first time this year," she said.

"It upsets me how entangled music and politics has become, but what do you think?"

"I've been struggling with this dilemma," Alejandra replied. "On principle, I can't justify going. On the other hand, I've heard that Jewish singers will be performing at the opera right in front of Hitler. For as a fan of Wagner's operas, he'll be attending the festival."

"Unfortunately. But I've also heard that the festival has not yet been subjected to the complete control of Goebbels' Chamber of Culture policies, maintaining independence. Emil Preetorius, a prominent Jewish stage designer, will be allowed to do his work."

"I respect you for separating Wagner's politics from his art," she said. "Still, you must have concerns."

"Not really. We would be among hundreds of opera fans. It's true some artists reject Wagner's work based on his prejudices, but I'm of the same mind as Bruno Walter. In fact, he'll be conducting *Tristan and Isolde* in Salzburg. My gut feeling is that we mustn't fall prey to the judgments of others and that as artists ourselves we must be true to our art no matter what the underlying currents may be. If we decide to go to Bayreuth, would you come with us?"

Alejandra paused since she also felt conflicted—Bayreuth being the most celebrated opera festival in the world. "I want to, but I'm not sure."

"It's not like we would be going off to war," he said. "It's a musical festival for God's sake, and we wouldn't have to stay for all of it. Anton tells me that, for the first time, ticket sales have been lagging due to the political situation."

She was unconvinced, knowing that the festival would probably be overrun with Nazi officials. And she suddenly remembered the Nazi officer she'd seen at the Adlon Hotel back in Berlin. She cringed at the possibility of running into him again. "Is Anton coming too?"

"Of course. Is there a problem, and why did you decline last week's invitation to dine?"

She was not about to tell Ben how she truly felt. Besides, this would be the last time she would be in Anton's company because when they traveled to Italy Richard would also be there.

"I'll give it serious consideration," she said. "I'll be on my own tonight as I have too much to review before the next rehearsal."

"If we go, I hope you'll come. You know that going to the festival is considered a rite of passage for exceptional singers, musicians, and conductors," Ben said. "It would be a pity for you to miss it because of politics."

"It's not just that." Alejandra thought Ben was a true gentleman even if he sometimes appeared autocratic and inflexible. So if he, being Jewish, saw no harm in attending, she could trust his judgment. What could go wrong?

D riving into Bayreuth in Northern Bavaria on August 2, Alejandra, in the company of her friends, noted on first glance that the eighteenth-century town was a magnificent example of Italianate architecture. As the former home of the enlightened Margravine Wilhelmine, the wife of the Margrave of Bayreuth, the city for the last fifty-seven years had been the theatrical setting for the Wagnerian Opera festival, attracting thousands of fans from around the world. However, in the summer of 1933, the town had been taken over not only by Wagnerian enthusiasts but also by the National-Socialist Party. Upon entering the city, travelers were confronted by swastika banners and flags hanging from every post and house.

Anton, who was driving, parked near the Hotel Bayrischer Hof. Alejandra stepped out in a light-blue dress and short-heeled shoes. Hannah, dressed in a brown skirt and white blouse ensemble, said, "I don't know about you, but I can already predict this will be contentious."

"I have to admit I did not expect such overt partisan visuals all over town, but this may be a time for tunnel vision," Ben said as he got out of the car. "We're here for one thing only, the opera. And we leave in two days."

"Despite the unseemliness of it all, I assure you there's nothing to be concerned about," Anton said as he opened the trunk of the car. He set four suitcases on the ground. "From this location, we can walk to Margravial Opera House, Villa Whanfield, old town, or Festspielhaus."

"Are you trying to reassure us?" Hannah asked. "Because it's not working."

"I'm sure we'll all have a wonderful time. Let's settle in first. We can reconvene in the hotel's lobby, say in an hour," Anton suggested. "I've made reservations for dinner nearby."

Ben picked up his and Hannah's suitcases, and Anton was about to carry Alejandra's luggage when she said, "Thank you, but I can manage."

"As you wish."

After settling into her room, Alejandra went into the lobby of the hotel, which was appointed with wood flooring, nineteenth century portraits, wrought-iron chandeliers, and low ceilings. With more than forty minutes to spare before meeting her friends, she decided to go in search of a music store for a Wagner book on the art of conducting and his well-known essays on Beethoven. She left the three-story brick building and, consulting a tourist map, headed south on Bahnhofstrasse and soon found a bookstore. Inside, the shop was packed with tourists and Nazi paraphernalia, including miniature busts of Hitler. Upset by the Nazi visuals in the bookstore, she considered leaving, but then, on the opposite side of the store, she saw a slim, well dressed, gray-haired man, whom she recognized instantly as Richard Strauss, one of Germany's most notable conductors and composers of the late Romantic period. She had been to one of his rehearsals in Berlin, although they were never introduced. He was standing by the children's book section. She moved toward him, hoping to make his acquaintance. As she perused the books on a shelf next to him, he turned to her. "*Verzeihen Sie Mir. Ich habe dich gesehen.*"

He recognized her, and she answered, "Yes. I was at one of your rehearsals with the Berlin Philharmonic. I was a student at the Stern Conservatory."

He extended his hand. "Pleasure to meet you. And what's your area of study?"

"Conducting. And it's nice to see you again, Maestro. I'm Alejandra Stanford Morrison."

"So, you were at one of my rehearsals, you say. Which one?"

She paused, recalling it was the rehearsal where he took over for Bruno Walter back in March, but decided not to mention it wanting to avoid a possible awkward moment, for it had caused quite a stir. And as if he had read her mind, he continued, "It's not relevant. Are you an American, and is this your first time here?"

"Yes, and I'm looking forward to you opening the festival with Beethoven's Ninth," she said. "It's among my favorite symphonies."

"Considering I learned from the best, Hans von Bülow, would you like to attend our rehearsal tomorrow?"

She smiled. "I'd like that very much. Would it be possible to bring a friend? Perhaps you know Benjamin Adelman. He recently debuted with the Vienna Philharmonic."

He took a couple of books from the shelf. "For my grandchildren," he said. "No, I have not met him, but I look forward to seeing you both tomorrow at eight."

"Until then," she said. Then Strauss walked away.

She had been in Bayreuth for only an hour and had met Strauss, and tomorrow she would be attending a private rehearsal. Perhaps this was a good omen, and the rest of the trip would go on without a glitch. She selected several books for her children, paid the cashier, and left the store.

At ten o'clock, Alejandra went into the garden of the hotel, landscaped with rows of blue and white cornflower plants. Lit by gas lanterns, the pathway had the appearance of having been built in the last century. She spotted Anton alone on a stone bench, smoking a cigarette. He waved, stood up and walked to her. He was dressed in a pair of black pants, striped shirt, and his familiar leather coat. "I'm so glad to see you," he said.

Since the intensity of the Viennese ball and her suggestive dream, she had tried her best to keep a distance and treat him as though he was a professional colleague. "I had no idea you'd be out here."

"Am I that awful to be around?" he asked, laughing.

"No. I just have a lot on my mind," she said.

"You hardly spoke over dinner," he said. "Let's sit for a few moments. No harm in that."

"I guess." She followed him to a bench surrounded by blooming potted trees. Taking in the earthy scent of the flowers, she sat next to him.

"I feel as though you're trying to avoid me. Did I say or do something to upset you?" he asked.

"No. I'm just worried about other matters," she said.

"What's troubling you? I hope you know you can trust me."

"Since our arrival this morning, I've felt ambivalent about being here," Alejandra said. "It was great to visit Margravial Opera House and stroll about town, and even discover where Franz Liszt lived. And to top it off, I met Richard Strauss, and I'm thrilled about that. But I can't shake the feeling that storm clouds are on the horizon."

"That's understandable given the political climate. Although, I don't think there's anything to worry about," Anton said. "We're leaving the day after tomorrow. What can happen in a little over a day?"

"Maybe I'm letting my worries get the better of me."

"Are you concerned about your meeting tomorrow?" he asked.

She paused for a moment. "Not exactly. When I spoke to Strauss earlier this afternoon, I couldn't help but think of the harsh criticism he has endured for accepting to conduct in this festival after Toscanini pulled out. Are we to judge every artist through a political lens? How are we to know their motivations and what's in their hearts?"

"It's rumored that Strauss agreed to step in as a conductor to insulate and protect his Jewish daughter-in-law and grandchildren from persecution," Anton said. "Strauss has spoken publicly about his disapproval of the government's racist policies, and he has refused to join the Nazi party, but he's walking a fine line. I'm afraid the choices are not always black and white, and everyone will have an opinion."

"I have struggled to place everything that's happening in a proper musical context," she said. "It's a delicate balance I'm learning to navigate while training. Tomorrow, I'll go to the rehearsal to focus on the music and to learn everything I can. I despise politics."

"I do sense your irritation, and I never realized how problematic it must be for you, but you have the strength to deal with it," he said.

She laughed ever so slightly, thinking she could handle professional challenges, but personal ones were another subject entirely. "Some things are beyond our control no matter how hard we try. I need to get some rest if I want to follow Beethoven's Ninth and Wagner's opera note by note, and the opera score is very involved."

"It calls for a first-rate tenor and soprano," he said.

"It calls for six tenors, nine basses, and two sopranos, plus the full orchestra. It was the largest score ever published in 1867. Hans von Bülow conducted Munich's premier of *The Mastersinger of Nuremberg*. I purchased the libretto this evening."

"You know the story's inspiration stems from a book about a mastersinger's guild and a real figure from the Renaissance," Anton said. "The protagonist of the opera, Hans Sachs, was a poet and song expert."

"I find it interesting that the opera, based on a story about a song contest and the beauty of poetry and music, can alter the character of a person and inspire a culture. I believe in art that's transformative," she said.

"And don't forget the contestants' real motivation," Anton said. "The victor gets to marry Eva, and as it turns out, his one true love."

"I think I should go," Alejandra said.

"Can you stay a little longer? There's something I want to tell you of a more personal nature," Anton said.

"Perhaps another day. I don't think I can deal with anything else right now."

"It will have to wait, then," he said under his breath.

She ignored his comment and walked away. He followed her to the entrance. "But brace yourself, Alejandra, the festival's opening could be chaotic."

"Now you tell me."

"I mean there will be thousands of screaming fans clamoring for their idols," he said.

The next morning, dressed in a gray skirt, turquoise-green jacket, and polka dot scarf, Alejandra walked through the tree-lined avenue toward Festspielhaus. From a distance she saw the opera house—an undistinguished, four-towered timber structure, built amidst incredibly appealing, lush surroundings. As she recalled, it was the reason why Wagner had chosen the site as the ideal locale for his operas so that the focus would be entirely on the music and the performances.

Upon entering the empty theater, she relished the peaceful silence and the absence of swastikas. Only a doorman was there so far; he bowed his head from afar but said nothing. Her gaze was drawn to the stage, flanked by arches and a double proscenium, giving it an incredible illusion of depth when designed for Wagner's opera *The Ring*. The theater was also a technical marvel regarding its acoustics, making the reverberation time last 1.55 seconds. She scanned the rest of the auditorium, noticing the Corinthian columns and descending rows of wooden seats, enough to accommodate more than sixteen hundred opera fans.

She approached the covered orchestra pit, an invention conceived by Wagner, and then proceeded down a few steps, taking a seat in the corner, away from the percussion section. While space was rather confined, it was large enough to accommodate the large orchestra. From her briefcase, she took two scores, Beethoven's Ninth Symphony and the opera *The Mastersinger of Nuremberg*, the original libretto, and the festival's program dated August 3, 1933. The names of the artists printed in the program included Richard Strauss, conductor, and Heinz Tietjen, artistic director. The cast included Rudolf Bockelmann, Alexander Kipnis, Willy Storring, Hans Wrana,

Gotthold Ditter, Harry Steier, Franz Sauer, Max Lorenz, Erich Zimmermann, Maria Müller, and Ruth Berglund.

She paged through the score, reviewing the various sections for flute, piccolo, oboe, clarinet, bassoon, et cetera, and then skipped to the chorus part, singing it to herself. Then Ben, in gray slacks, white shirt, and a black jacket, joined her. "As always, up and ready to go," he said.

"I wanted to have time to see it all before everyone arrived. How are you this morning?"

"I guess I'm all right. Have you seen this?" Ben handed Alejandra a flyer which read: "It is requested that there should be no singing of the Nazi anthem 'Horst-Wessel-Lied,' and no demonstration inside Festspielhaus that does not pertain to the works of Richard Wagner."

"Well, that's encouraging," she said.

"With its illustrious history, Bayreuth's festival has attracted the finest musicians and conductors from around the world. It's unfortunate one person can change all that," Ben added.

"One day we shall return to enjoy the entire festival under other circumstances, and today we'll enjoy listening to 'Ode to Joy' in this acoustically magnificent setting," Alejandra said. "As you've said, let's not think about anything else but the music. Here come the musicians."

Richard Strauss, casually dressed, looking like a university professor, approached them. "Guten Morgen, Fräulein Alejandra und Herr Benjamin."

"Guten Morgen," she said.

"Thank you for having us, Maestro," Ben said.

"I'm very pleased you're both here." Then Strauss proceeded with introducing Alejandra and Ben to the rest of the musicians as they came in. They were all very courteous, and as everyone took their positions Strauss marked the downbeat and began the rehearsal. After having studied the score in detail, Alejandra thought the opening of the symphony was as momentous and dramatic as the choral ending. From her notes, she was reminded of a quote from someone who reviewed the symphony during the world premiere. "Beethoven's inexhaustible genius has opened up a new world for us, has disclosed wondrous secrets of the holy art, hitherto unknown and wholly unsuspected."

For the next two hours she couldn't have been happier than to be learning from Strauss who was not only a gifted composer and conductor, but also seemed to be a kind-hearted man.

Later in the afternoon, as the orchestra prepared to perform the opening act of the festival, Alejandra, along with her friends, took their seats in the theater's balcony. With a bird's eye view of the stage and the crowd, she noted dozens of Nazi officials in the front row, including Adolf Hitler and Joseph Goebbels. Her first instinct was to walk away for she had not expected to feel so out of place, but when the first notes of Beethoven's Ninth began to reverberate in the hall, she immediately relaxed, as the music had the power to calm her down, like a lullaby to a crying infant. It was the first time in Bayreuth's history that the festival had opened with Beethoven's Ninth Symphony. She wondered if Beethoven with his generous spirit would have objected to having his grand symphony performed under the current political conditions. Would he be rolling in his grave as Anton had suggested? Or would he use the occasion to speak tolerance and patience? After all, it was the ideals of enlightenment that had propelled him to incorporate Schiller's poem, "Ode to Joy," into his music. No one, of course, could know what Beethoven would do. His music would have to speak for itself.

Then, as the music played, she thought of the many times Anton had criticized, rightfully so, the Führer's writings, policies, and overall ideology. So she entertained what she would have liked to say to Hitler given a chance. *You consider yourself an artist, a patron, and art enthusiast. You must know that creativity is a gift from God to man for the benefit of all humanity, and we are all God's creation. As you fail to comprehend this concept by excluding artists because of their race, I can only conclude that you lack understanding in the fundamental nature of creation, which is antithesis to destruction. You could dedicate your energy and power to a life of peace by encouraging tolerance among all human beings. Wouldn't that be a life worth living?* She fully grasped the naïveté of this, but fundamentally she believed it was possible to reason with even the most wretched of men, unless of course, they were evil or insane.

Her thoughts were interrupted when applause ensued at the conclusion of Beethoven's symphony. Then, immediately, the prelude to the first act of the opera *The Mastersingers of Nuremberg* commenced. As the curtains were drawn open, she saw a representation of the city of Nuremberg, designed in Renaissance style with diamond shaped fabric canopies, oversized trees, and mural paintings. A group of actors soon appeared, playing the roles of bourgeois artisans, poets, and musicians, who belonged to the prestigious artist guild, led by the noble cobbler, Hans Sachs, the expert song master, who would help Walther von Stolzing win the annual Meistersinger competition.

Sachs would also teach him the strict rules of the guild, write a song, and defeat the despot Beckmesser.

The opera continued for ninety minutes until the performance paused for the first intermission, at which point everyone dispersed, and many exited the venue. But to the dismay of Alejandra and her companions, another kind of theater was just beginning—political theater. Joseph Goebbels, the Nazi propaganda minister, used the occasion to speak on the radio to thousands of listeners across the country:

> *"There is certainly no work in the entire music literature of the German people that is so relevant to our time and its spiritual and intellectual tension as is Richard Wagner's Meistersinger. How often in years past has its rousing mass chorus 'wake… Soon will dawn the day' been found by an ardent longing, believing German people to be a palpable symbol of the reawakening of the German nation from the deep political and spiritual narcosis of November 1918? Of all his music dramas, The Meistersinger stands out as the most German. It is simply the incarnation of our national identity…"*

When the broadcast ended, they made their way outside and into the courtyard. In a most uncharacteristic tone and raised voice, Anton exclaimed, "Through their shameless exploitation of an authentic work of German art, Wagner's *Meistersinger* has been seized to symbolize the party's doctrine… and linked to Herr Hitler, who I fear will not advance my country."

It was at that moment she realized what Anton had been saying all along—how a government could exploit venerated masterworks that were skillfully wrapped around an ill-conceived partisan ideology.

Speechless and concerned that others might have overheard Anton's angry outburst, she glanced around the area, and to Alejandra's relief, most of the crowd seemed to have returned to the opera house for the second act. Anton, who was still beside himself and appeared to be without fear of re-crimination, impulsively held up the festival's handbook that showcased a picture, not of Wagner, but of Hitler. He frantically ripped it to shreds, contemptuously throwing the bits of paper into the air. As the pieces fell to the ground, he stomped on them with his feet, as if they were poisonous insects.

"Anton, calm down," Ben said. "It might be prudent for us to leave now."

"And don't look behind you, Anton, but we have a group of SA men and at least five pairs of eyes staring in our direction," Hannah whispered.

"If we leave suddenly, we may further raise their already apparent suspicion of us," Alejandra added.

Anton said, "Forgive me for putting you in a precarious situation. I was just too upset to ignore it, and I usually show better restraint. We should go back inside where I suspect it will be safe. We can then exit after the second act."

"We should stay until the end and exit with the crowd, which might provide some cover," Ben said. "I don't have the inclination to go through another beating like the one I got in Berlin."

"If we stay here, they will confront us," Hannah said.

"Again, please pardon me," Anton said.

"Ben's plan is reasonable. Let's hope for the best," Alejandra said.

Then, as they all returned to the opera house and she walked down the aisle toward the balcony, her heart nearly stopped when she caught an unexpected glimpse of the Nazi officer she had seen back in Berlin at the Adlon Hotel. She always knew he might be in attendance, for there were rumors that Hitler had practically commanded all the members of the party to attend the festival. He was in a seat behind the Führer. They looked so alike it was eerie. The only difference between them, now, was that he had shaved off his mustache. She thought he looked dangerous like Hitler, and something about the man's persona frightened her as he now stared and seemed to have recognized her with his creepy smile. She turned away and quickly walked past him. Thank God they were leaving the next day.

Once they made their way back to their seats, the lights dimmed again. Ben, who was two seats down, whispered, "As difficult as it may be, let's try to concentrate on the performances. We mustn't get sidetracked from our initial intentions." But that didn't calm her, for not only did they have to be concerned about potential repercussions of what Anton had done, but she also worried about coming face to face with that Nazi officer. She took a deep breath and did her best to enjoy the opera.

After several more hours, including another intermission, where the four of them stayed in their seats, and the opera advanced to the last scene of the third act, hundreds of choral singers and a procession of the guilds gathered for the finale. As Alejandra considered the entire production, she thought the visual pageantry stimulating, but the sound of the huge chorus reverberating in the theater was extraordinary. She was captivated by the energy and solid performances of the artists on stage, as well as all those behind-the-scenes personnel, including the orchestra. To her, their outstanding work only served to cement her belief that the only relevant factor was the expression of the art itself. In the end, whether the rest of the public realized it or not, they too had submitted to the essence of the art for they rose to their feet giving a standing ovation, lasting several minutes. Vigorous applauding continued as the entire cast stood onstage, bowing, and then the curtains came down for the last time. Breaking that magical moment of jubilation, Anton spoke, "We need to make our move now."

Amongst the rush of the crowd, they quickly left the opera house. Once they were outside the building, Alejandra was relieved to be among hundreds of fans who could still be heard praising the production and dispersing in all directions. Like a fugitive, she noticed Anton looking behind him and in every direction for the Brownshirts. "I think we're in the clear," he said. Then they walked toward their hotel for a block without saying a word. But when they turned a corner, they came in front of six SA men. Her heart raced when a Brownshirt with a square-shaped face, long nose, and broad physique, stepped in front of Anton. *"Wir brauchen Sie für die Befragung."*

"Befragung für das, was?" he asked.

Anton was wanted for questioning. With an expression of outrage, the man pulled shredded pieces of paper from his jacket, exposing a splintered image of Hitler.

"It was only a joke. I had no idea the Führer's picture was in the program. Do we no longer have a sense of humor?" Anton said.

"You need to come with us now," the man said.

"Then let these American tourists go."

The man glared at them, and with an upward dismissive hand motion, added, *"Du kannst einen Kommentar."*

Despite the fact he had dismissed them, Alejandra felt her stomach churning, afraid for Anton's safety. She remembered how violent these men could be as she recalled the incident with Ben a few months earlier.

"Please go, I'll be fine." Anton walked away with the SA men.

Once they were alone, Alejandra said, "Meet me in my room in an hour. I have someone to see who may help with this situation."

Ben and Hannah, both very shaken, nodded in agreement.

Later, at eight, they met in Alejandra's room, as planned. There was still no news of Anton. Hannah, who was leaning against an armoire, asked, "So where did you go?"

"To speak with Stewart Anderson who owns a music shop. He's the Englishman I met yesterday after dinner."

"How did you know you could trust him?" Hannah asked. "And what do we do if Anton is not back by tomorrow?"

"I just knew by our conversation," Alejandra replied.

"We can't leave him. We'll have to wait," Ben said. "Hopefully he'll be released soon."

"Stewart has been a resident of this city for the last ten years. He thinks Anton's situation may be of great concern if he is not out in a few hours. It's already nearly two. While he may be German, he's not necessarily safe if he's labeled a communist. They could transfer him to jail in Berlin or worse, to Dachau."

"Dachau?" Hannah questioned.

"Munich's Chief of Police Himmler opened this camp in March to house German political prisoners," she added. "It's a couple of hours from here."

"Surely, Anton can bribe himself out of prison," Ben said.

"I'm not so sure about that. According to Stewart, the SS take pride in flushing out enemies of the state," Alejandra said.

"Who could have ever thought that ripping up a flyer would lead to being arrested?" Hannah said.

"We need someone with influence to get him out. But who?" Ben asked.

"How about Winifred Wagner," Alejandra said. "I wouldn't go to her directly, but perhaps through Richard Strauss. As you know, they're gathering at her home, celebrating the festival's opening. If we wait until tomorrow, it may be too late."

"Are you crazy? You're going to go uninvited to Villa Wahnfried?" Hannah asked. "I knew you had guts, but you know the Führer could be there with his entire entourage."

"The important thing is that Strauss will be there too, and I hope that he may have some influence with Winifred," Alejandra said. "I'll discuss Anton's situation."

"You did seem to have hit it off with him this morning at the rehearsal. He was very gracious. I guess it's the only option we have other than to wait, hoping for the best," Ben said.

"Hoping for the best won't do," Alejandra said. "It's a tough call, but my instincts tell me that if we wait until tomorrow, we may never see Anton again."

"Would you like us to come along?" Ben asked.

"No, that might complicate things. I think it's best if I go alone. I'll wait until nine, and if I don't hear anything by then, I'll go through with the plan," Alejandra said.

With still no news of Anton's release, Alejandra proceeded with her plan. At thirty minutes past nine in the evening, she arrived at the two-story, neo-classical Villa Wahnfried, landscaped with shrubs and trees. At the center of the courtyard, a bust of Wagner adorned a circular garden. Set in stone at the front of the house was Wagner's motto: *Hier wo mein Wähnen Frieden fand, Wahnfried, sei dieses Haus von mir benannt*—Here where my delusions have found peace, let this place be named Wahnfried. Guards protected the compound, and when she approached the entrance, a uniformed man came up to her. With alcohol on his breath, he said, *"Guten Abend."*

"I'm here to see Richard Strauss," she said.

"Are you related?"

"No, I'm a fellow musician, and I have a pressing matter to discuss which cannot wait."

He studied her carefully. "Well, you seem harmless enough, and we like musicians." He opened the door, ushering her into the foyer. Another guard, dressed in a black uniform was standing by the door. "This lady is here to see Mr. Strauss."

"I'll take it from here," he said, scrutinizing Alejandra from head to toe. "Wait here."

While waiting, she glanced about the unusual vestibule, reminiscent of an enchanted forest from one of Wagner's operas. There were dozens of uniformed men and elegantly dressed guests who were frolicking and enjoying the festivities as if celebrating New Year's Eve. The cacophony of noise was so loud that when Richard Strauss met her at the door she barely heard his greeting. "Mrs. Morrison, what a pleasant surprise," he said and offered his hand.

She noticed a German pin, *Musikverein Siershahn* on the lapel of his tuxedo, which featured a harp and the year 1905. She wondered if it had anything to do with the premiere of his opera *Salome* that same year. At the

148

moment, however, that fact was of no importance. "Pardon the interruption. But I have an urgent problem to discuss, and you were the only person who I thought could help me."

"Oh! You sound as if it is a matter of life and death," he said.

"It might be," she said.

"It's too noisy here. There's a study where we can talk."

Alejandra followed Strauss through several rooms decorated with damask draperies, antique furnishings, and packed with people. At the end of a winding corridor, they entered a chamber with gray wallpaper, diamond patterned floors, and scarlet upholstered armchairs. "Please have a seat. How can I help you?" he asked, sitting next to her.

"Thank you for seeing me. A few hours ago, a group of SA men detained a friend. We're concerned he may have been considered a threat to the state."

He was silent for a moment, looking concerned. "Why would he be considered that?"

"Earlier today, outside the opera house, he ripped a program to pieces which included a picture of the Führer," she replied. "His action was considered suspicious, and the SA used it as justification to take him in for questioning."

"Is he of a questionable background?"

"Not at all. Anton is a German art dealer and a musician," she said.

"I admire your courage, but everything matters these days. What's his name?"

"Anton Everhardt."

"And your relation to him?"

"A dear friend," she replied, suddenly caught off guard using an affectionate expression to describe him.

"I fully understand your concern. One must be careful to avoid words or actions seeming anti-government," Strauss said. "Wait here while I make some inquiries."

"I appreciate it," she said.

While Strauss was gone, and feeling increasingly distressed, she tried to distract herself by looking at framed Wagner programs that hung on the walls—*Parsifal* 1884, *Die Meistersinger* 1892, *Lohengrin* 1902, *Tristan and Isolde* 1928, *Das Rheingold* 1931, and so on. Under other circumstances, she would have enjoyed experiencing the composer's home—a place where he had created some of his most revered operas. He was a man of endless creativity, for not only had he written complex musical scores, but also the librettos. Despite any personal shortcomings, it was his creative genius that had cemented his musical legacy.

Alejandra paced back and forth. It had been almost twenty minutes since she was left alone to ponder Anton's fate, and she felt a knot in her stomach at the possibility of never seeing him again. She imagined he was imprisoned in a dark cell, injured, or left to die in some remote place. Faced with those raw emotions, she was on the verge of crying when Strauss returned, closing the door behind him. As if in prayer, she joined her hands together and brought them to her lips, waiting for him to say anything. Caringly, he placed his hand on her shoulder. "I'm told your friend was not the most cooperative and was about to be transferred to Munich later tonight or in the morning. However, with a little gentle pleading, I've been assured he'll be released soon, but one can never be sure of anything these days." Feeling the tension in her shoulders relax, she sighed with relief and said, "Gentle pleading?"

"Let's just say persons of influence who intervened," he replied.

"How can I ever thank you?" she said.

"It was my pleasure from one conductor to another," he said. "Winifred would like to meet you. She was intrigued by your background and nerve."

"I don't know if it was nerve but rather a concern for a friend," Alejandra said.

"Well, he's fortunate to have you as a friend," he said.

"She wants to meet me tonight? I'm not sure I'd be good company right now," she said.

"It will have to do," Strauss replied. "Follow me."

Minutes later, Alejandra found herself in a reception room that also served as a library decorated with carved wooden shelves and crown molding, velvet furniture, and a black grand piano. Dozens of people had gathered, drinking and laughing. As she waited for the introduction to Winifred Wagner, Alejandra briefly revisited her biography—British-born orphan, Wagner's son Siegfried's wife, the family matron, and Bayreuth's festival official administrator. Alejandra walked with Strauss toward the forty-something brunette with a large figure, wearing a navy-blue dress with a laced collar.

"Alejandra Morrison, I'd like you to meet Winifred Wagner," Strauss said.

"Lovely to meet you, Mrs. Wagner," Alejandra said, extending her hand.

"Likewise, Mrs. Morrison," Winifred said, shaking her hand. "Please, join me. I'm thrilled to speak for a change in English, if you don't mind."

"Certainly." Alejandra smiled, sitting beside her on the sofa.

"Mr. Strauss tells me you're a pianist and training to be a conductor. I have to admit it caught my attention. I'm thrilled you and your friends are here for the festival. We want all opera fans to have the best experience possible," Winifred said in a no-nonsense manner. "We wouldn't want any negative publicity. We're very proud of what we have accomplished. It's an incredible legacy we must preserve."

"Indeed," Alejandra said. "The production was marvelous today. Congratulations! We immensely enjoyed the opera, as well as the opening by Maestro Strauss."

"Would you consider having tea with me? I'd like to know more about your experience and training," said Winifred.

Alejandra was hesitant, for they had planned to leave early the following day. However, she thought Winifred was a friendly person. "We will not be here for the length of the festival as we have other professional commitments in Vienna."

"Surely, you'll still be here tomorrow. How about tea at eleven? I would think that as an aspiring conductor you'd like to know more about the festival's history."

"Absolutely. My German grandmother was a big fan of the festival. She attended twice when she was a young girl," Alejandra said. "But, I don't want to take more of your time."

"Before you go, will you grace us with playing the piano? It would be a charming addition to our celebration."

She paused, finding no desire to perform. However, given that Mrs. Wagner had been apparently helpful in some way, she felt compelled to accept. She would play a composition of her choice and one that would send a subtle message to all the people who gathered there.

Mrs. Wagner made an announcement that Alejandra would be performing. Feeling all eyes on her, including about thirty other guests, she addressed Winifred as if she was there in some formal capacity. "Since Wagner himself chose Beethoven's Ninth Symphony as his inspiration for the laying of the foundation stone in his opera house, and as it was today's opening symphony, I'd like to play the symphony's second movement to honor Beethoven's memory and his love for all humanity. I feel this music is his greatest gift to the world."

"I see you are as devoted to Beethoven as we all are," Winifred said.

"Yes. He was not only a genius but an enlightened man," she said.

Then she slowly walked to the pianoforte and sat on the cushioned bench. Taking a deep breath, Alejandra placed her fingers on the keys, mustering all her energy, and she began to play. For the next six minutes and twelve seconds, she played the composition with such virtuosity and intensity as if Anton's very life depended on it. When she completed her presentation, she heard the applause and walked back to Winifred Wagner and Richard Strauss. "I'm very appreciative for your assistance and hospitality. It was lovely to meet you."

Winifred replied, "Bravo that was magnificent. Would you like to join us for a drink?"

"You're very kind, but I should return to the hotel. Two of my friends are probably waiting for me and very worried," Alejandra said. "I can't thank you enough for all you did."

"I'm looking forward to our talk tomorrow from one woman to another. I feel as though we will have much in common," Winifred said, patting Alejandra's arm.

"Yes, of course," Alejandra said.

"Remember you're always welcome at any of my rehearsals," Strauss said.

"Thank you again, Maestro," Alejandra said. "I'll never forget all your kindness."

"I'll walk you to the door," he said. "And please, be careful."

And just as she exited villa, she ran into the same Nazi official from the opera house. Wearing a black suit, he was smoking a cigarette outside the gate.

"What a coincidence to see you again, Mrs. Morrison."

She felt sick to her stomach. "And how do you know my name?"

"It's our business."

"How unfortunate! And I'm sure it will be the last time."

"Maybe not," he said, with an odd expression.

She quickly walked away.

Just before eleven, she was back at the hotel. Agitated and short of breath, she tapped on the Adelman's room. "It's me." Hannah let her in. "Ále, we've been worried about you."

"Have you heard from Anton?" she asked.

"Still nothing. You look awfully pale," Ben said. "Sit down and tell us what happened."

"Strauss said he would be released. Where is he?"

"What are you talking about?" Ben asked.

She forced herself to calm down and related the sequence of events of the last two hours.

"Unbelievable," Hannah said. "I don't think I could have gone through all that and be composed enough to perform."

"You have chutzpah," Ben said.

"Was Hitler there?" Hannah asked.

"He could have been, but thankfully, I didn't see him. I saw someone just as vile, but I don't want to talk about it," Alejandra replied.

"Yes. I know what you mean. And since the opera, I haven't stopped thinking of a whole litany of insults I'd like to say to Hitler," Hannah said.

"Me too," Alejandra said.

"You'd only say that if there was no fear of repercussion," Ben said. "I'm sure that many people would love to tell him exactly what they think, but they're afraid."

"That's why no one stands up to him," Hannah said. "But that's another conversation."

"Ále, you've done everything you can. Get some sleep. Hopefully we'll hear from Anton soon," Ben said.

Alejandra nodded in agreement and stepped toward the door. "Please let me know if you hear anything, even if it's late."

As she reached the door of her hotel room, she wondered if all her efforts had been in vain. Unlocking the door, and with only the light from the street lamps outside, she sat on the window bench. She reflected on the last five months. She had been on an emotional roller-coaster from heaven to hell and back again. While aware of everything that had happened, she had suppressed her emotions. But that night, the sum of all her experiences came crashing down in a myriad of emotions—anger, fear, frustration, and hope. Finally letting go for the first time, tears streamed down her cheeks, like a dam that had broken. Sobbing incessantly at the thought of never seeing Anton again, she realized she cared more about him than she had been willing to acknowledge. These emotions deeply troubled her because she loved her husband, and she wanted to believe that her feelings for Anton were merely affection for a friend.

After what seemed like an eternity of not knowing whether Anton would be released, she felt confined inside the dark and small hotel room. With her handkerchief, she wiped her face. She needed fresh air to clear her mind. Nature, like music, always soothed her. Still dressed in her street clothes, she took her coat and room key from the nightstand and left the room. First, though, she went to reception to inquire if Anton Everhardt had yet picked up his room key. The clerk informed her he was still gone, so she told him that she would be in the garden.

It was nearly midnight of a quiet summer night as she made her way to a secluded area in the orchard near a half dozen trees with little white flowers. The intoxicating scent of jasmine filled the air, and she felt a warm breeze on her face. And while everything appeared calm and peaceful, she was far from feeling that way inside. What was happening to her? Was Anton safe? Would he be freed? Her life had become too complicated.

NOCTURNE OP. 9, NO. 1 IN B FLAT MINOR

Anton sat in a cell at the police station, although he considered it to be more like a dungeon—dark, dilapidated, and moldy. Through the small barred opening, he could hear the shrieks of other prisoners, but he suspected they were also political dissidents, not criminals. Since Hitler's rise to power, there had been an increase in arbitrary civilian arrests, and it was a well-known fact that his administration ruled by intimidation and fear. Anton had been cautious in voicing his anti-Nazi views, so he never expected to find himself in such a predicament. Losing his temper was something he had never done publicly, except for when he confronted a bar patron in his adolescence, which landed him on the streets. He would take that anytime, rather than be in the custody of the Gestapo, who operated as judge, jury, and increasingly, as rumored, as executioner. Filled with anxiety at his illegal arrest, he rationalized they had nothing of substance on him to keep him imprisoned. He was no threat to the authority of the state, and he hoped it would be just a matter of time before he was released.

A lieutenant had questioned Anton earlier in the day. He went as far as attempting to bribe the man with an expensive work of art. The lieutenant had laughed and said that if they wanted any of his possessions, all they had to do was walk into his house and take them. Anton waited for another hour or more until summoned by a superior, who would conduct a formal interrogation. A guard led him to an office, and as he climbed the stairs to the main level, he saw through a small window that it was nighttime. Space throughout was equally drab and cold.

Two uniformed guards stood outside the door. One of the men said,

"The Hauptsturmführer will see you now." When he entered the office, Anton was shaking. Behind a large desk, cluttered with a bronze bust of an eagle with the Nazi emblem and stacks of papers and an envelope, sat a lean man who was pimpled-scarred and dressed in the familiar black uniform and swastika armband. A black and white picture of the officer with the Führer hung on a wall behind his desk. "Are you ready to talk now?"

With the door open, Anton sat on a wooden chair as requested. "I've answered all your questions to the lieutenant," Anton replied.

"You've said you're an art dealer in Berlin and a proud German citizen. Then why the hell haven't you joined our party? That can only mean one thing. You're a communist."

Anton laughed nervously trying to make light of the situation. "It can mean a lot of things, but I'm no communist. I'm a successful businessman who thrives on capitalism. How many times must you ask me the same question?"

"Until you confess who you really are. I've seen many communists like you who hide behind so-called honorable professions, and your actions today gave you away."

"The actions of an opera fan? I'm here like hundreds of others who came to enjoy the festival. And as far I know, Germany is still a free country."

The man pushed papers to the side of the desk, making room. Then he took an envelope and emptied its contents—the ripped musical program. Hitler's picture was broken up into little pieces like a puzzle. "How do you explain this?"

"That again? As I've said, it was a joke," Anton said.

"What kind of an idiot would think that ripping the Führer's picture would be a joke? It's nonsense, and you know it. You don't come across as a stupid man," he said.

Anton's frustration and anger were beginning to get the better of him, so he paused for a moment to collect himself. He then replied, "I didn't know his picture was in the program. I felt dissatisfied with the opera. I'm entitled to my opinion."

"That still doesn't explain why you so scornfully stepped on the Führer's ripped picture when it fell to the floor. The SA men watching you came to the conclusion you detested him."

"Why would I detest him?" Anton lied.

"You shouldn't," the officer said. "He and the administration are working on improving the country's economy and infrastructure. Transportation runs smoothly. He'll do great things for our country."

Anton would have loved to rebuke him, but that would be tantamount to suicide. He replied in a sardonic tone. "Yeah, and from your picture, I can see he's affable too. So I think we're done here. You have absolutely no reason to detain me any further."

"Who do you think you're dealing with?" the officer said. "And how do you explain dismissing two of your loyal servants back in the spring. Your chauffeur reported you'd fired them without cause, and he suspected it was because they supported our policies."

"I did have a reason, too many employees. I have enough in Berlin," Anton said.

"You're not convincing, and you can turn against us, if you haven't already," he said.

Anton, seething, replied, "How dare you question my patriotism? I fought for my country at Verdun. Do you have any fucking idea what that was like? Were you there? I doubt it!" He got up and was about to leave when the officer instantly stood up. "Stop right there." He then walked to Anton, grabbing his arm with a jerk, and struck him violently in the face. Anton almost lost his balance. "My questioning is done when I say so, you fucking liar."

Foolishly, Anton punched the SS man back on the jaw, inviting the guards into the room. They held Anton's arms while the other struck him in the face several times until blood gushed from his nose, splattering all over his clothes. The officer punched Anton's chest, rib cage, and stomach until he collapsed to the floor.

"I know he's a lying bastard," the Hauptsturmführer said.

The senior officer kicked him in the groin, and Anton curled into a ball, gasping. Then the other two men lifted him.

"You're a coward and a vicious brute," Anton spat out.

"You wait. This is nothing compared to what awaits you. Get him out."

Anton was cuffed and taken back down to his cell.

He managed to sit upright on the dirty concrete floor and lean against a brick wall. For the first time in his life, he was afraid. He was on the verge of losing his freedom and everything he had worked so hard for all his life.

Then he heard steps approaching and managed to get up and walk to the steel door. Through the opening, he heard two of the guards talking to each other and saying they would transfer him to Dachau. His heart was pounding hard, for Anton knew there would be no escape. He had been able to hold back his emotions, but now feeling devastated, he wept like when his father had been murdered. Could he also end up like him—killed by thugs? Then he thought of Alejandra when they were in church back in Vienna. She wasn't one to push her faith, but if there ever was a time to believe in a greater power, it was now. But he couldn't. Why couldn't he be more like her? Would he ever see her again? Why didn't he ever tell her he had fallen in love with her? What did it matter now if he never got out from this hell hole? He closed his eyes, and images of Alejandra's face appeared in his mind, her eyes filled with promise radiating unfettered optimism. But hope was not an option; for life had not been kind to him.

In that state of despair, he remained there for another hour until he heard someone unlocking the door. He was certain Dachau was his next destination. If miracles existed, he needed one now, but who was he kidding... that would never happen. Once you were under Gestapo custody, there was no chance of getting out alive. The lieutenant with the tiny eyes and oily hair who had questioned him earlier, glared at him. "You fucking communist. You're free to go," he said, taking off the cuffs. "I don't know why, except that you must have powerful friends. But know we'll be watching your every move from now on. If you ever make another false move, you won't be so lucky. I'll make sure of that! And one more thing... we expect you to join the party soon."

Anton thought he would never join their damned party. He would get the hell out before that happened. As he walked out, he couldn't explain his sudden good fortune. Had divine intervention saved him from what would have been a certain death? Had he been given a second chance? And for what reason? Outside the prison, he breathed in the night air; he would never take anything for granted again.

At the hotel, he climbed the flight of steps to the third floor, feeling a lot of pain in his rib cage. Before knocking on Alejandra's door, he considered the late hour, but soon his doubts were overcome by an overwhelming need to see and tell her everything. After several knocks with no answer, a bald, plump, and older man, dressed in striped pajamas, came out of the next room. "Sir, it's past midnight. Have more respect for those of us who are trying to sleep."

"Yes. I'm sorry," Anton said. Then he went to the Adelman's room around the corner. He rapped lightly on the door. "Ben, it's Anton, I need to speak with you."

Ben unlocked the door. "Anton, thank goodness you're safe… come in. You look awful. They sure did a job on you."

Hannah got out of bed and put on her robe. "Oh my goodness, you've been assaulted. What happened? Your face is a mess… and your clothes." Anton's face was bloodied and bruised, his shirt and leather jacket covered with dried blood.

"It's a long story, and I don't want to discuss it right now, but I thought Alejandra might be here. She's not in her room. Do you have any idea where she might be?" Anton asked.

"No. Can you stay for few moments? May I get you anything?" Hannah asked.

"No." he replied. "I just need to talk to her."

"You don't know what she did then?" Ben asked.

"No, what did she do?"

"At least let me clean your face," Hannah insisted.

He agreed and sat on the bed.

She left, and Ben related a detailed account of what had transpired since Anton's arrest and Alejandra's efforts to get him released.

"I didn't know how, but I knew she was involved. I need to find her," Anton said.

Hannah returned with a wet towel and carefully wiped the dried blood off his cheeks and around his eyes, nose, and mouth. "You can wait for a moment," she said. "And you might think about changing first, too."

When she had finished, Anton said, "Thank you." Then he left the room.

Later, after changing his soiled clothes, Anton returned to Alejandra's room and insistently knocked on the door, but like before there was no answer. The same man came out. "It's you again. Look, she's gone, give it up and let my wife and I sleep, you fool."

Anton's temper flared up again. "Dammit. Have you ever thought you might not live another day to see the woman you love? I've been through hell with fascist bastards."

The man looked shocked, walked to Anton, and said, "I'm no Nazi." He put his hand on Anton's shoulder. "I'm sorry for what they did to you and our country. But you must not voice your opinion so openly. Walls have ears around here."

Anton bowed his head to the man. Then he left, thinking the man was right, and he was a fool for losing his temper twice in one day and for believing things could be normal again in his beloved Germany. And he was also a bigger fool for falling in love with a married woman who did not reciprocate his feelings. But being in love with her was about the only thing that gave him meaning.

In the lobby, he asked the clerk if he had seen Mrs. Morrison and was told that she had gone to the garden. Anton then rushed to the area, but there was no sight of her there either. He sat on the bench where they had talked the night before thinking he wanted nothing more than to hold Alejandra in his arms. What would he tell her when he saw her? The truth? For even if he was a fool and it was a terrible thing to want the wife of another man, it was time to be completely honest about his feelings. He would not waste another moment of his life. He was perfect for her, and no one could ever love her more than he. It wasn't a conquest like many other women who had come and gone in his life; she was the only woman who had captured his being. So where had she gone?

Just then he heard a melody in the distance and noticed a nearly hidden pathway at the end of the orchard. He made his way there and through an abandoned garden, lit only by the moonlight, until he reached a building that looked like a former greenhouse with broken windows. He knew it was Alejandra by the way she played Chopin's Nocturne, op. 9—a velvety sound, melancholic and sublime. He opened the door and found her by an old battered upright piano, a little out of tune, under a dim light. "I've been looking for you."

At the sound of his voice, she stood up and walked a few steps to meet him. "Anton, I'm so glad to see you," she said with teary eyes. "Your face… what did they do to you?"

As she cried, he wiped her cheeks with his fingers. She was about to touch his swollen eye when he held her in his arms and kissed her passionately on the lips. For those brief seconds, he could not feel any pain, only the taste of her sweet breath. Then when they separated, his lower lip started to bleed again from a cut. Now it was she who gently wiped his lip with her index finger. Then Anton embraced her once again, feeling her slim figure so close and warm to him. He could have made love to her right then and there, but she pulled away.

It felt like being beaten up again.

"Please, I need to tell you what I've been feeling for months," Anton said. "I'm so in love with you, and you must know that you've captured my heart. As I laid there in the cell, not knowing whether I'd live or die, I could only think of you. Whatever happens, you saved my life, and you mean everything to me."

She caressed his bruised face. "I was so afraid I'd never see you again and what they might do to you. Please promise me you'll never do anything like that again. You mustn't expose yourself. It's dangerous."

"Yes. You're right. My ribs may be broken, but my heart is not."

"You're safe now, and that's all that's important," she said.

"I want to be with you, my guardian angel. May I stay with you tonight?"

She turned away for a moment. "Oh, Anton, I'm sorry, but no. You have been through a terrible ordeal, but I can't do this. I'm married, and I could never forgive myself. I'm not an angel, just a woman filled with mixed emotions."

"But do you want to? You kissed me back, and I know you feel something for me," he said. "I can see it in your eyes."

She briefly covered her lips with her hand. "I do care for you, perhaps even more than I thought possible. I never expected to be in this situation. But what happened just now between us came out of an unpredictable and extremely emotional moment after worrying and thinking you'd be hurt. Whatever feelings I may have for you, they can't go any further. Now if you wish, we can stay longer and talk. I'm grateful you're safe."

He sighed. They sat down together on the piano bench. He then kissed Alejandra's hand. "At least allow me this."

"When were you released?" she asked.

"Maybe an hour ago. Hannah and Ben told me everything you did."

"I did what I had to do, and I wasn't the only one who intervened."

"But it was at your initiation!" he insisted. "You were very courageous."

"What happened there?" she asked.

He told her everything.

"What will you do? I hope you'll now seriously consider leaving the country."

"Yes, but I have a lot to think about. Right now, I'm just thankful to be alive."

"As relieved as I am to see you, we both need to rest," she said.

"I'll walk you back to your room."

"No, you go on. I need a few moments alone," Alejandra said, squeezing his hand. "I hope you'll feel better tomorrow."

"I would if you were with me," he said.

"Go on," she said. "Please understand this is also tough for me."

Reluctantly, Anton walked away with a burning ache in his heart, and he wondered if it was his cruel fate to go through life without making love to her. He would never give her up no matter what she said. He would be patient, and someday, somewhere, he would have her love.

It was past one o'clock in the afternoon, and Anton was eager to put his plan in motion. Standing in a circle with Hannah and Ben, they waited in the hotel lobby for Alejandra to return from her meeting with Winifred Wagner. When she finally arrived, he waved to her. She joined them.

"Let's go," Anton said.

Ben said, "Slow down, Anton."

"Ále, how did it go?" asked Hannah.

"Mrs. Wagner was very cordial. We talked about the festival and how difficult it was after her husband died for her to manage it. We related well, discussing the challenges of being a woman in a profession of mostly men. Throughout our conversation I wanted to know her opinion about the politics of her adopted country. In the end, I didn't ask since it would have been inappropriate and even risky."

"Or why did she become friends with that madman?" Hannah whispered.

"I don't know anything about that," Alejandra said. "Perhaps Mrs. Wagner tries to maintain neutrality considering the enormous responsibility as the festival's administrator. Wagner's legacy and the festival mean everything to her. And she's in a difficult position."

Anton said, "I just want to get out of here."

"Did you change our train tickets? And what's our departure time?" Alejandra asked Ben.

"Anton has decided to drive us to Salzburg," he replied.

"I need to get away and figure things out. I can't show my face looking like this."

"All black eyes now," Hannah said.

"We're taking a small detour, if you don't mind," Ben said.

"What detour?" Alejandra asked.

"Anton thought that, while it might be a little strange given recent circumstances, it would be worthwhile for us to go back to the Rhineland," Hannah said.

"That's a long way from Salzburg," Alejandra said. "Is it safe?"

"Yes, it's still occupied by the French, but according to Ben you didn't have time to visit Bingen," Anton said. "Isn't that where your grandmother was born? I assure you that the Mosel region, monasteries, and vineyards that line the bank of the Rhine will be worth your time."

"You recalled," Alejandra said. "I believe you've been planning this trip for some time, and of course I'd like to go there to honor her memory."

"I think after everything that happened, we all could use a peaceful respite for a few days and leave with something beautiful to remember," Anton said.

"Spoken like a proud German," Alejandra said. "It is also where Hildegard of Bingen was born. Growing up, my grandmother often referred to her as 'the Sybil of the Rhine.' She was the first documented woman composer and playwright, among other talents. In fact, just last week I was reviewing several of her manuscripts."

Anton said, "And if that's not enough to catch your interest, there's also Goethehaus, and Schloss Johannisberg, and other castles of historical significance."

"You've convinced us, Anton," Ben said. "Let's go. But I think it's best if I drive."

"That would be best," Anton agreed.

THE ORIGIN OF FIRE

As she walked about the interior of a twelfth-century cloister with its vaulted ceilings, once only reserved for ordained monks, Alejandra admired the antiquities housed in several armoires. She was still in a state of inspiration from her morning visit to Bingen, at the confluence of the Rhine and Nahe rivers. It was the birthplace of her grandmother, and she could not have been happier than to have been there, driving through the town and seeing the lush, sloping countryside. While her grandmother's home, on the southeastern side of the river, was gone, she was able to go an hour away to visit Eibingen Abbey, where the famed Hildegard had lived. She saw the relics of the German medieval nun who had been a writer, philosopher, mystic, and theologian. Amidst the mystical ambiance in the sanctuary, Alejandra began to hum "The Origin of Fire," one of the seventy chants composed by Bingen.

Alejandra had always attributed her proclivity toward mysticism and her fascination with visiting churches, convents, and monasteries to her childhood experiences, stemming both from her paternal grandmother, who told her stories of Bingen, and also from her experiences when she lived in her maternal grandparents' Mexican, sixteenth-century hacienda. During four years of her childhood, she had visited, daily, the hacienda's ancient stone chapel. There, she had lived some of the happiest moments of her life, but as remembered now, it was also in that chapel, in later years, where Richard had made his marriage proposal to her when she was nineteen years old.

Since the previous night, she was laden with guilt. Had she broken her vows? Except for one kiss, she had remained faithful to Richard. She never imagined that she could develop tender feelings for another man, for she loved her husband without question. Perhaps being away came at a very high price. Could her marriage be in jeopardy? She wondered how she was going to explain such a blunder to Richard. She hoped he would forgive her.

The room was darkening as dusk set in, and Anton entered the cloister holding a lit candleholder. She smiled at the thought of him as a monk, albeit sans cassock, and how, given Anton's personality, he seemed the last person to seek such a restrictive calling.

"Were you trying to lose me again?" Anton asked. "I can understand why, with my face all bruised up. I must look like a boxer who lost."

"You didn't lose. It wasn't a fair fight," Alejandra said. "You know I have the bad habit of going off on my own without telling anyone."

"Yes, I know. At this moment, the candle's glow is enchanting your face, and if I were Rembrandt, I'd paint you immediately."

"And what would such a painting show?" she asked, instantly regretting the question.

"It would show a highly sensual woman with an air of vulnerability," he said.

She looked away for a moment, feeling as though he was undressing her under the flickering candlelight. She was determined not to succumb to her heightened emotions no matter how strong the temptation. Like the monks and nuns who had roamed through monasteries and the abbeys, she too would pray for strength and forgiveness. "About the other night, that will never happen again. I love Richard. And I'm sorry if in any way I led you to believe otherwise."

"I sense you have feelings for me also," Anton said.

"I do, but as a friend," she said, walking away.

He followed her to the arched window where he placed the candleholder on the ledge. From behind, he gently caressed her bare arms. She was wearing a rose-print dress.

"I can still taste your lips. You say its friendship, but friendship doesn't feel right to me."

She felt an electric charge through every bone in her body when he touched her. "Don't you see, no matter what I do I'll hurt someone? I was an emotional wreck with what happened to you and lost control. It was a mistake."

"I can be patient, and I'll never give up."

"You must! I'm not free to love anybody else. I'd never leave my husband. I can only hope he'll forgive me. Please don't make this more difficult."

He whispered, "How can you ask me to stop loving you? I feel alive for the first time. My heartbeat rises at the sight of you."

"You need to move on with your life, and from this moment we can only be friends, if that can even be possible. I admit I was drawn to you because you understand me as a musician. We do have that bond, but that's all. For the next days and weeks, whether or not you choose to accompany us to Salzburg or Florence, you must abstain from any physical gestures or comments about your feelings. That's the only way I can be near you."

She stepped back, determined.

"I can't imagine not seeing you, so despite your harsh conditions, I'll respect them."

A nervous tension fell between them until he said, "Am I to be a monk now, destined to a life of celibacy? Is this your final wish for me?"

She tittered, feeling a certain pleasure at the idea, but at the same time she hoped he would find someone else to love. "Certainly, you can manage that, can't you?"

"I don't know if that's possible," he said. "But thank goodness we're going to the monastery's wine cellar next. I need to drown my sorrows. Perhaps that's what the monks had to do to survive their austerity. Shall we?"

She nodded her head. "The candle," she said, taking it from the ledge. "You wouldn't want to be blamed for starting a fire."

After traveling through the Mosel-Saar Ruwer area, they ended the day in the wine region of Rheingau on the hills overlooking the Rhine River. They stayed at Zum Rüdeheimer Schloss—a family-run hotel. After checking into their separate rooms, they met at a wine-themed rustic restaurant, known for its nightly polka music and Rhineland cuisine. While the music rowdily played in the background, the maître de guided them through a narrow passageway until they reached a private dining room enclosed by stone walls. A linen-covered table, set with floral motif dinnerware, had been added to accommodate those guests who wanted more privacy in the former wine cellar.

"My goodness. You weren't kidding when you said we'd be alone," Hannah remarked.

Anton laughed. "I wanted us to have a relaxed dinner without prying ears, as I had to learn the hard way. You can't be too careful these days."

"You can hardly hear the music, so there's no need to worry about you asking us to dance," Hannah said.

"And that's a good thing. My father loved polka dancing, and he taught me how to dance it at twelve. I was a little clumsy to be sure and never quite got the hang of it," Alejandra said.

"But maybe with a few drinks, you'll change your mind," Anton said.

The waiter brought them a stack of menus and a bottle of Riesling from the Rheingau region. He served a sample for Anton to taste, and, after Anton approved it, filled the rest of the glasses. "This area claims to have the longest tradition of wine-making, which is why it was a popular locale for ecclesiastical and aristocratic estates during medieval times."

"Yes, I agree after our visit this morning to Burg Stahleck castle," Hannah said. "The views were spectacular. Can you envision waking up to that every morning?"

"It would be ideal for meditation," Alejandra said. "I could have lived in an abbey."

"The surroundings are stunning, but from what I've read, the restrictions by many orders were brutal. Once inside you were never allowed to leave," Hannah said. "So I'm not sure you'd have liked it all that much, Ále."

"Not so for Hildegard. She had unparalleled freedom for a woman of her times," Alejandra said. "She was the first author to discuss sexuality from a female point of view. Can you envision that?"

"Didn't she correspond with the pope, as well?" Anton asked. "The only way to pursue a higher level of education back then was to belong to a religious order."

"I'm not surprised, Alejandra, considering you once told me you wanted to be a nun," Hannah said.

"When I was six years old. My mother had a portrait of Sor Juana Ines de la Cruz in my bedroom," Alejandra said. "She was also a woman of prodigious talents, a Mexican Hildegard, you could say. The story of her life appealed to me."

Ben laughed. "That beats my boyhood fantasy of being a sailor."

"What's so wrong about that?" Anton questioned.

"Me, a sailor? Constantly moving from one place to the other, and always at the mercy of nature? I get nauseous just thinking about rolling waves."

"Isn't that what you're doing now as a guest conductor?" Hannah said.

"Everything has its price," Anton said.

The waiter returned. The men ordered the restaurant's specialty—Riesling-cheese-soup and Rheinischer Sauerbraten. Alejandra ordered Schlossduck with potatoes. Hannah wanted Königsberger Klopse and Bratkartoffeln.

When the waiter left, Anton said, "It would be intolerable for me to have no roots. That's why I'm hesitant to leave my country."

"So now what?" Ben asked.

"Either I leave or make powerful connections and pretend to be one of them."

"How could you possibly pretend to be one of them?" Alejandra said, aghast.

"I didn't mean that. A Nazi never," Anton said. "I love Germany. It's where I belong. My circumstances, growing up, were modest and devastating. I don't want to ever live like that again. It has taken me years of hard work to build what I have today."

"What good is all that if you get sent to prison again? Don't you already have some influential connections?" Ben asked.

"Many of my associates are deserting the country. There's never been a greater loss of artists and businessmen in our history."

"But again, the alternative of remaining in Berlin could be disastrous. What about selling off your estate and starting somewhere else?" Hannah asked.

"The economic depression has hit everybody pretty hard. I'm not willing to sell at bargain prices. All options are on the table, and I'm still hopeful once the people wake up this government will collapse. Perhaps I'll take a trip to New York to check things out. Ultimately, I'll do what's in my best interest. The world runs like that."

Alejandra wanted to say that not everyone acted only out of self-interest, since she considered that selfish, but didn't want to argue. She knew he was in a no-win position and only hoped he would make the right decision.

The waiter returned with their dinners.

When they were alone again, Ben resumed. "Forgive me for this question, and don't answer it if you don't want to. You've talked about your humble circumstances growing up, so how on earth did your father get his hands on the Stradivarius you now own?"

Anton paused. "I've never discussed it with anyone, but you have become trusted friends. My father was a gifted violinist and a charismatic man when he wanted to be. Before he married my mother, he had a relationship with a wealthy old woman who gave him the violin on the condition that he'd entertain her once a week until she died."

"Oh, dear. How long did that go on for?" Hannah asked.

"Until he died. That was one of the reasons my mother left him," Anton said. "I don't want any of you to worry about me. I'm a survivor. Let's enjoy this sumptuous dinner."

Later, the waiter returned to remove the dishes and brought another bottle of wine for dessert—1925 Dr. Burklin-Wolf Forster Kirchenstuck Riesling Trockenbeerenauslese—along with a platter containing a selection of tarts and gourmet cheeses. "Haven't you had enough wine for one night?" Ben asked Anton, who was now showing signs of being a little drunk.

"No. I need to drown my sorrow." Anton eyed Alejandra as he said this.

Alejandra, feeling distressed that he might expose his feelings in the open, changed the subject. "I'm not going to try to pronounce the wine's name, but it better be good."

Hannah attempted to recite the label, Burklin... with her accent, making a little fun of it. They all laughed.

"It may not be an easy name to say, but it's an intensely sweet wine made from grapes affected by botrytis," Anton said.

"Botrytis!" Alejandra said. "That doesn't sound appetizing."

"True, but this wine is the best you'll ever taste," Anton said, drinking his glass entirely. "Sweet wine like sweet lips."

Alejandra looked disapprovingly at Anton. "So what about tomorrow? We've been to Mosel-Saar-Ruwer, so should we just go straight to Salzburg?" she asked.

"And skip Cologne?" Anton asked.

"I'm sure it's beautiful, but I'm rather looking forward to the festival and Strauss's premiere of his revised version of *Die ägyptische*, and I'd like to see him again," Alejandra said.

"And for the first time at the Salzburg festival, Bruno Walter will conduct *Tristan and Isolde*," Ben added.

Anton ran his fingers over Alejandra's hand. "How can we forget a story of the tortured love affair between star-crossed lovers who, fortunately for the romantics, consummate their love in the second scene of the second act? And I think that should be us."

Alejandra pulled her hand away. "Enough, Anton!" she said, standing and taking her handbag. "Pardon me, but I need to leave. I'll see you all tomorrow."

RASTLOSE LIEBE, OP. 5 NO. 1

Hannah, who remained in the restaurant, felt that Anton's advances had gone too far, and she was prepared to confront him about it when he blurted out, "*Es tut mir Leid.*" But he still poured himself another drink.

"The hell you're going to have another drink," she said, pulling the glass away from Anton. "Yes. You've made a mess of things. I feel rather annoyed, because while I've sensed how you felt about her, I never thought you'd go this far."

"I'm sorry, but I love her even if she doesn't love me," Anton said.

"Look, she's a married woman, for God's sake. I know her too well, and she'd never leave her husband." Although she had to question if Alejandra did reciprocate his feelings at some level, even if she would never act on them. "I should probably go and talk to her."

"We should all go," Ben said.

"No. No. You go," Anton blurted out.

"We're not going to leave you here so you can end up in jail again," Ben said. "Why don't you wait, Hannah?"

"Fine!" She signaled the waiter, and when he came, she ordered coffee and the check.

Soon after, the waiter returned with three cups, placing them on the table.

"Now, drink!" Hannah said.

Anton finished his cup in three gulps. "I'm suuuch an idiot."

"Drink mine too," Hannah said. "And I agree with your statement."

"I understand how you feel, but you've got to let her go, my friend,"

Ben said.

"I don't know if I can," Anton said.

"If you don't control yourself better, you'll lose her friendship too," Hannah said. "She may even refuse that you go with us to Salzburg. Is that what you want?"

"No. That would kill me."

Ben placed his hand on Anton's shoulder. "You're a bit melodramatic right now. Didn't you say earlier you were a survivor? Well, you'll survive this too. Let's go." Ben paid the check and helped Anton to his feet. Holding his arm, he led him out of the restaurant.

A polka band was playing in the main dining hall, and Anton suddenly stopped and yelled out, "*Rastlose Liebe, Rastlose Liebe.*"

"Yes, I know all about restless love, but I don't think Schubert's music is what you need now. How about a cold shower, instead?" Ben asked.

"What to do with this inebriated romantic." Hannah shook her head. "Come on! We don't want any more trouble," she said.

At breakfast, Hannah and Ben were in the rustic restaurant with farmhouse style wood tables and benches. A collection of chime clocks adorned the walls, and with busy chatter in the background, it was loud.

"Did you talk to Alejandra last night?" Ben asked.

Hannah moved closer to Ben, almost speaking into his ear. "Yes, briefly… she was upset."

"It seems Alejandra has tightened up a bit lately. Is it possible she might actually have feelings for Anton?" Ben asked.

"I don't know for sure. My take is that if she ever reciprocated Anton's feelings it would have to do with how she sees him," Hannah said.

"What do you mean?" Ben asked.

"Richard and Anton could not be more different," Hannah said. "Obviously, Richard is a good man, but he's never suffered in his life. Everything has come easy to him, except Alejandra. He's conventional, and perhaps even self-righteous at times. Anton on the other hand… Alejandra finds him very human and vulnerable, and life has dealt him many blows. She'd never admit to this, but at some unconscious level she's drawn to Anton's vulnerability, which at some point might allow her to express her emotions freely. Here she comes."

"Good morning," Alejandra said, sitting down. "I'm so embarrassed about last night."

"Why should *you* be embarrassed? It was Anton who acted stupidly," Hannah said.

"I don't want you to get the wrong idea. Nothing is going on between us, and I wanted to make sure you both know that."

"I know you'd never do anything to go against your morals," Hannah said. "But you can't help how he feels."

"It's true that I care for him and was very emotional about the possibility of something terrible happening," Alejandra said. "I got a little carried away the night he was released. But I never meant for anything like this to occur. It's time to put distance between us. It would be best if he does not come with us to Salzburg. I'll tell him myself."

"Certainly, that's reasonable," Ben said.

"I don't want to change your plans," she said. "So, if you wish to go with Anton to Cologne, please do so. I'll meet you in Salzburg."

"No. We had already decided to skip it," Hannah said.

Just then Anton came into the restaurant and sat next to Ben. "Good morning."

Noticing his clean-shaven face and bruises, which were starting to fade a little, Hannah said, "And how are you this morning?"

An uncomfortable silence fell between them. "We've decided to skip Cologne," Ben said.

"Of course. And so that we can clear the rest of the day, I'd like to first apologize to Alejandra," Anton said.

"We'll come back in a few minutes," Ben said.

"No. That won't be necessary," Alejandra said. "Please, stay."

Anton continued. "My conduct was deplorable. And I'd like to assure you all that for the rest of our trip, and beyond, I'll be a perfect gentleman. Your friendship means everything to me, and I'd never want to jeopardize that." He paused, then turned to Alejandra. "I was in such emotional turmoil, and I was out of line. I hope you'll forgive me."

"Apology accepted," Alejandra said. "It might be best if we take the train to Salzburg."

Anton bowed his head. "I understand, but I hope to see you before you all go home."

"Of course you will," Hannah said. "There's still Florence in the forecast."

"Now, with everything settled, can we please order breakfast? I'm starving," Ben said.

"And when are you not?" Hannah said. She turned to Anton, and said, "We did appreciate our trip through the wine country. It was all incredibly beautiful, and we'll remember it fondly. We will always be good friends. Nothing will ever change that."

"I concur," Alejandra said. "And going to Bingen was a highlight for me."

Anton smiled. "Then I'm glad I at least accomplished something worthwhile."

"You see, life goes on," Ben said.

Five days later, they were back in Vienna, but Hannah noticed Alejandra had been distant since their return. With an envelope in her hand, she went to her bedroom and tapped on the door. "A telegram from Richard."

Alejandra placed the down coverlet on the bed and took the envelope from Hannah's hand. "Probably news on when he's coming."

"Do you have a few minutes to talk?"

"I have all afternoon," Alejandra said.

"You're terribly reserved lately," Hannah said, taking a seat on the window bench.

"I know. I felt sorry about having to send Anton away. And recently, I've been preoccupied with the upcoming concert and other issues."

"Forget about what happened with Anton. It was predictable. And now we can see it for what it was. It came to a crisis, but now everything is resolved. Then what about Florence? He's been asking Ben. He'd like to join us to say goodbye."

"We can all go forward now," Alejandra said. "If he wishes to join us in Florence that would be all right as Richard will be there. I'd like us to part ways on a good note. I can't believe we have only a couple of weeks left in Europe. Then it's time to go home. To tell you the truth I'm ambivalent about that. I've changed, and after having a taste of professional life, I wonder whether I can adjust back to a domestic one. Although, I'm thrilled to be seeing my family."

"I see. Well, you've accomplished the first step to becoming a conductor. So I can't fathom you going back to the life of a housewife."

"Nothing wrong with that. But I'd like to apply what I've learned. With only one major orchestra back home, I'm not sure how feasible it will be to find a job in the field."

"I'm sure you'll find something suitable. As for us, Ben is determined to seek a position with an opera company anywhere in the world," Hannah said. "I don't like it. This expedition has been rough, and I'm ready to go home and stay there. I'm not willing to leave my family for another adventure."

"Of course you will if Ben gets an offer. You're crazy for each other," Alejandra said.

"As much as Richard is crazy about you, would he follow you anywhere?"

"Not with his profession. It's different between a man and a woman. You know that."

"I suppose it's true," Hannah said. "But I still will not follow Ben just anywhere."

"Finding a balance between home and work won't be easy," Alejandra said.

"Everything always seems to work out for you," Hannah said.

"It may seem that way to you, but I assure you it isn't. Nothing is ever perfect. I've had my share of ups and downs, although I usually try to see the glass half full and to learn from my mistakes. Crying and moping was discouraged by both my parents."

Hannah laughed. "Not for me. There was always a drama, invigorating if you ask me."

"On a serious note. I want to express my appreciation to you and Ben for sharing your home with me. I couldn't ask for better friends. You're family to me."

"Likewise. We'll always be there for each other, but I should leave so you can read the telegram," Hannah said.

Unsettled by the conversation, Hannah thought that at some point she might need to go with Ben to wherever he found a job. She had been uncertain about it, but now upon further consideration she was not willing to leave New York again. In that aspect, she could not be more different than Alejandra. For if truth be told, while she had, in the beginning, liked living in Europe, she now hated it. She no longer felt safe and often wondered if the situation for Jews under Nazi leadership would worsen over time. She only hoped her refusal to accompany her husband elsewhere would never become a problem in their marriage.

SYMPHONY NO. 7 IN A MAJOR, OP. 92 –
SECOND MOVEMENT

Alejandra had finished packing most of her belongings in boxes that would ship to the United States. Scattered on the drawing room floor were dozens of musical manuscripts collected over a period of nearly six months. Every manuscript represented an experience now embedded in Alejandra's consciousness—attending a rehearsal, listening to a recording, or practicing at the podium with an orchestra. With a good ear, attention to detail, and in-depth analysis of the score, she had gained the respect of fellow musicians. While not a strict interpreter of the score, she strived to follow the composer's intention as faithfully as possible. But she also believed there could be an element of interpretation by experimenting with the tempo, for as Verdi had often said, "One must learn to read between the lines." After an extensive training in the art of conducting, she was well versed in the theory, but applying it to successful practice could be the challenge. From that treasure trove of musical compositions, she selected two manuscripts for her debut concert, for in less than two weeks she would finally accomplish her goal.

She had been up since six in the morning, and it was now two o'clock in the afternoon. Taking a break from packing, she read Richard's telegram, alerting her of his travel plans. He was expected to be in Vienna in less than a week, and like him, she too now counted the days. Although, as his arrival neared, she felt both excitement and remorse. She never thought it possible to have conflicting emotions. With the passage of time, she hoped to forget the incident with Anton. And of more immediate concern was whether to reveal that secret to Richard. The last thing she wanted was to hurt her husband.

The telephone rang, and she made her way to the parlor, careful to not step on her manuscripts, as though walking through a mine field. She picked up the receiver from atop a console table. "Hello, Richard? Where are you?" He was still in Minneapolis—due to a medical emergency with a longtime patient, his mentor, who needed immediate surgery. He had operated on Dr. Moore the previous day, and as a result, his trip was delayed. He would not join her in Vienna as planned but would meet her in Florence by the twenty-first of August.

Alejandra sighed. "I wish you could be here now. But I understand. It's only ten more days. Please don't give it a second thought. Wish him well for me. How are the children?" According to Richard, they were planning numerous surprises for her return.

He asked about their accommodations in Florence. "We're staying at a villa. Hannah and Ben went to visit Ben's relatives, Joshua and Sarah Oldenburg, at their cottage in Melk, Austria. They'll be back tonight, so call me before you leave, and I'll give you the address."

He expressed his desire to be with her and thought she sounded a bit grim. "I'm just disappointed you won't be here to see Vienna. I had so many places I wanted to show you. Give the children my love, and I'll talk to you soon. I love you."

She hung up the phone. He had said he would make it up to her, but it was Alejandra who needed to make things right between them.

The night before, Alejandra, Hannah, and Ben had arrived at a nineteenth-century villa on the outskirts of Florence. Built in 1898, the villa, with grand seating areas, four bedrooms, tile floors, a stone fireplace, whitewashed walls, and Tuscan décor, had panoramic views of both countryside and city.

At mid-morning and already at twenty-eight centigrade, Alejandra wore a favorite blue printed dress and went out to sit on the sunny terrace. The rich yellows, browns, and green landscapes gleamed under the hot Tuscan sky. Wearing sunglasses, she saw, in the distance, Palazzo Vecchio, the famed red-brick Duomo, and Basilica Santa Croce where Italy's most celebrated artists were buried. Florence was the birthplace of the Renaissance—a movement that had propelled a renewal of humanistic ideology based on Greek philosophical principles and classical writings. Many ancient documents were preserved, not only by monks, but also by the Moors, who ruled in Spain for several centuries. She thought human endeavor was at its most prolific when the contributions of all cultures were recognized. And she was pleased to debut her conducting skills in Florence, a city of such artistic prominence. How far she had come from those days in her adolescence when she imagined herself at the podium—so filled with dreams, conviction, and expectations.

Anton was expected to arrive at any time, and since his departure back in the Rhineland, she had not spoken to him. She was a little nervous about seeing him again, despite the fact she had made peace with her feelings. She wished they could learn to be the best of friends.

Just then he joined her on the terrace. "So, what's going on in that lovely mind of yours?" Anton asked, holding two packages. He set them down on the square wrought-iron table.

She turned to Anton who was dressed in a pair of navy-blue slacks, a short sleeve white shirt, and two-toned oxfords. "Always the charmer. It's good to see you all recovered."

"I'm glad to see you too. Ben mentioned your concert is on Friday. Congratulations."

He walked away, and with his back to her, said, "When is your husband coming? I expected he would be here by now."

"He had a last-minute surgery to do. But he'll be here tomorrow night," she said.

He turned to her and frowned. "I see. When do rehearsals begin?"

"The day after, so I'll barely have time to scratch the surface of this grand city."

"I brought you two gifts, one for your debut and one to say goodbye. The former you may open now if you wish, but the other I ask you to wait until you return home."

"Oh?" Alejandra took the box wrapped in a shiny white paper and opened it, revealing a black baton. "This is very thoughtful of you," she said, holding it with her right hand and twirling it in the air like a magic wand. Laughing, she asked, "Will all my wishes come true too?"

"Haven't they already?" he asked.

She nodded, placing the baton back in the box. "And Hannah tells me you'll be giving us a tour of the city today and tomorrow."

"Indeed. I'll do my best to compact as much as possible for your viewing pleasure," he said. "The tour is a prelude to a grand exhibition planned by one of my collectors, as I'm also expected to come up with a list of available Renaissance works by Medici supported artists."

"You're talking a span of two centuries," she said.

"My client has very specific instructions. He wants works by artists dismissed due to prejudice or controversy," Anton said. "He wants to show in an exhibit the grandiosity of the artists contrasted with the narrow-mindedness of those who opposed them."

"I'm interested to know what you find. Where are we beginning today?"

He pointed to the dome. "With Brunelleschi at the Cathedral of Santa Maria del Fiore."

Ben then entered the terrace and said, "I spoke with the concertmaster, and he'd like to meet us for dinner. His English is excellent, so he'll be able to translate at the rehearsals."

"You know how much I appreciate all your efforts for making the arrangements for the concert. I'm so grateful for the opportunity," Alejandra said. "We should probably get on with Anton's tour. We don't have much time."

After visiting the Baptistery and Giotto's Campanile, they arrived at the Gothic cathedral around noon and wandered through the main church, learning of its tragic history as the place where the radical Girolamo Savonarola made incendiary sermons and Giuliano de Piero de'Medici was assassinated. As they admired the richly painted dome, Anton explained that the church had stood without a dome for almost one hundred years due to the complexity of building such a heavy, octagonal structure. The task had eluded the talents of the best international architects of the day until a self-taught architect, Filippo di Ser Brunelleschi, surprised everyone. He studied the ancient dome of the Roman Pantheon and devised an original plan. While his innovative design was received with much skepticism, for it required a leap of faith, it was Cosimo Medici who finally awarded Brunelleschi the commission.

"He must have shown more than eloquence and clever plans to convince a Medici," Alejandra said.

"From what I've read, while lacking in physical presence, he was endowed with a brilliant mind and a will to accomplish anything," Hannah said.

"Perhaps that's the mark of someone possessing high intellect…" Alejandra said, "…to be able to use logic and problem-solving combined with self-awareness, then apply them to the common good."

"Are you saying that the more cerebral a person is, the less likely he or she is to hurt others?" Anton questioned.

"I'm not a philosopher, but I can't believe that someone of extraordinary intelligence could consistently wrong another," Alejandra said.

"I'll have to think about it," Ben said. "Surely heinous crimes have been committed by highly intelligent people. Perhaps a temporary regression to their primitive brain explains it."

"I do find it interesting that the Medici's thrived on supporting artists who served their power," Ben said.

"For better or for worse, that's part of history, like or not," Anton said. "Mussolini wants to take Italy back to the glory of the Roman Empire and Hitler wants to take Germany into an abysmal future of a thousand years," Anton said.

"Oh no. I think we're getting in too deep this early in the day," Hannah said.

"We got on this topic because Anton's client seems to want to expose current fanatics by contrasting them to those of the past," Ben said. "So, I think it's a relevant discussion. I'm rather intrigued by this subject."

"What was the reason for giving us all that background on Brunelleschi?" Hannah asked.

"He was probably one of those individuals who was underestimated most of his life until a Medici gave him a chance. I'm drawn to those characters in history."

"I see. Is that how you think of yourself?" Alejandra asked.

"Perhaps," Anton said. "I also would like to show you other painters of humble origins at the Uffizi Museum."

"But before we go, what work of art from Brunelleschi is your client after? The dome is out of his reach," Alejandra said.

"A crucifix," Anton said. "It's in a private collection here in Florence. I might have to steal it. I'm just kidding." He laughed. "But it would be fun to plan a heist of some masterpiece."

"I wouldn't put it past you," Ben said. "I'm kidding too... maybe." He laughed.

Later, they were in the light-filled Uffizi museum. As a former government building, built in 1560 by Cosimo I de' Medici, the galleries were appointed with high mural ceilings and wall-to-wall paintings. Most of the thirteenth-century works of art were on the second floor, and it was there where the works of Duccio di Buoninsegna, Cimabue, and Giotto were showcased.

Standing before the altarpiece *Ognissanti Madonna*, Alejandra, Hannah, and Ben listened to Anton who discussed the artist. "Giotto ignited modern painting, and his skill at imitating nature and illustrating figures with humanistic qualities in a three-dimensional setting would become the archetype of future works of art. It's well established that Giotto's perspective in figurative painting paved the way to Renaissance art. Pope Benedict XII recognized his genius and had him paint scenes from the life of Christ."

"So what's your collector's interest in Giotto's life?" Alejandra asked.

"Legend has it Giotto was discovered at ten years old while watching over the farm's sheep, but also immersed in drawing," Anton said. "And Lorenzo the Magnificent honored him by placing a marble bust on his tomb one hundred years later, therefore immortalizing in stone his famous words, 'art became one with nature.'"

"That would make an ideal title for your collector's exhibition. And by the way, who's this man?" Alejandra asked. "I'm becoming curious about his identity."

"I'm not at liberty to disclose his name, for I'm sworn to secrecy. For now, we can refer to my collector as Anonymous," Anton said. "He shares my political views, so he is cautious."

"He sounds tolerant to be sure," Hannah said. "And of Giotto's works, which would you recommend to Anonymous?"

"The Fresco of Dante. Both Dante and Giotto, who knew each other, had the distinction of showcasing each other in their works," Anton said.

"It was common practice for one type of art to inspire another," Hannah said. "Traditional thought at the time was to associate Greek and Roman cultural heritage with Christianity."

"But religious fanaticism also reared its ugly head then, and Botticelli destroyed some of his works," Anton said. "I know it's hard to believe, but Botticelli was affected, like many other Florentines, by the fanatic arguments of Savonarola. Fortunately, most of his works survived, including *The Birth of Venus,* commissioned by Lorenzo de' Medici."

"Since we're on the topic of fanatics, I'm reminded of one of Goya's quotes," Hannah said. "'The sleep of reason produces monsters.' And while that statement was a double reference to both the French Revolution and the Inquisition, it describes what's happening today."

"Savonarola is gone, but we have Mussolini, Hitler, and their followers whose reason has fallen by the wayside," Anton said. "Paintings have not yet been destroyed like books. But it would not be a stretch to predict that Nazism can evolve into something similar on a larger scale."

"That gives me the chills just thinking about it," Hannah said. "So, if you don't mind, let's talk about something else."

"On a lighter note, I've chosen for the concert Rigoletto's *La Donna e mobile*, and Respighi's pictorial suites inspired by Botticelli's *La Primavera*, *L'adorazione dei Magi*, and *La Nascita di Venere*."

"And which pieces have you chosen for your debut?" Anton asked Alejandra.

With a slight grin, she said, "You'll have to wait to find out."

Anton said, "This is as good a time as any to say that these months we've been together have been wonderful. I feel as we're old friends, and I hope that we will continue to be as such. In a few days, we will go our separate ways, but the memories will last forever."

Alejandra felt touched by his sentiments and would have liked to tell Anton that she too was changed in more ways than she thought possible. Her eyes met his, and she knew he understood she reciprocated those views.

"You've been an invaluable friend, and I admire your courage in these difficult times," Hannah said. "We should cheer our friendship over a glass of prosecco with a view of the Arno River at that quaint restaurant by Ponte Vecchio."

"Yes." Anton said. "Vasari's Corridor will have to wait for another time. For tomorrow, we'll spend the day on Da Vinci, the ultimate Renaissance Man."

"Leonardo. Magical, mysterious, and beguiling. He's a man for the ages," Alejandra said.

The next evening, Alejandra retired to her bedroom and changed into a beige, silk nightgown. It had been a marvelous day after visiting and walking about the city of Vinci and other sites in Florence's countryside, trailing the life and works of Leonardo Da Vinci. She was glad that Richard would arrive at any moment. Although, she was equally apprehensive on how best to reveal her secret. Exhausted, she went to bed, turned off the lights, and fell into mystical dreams.

Barefoot, with her hair down, and dressed in a semi-transparent flowing gown, like a ghost in one of Dickens' stories, she was flying over sunflower fields that extended into a misty distance. Soon, she found the cottage she had been looking for and landed outside its weathered door with paint peeling and the stain fading. She turned the knob and entered a light-infused studio filled with sculptures, blank and painted canvases, and hundreds of drawings scattered about on wooden tables. She scanned the open notebooks one by one, taking a mental survey of each—sketches of the graceful and the grotesque: animal and human figures, anatomical body parts, skeletons, as well as images of botanical gardens, architectural drawings, flying and military machines, and astronomical notations—thousands of pages that recorded the thoughts, visions, and emotions of a genius whose mind seemed to be in perpetual motion. For a moment, she considered that her casual attire was suited as a model for one of the artist's paintings. However, she recalled, she had entered Da Vinci's realm for one reason—to be an apprentice in the art of drawing. She heard a low-pitched voice. "Please sit here by me," he said.

Expecting to see an old man, she was struck by his vitality. He was bearded, in his late forties, and wore a loose white shirt and black trousers. She turned to the man, whose humble beginnings and lack of formal education proved to be no obstacle in attaining personal and professional prominence in his lifetime. Both now seated in front of his desk, she glanced at his hands... hands blessed by God. "Sir, I have several questions before we begin."

"Begin with one, and I shall see whether to go to the next," Da Vinci said.

She smiled, certain she must catch his ear. "I'm drawn to painting and sculpture, but uncertain which one I should pursue."

"'Sculpture is less intellectual than painting. These works cannot represent transparent or luminous bodies, nor mists or dark skies. Yet, this work can be as graceful and powerful in design, showing the magnificence of a human face or a human body. It requires as much dedication, and it is a rigorous process,'" Da Vinci said.

"Then, since nature inspires me to pursue art, I'd like to start with painting."

He took one of his notebooks, filled with landscape drawings and handed it to her. "First, you must master the art of drawing. Go into the fields, observe everything in detail, and retain it in your mind. Sketch those images in your own notebook by memory, thereby learning perspective and proportion. Come back in one month, and I'll review your work."

She took the notebook but remained seated, as she wished his advice on another matter.

"And your second question?" he asked.

As she stared at a gold-plated perspective-drawing device on his desk, with her index finger she touched the scroll design at one of the ends. "I'd like your perspective on a matter of a personal nature, a predicament of sorts."

He turned to her. "'If one wishes to see how the soul dwells in its body, let her observe how the body uses its daily habitation. If the soul is devoid of order and confused, the body will be kept in disorder and confusion.' What is your predicament?"

She gazed into his luminous eyes as if he held all the knowledge and wisdom of the world. "I'm burdened with guilt and uncertain whether to reveal a secret to a loved one."

He took a pencil, sketching the outline of her eyes on a piece of drawing paper. Then after a few moments, Da Vinci replied, "I have two answers to your question, but you must choose which is the most appropriate to your dilemma. 'First, be aware that when disclosing a secret, it puts itself at the mercy of the indiscreet listener. But if honor is what's at stake here, then you must know that no man has the capacity of virtue who sacrifices honor for gain.'"

She wanted to follow up with yet another question, but the image of Da Vinci began to vanish in the distance as if he was a fading drawing.

Awakened from her dream by the sensation of feeling another body next to her, she opened her eyes. In the moonlight, she saw Richard's face slowly coming into view. "Darling, I woke you up," he said, kissing her softly.

She took in his masculine smell and caressed his face with her fingers. Her heart was racing, and she moistened her lips. "I'm glad you did, but how do I know this isn't a dream?"

"What kind of proof do you require?" he asked.

"Another kiss might do the trick," she said, now fully awake and thrilled he was there.

Richard caressed her arm. "Is that all? We have all night, and I've missed you terribly. Let's leave any talking for later." He slowly undressed her like the first time they had made love, under the twilight of her dreams.

On August 22, 1933, Alejandra left the villa while Richard was still sleeping. She saw no point in revealing her secret just yet, not wanting to spoil their few remaining days together in Florence. Of more immediate concern was her upcoming rehearsal and concert, and for those events she must be in absolute control of her emotions and put all her dedication into her work. She must be alert and ready to direct a room full of men. She would be the only woman in the theater. The anticipation of finally realizing her dream of conducting raised the stakes. She had prepared for this occasion for the last twenty years, and now her heart was beating so hard she felt as though it would burst.

Across from Teatro Communale di Firenze, she was in a coffee shop, enjoying her second cup of espresso; the caffeine she had consumed in the last ten minutes was already working through her system. With only a few guests, she could hear most of the conversations, understanding a word here and there—*buongiorno, bellissima,* and *ciao*— as a group of friends spoke as they came and went. In a heightened state, she reviewed a few words in Italian that she would speak before the orchestra—*Non vedo l'ora al nostro concerto, grazie.*

She turned her gaze to the two-story theater, which was once an open-air amphitheater where some of the most famous operas were presented. Among those operas of note were: *Lucia di Lammermoor* by Gaetano Donizetti; *Don Carlo, Aida, La Traviata,* and *Rigoletto* by Giuseppe Verdi; and *La Boheme* and *Madame Butterfly* by Giacomo Puccini.

Florence, as the birthplace of Italian opera during the Renaissance, was an ideal place for the concert. Ben would direct most of the program, highlighting the music of Italian composers. And for the last part, she would conduct two works—one to give tribute to an Italian opera composer and the other to a German composer who had inspired and captivated her imagination since childhood.

Then from a distance, one by one, each of the musicians entered the theater, dressed casually. She was glad she had chosen to wear something simple—a white silk blouse, black trousers and flat, black shoes. It was time to join the musicians. She put her beige cardigan over her shoulders, paid the check, and left the café, crossing the busy street.

In the theater, the concertmaster, Luciano, a tall, distinguished man with brown hair, sideburns, thin figure, and perfect English, made all the introductions. Then everyone took their positions on stage. Alejandra stood before the podium and the orchestra ready to rehearse the first work—"Nessun Dorma." It was an aria with extraordinary musical range, the most celebrated song from the opera *Turandot* and the last, unfinished work composed by Giacomo Puccini. It would later be premiered by Arturo Toscanini in 1926 at Teatro alla Scala in Milan.

She held a white baton with sterling silver ends, a gift from Richard, and was about to begin the rehearsal when, suddenly, the tenor interrupted, making an unusual request. "May I sing a cappella before we begin with the full orchestra?" Alejandra, who had never heard the tenor sing before, looked at the robust man with wavy dark hair and round face, dressed in a black suit. He was young and inexperienced, it was said, but so was she. Six months of training to be a conductor barely scratched the surface, so why not accommodate his wish. Perhaps he was nervous like her. This situation, however, would give her the opportunity to become familiar with his voice and style of performance. Giving particular attention to soloists and singers was something she relished doing. She replied, "Please, Domenico, lead the way."

He then took his position center stage and instantly transformed himself into the role of Calaf, the handsome male protagonist who falls in love at first sight with the princess Turandot. Standing only a few feet away, he sang "Nessun Dorma." For the next three minutes, she listened to the aria that would become one of Puccini's most moving compositions from his entire opera repertoire. And Domenico sang like an angel who had just landed on earth to discover love: "*Even you, o Princess, in your cold room, watch the stars that tremble with love and with hope... Nobody shall sleep! Nobody shall sleep!*"

She thought he was an extraordinary talent, and Domenico's voice was as impressive as that of Enrico Caruso. With a focused and clean sound, the young tenor had mastered the piece with technical virtuosity, never straining on the high notes, but always showing profound sensibility and a relaxed facial expression. How fortunate that she would conduct this piece with such a vocal talent, ensuring he would prove his worth as an artist. And now she must prove herself; for the music must match the purity and grandness of his voice.

When she finished conducting the aria, she proceeded with the second work—Beethoven's *Symphony no. 7*, second movement. She briefly scanned the instrumentation: flutes, oboes, clarinets in A, bassoons, horns in A, E, and D, trumpets in D, tympani, and strings. It was a work that she had first heard performed live by the Minneapolis Symphony Orchestra, under the baton of Emil Oberhoffer. But it had been no ordinary day—it was her eighteenth birthday, December 17, 1920. At the time she was devastated, for not only had she broken up a marriage engagement, but more disheartening was the fact that she would not be going to London's music conservatory to pursue her musical studies. When listening to the music, in 1920, Alejandra thought it was the end of her musical aspirations, and she had wept silently to the tempo of the piece as she heard it. But, now, twelve years later, after many struggles and having studied at various conservatories, her long-standing dreams had become a reality. She was conducting.

She smiled, feeling grateful, looked at the musicians, and lifted her baton to mark the downbeat. Like in the past, the symphony's second movement, opening with A Minor Allegretto, provoked feelings of awe and mystery, but not melancholy. On her debut, the movement was seven minutes and fourteen seconds of happiness as the piece unfolded softly and rhythmically, building to climactic ecstasy, then back to a feeling of discovery, and returning to the hypnotic melody. As one of the most popular of Beethoven's compositions, other composers had described the second movement, including Wagner, who had written:

> "All tumult, all yearning and storming of the
> heart, become here the blissful insolence of joy,
> which carries us away with bacchanalian power
> through the roomy space of nature, through all the
> streams and seas of life, shouting in glad self-con-
> sciousness as we sound throughout the universe
> the daring strains of this human sphere-dance. The
> Symphony is the Apotheosis of the Dance itself: it is
> Dance in its highest aspect, the loftiest deed of bodily
> motion, incorporated into an ideal mold of tone."

When Beethoven premiered and conducted the symphony in Vienna on December 8, 1813, he considered it one of his best works, and so did the public, for they requested an encore of the second movement. On that date, it was a concert to benefit wounded soldiers who had fought in the Battle of Hanau, and Beethoven, to honor them, had said, "We are moved by nothing but pure patriotism and the joyful sacrifice of our powers for those who have sacrificed so much for us."

KYRIE

August 27, 1933 – Rome, Italy

Like many nights in the last six months, Richard woke up thinking about Alejandra, who was finally sleeping by his side. To make it up to her after delaying his trip, he had decided to surprise her with a visit to the Vatican where they would see some of the finest Renaissance art and where they would have memorable experiences of their own. For in Florence, he noticed, she was distracted, and any in-depth conversation about their time apart had been postponed for another day. But now they were alone with no one to interrupt or come between them.

He put on his plaid robe, noticing the austerity of the room in neutral colors with a wooden floor. A wrought iron double bed, two nightstands, and one armless chair seemed too much furniture for the small room. He stepped onto the balcony to smoke a cigarette. Across from him, he examined the architectural details of the Renaissance basilica designed by Bramante, Michelangelo, Maderno, and Bernini—an impressive structure financed by the monetary contributions of thousands of people in the sixteenth and seventeenth centuries in exchange for indulgences. He would gladly offer a donation if absolved of his sins. Although he winced at the very idea of such practices, Christ would have vehemently disapproved. But at least, the contributions were not wasted as St. Peter's was the most spectacular church he had ever seen and served to honor Christ's memory. He was pleased to be at the center of the former ancient Roman Empire, one of the birthplaces of Western civilization, the seat of the papacy since the first century, and the heart of Christianity.

Then at seven o'clock, as St. Peter's bells rang, Alejandra came from behind, surrounding Richard's waist with her arms, and said, "Good morning, darling, what a glorious to be awakened with." He turned to her. "Indeed it is, but even more so is that we're here together." He gazed at her figure, dressed in a soft, blue nightgown with a knitted white shawl draped over her bare shoulders. Physically she was slightly thinner and with longer hair, still lovely to look at, but different in her demeanor.

"How did you ever manage to have us stay so close to the Vatican?"

"I'll tell you," he said. "But let's go inside… I'm expecting room service any time now."

Inside, Richard heard a tap on the door and met a man with a shaved head and clothed in traditional monastic attire. He handed Richard a wooden tray with a coffee pot, cups, and silverware. Thanking him, Richard placed it on the nightstand. The man left without speaking and quietly closed the door behind him. Alejandra poured the coffee into white ceramic cups, and Richard took his cup back to bed and adjusted pillows behind his back. "Come and sit by me."

"I thought only priests were allowed to live here," she said, sitting at the edge of the bed. "I've never slept at a monastery before, and I like it."

"There are always exceptions, especially if you're interested in taking a course on the teachings of Saint Augustine, as I am."

"What are you talking about? You couldn't have changed this much in six months."

He laughed. "Why not? Are you the same person you were six months ago?"

"Is it that obvious? Am I so different?" she asked.

"You're the same sweet Ále I fell in love with, but there's a worldly character about you. I think you've learned to live without me."

She moved closer to him. "You're very perceptive, but my love for you hasn't changed."

He gazed directly into her eyes. "And no one else?"

"Why such a question?" she asked, turning away from him.

He reached out and held her hand. "I'm not blind, and I can't blame Anton for falling in love with you. Observing him over these last few days, it was obvious. In fact, I've sensed his attraction toward you since February. You have no idea how much I agonized over letting you stay, but I trusted you."

She felt as if her heart had dropped to her stomach.

"Ále, do you love him?"

She looked into his eyes. "I've grown fond of him as a friend. We share a passion for music, and he understands that part of me." She paused. "But I have to tell you that I did have a momentary lapse of judgment after a very dramatic situation."

"Oh my God! You didn't sleep with him, did you?" he asked in a raised voice.

"Of course not!" she replied.

He sighed. "I knew something like this could happen. It's never a good idea for a husband and wife to be apart for so long. But are you still committed to me?"

"Yes, and don't ever doubt my love for you," she said.

"I don't, but I need to be sure. And I don't want you to stay in touch with Anton either because he'll not stop his advances. So you must break with him completely."

"I'll do as you wish. I'd never want to be with anyone else nor jeopardize our life together. Let me tell you what happened."

"No! I don't want to know more," Richard said. "It's not like I don't know what temptation is. But I want you to understand I can never go through anything like this again."

"You forgive me then?" she asked, contrition in her voice.

"Yes. That's what love is," he said.

She sighed and caressed his face.

"Are you relieved?" Richard asked.

She placed her cup on the table, walked to the doorway, and replied, "I agonized over this moment for weeks, and perhaps you noticed I was preoccupied in Florence, and this was the reason."

"Of course I did. It was all so clear. So, do you think your training was worth it?"

"Yes. I know how difficult it must have been for all of you. It was something I needed to do. I regret causing anyone distress for my choices. But if I hadn't done it, I might have grown resentful over time. And that would not have been fair to you or our life together."

"Well, we both made the right choice," he said. "The children have missed you terribly, but they learned to accept your absence thanks to your mother who did a remarkable job."

"That's mother. So now tell me about your sudden religious conversion."

"Why are you so surprised? I'm not an atheist."

"Richard, since I've known you, not once have I ever heard of your interest in religion."

"When a man is without his wife for many months, he may find the comfort of another woman, if only temporarily, or turn to faith to keep him from straying. Obviously, there are other options as well, but fortunately for us, one of my patients, who became a friend, turned me toward the teachings of Saint Augustine. And I have to admit, for a sinner-turned-religious man, Augustine was a free-thinker."

"Thank goodness for Saint Augustine!" she exclaimed.

"I can relate to that. For I too spend a lot more time praying."

She laughed.

He joined her at the doorway and held her face. "I can't promise, however, the same steadfastness should you leave me again for such a long time."

"I won't," she said.

"How would you like if we informally renew our vows at the Sistine Chapel?"

"It would be lovely... like Venice again. You've made arrangements?" she asked.

"No. We don't need any witnesses. We did that ten years ago," he said.

"Was that the reason you brought me here?"

"Perhaps. I feared you had stopped loving me," he said.

"Never," she said, kissing him on the lips.

"This is what I had hoped for, overflowing love for me," he said, picking her up and carrying her to bed.

Mass ended at St. Peter's Basilica. For Richard, Alejandra, and countless others, St. Peter's was considered a pilgrimage for Catholics as well as for devotees of high art. As they ambled through the church among the crowd, he noticed how she took in the architectural details and overall decoration: domes, cast reliefs, ceiling frescoes, arches galore, marble columns, paintings, sculptures, mosaic tiles, and gold encrusted altar pieces.

"I could spend a week here," she whispered.

"We'll be here for three more days. Tomorrow, I'll spend most of the day learning how, since the fourteenth century, St. Augustine's writings have been applied to the Order. One of their tenets was to promote the arts and sciences. You're welcome to join me."

"You're not planning on becoming a priest, I hope," she said.

"No, but as a physician, that knowledge might be useful."

"Will they even allow a woman?"

"I don't see why not."

"Then I gladly accept. But first I'd like a quick stop at one of the chapels," she said.

They rushed through the basilica until reaching Michelangelo's *Pieta*— the life-size Carrara marble sculpture depicting the Virgin and Christ. He was impressed by the sculpture's grandiosity and the tender expression of the subjects, combined with the skill and representation of drapery lines, angles, and curves in a pyramidal composition.

"According to Vasari, a Renaissance artist and author, this work was never equaled by any other artist. He referred to it as "a miracle wrought from a once shapeless stone." Michelangelo's education, alongside Lorenzo de' Medici's son, was very influential. For later, Pope Clement VII, another Medici, commissioned Michelangelo's fresco of the *Last Judgment* on the Sistine Chapel. I knew of the Medici's impact on art, but not to this level."

"I suppose all that time spent with your friends was somewhat valuable," he said.

"Even you might have benefited," she said. "One of these days you're going to wish you had paid more attention to art."

"I'm trying. But if I sound a bit cynical it's because I'm envious I couldn't be there with you all this time, but we need to continue our conversation later. Otherwise, we're going to be late for the concert."

He took her hand, and they walked along a passage that led to the Sistine Chapel, entering through a door used primarily for cardinals, but with Richard's connections inside the Order of St. Augustine, they were permitted to go in through the chapel's private entrance. Richard, followed by Alejandra, quickly sat on a back pew. Exalted by the heavenly voices resonating throughout the hall, he was pleased with Alejandra's reaction as she gazed at the choir, composed of eleven tenors, nine basses, and thirty sopranos and contraltos, gathered around the lectern as they sang the sacred hymn "Kyrie." The choir's beginnings, traceable back to the Middle Ages, were as magnificent as described by his friend. He turned his eyes to the walls and ceilings, admiring the frescoes painted to perfection by Michelangelo and others, thinking the music seemed to complement the magnanimity of the consecrated place. For the first time, he enjoyed the art nearly as much as Alejandra.

When the concert ended, she said, "I don't know if it is divine inspiration, but being here, I can now envision a future commensurate with what I'm feeling, gratitude and humility to a God who has inspired all this splendor."

"Oh? And what future will that be?" he asked. "Haven't we had enough escapades?"

She laughed. "Don't worry. It's nothing that will take me away from you. Perhaps, for the near future, being a symphonic conductor back home might not be realistic, but a choral director is a path I can pursue. I'd like to assemble a group of twenty-four brilliant voices, six for each part, to interpret the greatest works of polyphony ever composed. Thank you, darling, for bringing me here."

"I can live with that," Richard said. "That night back in Florence, I don't think I've ever seen you as fulfilled as you were conducting at the podium, and I did wonder what your next step would be. I knew it was only the beginning. And today, you and I also have a fresh start."

Then Richard, in a black suit, led Alejandra, dressed in an embroidered, long beige dress, to the other side of the chapel. Standing under Michelangelo's fresco of the *Last Judgment*, they held each other's hands. He stared into her sparkling eyes full of wonder. In a soft voice they each pronounced the vows as they had ten years before—"to have and to hold from this day forward, for better or for worse, for richer, for poorer, in sickness and in health, to love and to cherish, from this day forward until death do us part. Amen."

ESTRELLITA

September 8, 1933

Alejandra stepped inside their home on Lake of the Isles Parkway. In Mediterranean design, the foyer with marble checkerboard floors, columns, and arches leading to other rooms, was a welcome sight after being away for so long. The children came running. Lydia Hannah and Delia Rose were holding yellow and white balloons. "Mommy! Mommy!" they said in unison. Alejandra embraced and kissed them. "I'm so happy to see you all." Her son handed her a bouquet of white orchids, and she breathed in the fragrant scent of the flowers. "Leidy, look at you! You're almost a young lady. Del, you've been under that hot summer sun, and Richie always with that big smile. I've missed you all very much."

Then Richard came in holding suitcases and took them upstairs to their quarters. Richie immediately offered to help his father. The youngest, four-year-old Del, impatiently pulled Alejandra by the hand. "We have a new puppy! You have to see him, Mommy."

"I will, but first I must put these flowers in water," she said as her mother Lydia came into the foyer. In her mid-fifties, Lydia was as radiant as ever and dressed to perfection with an ultramarine suit and pointed shoes. "Mother, it's so good to see you." She kissed her mother.

"Alé, thank God you're finally back," Lydia said, hugging her. "All right children, I know you're all excited, but dinner is ready. Go on and wash those hands. Who knows where they've been all day."

They frowned.

"Yes, Grandma," Leidy said, taking her sister's hand.

Alejandra said to her mother, "How can I ever thank you? Being away would not have been possible without your support. I'm so lucky to have you."

"There's nothing to thank," Lydia said. "I hope it was all worthwhile. You have no idea how much they've missed you, especially Richard. But you seem different."

"It was worth it, I assure you, but it did come at a high price. Let's talk about that later. I'd like to freshen up. It's been an exhausting trip. Crossing the Atlantic was choppier than expected, and the train ride from New York felt longer than ever. I'm so happy to see the children again. How I managed to be without them for this long is still a puzzle to me."

"I'll take care of the flowers," Lydia said. "From your letters, it sounds like a lot was going on, and I'm eager to hear all about it."

Later, after changing into a gray skirt and yellow blouse ensemble, Alejandra, carrying a rock crystal pitcher, was in the dining room pouring water into glasses. With her left hand, she touched the embroidered white tablecloth, a gift from her grandmother, and noticed the corners needed mending. Then her eyes turned to the tarnished candlesticks that needed polishing. A portrait of her father, Edward, sitting at an architect's table with a bowl filled with apples stood out in the distance, bringing forth some of the happiest memories of her childhood.

Soon she heard her childrens' loud chatter as the three of them came into the dining room, sitting in their assigned places. Her son grabbed a chunk of bread from the basket, practically swallowing it whole as if he hadn't eaten in days.

"Sorry to have made you wait. I know it's past your usual supper time," Alejandra said, placing the empty water pitcher on the sideboard.

"No, Mommy. We had a snack after school. Richie is always hungry," Leidy said.

Alejandra smiled at her oldest and most sensitive child. She resembled her grandmother Lydia with her dark hair and ivory tone complexion. Richie's character was as bold as Richard and physically a mix of the two. And Delia, the youngest, was high strung and the most inquisitive of the three. Physically she resembled Alejandra the most.

Then Richard came into the room, taking his place at the head of the table. "Who's that strange lady there? I don't recognize her," he said, reaching for her hand.

"Daddy, it's Mommy, you silly," Del exclaimed.

"It's only my reflection, smoke, and mirrors," Alejandra said, laughing. He kissed her hand. "Oh. It *is* you!" he said, winking at Del.

Alejandra walked toward the other end of the table and sat down in her usual place just as her mother came into the room and sat next to her.

"Would you like to say grace?" Richard asked Alejandra.

She nodded, tipping her head. "Thank you, Lord, for this meal, for the hands that prepared it, for bringing us together, and bless everyone at this table and keep in your care all those who are no longer with us. Amen."

"Where's Belin, Mommy?" Del asked.

"Berlin," Richard corrected.

"Berlin is a grand city in Germany, a country in Europe. It was once home to your great-grandmother," Alejandra said. "I've written it all down and plan to give you a detailed account as bedtime stories. But now, I'd rather hear about everything you did in my absence."

The cook and housekeeper, Millie, a woman in her forties with dark hair, thin figure, and of average height, came in holding a large bowl filled with an aromatic stew.

"I hate pot roast," Richie said in disgust as Millie served a portion on his plate.

"You'll eat it or go hungry," Richard said firmly.

"Just a little. It's good for you," Alejandra said.

"How was your debut, and what do you plan to do with all your new skills?" Lydia asked.

"She was sensational, and I'm very proud of what she accomplished," Richard said, jumping in. "I don't think I've ever seen her as happy as when she was holding a baton and leading the orchestra."

"Although, my greatest happiness was giving birth to my three adorable children. But I do plan to form a choral ensemble."

"That's an excellent idea," her mother said. "I was a bit concerned about your prospects here in town, especially considering that orchestral conducting is still limited to men."

"Just as long as you leave time for us," Richard said. "We need you here too."

"Of course, darling."

"What's a choral ensemble, Mommy?" Del asked.

"People singing together, like in church," Richie said.

"A children's choir?" Leidy asked.

"No, sweetie, an adult choir. Now please tell me about your first day of school."

One by one the children began to relate stories about their teachers and classmates, and she listened attentively to their stories, realizing how much they had grown up in such a short time. And while they were also happy to see her again, it was also easy for Alejandra to recognize that they were attached to her mother, turning to her for any decision. "Grandma, can we go to the lake house this weekend?" Richie asked.

"You'll have to ask your mother, now," Lydia replied.

"Can we go, Mommy?" the boy continued.

Alejandra thought it would take a little time for things to get back to normal. And she didn't mind at all. In fact, she felt some comfort in the notion that they had not missed her too much. "Of course," she said.

"I can't go this weekend, but you should all go," Richard said. "Take Millie with you. I can manage on my own."

"No, I'd prefer she stays and takes care of you, dear," Alejandra said. "It would give us time to catch up on all the summer happenings."

"Can we bring the puppy too?" Del asked when a small spitz came into the room, sniffing the little girl's hand.

"Yes, anything you want," Alejandra said. "And what's his name?"

"It's a girl, Mommy, and her name is Lulu."

Alejandra patted the dog on its head and turned to her mother. "You should come too. We have a lot of catching up to do."

"Yes, I'd like that," Lydia said. "But tonight I'll be going back home."

"Grandma, do you have to?" Del asked.

"Yes. I do. Your mommy is here, and you don't need me. I'm only a few miles away."

"You don't have to go, Mother," Alejandra said.

Lydia smiled. "Don't worry. I'll come by tomorrow."

The next morning, Alejandra was looking out through a Palladian window atop the stairway as the children climbed into Richard's brown Chevrolet Eagle. He would drive them to school, but before he got in himself he waved goodbye from the driveway. She glanced at the maples, which had begun to change color to a bright orange and yellow. It was a sunny morning, but with everyone gone, including her mother, she found the house eerily silent. She was about to turn on the radio when she suddenly heard a peculiar sound that seemed to emanate from the main floor. Walking down the steps, she approached the French doors, leading to the sunroom, and discovered a cardinal tapping with its beak on the window. As she watched the bird flying back and forth between two points, as though it was uncertain where it wanted to be, it brought into focus her feelings. While thankful to have united with her family, a part of her wished she was back in Vienna. She liked that life too. She visualized her friends' faces when they had bid farewell in Florence. She would see Hannah and Ben in a few months, but Anton would be best forgotten.

She went into the drawing room where several cardboard boxes, full of manuscripts and other memorabilia, remained. The room was appointed with new furniture: a brown leather sofa, two upholstered, plaid arm chairs, a Turkish rug in tones of ochre, brown, and royal blue, and two art-deco style tables. While the new décor was an improvement, strangely enough, she missed the old furniture. Between two arched windows, the fireplace, adorned with tile surrounds, was still the focal point of the room. Above the mantel, a new oil-on-canvas family portrait hung on the wall, signed by Lydia Merino Stanford. It was a perfect depiction of Alejandra and Richard seated at the piano with their three children beside them. Richard and her son were dressed in black suits, and her two daughters wore ivory-toned lace dresses. Alejandra wore a maroon velvet gown. She recognized the image taken from a photograph from the previous December to celebrate her thirtieth birthday. She would never have expected that just a mere seven months after the picture was taken, she would have fulfilled the first step to becoming a conductor.

Her memories turned back to the debut concert at the theater in Florence when she stood before the orchestra and conducted Beethoven's Symphony no. 7, second movement. It was one of the most exhilarating times in her life. The experience had imprinted on her consciousness, but it came at a great emotional expense. She was no longer the woman in the painting before her. Having savored the power of self-determination, she felt a certain freedom, but also a loss of naiveté about the world.

She began to unpack and came across a box marked "Mementos." On top of it, there was a package wrapped in white patterned paper. It was a gift from Anton who, on the day of her debut concert, had said "You can't play great music until your heart is broken." She had never experienced a broken heart, except when her father died. Might it be true? Was it essential for her to face absolute heartbreak to be a brilliant conductor? Or was Anton speaking from experience? She felt burdened to be the possible cause of his sorrow.

She sighed, turning to her favorite part of the drawing room—an alcove with raised floors where a black grand piano was housed surrounded by a curved wall partially of stained-glass windows. There, hanging on one of the walls, was a Beethoven portrait—one she had seen hundreds of time. He was holding a baton in one hand and clenching a fist with the other. His expression was as powerful as that of *Symphony no. 5*. But that morning, she saw something different in Beethoven's expression. Was it heartbreak? Heartbreak because of unrequited love? Disappointment in his fellow men? Or anguish with himself for not being able to develop his genius? What she would give to know, for Beethoven would always be her main source of inspiration.

She returned her attention to Anton's gift and considered opening it, but afraid that its contents might unsettle her emotions again, she hesitated. But curiosity got the best of her, and she tore the paper and removed the top cover, revealing a 1928 recording of the virtuoso Russian violinist Jascha Heifetz. The title of the record was *Estrellita* by Mexican composer Manual M. Ponce. She had played the composition over the years but had never heard a recorded violin arrangement. Then she saw a folded handwritten letter in the package. It read:

> *Alejandra, I'm sure by now you are perhaps stunned by my discovery of this recording by an artist you have heard me praise on many occasions for his expressive and impeccable technical abilities as a violinist. He is one of those rare individuals who lives only for music. I recently read that when he was touring Mexico, he came across this composition by Ponce. It enchanted him so completely that upon returning to his hotel he wrote a violin arrangement for it. Since then, it has attained international acclaim, making it a favorite among some of the finest violinists of our time. The melody is filled with sadness, tenderness, and love, which is what I feel when I think of you. The lyrics express what is in my heart. "Little star of the distant sky, you see my pain, you know my anguish. Come down and tell me if she loves me a little because I cannot live without her love. You are my star, my beacon of love! You know that soon I shall die. Come down and tell me if she loves me a little..."*

I hope you will forgive me for expressing these sentiments. It will be the last time. I promise. And always remember, you can't play great music until your heart is broken. Until we meet again, Anton.

Was this his intention—to haunt her for the rest of her life? She needed to forget, but wanting to hear the recording, she placed it on the Victrola and set the needle. As the notes of the melody filled every corner of the room and her being, she was moved to tears for a world and a life she had left behind and tears for a love that would never be. She read the letter again and placed it in the smoldering ashes of the fireplace until the letter caught fire and there was no trace of Anton's amorous confession. She would keep the expressive violin recording as a reminder that love must be nurtured, lest it slip away by its fickle nature.

She would never see or contact Anton again, but his words "You can't play great music until your heart is broken" would stay with her for a long time.

The doorbell rang.

Alejandra walked out of the drawing room via a hall filled with more paintings created by her mother, who soon greeted her warmly at the entrance. As always, she was dressed elegantly in a suit. "Ále, I brought you walnut bread and thought we might talk about your trip."

"Of course," Alejandra said, wiping her face and taking the pan from her hand. "Give me a moment." She went into the kitchen. When she came back, Lydia said, "Let's go into the living room. I assume you've seen the family portrait?"

"Yes. It's gorgeous. What a lovely surprise."

The music was still playing, so Alejandra quickly turned it off.

As they sat together on the sofa, Lydia asked "Are you all right? Were you crying? I was thinking about something you said yesterday. That being away came at a price?"

"I was feeling emotional. That's all." And while they were close, Alejandra didn't see any point in telling Lydia all that had happened, especially with Anton. It was hard enough to have discussed it with Richard. She would be ashamed to expose her misstep to her mother.

"I was referring to how much I've changed. At first, I struggled with staying in Europe and being apart from all of you. After a while, I liked my independence, although I never stopped feeling guilty about it. How did you manage to be apart from father, not for months, but years?"

"We haven't discussed this in a long time. I almost lost your dad. And I don't want you to make the same mistake. Richard is not like your father. He has shown his love to you by letting you be away to pursue your dream, but another separation won't be tolerated. I too enjoyed my independence. But over time, the sense of freedom is not as glamorous as it might seem in the beginning. Since your father's death, I regret the time we were apart, and I'd give anything to have him back. Things were more complicated for me as you might recall with a string of miscarriages. Your life is different, and your children need you. They will grow up, and if you're lucky enough to have a loving husband by your side as the years go by, don't tempt fate. You have everything here to be happy."

"Yes. And I am," Alejandra said. "What I was talking about also is the loss of innocence that comes with making choices regardless of what others may say or think. I was a little ambivalent as to whether I wanted this kind of life back or not. But I do because I love my family, and the choice of being without them would be heartbreaking."

"You know that I've been supportive of your professional ambitions, and you have accomplished a great deal," Lydia said. "And I'm not going to pry, but I hope that whatever or whoever might have caused this angst and doubt is now completely left behind."

"It is, Mother. You can be sure. I'll never do anything that could threaten the stability and love I'm fortunate to have in my life," Alejandra said.

They were interrupted when Millie, the housekeeper, came into the room.

"Mrs. Morrison, I've prepared a menu for the week. Would you like to see it before I go to the market?" Millie had been in the family's service for more than seventeen years, and she had never married. Alejandra was very fond of her. While she was in her forties, she looked younger with her dark short hair in bob style and a slim figure.

"I want you to know how much I appreciated all the work you did in my absence," Alejandra said. "Regarding the menu, I need a few more days to settle in, and I'm sure that whatever you have chosen will be perfect."

"Yes, madam. Good day, then," she said and left.

"Well, Mother, now that we've had our talk, how about if we now have a piece of that delicious bread of yours. I've missed it." Alejandra said.

Lydia smiled. "Now tell me all about your plans to form a choir."

MANZONI REQUIEM

December 2, 1933

Three months had passed with no unusual circumstances. Alejandra had settled into her domestic life, embracing her role as a wife and mother. She found the peacefulness of her hometown welcoming. Nationally, the news was of dust storms sweeping across the Midwest, deepening economic depression, and increasing unemployment. To address the economic downturn, President Franklin Roosevelt and Congress had passed legislation designed to produce government jobs in various industries. The New Deal enacted many domestic programs, including the Civilian Conservation Corps and Public Works of Art Projects.

From a recent letter, Alejandra learned that Hannah was participating in the Public Works Art program as project manager of a government task force to employ visual artists for the public muralists project in the United States. Inspired by the Mexican Modernist and Muralist movement catapulted by Diego Rivera, José Clemente Orozco, and David Alfaro Siqueiros, American institutions and influential individuals, such as John D. Rockefeller, Jr. and others, commissioned public murals throughout the United States. Works of note included Orozco for the New School for Social Research in New York, Siqueiros for the Plaza Art Center in Los Angeles, Rivera for the Detroit Industry at the Detroit Institute of Arts, and the most recent Rivera's *Man at the Crossroads* at Rockefeller Center in New York.

She was thrilled that these Mexican artists, whose work she had often admired during her youth, had brought their art and vision to the United

States, although not without controversy, as in the case of *Man at the Cross-roads*, which depicted political inclinations.

Seated at her roll top desk in an alcove next to her bedroom, decorated in the art nouveau style, Alejandra wrote:

Dear Hannah, it was so *wonderful to hear from you. From your letter, I gather you are happy to be back home and busy at work with the gallery and engaging new artists, who will play a dynamic role in future art projects in your city. Increased interest by the government to commission mural works seems to be aimed at engaging the public in new ways. I'm enthusiastic that you viewed Diego Rivera's mural painting* Man at the Crossroads *at Rockefeller Center, but troubled it has caused controversy. He has been vital in bringing forth a mural movement in America. But as we have seen, art produced in the public arena always seems to draw debate. I have not been an advocate of mixing art with politics, although I do understand it is a way to give voice to pertinent issues of the day. I often ask myself whether art is political by its creative nature. As individuals, we're always making a statement one way or the other.*

On another topic, I'm sorry to hear that Ben has not yet found a conducting position, but tell him to be patient, as he will be employed in no time at all. Our family is well, and I'm so pleased to be home again, even if it took a little time to normalize. I can't deny that the experience of being in Europe changed me in more ways than I care to admit. After having a taste of it, my professional ambitions have not in any way diminished, but they will have to accommodate my current home life. Perhaps I found something of myself there that I never thought possible—the need to be independent and self-sufficient in all manner and form. I'm content with my life, and that is thanks to Richard who is loving and supportive of my professional endeavors. He is very busy with his practice, and most nights he's not home until seven, and of late is taking extra shifts at the hospitals. As for our children, they bring me such joy. Leidy has become a remarkable pianist for such a young age. Richie is playing the violin but doesn't seem to be committed to the instrument, unless it is in competition with his sister. His interest seems to be more in the sciences like his father. As for Del, I'm not sure yet, although, I often hear her sing, which brings me to my latest endeavor.

Since my arrival, I have attended several rehearsals and concerts of the Minneapolis Symphony Orchestra, now headed by Eugene Ormandy. I have continued with my studies and training, alongside local directors, and now yearn for the opportunity to expand on the skills in the art of conducting. Despite the fact that opportunities for conducting an orchestra at this time are limited, I have begun a serious search for singers to form a choir of twenty-four voices. Being a choral director, I hope, will further my expertise in this area. I'd like to showcase choral works from composers around the world. I envision a chorus that can perform in concert halls, churches, schools, and hospitals alike, and that will sing religious as well as secular music. I want to call it Opus Dei. And in case you're wondering about the religious name, my reasoning is simple—work of God and a philosophy that ordinary life leads to a path to blessedness.

This morning I feel so encouraged by a concert of the Minneapolis Symphony Orchestra that we attended last night. It was no ordinary concert for fellow Minnesotans or me. It was in memoriam of the orchestra's German-born founder Emil Oberhoffer, who served as permanent conductor from 1903 to 1922. I felt terribly saddened at his passing, and last night, overwhelmed with emotion as I recalled he was one of my inspirations to become a conductor when I was thirteen years old. The program was of particular significance as the Twin City Symphony Chorus, and Rupert Sircom, performed Giuseppe Verdi's Manzoni Requiem for four solo voices, chorus, and orchestra. The piece was exquisite and personal. It perfectly honored Oberhoffer's memory. The program ended with: "Requiem e Kyrie," "Dies Irae," "Domine Jesu," "Sanctus," and "Agnus Dei." Oh, what angelic voices I heard.

The entire program was a perfect tribute to a man who contributed greatly to Minnesota's cultural life. He brought so much beauty through music, reminding me more than ever of the importance of giving oneself to our professions, and that is something I hope to do. It is what still keeps my dreams alive. I find it remarkable that beginning next year the Minneapolis Symphony Orchestra will be making recordings of some of the best music ever composed. Music that everyone can enjoy from their home. How far we've come!

As for your invitation to come to New York to attend the world premiere of a new work for violin and orchestra on April 12, we're happy to accept. We're looking forward to seeing the Philharmonic's famous Italian conductor. The opportunity to observe Maestro Arturo Toscanini's rehearsals was something we discussed in Vienna, but I never imagined it would happen. Please thank Ben for making this possible.

I miss you both, and I will always cherish our time together. Please extend my best wishes to Ben and the rest of your family. May you have a season filled with harmony and peace. With all my affection and gratitude, Alejandra.

CONCERTO GROSSO IN G MINOR

*F*ebruary 1934 – Berlin, Germany

In a warehouse filled with sculptures, paintings, and decorative arts, Anton was browsing through objects that would go on auction in the next week. Arranged in periods from antiquity to medieval, Renaissance, baroque, and modern art, he took a maritime painting that needed restoration. He then went to the studio, next to the warehouse, where Karl Schmidt, a professional painter, was working on a contemporary portrait. The sixty-year-old man with stained clothes, deep facial creases, yellow teeth, and often a disgusting body odor looked other than the gifted artist that he was. While he was unreliable due to his drinking, Anton had often considered dismissing Karl, but his work was extraordinary.

"If you can have this painting restored soon, I'd appreciate it," Anton said, placing the painting on an empty table next to Karl.

Karl nodded.

Anton then turned to Isolde Beckman who was posing for Karl, as he started another nude painting of her in the style of Matisse's odalisques, inspired by the artist's time living in Morocco. Anton noticed Isolde's posture, lying sideways on a colorful tapestry. But like the day before, she needed a little prodding as to the exact position.

"Isolde, place one hand sustaining the side of your head, and let the other loosely fall in front of your abdomen," Karl said. "Allow the tips of your fingers to touch the fabric. Bring your right knee up toward your face, and your expression must be one of innocent seduction as though you're unaware of your natural beauty."

She sighed. "All right."

Karl continued with the large canvas painting—an image of a young woman portrayed as a nude fairy maiden with her blond curly hair falling loosely to her waist. She appeared to be part of a supernatural landscape surrounded by white and purple lily pads, like a Monet that served as the backdrop. With his brush embedded in white and yellow paint, he highlighted the morning light that shone on Isolde's chest, accentuating her ample breasts.

Anton observed Isolde who waited to get her orders—to get dressed or move elsewhere. He thought she had become, in some perverse way, his possession like the rest of the objects in his warehouse. For not only did he support her financially, but since she gave up prostitution at his request she had become dependent on him and willing to please his every need. He cared for her as someone in need of protection and often encouraged her to pursue a singing career, which she had consistently refused to do. He considered her to be simpleminded and coarse. However, as a private concubine, she had maintained his continued interest. As far as he was concerned, it was a relationship of mutual convenience.

Anton looked at his watch when Karl said, "I have an appointment and must go."

"You've been here for less than two hours. At this rate, we won't get anything done, and I've promised this painting would be ready this week," Anton said.

"You like it, don't you?" Karl asked and put away his brushes.

"How many more chances must I give you?"

The man shrugged. Anton placed a roll of reichsmarks on the tray as Karl turned to walk away. "Now don't spend it all in one night, and I expect you tomorrow by nine. Work on the restoration piece first!"

"I'll show up," Karl replied. Then he shut the door, leaving the studio.

Isolde walked to the painting. "Oh. Is that really me? May I dress now?"

Anton lustily approached her, staring at her behind. "Whatever for? I like you best this way." She turned to him and grinned. "I'm all yours." She unbuttoned his pale-blue shirt while he lifted her, carrying her to a leather-tufted platform bed on the opposite side of the studio. She lay on the mattress with a loose sheet beneath her. Then she stretched her arms and opened her legs invitingly. "Why do you have a poster bed here?"

"I bought it with the intention of keeping it for myself, but with its regal history, I decided to sell it. It will go to auction this week."

"Owned by whom?" she asked.

"A king... no more questions," he said, pulling down his pants.

Holding a glass of cognac, Anton went to his library, softly lit by lion-paw Bakelite floor lamps. The spacious room was furnished with a carved wooden desk, bookshelves, and two mahogany-toned club armchairs. As he placed the glass on a side table, next to a letter, he sank into one of the armchairs, leaning back and resting his eyes. It had been a long and fruitful day for he had sold two more of Karl's original paintings of female nudes in Turkish harems, but business had become complicated. Now more than ever, he felt he was at a crossroads both professionally and personally.

Last fall Anton had made powerful connections in the government as art collecting had become a frenzy among high-ranking Nazi officials. But highly destructive policies had been recently implemented that affected his business. The Reich Culture Chamber, Reichskulturkammer, a governmental agency, was established in September, headed by Joseph Goebbels, the propaganda minister. The chamber developed policies affecting the arts—music, film, literature, architecture, and the visual arts. In the latter, a new attitude was emerging among the establishment... a policy that would define good versus bad art. Traditional art was praised whereas modern art was tagged as "degenerate." It went so far as to identify unacceptable members of the art community by removing them from their museum posts and replacing them with Nazi supporters who believed in a "racially pure" approach to art. Anton was concerned that the policy of "art purification" based on current politics was a dangerous trend. He wondered what would be next—purge modern works of art from museums and raid private business? Up to now, he was convinced the government would disintegrate due to its totalitarian policies, but with their tactics, the fascist movement had gained strength. And he could not accept the discrimination against other German citizens. It was time to consider going to America in search of business opportunities and leaving his homeland for good.

Anton looked at Hannah's letter she had written recently inviting him to New York. It was not the first time since they had parted ways in August. Twice, he had postponed the trip. But this time, he had the impetus he needed to make the long trip abroad. Hannah wrote that Alejandra would be visiting in the spring to attend rehearsals and the premiere of Francesco Geminiani's Concerto Grosso in G Minor for violin and orchestra. He sighed thinking about Alejandra, who he yearned to see again. Since their Florentine goodbye, five months earlier, he had written several letters, but all had been returned. What had become of her? He was troubled that they had lost all communication, and it hurt. Had they gone through so much to end up like strangers? He dealt with her unexplained rejection the best way he could— devoting all his time and energy to his business, and for those lonely times, he had Isolde. But nothing would be as satisfying as having a connection with Alejandra. He had accepted platonic love, and he must do something extraordinary to salvage their friendship.

With the anticipation of traveling to New York to see Alejandra once again, he picked up his violin and bow from a side table and began playing the vigorous violin solo part of Geminiani's baroque composition, as though playing music, instantly, connected him to her. Surely, there had to be a way to win back her favors.

BABY

*A*pril 11, 1934

In a parlor of a tenth floor, Upper West Side Georgian-style apartment, Hannah, dressed in a loose polka dot black and white dress and flat shoes, was drawing the curtains open, showing the city lights that glowed brightly across Manhattan. The room painted in green, parquet floors, Japanese scenic wallpaper, and geometric upholstered light gray furniture, was decorated to her taste. Small niches in the living room showcased her Chinese and Japanese blue pottery collection.

To accommodate a growing family, they had acquired the new flat after a quick sale, making it not only affordable, but also a good investment, and more importantly the home of their first child. Hannah placed her hand over her abdomen, happy that she had finally passed through the first trimester. She now could imagine her baby crawling about the room or sleeping on the floor by the sunny window in the corner.

She was thrilled to share her news with Alejandra and Richard, who were expected to arrive at any moment. Ben came into the room holding a tray filled with a variety of cheeses, olives, a platter of pastrami, and rye bread. He placed it on the cocktail table. Then he walked to her and kissed her. "You've made me the happiest man alive."

"And I'm the happiest woman alive," Hannah said.

The doorbell rang, and Hannah opened the door and embraced Alejandra, who was dressed in a long-sleeved chiffon salmon-toned dress, belted at her waist, and pumps. She was holding a raincoat. "Welcome to our humble abode," Hannah said, hugging Richard and taking their coats.

"You look fantastic, Hannah. There's a glow about you," Alejandra said.

"Good evening," Richard said.

Hannah took Alejandra's hand, placing it on her tummy, and smiled.

"Oh. My God! Why didn't you tell me? This is great news. Ben must be in heaven."

"I wanted to be sure, considering how difficult it has been for me to conceive. We'd given up. The baby is due in early October," Hannah said.

"Congratulations," Richard said.

As they stepped into the drawing room, Alejandra said, "This is gorgeous. You can come and decorate our house anytime. I suppose being back home has suited you divinely."

"Yes. But as for the decoration, I can't take the honors," Hannah said. "The former owner was an interior designer. She moved to France in a rush. But there's more to this acquisition than meets the eye. The best part is down the hall." She led them to the end of a corridor, and with the excitement of a young girl, Hannah showed them the nursery painted in soft pastel colors. A crib pushed against a wall was surrounded by impressionistic black and white sketches of children of all ages playing in Central Park. A stained-glass window, framed by soft white transparent draperies, was one of the earliest windows made by Louis Comfort Tiffany's glass company.

"It's beautiful. I especially like the window with the waterscape design," Alejandra said.

Hannah took a yellow and white knit blanket with a star from the crib and unfolded it. "My mother made it."

"How are your parents?" Alejandra asked.

"They couldn't be happier. That's all my father talks about... their first grandchild."

"I need to congratulate Ben. Where is he?" Richard asked.

"In the kitchen making one of his favorite delicacies," Hannah said.

"I'll excuse myself. I'm sure you have much to talk about."

Hannah walked to the white-painted chest of drawers and pulled out a small box containing a sterling silver Jewish star pendant. "Ben's mother gave it to him before she died, for her grandchild, she said. And now after all these years, it's finally going to happen." Hannah teared up.

"What a joyous occasion," Alejandra said. "I always believed it would."

Hannah pointed to the tiny inscription on the star—"B.A." "It belonged to Ben's grandfather." Feeling emotional, she wiped her eyes and put the pendant back in the box. "This is all I have dreamed about for the last ten years. We have names picked out, but no one will know until the baby is born. Oh. That sounds so good to say, doesn't it?"

Alejandra put her arm around Hannah's shoulder. "I can't believe you kept this secret for so long. I'm going to love this baby as though I was the godmother."

"Well, we may not have that tradition like you Catholics, but as far as I'm concerned, you can be our child's godmother… why not? You might as well be, considering you're a sister to me."

"In our faith, we take the role of godmother very seriously, as you know. So I'd like that very much," Alejandra said.

Hannah thought that if ever anything happened to her or Ben, and her parents were unable to care for their child, Alejandra would be next on her list. They didn't have a large extended family. Was this the sort of thing parents thought about all the time? Nothing would happen to Ben and her but there was comfort in knowing her child would always be loved. "Well, you better be here when he's born."

"He?" Alejandra asked, playfully.

"Or she. Let's go and join our husbands," Hannah said.

After dinner, Hannah came into the parlor, holding two glasses containing amaro, as Alejandra and Richard stood by the window. Richard had his arms around Alejandra's waist. "So what are you two chatting about?" Hannah asked, placing the drinks on the cocktail table. "With so much affection, one might think you were just married."

"You could say that," Alejandra said. "Our trip to the Vatican turned into something very special."

Hannah glanced at Alejandra, noticing she seemed at peace and content alongside Richard. And she was glad to see them in a happy marriage. For when they were in Europe, Hannah worried that Alejandra had fallen under Anton's charm, even though she'd never act on those feelings. And, while Alejandra had always been principled, anyone was capable of making mistakes. Anton was clearly not over her, for the last time they spoke on the phone, he had asked a lot of questions about her. Thank God he wouldn't be coming to New York for another week. It could be very awkward, considering Richard expressed animosity toward Anton earlier during their dinner conversation.

"So, what happened in Rome?" Hannah asked.

"I know it's not a common thing to do, but we informally renewed our vows under Michelangelo's the *Last Judgment*," Alejandra said.

"The last judgment, ha?" Hannah said. "A little melodramatic?"

Ben joined them. "What are you all talking about, the last judgment?"

Alejandra laughed. "I hope none of us have to worry about it for some time, but just in case we all better be good."

"And when haven't you been Miss Goody Two-Shoes?" Hannah said. "Remember when we had our first taste of whiskey in a speakeasy at seventeen?"

"How can I forget. It led to a week of atonement after your father imposed a curfew after we broke the law," Alejandra said.

"So did you gals ever go back to any other speakeasy?" Richard asked.

"Not me, I'd have been too embarrassed to face Hannah's father again," Alejandra said.

"I did many times with Ben," Hannah said. "I don't think my father approved of Ben at first since he was the one who perverted us, as he would often say."

Ben laughed. "I did have to express my regret countless times."

"Those were the days of careless fun," Hannah said.

Ben then took his drink. "Here is to our child, who I hope is as witty as my dear Hannah and never knows his father's shortcomings."

"Not shortcomings, honey. I've told you before, just a lot of experiences and brilliance. Better yet, I hope she plays the violin with the same perfection as you do," Hannah said.

"I don't care if it's a boy or a girl or pretty or not, just as long our child is bright and happy is good enough for me," Ben said.

Just then the telephone rang, and Ben walked to the console table and answered. "Hello." He paused. "We were not expecting you for another week. We've just finished dinner, and we're going to the Cotton Club a bit later. Why don't you join us there? We'll be there at nine." A few seconds of silence more. "Great, see you then."

"Was that Anton?" Hannah asked.

"What?" Richard exclaimed. "I thought you said he wasn't coming for another week."

"That's what he said in a telegram," Hannah said. "It would be nice to see him and tell him our news. I hope you don't mind, Richard. We're just all good friends."

Hannah noticed Richard tensing up so that Alejandra took his hand, looking a bit shaken herself.

"We can call it off if you prefer," Ben said.

"No. I was not expecting to see him ever again. But I don't want to dampen anybody's spirit, especially on a night like this. It's fine, really," Richard said.

"Besides, with the music and all, you won't even notice he's there. And you don't want to miss tonight's performer either. Her show is a hit," Hannah said.

"Of course," Richard said.

"And who's the performer?" Alejandra asked.

"Adelaide Hall. You remember her from her Broadway days?" Hannah said.

"She's marvelous. It will be a splendid night," Alejandra said.

T he Cotton Club was the premier jazz venue of the time, bringing Broadway to Harlem. Duke Ellington and the Cotton Club Orchestra had been a smash since 1927, and with that success, by 1932 they were touring in Europe. On that night it was the Jimmie Lunceford Orchestra performing, starring Adelaide Hall. Most nights it was standing room only, but Ben had made previous arrangements with a long-time acquaintance who was now the manager and who had assured him a table for four. Hannah was elated, as the jazz club was her favorite venue in New York.

When they arrived at the smoky and lively club, the orchestra was playing "Rocking in Rhythm" and "Bugle Call Rag." Hannah, who had been there before on numerous occasions, scanned the audience—half black and half white, not a surprise. She was thrilled to be among such high-spirited people, especially on this day of celebration. Soon, Ben's friend "Rocky," a tall black man, fashionably dressed, greeted them with a big smile and led them to their table in front of the stage. "Wow," Hannah said. "That's a first."

"Only the best for my pregnant wife," Ben said. "Thank you, my friend. We will need one extra chair, please."

"So that's the special occasion. Congratulations to you both," Rocky said.

"These are our friends Alejandra and Richard Morrison," Ben said. "Rocky and I go way back to our high school days."

Soon, Rocky brought an extra chair, placing it next to Hannah. They took their seats and ordered drinks, except for Hannah who ordered coffee. One drink during dinner was enough for her. The last thing she wanted was to feel tipsy at a time when she wanted to enjoy every moment to its fullest. "What do you all think about this club? Isn't it amazing?"

"Yeah. It's wild, but I like it," Richard said.

"You're awfully quiet, Ále," Hannah said.

"I'm just taking it all in. The music is fabulous, upbeat, and very danceable."

"Is that a proposal?" Richard asked. "I used to be like that man on the dance floor, agile, fast, and with a crazy streak. But now it would take a few drinks."

"No kidding?" Ben said. "So what happened?"

"I got married." Richard laughed.

"Hey, I wouldn't mind seeing that crazy side of you more often," Alejandra said.

The waiter brought them their drinks, and Ben added, "Here's to the end of prohibition."

"It's been only four months, and we're already seeing an influx of drunks at the hospital," Richard sneered.

"Once the dust settles, I'm sure things will calm down. I suspect people are making up for lost time, although thirteen years of prohibition didn't stop anyone from drinking," Ben said.

"It certainly didn't," Richard said, downing his glass of whiskey in one swift gulp.

"Well, I don't miss getting drunk. I'll tell you that," Hannah said, turning to the stage as the upbeat song ended. The musicians began to play an instrumental version of "Baby" from the Broadway show *Blackbirds*. She couldn't remember a happier time, and as she did several times a day, she placed her hand over her stomach, feeling the life growing inside of her. For a moment she closed her eyes and imagined holding that little being in her arms and wondering what kind of temperament he or she would have. As she listened to the melody, she did wish her child would be less like her and more like Ben, calm, collected and musically endowed, even if he had a few flaws like everyone else. She never felt as much love for him as she did since she had become pregnant. He loved her unconditionally, despite being childless for a long time, but now she had finally given him what was missing in their life together.

"Are you all right?" Alejandra asked.

Hannah opened her eyes and leaned toward her friend. "Yes. I was enjoying this moment. I wake up every morning thinking how lucky I am and what a beautiful life we have."

"This is only the beginning, Hannah, my dear," Alejandra said.

Just then Hannah noticed Anton approaching the table, dressed in a chic gray suit, Prussian blue shirt, and tie. He had let his beard grow again, and his eyes immediately fell on Alejandra who had not yet seen him. Just by the way he looked at her, Hannah could tell he was still in love with her. How lucky, or maybe not, was Alejandra—to have two men so completely devoted to her, but only one could have her love. For it certainly would be a torment to love them both.

"Good evening," he said, shaking everyone's hands and taking a seat across from the Morrisons and next to Hannah.

"Anton, it's so good to see you," Hannah said. "But you've got us all a bit rattled by your sudden appearance."

"I had some business dealings that could not wait," Anton said. "I'm on the trail of two paintings by Spitzweg von Kaulbach and Boecklin here in town of all places. And that art is very popular back home. I hope I'm not intruding. I was eager to see you all."

"What a coincidence," Richard said.

"What would you like to drink?" Ben quickly asked.

"A glass of Sanderman. So what's the happy news?" Anton asked.

"We're expecting a baby," Ben said. "How is that for a big surprise?"

"As you Americans say, wow! Congratulations. I wish I would have known and brought the baby a first violin," Anton said. "Next time."

"Next time? So you're finally moving here?" Hannah asked.

"Is this your first time in New York?" Richard asked.

"Yes," Anton replied. "I've heard you describe the long trip, train to Liverpool and then another six days to cross the Atlantic, and yes it's exhausting. And I got a bit seasick. I'm sure you don't want to hear about that. Although I could go on and tell you some of the more interesting adventures..."

Hannah thought Anton had a way with words, a charmer to be sure, who made everyone laugh except Richard who was not amused and seemed put off by his presence. Alejandra was completely silent until Anton turned to her. "How is your trip going?"

"We've been here for a couple of days, and it's been marvelous," she replied.

"They were at Toscanini's rehearsal earlier today," Hannah added.

"Oh! Is it true what they say about him?" Anton asked.

"Indeed. Toscanini's focus is intense, and he approaches both rehearsals and performances as sacred rituals. He's a literal interpreter of the score," Alejandra replied.

"Thank goodness Toscanini was finally allowed to leave Italy. Had Mussolini confiscated his passport any longer, he may have never ended up here," Hannah added.

"And the music? I suppose it will be a fantastic premiere tomorrow night," Anton said.

"You must join us," Hannah said.

"I'd love to if it's still possible."

"I'm sure I can arrange it," Ben said.

"And what news from Berlin?" Richard asked.

"Nothing has changed. I'm trying to escape it and am exploring the idea of moving here."

"Are you serious about that?" Hannah asked.

"Nazi ideology has totally perverted the art scene. Everything is political," Anton said.

"There's a little of that here too. Diego Rivera's mural has caused a stir," Hannah said.

"I'm not familiar, but it can't be as bad as what's happening back home," Anton said.

"Of course not, but it's unsettling to think that a marvelous mural like *Man at the Crossroads* could be destroyed at the heart of New York," Hannah said. "The controversy stemmed from having the image of Lenin at the center of the painting. I think the idea was to give some attention to communism."

"Didn't you say Rivera offered to replace Lenin with Lincoln's image?" Alejandra asked.

"He did, but who knows what happened in the end," Hannah replied.

"I'm glad I took photos of it when it was available for viewing," Hannah said.

"Public art will always be laced with controversy for one reason or another. But here's to being together again and for all the good things to come," Ben said, lifting his glass.

"You're awfully giddy tonight," Hannah said to Ben.

"How could I not be? I'm going to be a father."

"It's a pleasure to be with you all. I was inconsolable after we parted ways," Anton said.

"You won't have to miss us if you move here, Anton," Hannah said. "But either way, you'll have to come back in the fall for the baby's naming," she said.

"Of course. I wouldn't miss it for the world," Anton said.

AS LONG AS I LIVE

Alejandra, who had been mostly silent, turned to the orchestra as they finished the instrumental piece and one of the musicians introduced the famed jazz singer, Adelaide Hall. With a silky black complexion and curly hair, and dressed in a red sequin dress, she stepped on stage. An enthusiastic applause ensued. After a brief musical introduction, she took the microphone and began singing "As long as I live," as Alejandra sipped her drink. *"Maybe I can't live to love you as long as I want to. Life isn't long enough, baby, but I can love you as long as I live. Maybe I can't give you diamonds and things like I want to, but I can promise you, baby, I'm gonna want to as long as I live..."*

Alejandra noticed that Anton's handsome looks had apparently caught the singer's attention for she climbed down to the floor level, and with a confident gait she approached him, running her fingers through his light brown hair. With her curvy figure and a smooth voice, she could melt any man on the spot. Whether it was her intention or not, Anton seemed mesmerized by the singer's sensuality and enjoyed the attention. He smiled back at the singer. And Alejandra, who had never expected to see Anton again, was pleased by the scene unfolding before her. So what did it matter that Anton was there? She had made peace with their past, and he seemed to have moved on. She was glad to see him again as a friend, having a marvelous time. Then, Richard held Alejandra's hand as he mouthed, "I love you."

"As do I," she whispered.

A couple of hours later, before midnight, the five companions were outside the jazz club, in high spirits and bidding farewell. The streets were busy. It was a clear night, although a bit cold Alejandra thought, placing her hands inside her coat. Feeling herself a little tipsy, she found it rather humorous to be standing between Richard, to her right, and Anton to her left. Richard, with a hint of sarcasm, said to Anton, "Another coincidence you're staying at the Waldorf?"

"Not really, it's the best hotel in midtown," Anton said. "But if you have other plans, I can take my own cab."

"Nonsense. I can drive you all to your hotel," Ben said. "I insist."

"That's kind of you, Ben, but it will be easier for us to take a cab to the hotel," Richard said. "We might want to stop somewhere to get a bite to eat, and Hannah should be home."

"I *am* a little tired," Hannah said. "But it has been terrific being with all of you."

"All right, have it your way, see you tomorrow," Ben said, shaking hands with the two men. "We'll get you a ticket for the concert."

Hannah and Alejandra hugged each other goodbye.

"Until we meet again," Anton said.

Then the Adelmans walked to their car a block away. Turning a corner, they disappeared from view.

Richard then hailed a taxi, but it failed to stop. For the next few minutes, he waved to several more, but every single one was occupied. "Maybe if we walk to the intersection we might have better luck," he said, taking Alejandra's hand.

"Yes, probably more chances there," Anton said, walking beside Alejandra.

They walked toward the intersection of 142nd Street and Lenox. From there, an empty cab was coming from the opposite direction, and Richard ran toward it, but in his haste, he did not see a 1934 black Chevrolet which had just turned the corner from his right side, swerving at high speed. Alejandra, who was looking at Richard, gasped. Then Anton, who was next to her, sprinted toward Richard pushing him forward, preventing him from being run over by the car. However, Anton, who was in the middle of the road, was violently struck by the same vehicle, throwing him ten feet away. Alejandra watched as he landed hard on the asphalt. "Oh, my God!" she yelled as the vehicle vanished around another corner. Everything happened so fast she was momentarily in shock, seeing both Richard and Anton on the ground. Alejandra ran toward Richard. "Are you all right?" He stood up, dusting off the gravel from his hands and suit. "I am, but I'm afraid your friend is not." They both turned to Anton who was still motionless on the ground and rushed to him as people gathered. Richard pushed himself through them, and Alejandra followed behind him. He kneeled down next to Anton, taking his pulse from his wrist. He was alive but unconscious. "Can someone call an ambulance?" Richard shouted. "How close is the nearest hospital?"

"Not too far from here," a black man replied. "I'll make the call."

Richard then took off his coat and spread it over Anton.

Later, in the hospital lobby, Alejandra waited to hear about Anton's condition. Other visitors who were scattered around the seating area also seemed eager to speak to a nurse or physician. She noted a young woman crying as her husband consoled her by saying, "Our boy is going to make it."

What about Anton? *Was he going to make it?* she wondered, knowing he was in critical condition. She could not abandon the feeling that their lives were now irrevocably intertwined. Although, she was relieved that Richard had been spared from a potentially fatal accident. He could have been the one in peril. Everything had gone terribly wrong in a matter of seconds. Fifty agonizing minutes transpired before she finally spotted Richard from a distance as he came out of the emergency room. His face was grim, and she feared the worst. "He's going into surgery, and he has a concussion."

"He's going to live, right?" she asked.

"Yes, but he has a comminuted femur fracture."

"What's that exactly?"

"The bone is broken in more than two places, and there's a high risk of infection. They will have to insert a rod in both ends of the fracture."

"Are you going to be there in the operating room?"

"No, but I'll be able to watch from a window in the next room," he said, gently pressing her shoulder. "Don't worry. He's a strong man."

"Thank you for being at his side," she said.

"It's the least I can do," he said. "Oh, one more thing, the police want a report. Can you do that? I told the officer to talk to you as I have to go now."

"Yes," Alejandra said.

Not long after, she gave the policemen a full account of what she had seen, including a description of the runaway car. The police said they would investigate, but the vehicle was all too common. With no license number, it would be difficult to find. It was four o'clock in the morning when a nurse approached Alejandra. The older woman with a tan complexion and hoarse voice, dressed in a white uniform, asked, "Are you Alejandra Morrison?"

She nodded.

"Mr. Everhardt has been asking for you. He's still a little drowsy and talking a lot of drivel which I can't understand. He's stable. Follow me," the nurse said. "Is he related to you?"

"No. He's a friend," she replied. "Do you know where my husband, Dr. Morrison, is?"

"He's talking to the surgeon."

They walked along a disorderly corridor filled with wheelchairs and metal trays that had been left randomly on the wooden floor until they reached Anton's unit.

"He's at the end of the hallway," the nurse said.

Alejandra entered the single dark room that had a strong smell of disinfectant. She sat on a chair, next to the bed, and placed her hand on his arm. "Anton, can you hear me?"

He barely opened his eyes.

"You're going to be all right," she said.

He uttered some words that she could not make out. She leaned her head forward, and he spoke again under his breath. "*Bleib hier.*"

He wanted her to stay with him, and she felt grateful to see him breathing, even though he looked helpless and broken under the faint light. His face was swollen, reminding her of the last time he was badly beaten back in Germany. The IV stuck in his arm had caused some allergic reaction. He tried to talk randomly and occasionally twitched, but he quieted down whenever she stroked his hand. Seeing him injured brought back a flood of emotions.

At the break of dawn, Ben and Hannah walked into the room. Hannah gasped at the sight of him, covering her mouth with her hand.

"How is he?" Ben asked.

"Not the best, but the surgery went well," Alejandra said. "He can hear you."

Hannah stepped next to Anton on the other side of the bed. "I'm so sorry."

He opened his eyes once again. "*Wo bin ich?*" Anton asked.

"You're in the hospital. Just rest for now," Alejandra said, gesturing her friends to meet her out in the hall.

Outside the room, Ben asked, "What's the prognosis?"

"I don't know yet," Alejandra said. "Richard is racked with guilt. He said this wouldn't have happened if we had just driven with you to the hotel."

"It's not his fault. It was an accident, plain and simple," Ben said.

"I've told him that repeatedly, but it seems there's nothing I can say to change his mind."

Richard then greeted them and said, "He's stable, but he's going to be here for a week. Ále, you look tired. You need to eat and get some sleep."

"And you!" Alejandra said to Richard.

"You both need a break. We'll stay," Ben said.

"Yes, that's a good idea," Richard said.

Alejandra returned to the room and leaned toward Anton. "Hannah and Ben will stay here with you, and we'll be back soon."

"Ja," he murmured, falling back asleep.

After showering and getting dressed, Alejandra was combing her wet hair in front of the dresser mirror in the hotel room. She noticed dark circles under her eyes as she had only managed about two hours of sleep. Richard had been on the phone most of the morning talking to his colleagues back home, informing them about the accident and making arrangements for another physician to cover him at the hospital for the next week. After hanging up the phone, he sat next to a small round table with a tray filled with plates of fresh fruit and pastries. "Come, let's have breakfast."

"I'm not hungry," she said.

"Please, you've got to eat something. We need to talk."

Alejandra placed the hairbrush on the nightstand and joined him at the table, serving herself a few pieces of fruit and one croissant. "I'm glad it's not me in the hospital, but it should have been. How could I have been so distracted? One too many drinks, I suppose."

"Richard! It was an accident. You have to stop blaming yourself!"

"I feel responsible. I've given it a lot of thought, and it's the only solution."

"I don't understand," she said.

"Anton is in no condition to travel back to Germany. He may not be able to walk for several weeks or perhaps a month or two. He will require close attention and personal care. We obviously can't stay here in New York, and we can't afford to have him stay here."

"Absolutely not!" Alejandra shouted, realizing what her husband was suggesting.

"Ále," Richard said, reaching out to hold her hand. "I know I'm asking a lot. But back home, we have a large house, and he can stay in the guest room next to the kitchen. Millie can help, and I'll hire a nurse, at least initially when the risk of infection is the highest. I feel it's my obligation to make things right. Please understand me."

"Of course, I just wish there was another way. I don't know that I can do it."

"Yes, you can. Why are you so hesitant?"

She paused, thinking she must do her best to separate her feelings from those of her husband. "I thought you didn't care much for him. And how do you know he'll even accept?"

"I didn't care much for him, but now that has changed, hasn't it? As far as accepting, of course, he will. He loves you. I've known it since Florence. Do you think it was a fluke that he showed up here when he did? I confirmed it last night after surgery. He kept repeating your name. Even though he spoke German I understood '*Wo ist, Ále?*' You know it's true don't you?"

Placing her hands together, she added, "I had hoped he had moved on. But then why bring him to our house?"

"Honor. It's the right thing to do. Although he may love you, you're my wife. You were on your own for six months. If you managed then, you can certainly manage having him around at our house. I trust you completely."

She took a deep breath. "I'm not sure of this plan, but I do understand. Let me be very clear. I'm doing this for you and only you. This is very noble of you."

"I know. Anton won't be ready to travel for another week, but we'll speak with him tomorrow when he's more alert."

"What will we tell the children?"

"The truth. That he's a friend who is going to stay with us until he recovers."

Late the next morning, Alejandra and Richard returned to the hospital. Anton had been moved to another room on the fourth floor, as his condition had improved. In fact, when they entered his room, he was already up and eating breakfast from a tray on his bed.

"Good morning," Richard said.

"Hello to you both," Anton said.

Alejandra sat next to him, and Richard brought another chair from the hallway.

"How's the pain?" Richard asked.

He wiped his mouth with a napkin. "I can hardly feel it with the drugs they're giving me," Anton replied. "But I'm eager to know when I can get out of here."

"That's what we're here to talk about," Richard said.

"Dr. Blasdell discussed the fracture and the concussion, although he didn't say much about the recovery. Should I be concerned?" Anton asked.

"Frankly, yes. You won't be able to walk right away, and you may have some lingering pain in your leg and short-term headaches. I'm truly sorry," Richard said.

Anton sighed. "How long before I can walk?"

"Three to six months."

Anton leaned his head back. "Can I travel back home?"

"Possibly, but I wouldn't recommend it, especially such a strenuous trip. It would be very difficult and risky," Richard said. "You're not, as we say here, out of the woods. However, we do have a plan."

"What plan?" Anton asked.

"First, let me say how grateful I am for what you did. If not for you, it would be me in your place or possibly worse," Richard said. "I feel responsible, and I want to see this through."

"You're not responsible for me, and under the same circumstances I'd do it again."

"Regardless, I want to see you fully recover, and we suggest that you return with us to Minnesota," Richard said. "We have a spacious house that can accommodate you, and I'll hire a nursing staff that can assist you until you can walk on your own."

Anton paused for a moment, turning to Alejandra. "I don't want to put you and your family out like this. Do you agree?"

Alejandra turned to Richard, who nodded, confirming his decision. "Yes. And even if you could travel to Berlin, things are dicey there. What if you needed additional medical care? How would that work, considering what happened back in August with the SS officers?"

"I'd forgotten about that," Richard said. "Another good reason to stay until you're completely recovered."

"I only accept if I'm allowed to pay for my expenses. This plan is truly an incredibly generous offer, and I'm extremely grateful to you both," Anton said.

"Naturally, if that's what you want," Richard said. "It's me who's grateful."

SONATA IN C MAJOR NO. 1 OP. 12

Anton, wearing black trousers and a gray pullover, sat in a wheelchair in the guest bedroom of the Morrison residence, reading the newspaper. The bedroom was appointed with a single bed, two nightstands and a silk brocade armchair. They had arrived the previous night, after traveling by train for almost three days. He had not slept well, and despite his convalescing condition, he was glad to be there and away from everything he loathed back in Berlin. He looked out of the window at the rain. Birds chirped, but he could not see them. The newly cut lawn looked astoundingly green, and the tiny white flowers of a magnolia reminded him that beauty could still prevail in the world. He felt strangely comfortable and looked forward to the months he would spend there.

That morning Millie brought breakfast to his room, but now it was nearly noon when he heard a knock on the door. "Come in." A middle-aged woman with graying hair, a pale face, and a full-bodied figure, entered. "Mr. Everhardt, I am Gerda Nilsson, and I'll be your nurse. Mrs. Morrison would like to invite you to join her for lunch."

"Yes, I'd like that," he said, putting the newspaper on the nightstand. Gerda wheeled him through the hallway and into the dining room, which was painted in soft yellow tones. Alejandra appeared wearing a navy-blue suit and said, "I can take it from here." She positioned the wheelchair at the end of a polished dining table and poured him a glass of iced tea.

"Thank you," he said to the nurse as she left. He looked at Alejandra and asked, "Is she Swedish?"

A little coldly, Alejandra replied, "American."

From several platters on the sideboard, Alejandra filled two plates with green salad and spaghetti and placed them on the table. "I hope you like it. We're big on Italian food here," she said and sat next to him. "I'm going to the market before I pick up the children from school. So please write a list of anything you may need."

Anton took his napkin and placed it on his lap. "I hope I won't be too much of a burden."

"No. We just want you to get better. How was your first night?"

"I can't complain about the accommodations. The room's décor is lovely and comfortable. Although to tell you the truth, I didn't sleep much."

"Oh?" she said.

"I'm not sure if I should rejoice at my misfortune," he said. "I've been thinking about everything that has transpired, and I need to confess something to you. Before leaving Berlin, I said to myself I'd give anything to maintain a connection to you."

"Anton, please. This is going to be challenging as it is. You must know, it was my intent that we'd never see each other again, and I only agreed to this because Richard insisted. Let's be friends and devote our energy to getting you back on your feet."

"Of course. Please forgive me, but it just seemed that divine intervention led me here. But why should I deserve such kindness from you and your family? It's beyond anything I could expect. I won't talk about it again."

"I've asked myself similar questions," she said. "I do find it curious that many years ago, Richard intervened in a similar fashion, preventing a child from being hit by a vehicle. My father too had an accident, injuring his leg, although in his case it was from a fall. God works in mysterious ways."

"Your husband is a gentleman, and he has earned all my respect," Anton said.

"Indeed he is. I love him, and I'd never hurt him," she said. "Were you able to contact your associate this morning? What's his name again?"

"Frederick Huntsman. He told me I had nothing to worry about. I'm not sure how much I can trust him, but I don't have a choice. On the other hand, this will give me the opportunity to see how things might work if I decide to relocate my business to the United States."

He started eating his salad, looking at Alejandra from the corner of his eye. He had never noticed before how she ate with delicate bites. Her pink and supple lips moved slowly. It was going to be so difficult being near her every day and not express his feelings. He would do his best to suppress them and be the perfect gentleman.

"I was wondering if you'd like me to borrow a violin from one of my friends. It would give you something else to do," she said. "You're going to have a lot of free time."

"I was thinking the same thing. I should have mine shipped. When do you rehearse... in the mornings?"

"Yes. Every day at ten, but you don't have to follow my schedule."

"Perhaps you'll allow me to play with you sometimes once or twice a week," he said.

"I don't see why not," she said. "And why don't you select the music on those days. You'll find a huge selection of manuscripts on the bookshelf in the drawing room."

"At what time do your children get home from school?"

"At two thirty, and be prepared because it can get quite hectic."

"I'll try my best to stay out of their way," he said, playfully.

"You don't need to do that unless you want to," she said. "They'll get used to you. The question is, can you get used to them with all the commotion after being alone all your life?"

"I might miss the silence, but for now I enjoy the company," he said. "I'm looking forward to meeting them."

She finished her meal. "I have to go soon, but feel free to do as you please. The porch is the best spot to be in the house, and it's especially pleasant for reading or simply looking out at the cyclists and walkers who circle the lake every day. Just be glad you're here through spring and summer and not winter."

"That's fortunate," Anton said.

Alejandra picked up his empty plate and placed it back on the sideboard. "I'll get Gerda for you, and be sure to pronounce her name correctly. I hear she's quite the general and very meticulous about her work." She laughed. "And probably a good thing if you're to get on your feet soon."

"Just what I need, right?" He too laughed.

"I'll see you for dinner," Alejandra said.

After two weeks, Anton had settled into a comfortable daily routine. Gerda worked from nine in the morning to seven in the evening. She was responsible for health related and housekeeping chores. He preferred to have breakfast in his room, lunch with Alejandra on most days, and for dinner, he always joined the rest of the Morrison family. He thought the children were smart and extremely well behaved, except for the boy who required more attention. Anton had found something in common with him, and despite the fact he never had any family of his own, he liked being around them.

According to the physician, one of Richard's partners, his leg was healing well enough that he might start walking with crutches shortly. With assistance from Gerda, he spent considerable time every day in physical therapy, working on strengthening the muscles of his leg. Most of the bruises on the rest of his body had disappeared.

On the second of May, Anton heard Alejandra practicing the piano. Listening to her every morning was something he relished. It was probably the first time in his life that he didn't feel lonely. He heard the doorbell ring. With both Millie and Gerda gone, he attempted to get up on his own to open the door and took his crutch, but feeling light-headed, he fell, feeling excruciating pain in his leg. With his bedroom only a few feet away from the foyer, moments later, he heard Alejandra speaking to the postman who was delivering a large package. Soon after, she knocked on his door. "Anton, your violin is here. May I come in?" He tried again to get up from the floor but let out a loud groan. Instantly, Alejandra came into the room. "Oh my goodness, what happened?" He replied, "I think I might have injured my leg again. I thought I could walk with crutches, but I felt dizzy and lost my balance."

With considerable effort and care, Alejandra helped him get back to bed. His leg, affixed with rods, had not required a cast, but there was a risk of hardware irritation on the muscles and tendons or misalignment of the broken bones. He leaned back and stretched his legs.

"It was so stupid of me," he said.

She covered him with a blanket and fixed the pillows behind his back. "Don't be too hard on yourself." Then she picked up the crutch, placing it in the far corner of the room. "Can I get you anything?"

"Another injection of morphine would feel good just about now," he said. From a tray in the nightstand, he took a syringe and an ampule of morphine and injected himself in the arm. She poured a glass of water for him. "I hope you didn't do damage to your leg. You should rest."

"Please stay and read to me. That will distract me," he said, handing her *Brave New World* by Aldous Huxley.

Seated next to him, she opened the book where the bookmark was and read aloud.

"Art, science–you seem to have paid a fairly high price for your happiness," said the Savage, when they were alone. "Anything else?"

"Well, religion, of course," replied the Controller. "There used to be something called God–before the Nine Years' War. But I was forgetting; you know all about God, I suppose."

"Well ..." The Savage hesitated. He would have liked to say something about solitude, about night, about the mesa lying pale under the moon, about the precipice, the plunge into shadowy darkness, about death. He would have liked to speak, but there were no words. Not even in Shakespeare...

Feeling sedated by the medication, he closed his eyes. When she finished reading from the chapter, she put the book away and caressed his forehead with the back of her fingers. Instinctively, he grabbed her hand and kissed it. She quickly pulled her hand away. "I thought you were sleeping," she said.

"I was until I felt your warm touch," he said.

"Go back to sleep," she said and left.

$\mathbf{B}$efore ten the next day, Anton was in the drawing room waiting for Alejandra to begin their practice together. Seated in the wheelchair, he moved around the room noticing several paintings, including a family portrait above the fireplace. Then something else caught his attention next to a stunning Beethoven painting—a framed musical score. He wheeled himself closer to it and carefully analyzed a signed manuscript of Beethoven's "Moonlight Sonata." How in the world did she acquire such a manuscript? Was it genuine? And if so, what was its provenance?

Then Alejandra arrived wearing a mint-green knit dress with her hair up in a chignon, looking like a school teacher ready for her first lesson. "Are you're feeling better today? Richard said you didn't do any harm to your leg, but that you should be careful."

"Yes. Richard scolded me," Anton said.

"He wants to see you get well. That's all."

"I'm not so sure I want to get well after yesterday morning," he said.

"Oh, that! Don't read too much into it. So I slipped, and you noticed. But it was merely a small gesture of compassion after seeing you in such pain." She laughed, walking to the piano.

"Only compassion?"

"Yes. Can't I care about the well-being of a friend?" she asked, now sounding annoyed. "Are we going to play or not?"

He felt embarrassed for having stepped over the boundaries. "I thought we'd start with Beethoven's sonatas for piano and violin. Can you please hand over the violin?"

She nodded, giving him the violin and bow. She took the manuscripts, placing his part on the music stand and taking the piano part with her.

"I'm curious about your framed manuscript," he said.

"That was a gift from a friend."

"Do you know how she got it?"

"It was a wedding gift from Franz Wensing. He and his twin sister are longtime friends. We were inseparable in our teens. Their parents immigrated from Germany in the early 1900s. You might meet them on Mother's Day. He'd probably know the answer."

"You know that manuscript is worth a small fortune," he said. "One of my collectors would love to get his hands on it."

"It's not for sale, but is he the same collector you have often talked about? Anonymous?"

"Yes, as a matter of fact. You remember?"

"I'm starting to think he's a figment of your imagination. What ever happened to his exhibition?"

He laughed. "I assure you he's very real and a bit of a cad. He's still busy acquiring pieces. He's also interested in various works owned by private collectors in the States. I'm working with Hannah on a couple of paintings."

"Is he planning on revealing his true identity? I'd love to meet him someday," she said.

"That's a good question, and I'll be sure to ask next time I see him."

Alejandra turned to the manuscript before her and read the title aloud: "Sonata in C Major no. 1, op. 12. Is there any particular reason why you chose this piece? You never do anything randomly." She smiled.

"I recalled your desire to live at a time when salon music prevailed. Beethoven's sonatas were created to bridge the worlds of the salon and the concert hall. Perhaps it will also help us to bridge our two worlds, as well."

"What two worlds?" she asked.

"Our inner and outer worlds," he said.

Ignoring the remark, she signaled the first beat of the sonata.

He put all his concentration into playing and couldn't help but wonder if her affectionate gesture on his forehead the previous day meant she loved him a little. She'd probably deny it for the rest of her life. But what did it matter? For now, he was next to her, and through the music he would express his love to her. That's all he could do. They played in such harmony as if they had been playing together all their lives. The cadence of melodious notes flowed between them, and he sensed their joined existence where no prose or poetry was uttered or needed.

HUNGARIAN DANCE NO. 5 IN G MINOR

Standing before a marble table in the hallway and dressed in a laced, beige, ankle-length dress, Alejandra placed a dozen white roses in a crystal vase. From that vantage point, straight ahead into the drawing room, she could see family and friends gathered for a Mother's Day celebration. She was overjoyed to see many whom she had not seen in more than a year, including her closest friends during adolescence—cousin Stephen Johnson, his wife Olga, and her twin brother Franz Wensing. Franz, whom she had almost married before dating Richard, had an aspiration to own a theater company. In the end, she broke off the engagement, and Franz moved to London to pursue his profession. He was married thereafter, but years later he divorced and had no children.

Richie practiced violin in the library. Anton was coaching the boy, as he had done for the last few weeks, with unexpected dedication. As a result, her son had taken a greater interest in music, improving impressively in that short period. Anton's daily attention had also made a positive improvement in her son's overall attitude. The unlikely pair had bonded so well that when her son came home from school he went straight to Anton.

As she entered the library, she asked, "Are you ready to entertain us, my sweet boy?"

"Yes, Mommy, but why won't he play with me?"

"Because you're ready to play on your own," Anton said. "You've made real progress."

"Your father and I are so proud of you," Alejandra added, kissing her son on the head. "The family is all waiting for you. Shall we go?"

Richie rushed out of the library, holding his violin and bow.

Anton stood up on his good leg, took his crutches, and walked out of the library alongside Alejandra. Upon reaching the drawing room, she introduced Anton to Franz Wensing, a blond, blue-eyed thirty-four-year-old. "How wonderful you're visiting. I think you and Anton will find many things in common, poetry for sure."

"Pleasure to make your acquaintance," Anton said to Franz, shaking his hand.

"Likewise," Franz said, turning to Alejandra. "Congratulations. Olga told me you have finally realized your dream of being a conductor."

"Not quite. I'm working on it. I understand congratulations are in order for you as well. I heard you now own a theater company specializing in Shakespeare."

"I guess we both now have everything we wanted, don't we." Franz said.

"Yes, we do," Alejandra said.

Olga Johnson, a redhead with a voluptuous figure, interrupted their conversation. "And who is your friend, Ále?" she asked, looking at Anton from head to toe.

"Anton Everhardt, meet Olga Johnson, twin sister of Franz," Alejandra said. "She has a lovely voice and has agreed to be in the choir that I'm forming. It's good to see you again, and your children are as energetic as I remember." Olga had four children who were running around the room.

Anton said, "*Es freut mich, Sie kennenzulemen.*"

"Oh, a compatriot, how delightful. The pleasure is all mine," Olga said. "Perhaps you can bring Anton for lunch at my house. I'm sure he'd love to hear about our youthful indiscretions."

Alejandra laughed. "I'm sure he would."

Anton turned to Franz. "So tell me about the provenance of Alejandra's Beethoven manuscript. It was a gift from you, I understand."

"Indeed," Franz said. "Let me just say it was a family heirloom. If you ever visit London, you can inquire about its history from my uncle who procured it from a collector in Germany."

"I know the story well," Olga said. "Uncle Hanz told me years ago. It's a long one, so why don't you come over tomorrow," she suggested.

"Yes, if Alejandra can drive me there," Anton said.

"And if she can't, I'll pick you up. It would be no bother."

Alejandra noticed Olga was impressed with Anton, and she was going to find every excuse in the book to spend time with him. As far as Alejandra was concerned, that was fine, so long as she didn't discover anything about their complicated friendship. That was the last thing Alejandra wanted. Olga had a way of not only making trouble for herself but for other people with her busy-bodying.

"Since you're all introduced, I'm going to excuse myself. My children have been working hard to entertain us, and I see Del waving. Please enjoy," Alejandra said.

A few minutes later, the rest of the family, now in the drawing room, waited for the recital to begin. Alejandra sat next to Richard who took her hand. "I remembered how sullen the children were last year in your absence, but today they're thrilled to impress you."

"I know. They're adorable. Del wants to be the next Shirley Temple."

"Since I took her to see *Kid Hollywood*, that's all she talks about," Richard said. "Although, I'm not sure I'd be in favor of that kind of public exposure at such a young age."

"I agree, but there's no harm in her singing for us."

Alejandra glanced at all the guests who were now seated. How odd, she thought, that at this particular time both Anton and Franz were there, along with her husband Richard. Each one of them had played a significant role during parts of her life, teaching her lessons about friendship, dreams, disappointment, love, and about herself. She thought about the personal choices she had made of which none exist in a vacuum, for inevitably they are linked to experiences and reactions with others. Now that she could see everyone and everything with a clear perspective, she was thankful and certain she had chosen the best path for her life.

Soon after, Leidy, her eight-year-old daughter, wearing a pink cotton dress, made her appearance on the makeshift stage next to the piano. "Happy Mother's Day, Mommy, Grandma, and Aunt Olga. For our first act, my sister will sing 'Baby Take a Bow.'" Everyone applauded as Del, the youngest, stepped on stage in a ruffled yellow dress. She bowed and with her big voice sang, "*Nobody gave me a mention until they saw me with you. Paid me a bit of attention until they saw me with you...*"

As her young daughter performed, Alejandra was overcome with emotion as she looked at each one of her children in turn, considering their individual temperaments, personalities, and talents. Perhaps she had been too focused on her goals to see that everything she needed to be happy was right

234

here at home, just as her mother had said. Had she been selfish? Would she need to sacrifice her professional ambitions in order to nurture those of her children?

When Del had finished singing, she ran to Alejandra, her face aglow and framed by dangling curls. "Mommy, did you like it?"

"Did I ever," Alejandra said as she picked her up, sitting her on her lap. "That was astonishing." The girl giggled.

Then Richie, with his golden locks and supreme confidence, came in. Dressed in a crisp white shirt with short pants and suspenders, he lifted his head high before placing the violin under his chin. Then, taking a bow, he played Mozart's "Eine Kleine Nachtmusik," the first movement. Despite a few errors at the beginning, Alejandra thought he showed real promise. He not only played well technically, but also appeared to enjoy himself. Previously when she had heard him playing it was mechanical, just going through the motions. But this time, he played the composition as though he was one with the music. After almost four minutes, his performance came to a conclusion. Everyone applauded, and he too rushed to his parents.

"My goodness how did you ever get so good?" Richard said, patting him on the head.

Richie raised his eyebrows mischievously, grinning and pointing to Anton.

"That deserves a big kiss on the cheek," Alejandra said, hugging the boy. "I can see you and your sister playing together in the future. Would you like that?"

"No, Mommy. I want to play with you," Richie said.

"I'd be honored," Alejandra said.

Then Richard whispered in Alejandra's ear. "You know, I never thought I'd say this, but Anton has behaved respectably. I had my doubts, but he's a good man. I'm especially pleased with how well he has gotten along with our son."

Alejandra nodded, thinking Anton had indeed accomplished something significant. She turned to Anton with unspoken appreciation. He tipped his head, smiling.

Then Leidy addressed the audience one more time. "The next piece is for my mother who's my favorite musician," she said. Then she sat at the piano and played Brahms' "Hungarian Dance no. 5." Alejandra became teary-eyed as the music reminded her of an incident the previous fall when her daughter had stubbornly refused to play the piano for one month. Leidy, who dreaded practicing scales, had decided the effort was not worth her time. One day, Alejandra told Leidy that playing a musical instrument was a privilege that required dedication. She gave her a challenge—if Leidy learned to play the Brahms' composition in its entirety with perfection, she would never be asked to play another piece and could make her own choice of continuing or ending piano lessons. Leidy accepted the challenge even though it was a difficult piece. Not only did she learn it, but it made her understand that perhaps she did possess the talent to someday be a concert pianist, and as her mother always told her, music was a gift to be shared with others.

As Leidy continued to play, Alejandra realized that by being a consummate musician herself she had taught her children to believe in their natural aptitudes and had given them a reason to dream.

When the recital ended, Alejandra invited everyone to lunch in the dining room. Olga walked to Alejandra who was collecting empty glasses and putting them on a tray. "That was very impressive," she said. "Your children are very talented."

"Yes," Alejandra said. "Thank you."

"Perhaps now you'll be inclined to stay home like a good mother and nurture that talent," Olga said.

Alejandra, surprised by her unkind but truthful remark, was used to Olga's often harsh comments, but she knew she meant well, so she replied, "I was thinking about that too. Maybe it's time for me to slow down."

Then Anton joined the conversation. "Slow down? Now that you've accomplished so much? I don't think so. I've spent a lot of time with your son, and he's fascinated by his piano playing mother who's starting a choir. And I'm sure your two daughters feel the same way."

Alejandra noticed Olga looking at Anton. "And how did you two meet?" Olga asked.

"My dear, you're always so inquisitive. That's what I love about you. Perhaps you remember my friend, Hannah. We all met at an auction."

"I'm looking forward to hearing more about it tomorrow," Olga said. "Anton has agreed to come over for lunch."

"How unfortunate. I can't. Several singers are auditioning for the choir," Alejandra said.

"Then I'll be happy to pick you up, Anton," Olga said.

"That's nice of you, but we can wait until Alejandra is available," Anton said.

"I'll call you later," Alejandra said. "I might even have dates for our first rehearsal."

"As you wish," Olga said. "But for now, come with me, Anton. I want to hear all about your art dealing business, and I'll tell you about the provenance of that manuscript."

"You're trouble, aren't you, Olga?" Anton said, laughing.

"Absolutely," Olga said.

Alejandra laughed, glad that Anton would turn his attentions to one of her friends. The two walked away.

I'LL BE GOOD BECAUSE OF YOU

July 6, 1934

With a view of Lake of the Isles, Anton, wearing sunglasses, off-white slacks, a loose white shirt, and slip-on moccasins, was seated in his favorite wicker chair on the terrace under a canopy. Nearly three months had transpired since he arrived in Minneapolis, known for its long winters and fickle weather. But for Anton, it was paradise. For despite lingering pain and a difficult struggle to walk again without crutches, he was grateful for the opportunity to have experienced a different kind of life, free to speak openly about anything, to dream and never live in fear—the kind of freedom most people take for granted. It was a life he would choose if he could, but for now, circumstances dictated he must return home to an unknown future and to a place where he no longer felt he belonged. Amidst those thoughts, he recalled every moment shared with Alejandra, even if from a distance. It was always the thought of being near her that gave him a reason to get out of bed each morning. He knew almost everything about her—how she walked, how she laughed, and what she liked and didn't like. Day by day, as she and others nursed him back to health, he had become a changed man. He closed his eyes, replaying in his mind the words to a new and catchy popular song that he had been listening to on the radio that morning. *"The very thought of you and I forget to do the little ordinary things that everyone ought to do. I'm living in a kind of daydream. I'm happy as a king, and foolish though it may seem, to me that's everything, the mere idea of you. I see your face in every flower, your eyes in stars above. It's just the thought of you…"*

Without realizing it, he began to whistle the melody as Alejandra, dressed in a sleeveless, floral, pale-yellow dress and sandals, appeared on the terrace. "What's that you're whistling?"

"Some tune I can't get out of my head," he said.

"Are you ready for your walk?" she asked, squinting. She then took a pair of white-rimmed sunglasses from her pocket.

"Another beautiful day. I'm going to miss everything about this house, the terrace, and especially the view," he said, looking at her.

"Even domestic life?"

"A glamorous life may sound good, but it's not real. A domestic life on the other hand, puts everything into perspective, and that's where our best experiences reside," he said.

"We certainly have shared that. And it's true. If not at the piano, I'm the happiest when I can be with the family out here or at the lake house."

He slowly stood up, taking his black cane, but almost lost his balance.

"Be careful!" she said, holding on to him. "We don't want to see you start over."

"Don't worry," Anton said. "But who cares if I did start over. It would be better than what comes next."

"We've been through this topic many times. Cheer up. You're just going to go back, close shop, and move to New York. Right?"

"If it were only that easy," he said.

They walked down a few steps onto a path, passing a fountain with brown and turquoise tile work and a mermaid sculpture.

"Let's take it slow," she said. They exited the yard through a wrought iron fence, steering toward the right side. Walking along the concrete pathway, several feet from the shoreline, he noticed the trees now in full bloom.

"I could see myself living here rather than New York. I now understand why so many other Germans immigrated here. And I'm not sure which lake, of the few I've seen, is the most scenic, but I think the lake where you have your cottage may be the one. It was so peaceful."

"It was once a prime destination for East Coast travelers at the turn of the century. At its height of popularity, there were dozens of hotels."

"What was the name of it again?"

"Lake Minnetonka," she said. "Great water in Dakota language. How soon do you expect to move to New York?"

"I don't know. I have to see how things are back home. From my communications with Frederick, it seems that business is booming."

They came to a wooden bench surrounded by big maples, providing shade from the hot sun. Before sitting down, he placed the cane on the bench at his side as he looked toward an abandoned Lutheran church across the street. "Wasn't that the church you were hoping to use for your rehearsals?" Anton asked.

"Yes, I was hoping to rent one of their rooms, but the congregation recently disbanded," Alejandra said. "A few of the choir members belonged there and told me they had financial problems. Even the pipe organ was sold off. I'll find another place, but this would have been ideal so close to home."

"Yes, I remember Gerda talking about it. It was her church. I'm going to miss her daily orders and wicked sense of humor."

"You needed her. She's sorry to see you go. I think she has a crush on you," she said.

"I suppose everything comes to an end sooner or later. This is one of those times I wish I had faith in something, because I fear for the future."

"I can empathize with that, but you have options… remember that."

"I have to tell you something, because we might not get another chance to be alone. In just a couple of hours we say goodbye," he said. "These last three months have been the happiest of my life. You and your family have taken me in as one of your own. I had no concept of what it was to be part of a family, but I do now. I leave knowing that even though there can never be romantic love between us, there's love of a different kind. I'll carry it with me forever. I'll always be grateful to you and Richard for your kindness and patience during my recovery."

"There were some challenges, but Richard was right to insist you stayed with us. I think he might just be a little fond of you too, now that he's more at ease with our friendship. He'll definitely miss his chess partner. I never thought I'd see the two of you bond over nightly chess games and a glass of scotch. We have all enjoyed your company, and I'll miss our morning ritual of playing together. It has been so gratifying to have someone around who shares that passion. You understand that side of me. Your input and help in choosing singers for my choir was invaluable. You weren't the only one who benefited from this unpredictable arrangement."

"When do you expect to have your first choral concert?" he asked.

"I'm hoping by Christmas. It's a start of something promising. We'll have our first rehearsal in the fall once the children are back to school. They'll miss you, especially Richie."

"I'll miss them too. I'll try to visit once a year if that's acceptable to you. I don't think I'll be able to return in the fall for Hannah and Ben's baby naming but count on a visit next year if I haven't moved to New York by then."

"She'll understand. I hope you'll be yourself in no time and the pain soon vanishes. But please do be careful. I don't think it will be safe for you in Berlin as things are now."

He placed his hand on hers. "I can handle it. I'm stronger than I look."

"You don't sound too convincing."

"I'll never be like my old self again," he said.

"You've changed?"

"I don't think one can change one's core character, but we can change our views and attitudes," he said.

"What do you mean?"

"I do think it possible now to do things for a greater purpose, and to not always act purely out of self-interest," he said. "You and Richard have taught me that."

Tears fell on her cheek. "I'm sorry to be so sentimental, but I've been holding back all these months, and now that you're leaving I'm sad," she said.

"Does this mean you love me a little?" he asked with a smile.

She wiped her eyes. "Yes, I do, as one of my dearest friends. Please take good care of yourself and find your happiness. A good start would be a wife and family. You deserve that. But know we'll always be here for you."

"That fills my heart with love more than you can imagine. And you promise to not return my letters this time?"

"Yes. Those were different times. We're in a better place now. We've changed. You and Richard are friends too. It's really a happy ending for all of us, if you think about it," she said.

"It's not the happy ending I want, but I'll take it," he said. "May I kiss you goodbye on the cheek?"

She nodded.

He placed his lips on her soft skin for a brief moment, but a memory of a lifetime. "Until we meet again," Anton said.

PART
TWO

AS TIME GOES BY

December 17, 1937

Internationally, the balance of power was increasingly fragile. With the rise of fascism and Nazism, new conflicts were on the horizon. Italy withdrew from the League of Nations, and Spain was in the midst of a civil war. The distrust between communism and capitalism had become more intense in the dialogue and actions of politicians from the Soviet Union and the United States. Franklin D. Roosevelt had been sworn in for his second term in January of 1937.

Considering world affairs, which were pointing to a second war, or so it was rumored, national news reported that Roosevelt was hesitant for America to be involved in the political affairs of Europe. That may have given Alejandra a false sense of reassurance, but it was preferable to the thought of entering into another disastrous world war. However, having lived in Europe and experiencing first-hand the policies of foreign nations, she was acutely aware and worried about the potential impact on neighboring countries.

In other national developments was the unprecedented news that Howard Hughes had made a record flight from Los Angeles to New York City, lasting less than eight hours. But Amelia Earhart had disappeared over the Pacific Ocean after attempting to be the first woman to complete a flight around the world.

Fortunately, women were making considerable progress in the music profession. Alejandra was living in a time when female orchestras were prevalent and where other women were making significant strides as conductors. Women's orchestras and ensembles had grown incrementally in the United States and Europe in the years following the Roaring Twenties. Among the best gender-exclusive orchestras were the Los Angeles Women's Orchestra and the Chicago Women's Symphony Orchestra. Antonia Brico had been appointed conductor of the Women's Symphony Orchestra with the support of the first lady, Eleanor Roosevelt, in 1934. Ethel Leginska secured many engagements with European and American orchestras, establishing the National Women's Symphony Orchestra in New York in 1931. Gena Branscombe established the Branscombe Chorale in 1934. Other notable women conductors included Eva Anderson, D'Zama Muriele, and Nadia Boulanger, the first woman to conduct the London Philharmonic Orchestra in 1936.

And now on this her thirty-fifth birthday, while not keen on celebrating her day, Alejandra was grateful to have been able to break down barriers in her profession. Despite prevailing attitudes about female conductors, she overcame prejudices and stereotypes with determination and skill in the art of conducting. She had continued with her studies and had established herself among orchestral musicians as someone to be trusted because of her knowledge of music, leadership skills, and respect for others in the same position. In the last two years, she had participated as guest choral and symphonic conductor of various orchestras, many of which were exclusively composed of women. And to add to her accomplishment, after a year of trial and error, she had established her twenty-four voice Opus Dei Chorale. The chorus served as a model in featuring the music of women and men alike, whose work was neglected or forgotten. And through her choral programs, she had endeavored to showcase the contributions of female pioneers and the music of women whose creativity, talent, and dedication were of historical significance. The partial list of past luminary composers included Hildegard von Bingen, Beatriz de Dia, Gaspara Stampa, Lucrezia Orsina Vizzana, Princess Wilhelmine of Prussia, Maria Anna Walburga Ignatia Mozart, Isabella Colbran, and Sophia Dellaporta.

Alejandra was at a point in her life where everything in her professional career and personal life was as harmonious as the polyphonic voices of her twenty-four-voice chorus. Seated at her desk in the library of her home, she was finishing the program notes for her upcoming Christmas concert that would showcase "Madre, La de Los Primores," a choral piece composed by the seventeenth century Mexican poet Sor Juana Inéz de la Cruz, who was also considered the first published author in the new world. Next came "T'amo mia vita," by Vittoria Aleotti, "Chant," by Ruth Crawford Seeger, "The Lord's my Shepherd," by Jessie Seymour Irvine, "Two Sacred Works for Treble Voices," by Maria Francesca Nascinbeni, and "Drei Gemischten Chöre," by Clara Schumann.

Richard came into the room. "Happy birthday, my dear," he said, leaning over to kiss her. She thought that Richard had made a full circle, for not only did he support her endeavors, but he also accompanied her on guest conducting appearances throughout the States, despite the fact that he was busier than ever in his medical practice. "Thank you for the roses," she said, embracing him.

"Oh my," he said. "So affectionate, are we? What are you writing about?"

"I thought I'd dedicate the Christmas program to women composers," Alejandra replied. "And I'm also writing a historical perspective on women's accomplishments in conducting."

Richard smiled.

"I know that expression. What do you have up your sleeve?" she asked.

He leaned on the desk. "Well, I have one more surprise for you," he said. "Hannah was hoping to be here today, but she was delayed and will arrive tomorrow in the afternoon, instead."

"What? Are you serious? Splendid," Alejandra said.

"She wanted it to be a surprise, but I thought you'd like to know. She's traveling as we speak," he said.

"I have so much to do to prepare," she said. "I also promised to take the children sledding after school." She then looked out the window, noticing it was snowing heavily. "They'll be disappointed if they don't go."

"Why don't I take them to choose the Christmas tree, and you take care of whatever you need to do before Hannah's arrival. We'll keep our plan to have dinner at your mother's."

"That sounds terrific," she said.

They were soon interrupted by their children's voices as they came running into the library after arriving home from school.

"Mommy, Mommy, happy birthday," Del said. "And Daddy, you're home early."

Alejandra bent over to kiss her youngest daughter who was now seven years old. Her son, Richie, now nine, gave Alejandra a handmade ornament in the shape of a star with her name and the year 1937 carved on it. "Happy birthday."

"Here, Mommy, for you." Leidy, her twelve-year-old daughter, handed her a card. "But don't read it until later."

"Thank you, my darlings. I baked your favorite, apple crisp," Alejandra said, directing them to the kitchen to wash their hands.

"Guess what you're doing later on," Richard said.

"Sledding," Richie said.

"No. Even better, you're helping me to choose a Christmas tree," he said.

"Oh, goody," Del said. As Richard picked her up, she laughed.

"And I want to help with the ornaments," Del said.

"Of course, I wouldn't think of doing that without you," Alejandra said.

An hour later, after Richard and the children had left in search of a Christmas tree, Alejandra, with Millie's help, brought to the drawing room several boxes filled with Christmas decorations. Before starting to unpack them, she took the birthday card from Leidy and read it.

*D*ear Mommy, Happy Birthday. Yesterday I liked being there with you at the rehearsal. I really like to *hear* all those people singing, and some-day I want to be like you directing my own choir. But first I want to learn how to hold that baton, will you teach me soon? And one more thing, I love you. Leidy.

Moved by her daughter's words, Alejandra felt blessed that each of her children had continued with their musical studies. All three had taken roles in activities relating to the chorus, but it was Leidy who nearly always accompanied her to rehearsals, where she obviously was not only learning, but enjoying the experience.

Then as she started emptying the boxes with decorations, she came across the music box Anton had given her years before. In a moment of sweet remembrance, she opened it and let the melody carry her back in time. As she recalled, "In Dulci Jubilo," in sweet rejoicing, was a fourteenth-century composition that had become a favorite German Christmas carol since the day the manuscript was discovered in Leipzig University's library. She thought of Anton, who seemed to have fallen off the face of the earth. They had maintained contact for the first two years since 1934 when he returned home. But they had not seen each other in more than three years. In his last letter, dated August 1, 1936, Anton expressed deepening concern that the German army had occupied the Rhineland in March, undermining the peace treaty of Versailles of 1919. He was alarmed that his country was preparing for war. She followed with a reply, but all her letters went unanswered. Had he made a new life for himself elsewhere? She hoped so.

At ten that night Alejandra and Richard retired to their bedroom. It was painted in a warm gray, accentuated by art deco paintings in whites and yellows. Two nightstand lamps softly illuminated a gray, leather tufted headboard and a bed covered with a silk, beige bedspread. The flickering light from the wood burning in the fireplace gave the room a radiant golden glow. A 1931 recording of Rudy Vallee was playing on a portable wind-up-gramophone—"*...the fundamental things apply, as time goes by. A kiss is just a kiss; a sigh is just a sigh. And lovers still say I love you. No matter what the future brings...*"

In a seating area off the bedroom, they relaxed on a swan fainting couch upholstered in brocade jacquard fabric.

"Did you have a good birthday?" Richard asked.

"How could I not? This year has been the best. I have everything I've ever wanted," she said. "Is it possible to be this happy? Sometimes I'm afraid of it."

"Hush," Richard said, placing his index finger on her lips. "Why shouldn't we be? You may recall it wasn't always this perfect. I too had my doubts, but now that we have finally come to this point in our lives, let's enjoy it." Then, from the side table, he took a small box wrapped in sparkly silver paper with a pink ribbon and gave it to her.

She unwrapped it and found a box holding a pink sapphire pendant in cobblestone design. "It's gorgeous!"

"Now, this is just my opinion, but I think it would look better if you put it on with nothing underneath," he said.

"Ulterior motives I see. A seduction, complete with background music and all your charms." He put the pendant around her neck and kissed her again.

She stood, turning toward him as she slowly unbuttoned her fuchsia silk dress until it fell to the floor. As he also undressed, bringing her closer to him, he said, "Are you ready to play me like a fiddle?"

She laughed. "As you wish, my lord."

"I'm yours to do with as you please, my bewitching angel," he murmured.

CONCERTO FOR PIANO AND ORCHESTRA NO. 4

Setting up tea service in the drawing room, Alejandra, wearing a burgundy dress, placed a platter of cookies and small cakes on the cocktail table. Lydia, in a light-brown suit, followed with a tray containing a silver-plated teapot, cups, creamer, sugar, and utensils. Hannah and her son, Joseph, were in the guest room.

"I haven't seen your friend in years," Lydia said.

"Wait until you see her son... he's adorable. He looks just like Ben," Alejandra said, noticing a silver angel ornament that had fallen to the floor. She picked it up and placed the ornament at the center of the Christmas tree, fixing a ribbon.

Lydia filled the cups with mint tea. "And Ben?"

"He's in Vienna," Alejandra replied just as Hannah, in a green wool suit, entered the room. Right behind her, a three-year-old boy followed, dressed in long pants and a red sweater. He ran in toward the tree and started playing with the colorful ornaments.

Rubbing her hands, Hannah said, "Mrs. Stanford, so lovely to see you again."

Lydia embraced Hannah. "You haven't changed a bit. Still as pretty and perky as I remember. And so this is Joseph. He does look like Ben, but with curly hair."

Alejandra picked up the boy with big brown eyes and kissed him on the cheek. "And how's my favorite godson?" she said, noticing the Star of David hanging from his neck.

The boy giggled. "Cookie, cookie," he said, reaching down toward the platter on the table. Alejandra grabbed a ginger cookie and gave it to him. Then she put him down, and the little boy started running around the table with the cookie in his hand.

"This is how he is all day, running in circles. I think he turned out to be more like me than his father," Hannah said. "Maybe Millie can take him for a little while so we can talk."

"Sure. Come, Ben," Alejandra said, holding his hand. Millie came into the room, holding a platter of small sandwiches and placed them on the table. "Millie, please take him to Richie."

"You want to see a puppy?" Millie asked, taking the boy with her.

Alejandra sat next to Hannah, giving her the cup and saucer. Lydia took her cup, sitting across from them. Taking an aniseed ball from one of the plates, Hannah said, "You know sweets are my weakness, and I'm afraid I've put on a few extra pounds since my pregnancy that I've not been able to shed. How did you do it?"

"Starving myself," Alejandra replied.

"And how was your birthday?" Hannah asked.

"Terrific and even better now that you're here. But what about you? How's your father? We've been concerned about his condition since your last letter."

"He's stable, though very frail. He sends his regards. As I mentioned, he's been homebound since he was diagnosed with advanced emphysema. My mother is there along with staff around the clock."

"I'm so sorry to hear that," Lydia said. "It must be difficult for someone who was always so active."

"Indeed. Our lives have changed. I hate seeing him deteriorate like this," Hannah said. "He's even lost interest in most of his previous social pleasures, especially having morning coffee with his buddies. His grandson is the only person that brings him joy."

Alejandra took a sip of her tea. "And how's Ben?"

"Good, I suppose. But I'm in a bit of a quandary. He's been begging me to go to Vienna since last summer," Hannah replied. "He loves his job, opera day and night, and finding a conducting position with the Mozart Orchestra was something he always wanted. But I told him I didn't want to leave New York again. Europe is becoming more unstable."

"Yes, that's what I've heard. Isn't Ben concerned?" Alejandra asked.

"Not in Vienna. He likes it there very much." Hannah sighed. "And I feel terribly guilty. His son misses him too. It's not fair to keep them apart for so long. This situation has created hardship for us. I'm not sure what I should do or whether I can even go."

"What's preventing you from going there, besides not wanting to?" Alejandra asked.

"The gallery needs an interim manager. Obviously, my father is no longer able to carry out the duties of such an enterprise, and I've been doing so up to now." Hannah turned to Lydia. "So my father, knowing I was coming to visit, suggested that I ask you to consider taking the job either temporarily or permanently if you're interested."

"Me?" Lydia asked, stunned.

"Yes, Mrs. Stanford, you'd be ideal. My father has been an ardent supporter of your work for years. After all, you studied art at the Sorbonne in Paris, you have the experience, and you're a trusted friend," Hannah said. "Not to mention you also speak French and Spanish fluently."

"It's true, Mother. Not only did you open the Stanford Gallery but also administered it to great success. If it wasn't for the depression, it might still be open," Alejandra said.

"Those were other times. It was a way for me to deal with your father's passing. That was ten years ago. In the past, I've entertained the idea of returning to the profession. It's a fabulous opportunity, but I'm not so sure how I'd deal with living in New York so far away from my daughter and grandchildren, although it would allow me to see my son more often. As you may know, he lives in Milford, Connecticut."

"Yes, of course, your younger brother," Hannah said to Alejandra.

"I was an only child for fifteen years," Alejandra said. "And I'm sure Eddy feels that way now, so he'd love to have his mother close by for a change."

"We have a furnished apartment in Manhattan that we have used in the past for out-of-town clients. It would be yours, should you accept." Then Hannah handed her a sealed envelope. "This contains the terms of the position. Please let me know if you have questions."

"Mother, ever since Father died, you've been dedicated to us. It's not too late for you to start a new life. You're as vital as ever, and if I remember correctly, you always wanted to live someplace other than Minnesota. Well, this is your chance," Alejandra said.

Lydia nodded in agreement and took the envelope.

"Give me a couple of days to think about it. I need to excuse myself, as I have a meeting with some friends at the museum for an upcoming exhibition."

"Yes," Hannah said, standing up. She hugged Lydia. "It was a pleasure to see you again."

"We'll see you later for dinner," Lydia said before leaving.

"I do hope she accepts. She still has so much energy. I'd miss her, though," Alejandra said. "And I wouldn't mind if she'd find someone. She's been lonely since Father died."

"She'd be terrific, and she seems to be in fantastic shape too," Hannah said, sitting.

"I agree," Alejandra said, placing her hand on Hannah's. "When you arrived, you mentioned that Ben had seen Anton last fall. Where? And how is he? I've written but haven't heard from him in more than a year."

"There's a good reason for that," Hannah said.

Alejandra leaned forward, concerned.

"Well, first off, he's been living in Vienna for some time. I don't know if it's an ongoing pain in his leg, but he's fallen on hard times. From what Ben tells me, not financially."

"Then what?" Alejandra asked.

"His health. He's addicted to morphine, and he didn't want you to know."

"Richard warned me of that possibility," Alejandra said. "That's terrible news. What else can you tell me? Has he had any treatment?"

"I don't know anything more. There's not much we can do but pray that he finds a way out of that hole," Hannah said.

"Perhaps there is, if you end up going to Vienna," Alejandra said.

"It might help if you write him a letter. I can deliver it in person, if I go," Hannah said. "We're the closest he has to family. So we must try. But everything has to fall into place. But don't worry too much. It wasn't my intention to bring unpleasant news. You know he always seems to pull through no matter what happens to him."

"I was hoping by now he had found a wife, maybe even have children," Alejandra said. "It does make me sad. I'll be praying for him. And if you decide to go, please be careful."

"I assure you that I'm not planning on staying there for as long as I did last time, not when my father is ill," Hannah said. "My real motive is to convince Ben to come back home. Somewhere deep inside of him, he thinks he should be the one supporting us and not the other way around. He's very old-fashioned that way. Back in New York he gave violin lessons, but that was never too rewarding either. He has to understand that what good is having an income versus not having a family by his side."

"Ben is reasonable. I'm sure he'll also come to that conclusion," Alejandra said, placing her arm around Hannah's shoulders. "Now, let's go upstairs and see what our children are up to."

"I'm sure my Joseph is up to no good," Hannah said. "Although, I like that he knows what he wants."

Over a month had passed since Hannah had gone back to New York, but Alejandra had stayed in touch with Hannah, who had decided to return to Vienna in a couple of weeks. She had a written a letter to Anton, and Alejandra planned to give it to her mother who had accepted the position as manager of the Mendes Gallery in New York. Lydia was expected to leave in three days.

On this night, Alejandra and Lydia were seated in the fourth row of Cyrus Northrop Memorial Auditorium, waiting for a concert to begin. As the home of the Minneapolis Symphony Orchestra, it was located in the heart of the University of Minnesota campus. The venue, with a proscenium arch in classical revival style, could accommodate over 4,800 attendees, and it was filled. An Aeolian-Skinner pipe organ, the second largest in the Midwest, served as a backdrop to the stage. Since its founding in 1903, the orchestra had become one of the best in the country. As part of Alejandra's continued training, she had often attended rehearsals under the baton of the orchestra's current conductor, Greek-born Dimitri Mitropoulos, who was a composer and a prominent force in conducting Mahler's work and operatic repertoire. Mitropoulos also had the distinction of working for the Berlin State Opera, and as a pianist he had performed with the Berlin Philharmonic. With a prodigious mind, he memorized the scores, never using a baton. A thin man with deep eyes and shaved head, he not only looked like a monk but had almost become one. Though deeply religious, he instead devoted his life to music.

Alejandra, while feeling nostalgic about Lydia moving to New York, was happy that she had stayed to see her favorite pianist—Polish-born, Arthur Rubinstein, who shared her affinity toward Spanish and Latin American composers including Granados, de Falla, Albéniz, and Villalobos after he toured through Spain and Latin America. Alejandra had met Rubinstein that morning for rehearsal and had the opportunity to also celebrate his fiftieth birthday with him. He took every performance as living in the moment, and he had said he wanted to risk, to dare, and to enjoy the concert more than the audience.

Then Lydia said, "It's a shame the organ will not be in use tonight. I love that sound. I have very fond memories of visiting with your father in London, listening to Bach's music at church. Did Beethoven ever compose anything for the organ?"

"Oh, Mother. That seems like a lifetime away. Yes, Beethoven wrote one solo, Fugue in D Major," Alejandra replied. "You'll not be disappointed tonight as Rubinstein is described by critics as a virtuoso pianist with a rare talent. He'll be playing a Beethoven solo. And when I heard it this morning I thought it was incredibly spiritual."

"On another note, are you all right? You seem a little preoccupied with something else."

"To tell you the truth I have mixed feelings about you going," she said. "But, it will be wonderful for you. I'm worried about Hannah and Ben, and Anton too. He's not doing so well."

"I'm sorry to hear that. I'm kind of surprised Hannah decided to go. She seemed adamant about never going back," Lydia said. "As for me, my dear, I'm a little nervous but content to start a new life. Your brother is thrilled. He'll pick me up at the station and then have dinner."

"That's marvelous, Mother. I wish I could see him more often. Now Richard and I will have more reasons to go to New York," Alejandra said.

"That would be lovely," Lydia said.

Then Alejandra turned to the program, and as she leafed through the pages, with great surprise she noticed that the next guest soloist to appear on stage with the Minneapolis Symphony Orchestra, on February 24, was none other than Jascha Heifetz—Anton's favorite violinist. How strange that Heifetz would be performing in Minneapolis of all the places in the world, just as she had learned of Anton's whereabouts. Since December, she had not stopped thinking about Anton and his health problems. Not that she was superstitious, but it seemed a remarkable coincidence. Was it a sign? But what could she do when she was thousands of miles away? Maybe she couldn't do much, but she hoped her letter and Hannah's intervention would make a difference.

Then, Arthur Rubinstein finally stepped on stage. He took his seat at the piano and began to perform the long solo part of Beethoven's *Concerto no. 4.* When the full orchestra joined in, revealing a reflective melody infused with a kind of deep spirituality for which Beethoven was known, she listened to the grand opus—music interpreted as someone trapped in hell daring to look up, seeking the light. Perhaps, upon hearing it again, she could not help but imagine Anton being such a person trapped in hell and waiting for absolution.

It was nearly eleven o'clock when she returned home. Richard was already sleeping, but she could not go to bed until she wrote another letter to Anton. The one she had written, weeks before, seemed too formal and devoid of the emotions she was now feeling. Alejandra went to the library and under the light of a desk lamp, she took pen to paper and wrote:

January 28, 1938. Dear Anton: A new day is almost upon us, and as you begin your day, I hope life will show you kindness. It is my wish that this letter will find its way to you to remind you how much your friends care for you. We've just returned from a concert featuring Beethoven's Concerto No. 4, and as I listened to the music so filled with hope and tender love, I could not help but think of you. Love of the kind that wants to see a newborn smile, or feel the touch of an aging parent who can't remember names or prayers, or to hear of a friend's troubles. The kind of universal love that is unspoken but is always there inside us with every beat of our heart.

I don't know all the details or circumstances that led to your current predicaments but know we would like to help you if you let us. Please don't hesitate for a second to reach out to us with whatever it is you need. There's a solution to every problem and a way out of every difficulty. I know you have the strength to confront it, especially with a little help.

You once told me, "You can't play great music unless your heart is broken," and now, I say to you, you can't play great music if your heart stops beating. So let us hear once more the sound of your sweet vibrato and spirited staccato as your hand and bow play upon those strings that sing your favorite Mozart melodies. We will be praying for you and wishing you a speedy recovery my dearest friend. -Alejandra.

She placed her hand on her heart and hoped that Hannah and Ben would come to his aid and make a positive change in his life. Although, her intuition told her otherwise, and with an emerging sense of angst, she placed the letter in an envelope and sealed it. Would their efforts be too late? She closed her eyes and envisioned the last time she had seen Anton. Would she see him again? "Oh God, please make it so," she said under her breath.

THINE BE THE GLORY

T he melody and words of the hymn "Thine Be the Glory" by George Frideric Handel and Edmond Budry resonated loftily around her as the chorus sang *"Shall I still fear? He lives forever. He is my Victory, my Reliance, my Life and my Glory. No. I fear nothing!"*

Alejandra was standing before a podium, inside a small church with stained glass windows, directing her choral ensemble composed of twelve women and twelve men, who varied in age from twenty to fifty. Dressed in a white and black ensemble, they rehearsed for the upcoming concert on Good Friday that would take place at Lady of Lourdes Catholic Church. With its soaring spires, the sanctuary, high on a hill and overlooking St. Anthony Falls, was built in the late nineteenth century, making it the oldest church in Minneapolis. It sat on the east bank of the Mississippi riverfront.

She was suddenly interrupted by the secretary, Lauren. "Mrs. Morrison, your mother's on the phone. She says it's urgent. You can take the call in my office."

Her mother, Lydia, who was managing the Mendes Gallery, had only been in New York for two months. And according to her mother everything was going smoothly. So what was the emergency? She never called in the middle of rehearsals. Realizing it was almost lunchtime, Alejandra said to her chorus, "Why don't we call it a day? Thank you for coming. I'll see you tomorrow at the same time. Please excuse me."

The chorus began dispersing toward the entrance, and Alejandra made her way into the office in the back of the church and closed the door behind her. She quickly dropped the manuscript on a cluttered desk and picked up the telephone receiver.

"Mother, what's the matter?"

Hannah, Ben, and Joseph were missing. Two weeks before, on March 12, the Third Reich had annexed Austria. The Anschluss, as it had been termed and reported worldwide in the media, had created a panic among its population after the Nazi administration instituted anti-Jewish policies, expelling Jewish citizens from any cultural, economic or social life. Her friends were supposed to have left in early March, but there had been no word from them since March tenth. Terrified by her mother's information, she took her handbag and coat and left the church.

Two hours later, from her home, Alejandra spoke with Mr. Mendes, Hannah's father, who implored her to telegram Anton, as he might be helpful in finding them or knowing their whereabouts. According to Mr. Mendes, Hannah had been in touch with Anton before their expected departure from Vienna.

At the desk in her library, she began to write a draft of the telegram, but then ceased as she recalled news that reported that Nazi officials opened every correspondence that came in within their region of influence, and Austria was under their total control. She could not directly allude in the telegram to her missing friends, but she needed to come up with an excuse that would not raise any suspicion. After careful consideration, she wrote:

March 29, 1938. Dear Anton: Urgent business proposition. Beethoven signed manuscript. Friends unreachable. Call me. Alejandra.

That evening, Alejandra waited in the dining room for Richard to arrive from work. She had served dinner to their children and had sent them to bed. Not wishing to discuss the matter over the telephone, she was anxious to talk to her husband. As soon as she heard his footsteps, she met him in the foyer. "Hello, darling," she said, taking his coat.

"What's for dinner?" he asked. "Something smells awfully good."

"Scalloped oysters with pickled beets and mashed rutabaga turnip," she said.

"So what's the delicate matter you wanted to discuss?"

"Perhaps you should eat dinner first," she replied.

"By your demeanor, I can tell something is obviously wrong, and I don't think that I can eat knowing you're upset," he said.

They both walked to the dining room already set for dinner and sat next to each other.

She momentarily closed her eyes. "Hannah, Ben, and their son are missing. They were supposed to have left Vienna weeks ago, and they should have arrived in New York by now."

"Maybe they're just in transit somewhere without a means of communicating. I don't think you need to worry. They're American," he said. "They can surely go to any embassy."

"You would think so. I'm glad mother is with Hannah's parents. I spoke with Mr. Mendes earlier today, and he suggested I telegram Anton."

"But we haven't heard from him in more than a year," Richard said.

"When Hannah was here she told me Ben had seen him," Alejandra said. "He lives in Vienna, now." For the moment, she decided to withhold the information about Anton's addiction, for she did not want her husband to feel responsible in any way. She hoped Anton was in better condition, but she could not be sure.

"I see. You sent him a telegram, then?"

"Earlier today."

"I hope you were careful in what you wrote," he said. "Things are pretty messy there right now. Where did you send it?"

"To his last known address in Vienna."

"What do you think he can do?"

"I don't know, but he can certainly do more there than we can here," she replied.

"I guess we can only wait," Richard said. "Try not to worry. I'm sure they're fine."

"Mr. Mendes was beside himself when I spoke with him. I hope you're right. Let me get your dinner."

The following Saturday, in early afternoon, Alejandra was reading to her youngest daughter in the drawing room when Richard came in and gave her an envelope. "I think this is the response you've been waiting for," he said. "You go on. I'll stay with Del."

"Mommy, what about the story?"

"Your dad will finish it, sweetie," Alejandra said, as she left the room.

In the library, she tore the envelope, pulled out the telegram, and read.

April 2, 1938. I managed to send this telegram from outside Vienna. I guess this might have to do with our friends. I have powerful connections if someone else can take the lead. I'm gravely ill. You know where to reach me. Love, Anton.

259

Disheartened, she sank into the leather chair thinking of her options. First, she could wait and let things develop, hoping that by a miraculous turn of events her friends showed up in New York. However, the more time that elapsed, the more dire the situation. Their families were unable to travel for health and other reasons. Anton was gravely ill. As a last resort, might she have to consider going herself since she knew the area and spoke the language? Mr. Mendes had pleaded with her to do everything in her power to find them. She knew she couldn't live with herself knowing that Hannah and her family were in danger, and she had done nothing. However, Alejandra knew Richard would never approve. She left the library and returned to her husband and daughter. "Sweetie, please go upstairs to your room. I need to speak to Daddy."

"Yes, Mommy," the girl said, running out of the room.

Richard put the book down on the side table. "What's the verdict?"

"He can't do it himself, but has connections," she said, sitting next to Richard.

"What do you mean he can't do it himself?" Richard asked.

She clasped her hands. "I didn't want to tell you before, and I don't know exactly how severe Anton's condition is, but he's been incapacitated due to morphine addiction. I had hoped that Hannah and Ben would have helped him with treatment, but that was before current concerns. He said he was gravely ill. Could he die?"

"Of an overdose, sure," Richard said.

"Naturally, I was hoping for another answer," Alejandra said.

"I was afraid something like that might happen, which is why I had insisted he not take prolonged narcotics. Why can't Mr. Mendes hire someone to go there on his behalf? Has he been in touch with the embassy?"

"Yes. They don't have any information, and the staff is overwhelmed with thousands of requests and reports of missing persons. He attempted to hire someone, with no success."

"Oh, Ále, I'm so sorry. I feel terrible about the situation, and I can understand how you must feel," he said. "You have to remain hopeful that they're going to be all right as there's not much we can do. As for Anton, he'll find his way. He loves life too much to just let it slip away."

She paused. "There's something I can do," she said, finally.

He looked at her, reading her thoughts. "Absolutely not! I know what you're thinking, and it's crazy and out of the question!"

"Do I ignore Mr. Mendes' plea? I couldn't live with myself if something happens to them when I could have done something. They're family to me."

"And what about us? Your husband and your children? We need you too. Just the thought of it is madness! You'd be going to what very likely will be a war zone. It's chaos now, and from what I read will soon be hell! Do you know Poland is their next target?"

"I'd go to Vienna to make inquiries and hopefully find them and return in a month."

"Ále, I admire your bravery and good intentions, but it's naïve to think you can pull this off without significant risks. Do you want to leave your children without a mother, and me without a wife? I'll never approve. Never!" He stormed out of the room.

Attending Easter Mass at the Basilica of St. Mary's in Minneapolis, Alejandra and her family, all formally dressed for the occasion, were seated in the back pew of the Renaissance-style cathedral. She listened attentively to the priest as he referenced Philippians 1:27-28, invoking the faithful to… "Lead a life worthy of the gospel so that when I come, I may find that you stand firm, unafraid of any of your opponents. The gospel makes us bold, courageous, and unafraid." The priest's message of courage reinforced the decision she had made the night before. She had resolute faith and was not afraid of whatever may come.

It was a bright spring day with blooming lilac trees all around the church. As she walked through the archways and down the steps of the basilica, holding her two youngest children's hands, she gazed at their innocent smiling faces. "Mommy, are we still going to Grandma's house?" Richie asked. "Yes," she said, turning to Richard and Leidy, who were steps ahead of her, climbing into their Ford. How easy life was here, and she wished it would continue that way. Life was as perfect as it had ever been, but now things had changed. How could she ignore present circumstances and enjoy it knowing Hannah and her family were missing?

Later that evening, Alejandra and Richard were home, but without the children it seemed barren and strangely silent. The children had stayed for the night at their grandmother's house as Lydia had returned to Minnesota to spend Easter with the family.

Alejandra felt consumed with guilt as she had to explain to Richard the most difficult decision of her life. There was already a distance between them since their recent argument, for Richard had purposefully avoided any further discussion on the subject. She gathered herself together and approached her husband, who was reading one of his medical journals in the living room, drinking a glass of scotch. Extending her hand, she said, "Richard, we need to talk."

He sighed and placed his glass on the table next to a bouquet of purple hydrangeas.

Then he squeezed her hand. "Thank you for such a lovely day."

"It was. Mother was so happy to see the children," Alejandra said.

"I'm sorry. I've been difficult the last two weeks, and I just couldn't bear the thought of you leaving us again. It scares me."

"I understand, and I don't blame you. Please don't get angry again, but you know it's something I must do. I've gone over it a thousand times in my head, and it's the best option."

He tensed up again. "No. I'll never understand. Why do you have to sacrifice everything and be a martyr? I'm completely against this!" he said, standing up. "So, you've made up your mind, and I can't stop you?"

She stood up and faced Richard. "I'm not trying to be a martyr. What an awful thing to say. I need to know they're safe. If it were your brother or sister, you'd do the same."

"Are we less important?" he asked, walking away toward the door.

"Of course not. You and the children are my life, but no one here is in danger, thank God. I talked to my mother this afternoon, and like you, she's against it, but she'll stay until my return. I'm sure Mr. Mendes will understand she will not be returning to New York for the time being."

"Of course he will," he said, bitterly.

"Is that all you can say?" she asked, running her fingers over his arm.

"What do you want me to say?" he asked.

"I don't want these to be the last words between us," she said. "I assure you everything will be fine, and I'll be back soon."

He was silent briefly, then said, "Ále, you can't make that promise... no one can."

"You're right. I can't, but I need to know you'll be here when I come back."

"How could I not? You're everything to me. So if you go, I'm going with you," he said.

She took both his hands. "Under other circumstances, I'd accept, but as you've said, there's a risk. I don't think it wise for both of us to go, leaving our children without a parent during such perilous times. I'm the one who speaks German and has some connections. I need to know the children have you, should something happen to me. That would give me courage."

Richard took a deep breath. "I don't want you to go, but since you insist, I'll make provisions for you to be met by an Augustinian canon. He can arrange for you to stay at a guesthouse in Vienna or close to the Klosterneuburg Monastery. Being connected to an affiliate of the Catholic Church will offer protection, even though the clergy aren't safe anymore."

"It's clear you've been preparing for this all along," she said.

"I'd hoped it wouldn't come to this, but you're too stubborn and loyal to your friends, so I knew nothing I said would dissuade you. I decided to check into several prospects last week."

"Thank you. If by June I have no news, I'll return. I love you."

"Just keep me informed often and promise that you won't take any unnecessary risks."

"I promise and don't be afraid," she said. "Because I'm not."

"Oh, Ále. Sometimes I wish you *were* afraid," he said, embracing her with all his love.

TOCCATA AND FUGUE IN D MINOR

*A*pril 26, 1938 – Vienna, Austria

*A*t a few minutes past nine in the morning, Alejandra left a private residence affiliated with the Augustine Order located in the Landstrasse, third district, near Stadpark. The neighborhood, known as Vienna's diplomatic quarter, was surrounded by churches, monuments, and palaces. It was one of the oldest sections of the city, rich in imperial history. Alejandra was more grateful than ever that Richard had made all the arrangements before she departed the United States.

The night before, a man in his forties, Nicholas Kroberger, a canon of the order, met her at the train station. As such, he was mild mannered, quiet, and someone who could be trusted to assist her with the investigation during her planned month stay in Vienna.

Walking through the park, dressed in a striped white blouse, a cardigan white jacket, and black pants, she noted the numerous statues of Vienna's legendary composers. Then in the distance, her view shifted to Prince Eugene Savoy's Belvedere Palace. Five years earlier, she had visited the palace in the company of Hannah, Ben, and Anton. She remembered it was a time of peace and harmony, but that was before the Nazis came into power. Now another country was part of the Third Reich and plagued by offensive displays of swastikas, inhibiting the city's natural beauty. The whole concept symbolized by the equilateral cross of good existence had been turned on its head, now symbolizing the exact opposite—an abhorrent ideology that led to appalling conditions for many of the city's citizens. The air seemed heavy, and even the Danube could not wash away the growing moral decay of hundreds of uniformed men who wandered the streets, spreading distrust and fear, determined to wipe out any vestige of non-Aryan existence.

After exiting the park, she turned onto Landstrasser Hauptsstrasse, noting it was a busy section of town where rows of vehicles, stuck in traffic, sounded off on their horns. People walked about, heading for work, ignoring a group of SA men with barking Labradors that were sniffing for prey. She quickly moved out of their way, stopping at a newsstand from where she observed them accosting a passerby for no apparent reason—something she would have to, unfortunately, ignore.

Glancing at the directions she had written on a piece of paper, she realized Anton's address was now only two blocks away. She continued for another block until she spotted Erdbergstrasse, where she turned left. Walking a short distance, she reached an old brownstone building and entered the four-story apartment complex.

Her heart beat quickly, and she feared what she might encounter. To help calm herself, she took the elevator up to the third-floor apartment rather than climb the steps that she would normally prefer. Minutes later, she was standing outside apartment 3B. She knocked. A young disheveled woman opened the door just enough to peak outside. "Oh! I remember you, but I don't recall your name. Come in," she said. Alejandra recalled her too. She was Isolde Beckman, though now nearly unrecognizable. She seemed to have aged ten years. Her hair, oily and languid, hung down to her shoulders. Her eyes were sunken and without spark, and her complexion had a sickly yellowish hue. Her dress was stained and ripped at the hem.

"Isolde? I'm Alejandra Morrison," she said.

She stepped into the flat and cringed at the living conditions—dirty clothes and dishes were scattered on the floor like discarded wrappers. The furniture was caked in dust and crusted with spilled food. Syringes lay on the floor. Empty bottles of liquid morphine and other pills were scattered about the room. A pungent odor of putrefaction overwhelmed her. "Where's Anton?"

"In the bedroom," Isolde replied, speaking and moving as if in a fog.

Cautiously, Alejandra made her way to the bedroom. The door was half open, but the room was dark, and she could barely make out the shape of a man lying under heavy blankets. As she walked in, she teared up upon seeing Anton, gaunt and in an almost catatonic state. She approached him, placing her hand on his clammy forehead. His chest was barely moving, and his breathing was shallow. "Anton, can you hear me?"

He opened his eyes, showing constricted pupils. *"Es tut mir Leid."*

He was sorry, but so was she seeing at him in such deplorable health and living in appalling conditions. This was unexpected, and not only was he gravely ill, he was on the verge of dying. She agreed with Richard, he loved life too much to allow anything like this to happen, so what had caused this change in his character? She wiped her eyes.

"Rest, I'm going to get help," she said.

It was clear, he was in no physical or mental condition to talk, much less help her to find their friends. He needed immediate medical attention, but hospitalization was a risky option. Richard had prepared her for this scenario. The reality was much worse than feared. Where to find a trusted physician would be a challenge.

Alejandra went to Isolde, who was in the filthy kitchen chewing on a piece of bread over the sink. "How long has he been like this?" she asked.

"For several days... I don't remember. He'll get better for a while, and then he'll be like this again, but this is the worst I've seen him."

"Are you using drugs too?"

"Here and there, although no morphine."

"Are you living here?"

"No. I just come for the day, buy groceries, make him meals, and tidy up the place."

Alejandra frowned.

Embarrassed, Isolde continued, "I only clean up after him when he vomits or whatever else comes out of his body."

She felt sympathy for the young woman, who seemed to have been caring for Anton for a long time. "You must be exhausted and could use a break," Alejandra said.

"I can handle it," Isolde said. "Is he going to be all right?"

"I hope so, but he needs urgent medical attention. I'll be back soon with a physician. Please stay until my return," Alejandra said. She then opened the kitchen window to let fresh air in before leaving.

By early afternoon, Alejandra returned accompanied by Dr. Schumann, a man of short stature, bald, with impeccable manners, and in his sixties. Isolde let them in. "Please doctor, follow me," Alejandra said, rushing into the bedroom. The physician examined Anton. He took his pulse and pulled up his eyelids. "If we don't get him into urgency care, I don't think he'll make it through the night. He needs detoxification and treatment."

"Do whatever you need to do. Just get him well again," Alejandra said.

"I'll need assistance moving him out to my clinic. Stay with him until I return," he said.

Alejandra approached Anton and held his hand. "Anton, hang on. You must." Then she accompanied the physician to the door. Isolde was in the sparsely furnished living room, which had now been moderately cleaned. The putrid smell had diminished.

She asked, "Is he going to get better?"

"Yes. We're going to do everything we can," Alejandra said.

"Where are you taking him?" Isolde asked.

"Someplace where he can be treated," Alejandra said.

"I want to go," Isolde said.

Dr. Schuman's clinic was in the Jewish Quarter, and it served predominantly Jewish patients. He had told Alejandra that it was only a matter of time before his clinic was ransacked and shattered like other Jewish establishments. So she did not think it would be a good idea to bring Isolde there at this time and tip off the clinic's location. "Of course, but for the moment he'll have the medical care he needs, and you've been through a lot. It might be more helpful if you can get some rest for now so when he's out of the hospital you can assist in his care and recovery. Can you please pack some of his clothes?"

Isolde nodded. "All right, but I'll be back here tomorrow so you can give me an update."

"Why don't we meet in the evening, say at seven?" Alejandra said.

Isolde left to pack Anton's clothes. She returned with a small suitcase, gave Alejandra an apartment key, and timidly said, "*Auf kurz auf Geld.*"

She reached into her handbag and from her wallet gave Isolde fifty schillings. "*Bitte pass auf dich auf.*"

When she left, Alejandra returned to Anton's bedside. He was unmoving, like a corpse. She leaned over to hear he was still breathing. What happened to the strong man she knew? And what if he didn't make it? "Oh, God, please, don't let him die," she whispered.

Later that afternoon, she was in a small clinic with limited lighting, broken bulbs, paint peeling off the walls, and loose tiles on the floor. Several people waited, looking homeless, as the doctor attended another patient in one of the two private rooms. She wondered whether Anton would have the appropriate care there. Dr. Schumann had said the first three days would be the most critical and grueling for both patient and caregivers. Many times had Anton's life been in jeopardy, yet somehow he had survived. She went into Anton's room and found him on a stretcher. Two older nurses, dressed in white uniforms, were also there. The younger of the two, a petite woman with glasses, hooked him up to an IV, while the other nurse, tall and thin, was closing the stained curtains. "Are you staying for the night?" she asked.

"No," Alejandra said.

Dr. Schumann joined them. "We won't start treatment until he's more stable."

"Is he going to pull through?" Alejandra asked.

"I think so. There's not much you can do now. Go get some rest," the doctor said.

Alejandra walked to Anton's bedside and gently stroked his arm. "Please, Anton, I need you to get better. We're all counting on you. I hope you know how much we care for you. I'll be back early in the morning."

The next day, carrying an orange and yellow Gerbera floral arrangement, she walked into Anton's room. He was sitting up and more alert but trembling all over.

"Ále, it is really you! The physician told me you were here. I could hardly believe it."

"It's good to see you," she said, placing the flower basket on a water-stained nightstand.

"You must be shocked by my pitiful appearance," he said.

"A little," she said.

"I have so much to explain," he said. "I'm so ashamed of myself."

"You can be ashamed later. Has the doctor spoken to you about the treatment?"

"Yes," he said. "It's something I thought about doing a long time ago upon receiving your letter. And I almost did, but I just didn't have the strength to go through it. You'll stay with me, then?"

"What about Hannah and Ben? Have you see them recently?"

"After her initial visit, she never came back."

"My time here is limited, but I hope you'll soon be well enough to help us find Hannah and her family. They're missing. They were supposed to leave Vienna in early March, but there has been no news from them since then. I spoke with Hannah's father last night and still nothing."

"I'm so sorry," he said. "I can't believe everything that's happening. And I don't understand how they could have disappeared. But we'll get to the bottom of this." He sighed and reached out to touch her hand. "Ále, my guardian angel."

"It's not me, I assure you. It's someone up there watching over you," she said.

"Still trying to make a believer out of me?"

"No. That, you'll do on your own," she said. "But for now, you must be strong. I'll see you tomorrow or the next day."

"Must you go?"

"Isolde is waiting for me at the apartment, and she's eager to know your condition. She obviously cares about you. The important thing is that you're in good hands now."

For the next three days, in short intervals, Alejandra watched as Anton was treated for his addiction, causing symptoms so severe she didn't know how he could survive. The first day his cravings and severe anxiety caused him fits of uncontrollable crying. By the second and third days, he suffered from muscle cramps, twitches, chills, nausea, vomiting, and insomnia, as well as dysfunctional breathing and unremitting pain. His relentless craving for morphine could only be stopped by the medical staff, who watched and restrained him twenty-four hours a day, while closely monitoring for possible coronary or pulmonary complications.

She had never witnessed someone going through withdrawal and couldn't imagine it being any worse, but Dr. Schumann assured her the reaction was normal. However, he warned her that after the physical addiction was over, the hard part was only beginning. He must deal with the long-term psychological issues of his addiction and the chronic pain in his leg.

By the fourth day, Alejandra had met with Isolde twice and reassured her he had improved to the point where he might be back home in less than a week.

With the first part of his treatment completed, Alejandra returned to the clinic. As she waited outside his room, her thoughts focused on the long-term recovery. Anton needed someone trustworthy who could provide support and even monitor him on a regular basis. But who?

Dr. Schumann met her outside the door. "You may see him now."

"Thank you for everything you've done," Alejandra said.

Despite the early morning hour, the room was dark, lit only by a ceiling lamp with all broken bulbs except for one. "You made it," she said, pulling a chair next to him. He was very pale and under the cover of ripped blankets, but a smile surfaced. "What day is today?"

"It's very cold here," she said, putting on a black cardigan over a white blouse and gray trousers. "It's Tuesday, May third, and you've been here for five days. How do you feel?"

"Strange. I don't think I've been this alert in months. When can I go?"

"In a couple of days. The doctor wants you to leave with an appetite. He also said your chances of physical recovery from morphine addiction are far better than other drug addictions, but that you must now deal with the psychological component, which is a longer proposition."

Anton sighed. "I've been living in hell and unable to get out."

"How much was the lingering pain in your leg a factor?" she asked.

"A minor one. But how do I begin to deal with this and confess all that has transpired in my life in the last two years?"

"You don't need to confess anything to me. That's in the past, but if you allow me, there's someone you should meet who can help you," she said.

"That's the problem. I've kept everything inside, unwilling to talk to anyone. I trust you, but I'm ashamed of what I've seen and done."

"Don't torment yourself. You don't owe me any explanations. We don't have to talk about this," she said. "Just get well. We must focus on finding Hannah, Ben, and their little one. That's why I'm here, and I fear for them every day that goes by. Who are the powerful connections that you alluded to in the telegram?"

He remained silent for a moment. "It's all tangled up, and I need to tell you what happened. It's been killing me, and you need to know why I fell as low as I did."

The nurse interrupted and gave him several tablets and a glass of water. "This will help to settle your stomach before lunch."

"Thank you," he said. "And please close the door on your way out."

He turned to Alejandra and leaned toward her. "Three years ago, I met the second most powerful man in Germany. Do you know who I'm talking about?"

"Several come to mind, but I'm not sure," she replied.

"His name is Hermann Göring. He was a veteran of the war, and he's now commander-in-chief of the Luftwaffe, the air force. He's also in charge of Germany's economy and building up the country's military might. Next to Hitler, he's the second biggest art collector. That's how I met him. I feared for our future, but never in my wildest dreams did I think that things would go so awry. I admit I was blinded by my own greed."

Anton went on to explain how the Nazis' relentless crusade for purification had made its way into the art scene when they began purging so-called degenerate works or art from museums. They were some of the biggest names in modern art such Picasso, Matisse, Beckman, and others. Their paintings were put up for sale on the open market and sold to the highest bidders to help finance the country's growing military appetite.

After drinking a glass of water, he continued. "And, if that wasn't enough, they now have a wish-list of works of art from all over Europe. Do you know what that means? Their ultimate plan is to invade Europe and plunder from museums and private collections alike. Hitler's ambition is to build the world's greatest museum in Linz, Austria and to own the greatest art ever created. The Anschluss is only the beginning. Once I realized there would be no end to their madness, I felt laden with guilt and shame that I'd participated in this for my own profit. I had falsely convinced myself it was about art taken from museums and that I was somehow saving the art from being destroyed." He paused again. "Everything became shockingly clear when the German Army marched into Austria. That's when I had enough."

"What do you mean?"

"It was unlike anything I'd ever seen before. There has been plundering of hundreds of works of art from private collections. Jewish homes and businesses are being vandalized. I could no longer be a willing participant in their mad scheme."

He sighed, as if unburdened by a great weight. "I had dug myself a deep hole, but rather than stop digging, it was easier to escape into morphine and to forget it all. No amount of wealth could give me peace of mind. With what had happened and what I could see coming, there was no reason to live. Your letter said everything had a solution, but I couldn't see it."

She was speechless.

"You see, you hate me!" he said.

"I don't hate you. But to be clear, did you ever participate in the exchange or sell any looted Jewish property?" she asked.

"No," Anton replied. "But I have to tell you that my associate might have been doing that. I agree that anyone who buys and sells art from these sources is complicit in a terrible crime. It's also true that some works of art were bartered to save Jewish lives."

"Is Frederick handling your auction house?" she asked.

"Yes, and he's probably waiting for me to die. I'm certain he continues to do business with the government and cannot be trusted. He has been a good cover for me, as he has no idea of my anti-Nazi views. So far, I have not joined their political party. He just thinks I'm a sick addict, so I'll have to be very careful as to how I get myself out of this mess."

"What do you plan to do?" she asked.

"First, find Hannah and Ben. Then get the hell out of here," he said. "I'll need to get a visa to enter another country, but I'm told all foreign embassies are flooded with requests, so that could take some time. I was an idiot for not heeding your advice years ago!"

"I've just met someone who can assist you throughout your recovery," she said.

"And who might that be?" Anton asked.

"Nicholas Koberger," she said. "He's a canon regular of the Augustine Order. He was the one who recommended the doctor who has been caring for you."

"How do you even know he can be trusted? You must know everyone is under suspicion, even Catholic priests," he said.

"I know, but he's told me he's a collaborator of Roman Karl Scholz, a canon of the order, who is secretly leading a resistance movement here in Austria," she said. "Obviously, I'm not involved in that, nor do I know when this movement got started. But I'm sure he'll help us in any way he can," Alejandra said.

"I accept! Although, I'm not hopeful they can succeed with their resistance. It's futile."

"Don't say that! You, and he, and everyone has to have hope," she said. She took out a small prayer book with a leather cover from her handbag. "Nicholas gave it to me and said that in times like these, prayer can go a long way to diminish our doubts and anxieties. I know you're not a believer, but I want you to have it. It might help you to get through this."

Anton took the small prayer book and placed it on the nightstand. He smiled. "I guess you expect me to read it too?"

"Naturally. It's not a decorative item." She smiled too.

He extended his hand to hers. "You still love me a little then?"

"Only as a friend," she said, shaking her head.

Rising gracefully in a valley, stood the Stift Klosterneuburg monastery and its twelfth-century abbey that had served for centuries as a center of spiritual life for the Augustinian Order of the Roman Catholic Church. Located in the small town of Klosterneuburg, just kilometers from the Danube River outside the city, the monastery was also the largest and oldest winery in Austria. Within the monastery, five meters below ground, lay the ancient wine cellar.

Inside the expansive basement, outlined by thick brick walls and surrounded by hundreds of oak barrels and dim lighting, Alejandra, Anton, and Nicholas sat around a worn wooden table. Since their first meeting a week before, Nicholas, as the winery operations manager, had suggested the cellar as a preferred location to conduct discussions on their investigation. Alejandra watched as he opened a bottle of Zweigelt Tattendorf. He was a kind man who had a distinctive mole on his chin and a round and rosy face that made him look years younger. By now, as she had discovered, Nicholas was not as serious as he had first appeared, but he had a dry sense of humor that served him well in his dealings with people.

He poured the red wine into the glasses. "I hope you don't mind, but it calms me down a bit," Nicholas said. "A man does not live by prayer alone, especially these days."

"I'm actually more reassured by your weakness for wine than by prayer," Anton said. "I have not always trusted men of the cloth."

Alejandra was glad to see Anton back to his old self, despite still being awfully thin and gaunt. "You see, I said you'd like him," she said to Nicholas.

"You're not the first one to tell me that. In fact, of late I've received many complaints as to why the church doesn't speak out more strongly about what's happening in Germany and Austria. It's a delicate matter as to how we should proceed. Religion is of no use to the Nazis, and we too may be considered enemies of the state. Have you given any consideration to becoming a member of the resistance, Anton?"

"I'm impressed by your commitment, but at the present our attention must be on finding our friends," Anton said. "However, I believe in your cause, and for the time being, you can count on my financial support."

"We appreciate it, but when the time comes, we need to recruit as many members as possible if we want an independent Austria again," Nicholas insisted.

"I managed for years to escape on weekends by having a place in Vienna, thinking I was safe here," Anton said. "Even Chancellor Schuschnigg tried to reassure the people nothing would change, but we were all wrong, including him. He was arrested and taken to Dachau. So yes, I do hope you'll succeed in your efforts."

Alejandra interrupted. "I also hope and pray for that, but a more immediate concern is coming up with a plan to locate Hannah and her family. That's the reason I'm here, and I promised my husband to return by June."

"And two weeks are gone, thanks to me," Anton said.

"You know that's not what I meant. I'm just concerned that the more time passes without hearing from them, the less likely it is we'll find them alive."

"What did you find out from the American embassy?" Anton asked.

"We've been there several times this week, they've checked several lists, and their names didn't come up anywhere," Alejandra said. "We did report them as missing and gave them Nicholas as a contact should they show up on a list or at the embassy."

"The embassy is swamped with visa requests from thousands of people trying to get out," Nicholas said. "They are way behind. And to make things more difficult for these people, they're required to leave everything behind and to also pay a high departure tax. It's just disgusting."

"I also went to the Mexican embassy with the hope that they may be able to help you to get out of here. Perhaps you remember I met Octavio Fuentes, the chargé d'affaires, at the Viennese ball several years ago," Alejandra said to Anton.

"Yes, I do. Did you speak with him?"

"He was very helpful. The Mexican government was the first to protest Germany's annexation of Austria."

She went on to explain that the Mexican diplomat Isidro Fabela made a formal complaint to the League of Nations a few days after the annexation, and that Lazaro Cárdenas, the Mexican president, would meet with Roosevelt and other international delegations at the Evian Conference in France to discuss the Jewish refugee situation. Mexico may support refugees fleeing the Nazis, as well as those fleeing the Spanish Civil War. The Mexican government provided temporary asylum to more than 460 Spanish children in the past year.

"What did you find out on your end?" Alejandra asked Anton.

"From what I've gathered so far, there are two possible scenarios that could explain Hannah and Ben's disappearance. If they left before the Anschluss, we'll have more difficulty finding their whereabouts. If, on the other hand, they were in Vienna when Göring ordered the borders shut, they could have been apprehended along with thousands of others who were sent to Dachau and other places."

Alejandra placed her hands on her face. "Why? They're American."

"They are also Jews, yes? Or just being at the wrong place and at the wrong time," Nicholas said.

"Pardon my impatience, but what's your plan?" Alejandra asked.

"I'll return to Berlin tomorrow evening and select my best work of art to send to Göring as a gift, hoping he'll agree to meet with me," Anton replied.

"What if he refuses?" Nicholas asked.

"He won't as long as he thinks I'm still useful," Anton said. "He's more invested in his own power than anything else."

"And if he does?" Alejandra asked.

"I'll meet with him, and all he'd have to do is pick up the phone and make some inquiries. They are meticulous record-keepers after all. Knowing Ben is an American conductor, he won't have any qualms in having him released, although perhaps at a price."

"I'd like to go with you and make some inquiries at the embassy in Berlin. There's nothing more I can do here," she said. "I can put pressure there too with the time I have left."

"Are you sure?" Anton asked.

She nodded.

"I cannot assure your safety unless you stay with me."

She hesitated at his suggestion. "I must be honest. What if you have a relapse? I couldn't go through that again."

"I do understand, but I assure you that won't happen. I know what it's like to live with an addict. Is that your only concern?" Anton asked.

"Yes, it's not like we haven't lived under the same roof before," she said.

"Well then, it's settled. We leave tomorrow on the ten o'clock train to Berlin."

"And what can I do?" Nicholas asked.

"You've been incredibly helpful, and I appreciate everything you've done in the last weeks," she said. "Just call us if you hear anything from the embassy."

Before leaving the wine cellar, Alejandra asked the priest, "Do you think we could stop at the abbey for a few minutes. Recently, I've taken to prayer, and I'm sure we might need it."

Nicolas glanced at his wristwatch. "You might even hear the organist playing the seventeenth-century instrument. Some say the organ rivals the famed Verdun altar."

"That would be lovely," she said.

A few minutes later, when they arrived at the ancient baroque-style abbey, Alejandra heard the heavenly notes of Toccata and Fugue in D Minor by Johann Sebastian Bach. The organist was practicing the piece for the next day's Mass. The music resonated in the church as if the angels were playing, easing her anxiety. While smelling incense, she looked around the priory and its magnificent imagery filled her spirit with inner peace. She walked to the winged altarpiece with painted panels dating back to the Middle Ages and kneeled before the enameled gold altar. With head bowed, downcast eyes, and hands together, she prayed for her family, the safety of Hannah, Ben, little Joseph Adelman, and for their journey ahead.

VIOLIN CONCERTO IN DE MAJOR OP. 35

Early in the morning, on May ninth, Anton unlocked the door to his house in the Tiergarten district, allowing Alejandra in first, then followed with two suitcases, setting them on the floor. Alejandra said, "The last time I remember being here was with Richard, Hannah, and Ben. That was more than five years ago. Please, tell me our friends are alive." Frowning and looking around the entryway, Anton replied, "Of course they are. We'll find them."

"I couldn't sleep at all last night thinking about them," she said. "In fact, that's all I can think about. Why so much madness around us?"

"Because we're dealing with lunatics with enormous power. And I'm afraid we must prepare for the long haul," he said. "Let me show you to your room. He picked up her suitcase and led her to a guest bedroom where he pushed the door open with his foot and placed her bag by a closet, switching on the lights. "Sorry for the stale smell and mess. As you can see, no one has been here in years." Heavy draperies covered the window, making the room dark. The bed was covered with a brown coverlet. The nightstands and headboard were lined with dust.

"Don't worry about it. I'll clean it up," Alejandra said, opening the window. She took off her coat, dropping it, along with her handbag, on a dusty upholstered chair. "I'm tired."

"If you need anything, remember the kitchen is next to the dining room."

She nodded, and he left.

At noontime, Anton, dressed in gray pants and a white shirt, had just returned from shopping, and he was in the kitchen putting away groceries.

He was trying to be quiet, but he dropped a can and said, "*Scheisse.*" He then set up a small table with a view of the street. He poured a cup of coffee and walked from the kitchen out into a small garden that had been neglected and engulfed by weeds, dead grass, and piles of plant debris. "It's time to sell," he said under his breath. Yet, for the first time in a long time, under a sunny sky, he felt lucky to be alive and grateful to be at home with the only woman he had ever loved. But he was also afraid of relapsing. Eliminating the urge to consume morphine would be a struggle that would require more than a strong will. He didn't care much about anything or anyone, except for Alejandra—so for her he would stay straight. And now that Alejandra was back in his life, he was more convinced than ever it was fate. Hadn't he suffered enough? But how could he be so selfish thinking about Alejandra this way when her friends were missing. He cared for them, and he would give it his all to find them. Life had not been fair to them either.

He came back into the kitchen and found Alejandra leaning on the doorframe. With wet hair falling to her shoulders, no makeup, and wearing a floral dress and oxford shoes, she looked like a woman in her twenties. He noticed her expression was unusually reserved.

"Did I wake you up?" Anton asked.

"Yes, but I'm glad you did. We have work to do," Alejandra said.

"I hope you're hungry." He started stirring potato soup on the stove.

"Yes, and coffee too, please," she said. "Anything I can do?"

"I can manage," he said, giving her a cup of coffee.

"Now that's something I thought I'd never see," she said.

"A cook and a butler all in one? In times like these all pretenses are dropped, and not a bad thing either," Anton said, bringing her a plate with bread, cheese, cold cuts, and fruit.

"What happened to Wellington? That was his name, right?"

"Yes. He went back to England last year. He couldn't abide the foul atmosphere here. He insisted I go with him, but yet here I am," Anton said.

"And your friend Sacha?"

"I haven't spoken with him in two years. He too would rather stay away from here."

He joined her at the table, and for a few minutes they ate their meal quietly, until she said, "I was also thinking about Isolde this morning. Did you see her before we left yesterday? What's to become of her?"

"I told her she could stay in the apartment for as long as she wanted, and

I gave her some money to last for a while. I feel terrible for what I put her through. It wouldn't have been wise, however, to bring her with us. She has many shady acquaintances. Spies might be a better description, but I don't think she realizes that. She's a good person."

"She has a job to support herself?"

"Yes, but one I'd rather not talk about. And you, did you speak with Richard yesterday? He couldn't have been happy knowing you decided to come to Berlin with me."

"Scoundrel, always a scoundrel." She laughed.

"What? Are you trying to offend me, or are you kidding?" he asked.

"A little of both," she said. "Look, you know the only reason I'm here is to find Hannah and her family. I'm so glad you've recovered your health. But there's nothing between us, and Richard knows it. He's aware of our plans, and to be honest, he also thought it would be safer for me to stay with you. He was opposed to me coming on this trip, but now that I'm here he wants us to have answers soon. For goodness sake, wasn't he the one who brought you into our house? Have you forgotten that? He obviously cares about you too."

"You can't cover up the sun with a finger," he said. "Sooner or later, you have to confront your feelings."

"What's that supposed to mean?" she said, upset. "I have faced my emotions. I care for you as a dear friend. Period. So let's cut to the chase. When will you be in touch with Göring?"

"I suppose you're right. With this pitiful appearance in which you found me, I'm no threat to anyone," Anton said. "But you must know that seeing you again brought up a whole bunch of feelings and memories. I'm sorry. I'll do my best to avoid this subject. I have to go and meet with Frederick in a couple of hours. I'm sure he'll be shocked to see me, probably hoping I'm dead. But before I contact Göring, I need your opinion on something."

She nodded.

After they finished their meal, Anton led Alejandra to a large stockroom, connected to the library that was hidden from view and accessed through a door behind a hunting-themed tapestry. Brightly illuminated, the warehouse with wooden floors was filled with paintings, sculptures, porcelains, tapestries, Turkish rugs, carved furniture, decorative arts, and a stuffed leopard. They were neatly arranged on tables and shelves according to the age of the objects, from medieval, Renaissance, and baroque, to Modern. One table included miscellaneous objects—a centerpiece for sorbets with shell tiles, a lidded tankard in ivory, a pair of silk vestments, and a flintlock rifle with a monocle.

Amazed by the assortment and quality of the objects, she said, "Please tell me this collection came from legitimate sources and purchases, and they're not the result of looting."

"Everything you see here was bought some time ago. Although, as I told you before, I cannot promise the same of the other stockroom at the auction house that has been managed by Frederick. I can now say candidly some of the paintings are fakes, and some of my profits came from selling them to Nazis." He grinned.

"You've found a way to rationalize your illicit behavior. And what about Hannah's Rembrandt? Or other trusting clients?" she asked.

"No. I swear hers was legitimate," he said. "I'm not all bad."

"Just a little, ha? That explains why you were never an art collector," Alejandra said.

"I only started selling forgeries of late. But I can't say I'm ashamed, knowing they all went to unscrupulous collectors."

"But what about the objects in the auction house? What will you do with those?"

"I wish they could be returned, but obviously not. There's so much to sort out. Let's first choose the bribe to Göring," he said. "Considering he's a hunter, I was thinking of the flintlock with the monocle. It once belonged to one of the Habsburgs."

Alejandra, holding a large envelope, leaned against a pillar. "Choose whatever will get the job done. There's nothing here that he deserves, except perhaps that hideous stuffed leopard."

"I understand your disgust, but we must be strategic if we wish to locate the Adelmans."

She sighed. "If Göring is an art connoisseur as you've said, what could you possibly give him that would pique his interest enough to see you? He has access to everything he'd ever want. Perhaps it should be something else?"

"Like what? He likes Dutch cigars and gold bullion," Anton said sarcastically.

"Something so German and historically significant that he could not reject it," Alejandra said. "Like the first edition of Kant's *Kritik der reinen Vernunft* or *Die Methaphysik der Sitten*. I noticed them in your library."

"He might throw the *Metaphysics of Morals* straight in my face and wonder if I was just a smart ass."

"Maybe he needs a large dose of pure reason," Alejandra said. "I'm glad you still have a sense of humor. You've mentioned many times that one of your clients has an extensive collection of original manuscripts by German composers, so another possibility could be an original or signed copy of a Beethoven manuscript if you can get your hands on it."

"Such as?" he asked.

"Two come to mind... the symphony "Eroica" or the opera *Fidelio*, Alejandra said. "As to the first option, there's a copy of the score in which Napoleon's name was scratched out after Beethoven became disillusioned with him when he proclaimed himself emperor. The second, *Fidelio*, is a story of sacrifice, freedom, and heroism inspired by the French Revolution."

Anton's face lit up. "Yes, that might be ideal. Your instincts are right on. Not only is Göring an opera afficionado and considers himself to be a man of high culture, but as Minister of the Interior of Prussia, the Berlin State Opera falls under his jurisdiction. No question, he'd be intrigued by such a unique gift."

"Do you have access to an original?" she asked.

"I think so. But I might need to barter for it. I should go, but stay here as long as you like."

"No. I've seen enough," she said. "But before you leave, I want to give you my signed Beethoven manuscript of "Moonlight Sonata." You said it could be worth a princely sum. If you can use it in any way with your collector as part of a trade for a more valuable piece, or as funding for the investigation, please do as you see most appropriate." She handed him the letter-size envelope.

"I thought this had significant sentimental value for you," he said.

"It does, but so long as Hannah and her two men are missing, it's irrelevant," she said.

"I can assure you that this will definitely be helpful in my negotiations," he said.

That evening, Alejandra was in the living room writing a letter to Richard when Anton joined her. "This place looks so much better," he said.

"No more filthy dust covers and floors," she said.

"You've been cleaning all afternoon? I was expecting to see you playing."

"Yes. I did sit at the piano earlier today, extremely out of tune, but there was something eerie about being here alone, recalling Hannah playing the cello that night and Ben turning the pages as I played."

"It might have been more than five years ago when we met, but I remember it as if it was yesterday. That was when I first fell under your spell," Anton said.

"Please, Anton," she said. "If you don't stop this nonsense, I don't care how dangerous it might be, I'll move into a hotel."

"Can you even understand how hard this might be for me?" he asked.

"I do. You're coming off a series of terrible circumstances, but can we go back to where we were the summer of 1934? Loving friends?"

"No. I don't think I can. I'm at a different place," Anton said. "But for the sake of Hannah and Ben, I'll do everything in my power to accomplish what you came here to do, to find them and bring them home safely. I'll abstain from expressing any of my feelings."

"So, I have your word? I don't want to spend whatever time I have left arguing with you. My friends are all that matters to me right now," Alejandra said.

"I promise," he said, walking up to a console table behind the sofa. From a tray, he took a bottle of brandy and poured himself a glass. "I need a drink or two. It's been too tense lately. Would you like one?"

"Yes," she said. "How was your meeting with Frederick?"

Anton gave Alejandra her drink. She was standing by the glass étagère containing more than a dozen violins.

"He was surprised to see me," Anton said. "But it was me who was more stunned after seeing our other art depository practically empty. At first, I thought he had stolen the funds from the sales, and I'm sure he did a little, but I was on time to transfer the remaining monies to my private account. Had I been gone longer, I have no doubt he'd have embezzled everything."

"And did he say anything about where the art came from?" she asked.

"They were mostly acquisitions from private sellers and through several auctions, but I saw no point in asking their provenance. The art is gone," he said. "You don't trust me, do you?"

"I'm not sure," she said.

"Ále, I've made some bad choices, but please know, I'll never do anything to hurt you. I've shared with you things I've never told anyone. But just so there are no more secrets, I'll tell you everything about my early life."

"You don't need to do that," she said. "But I'm curious about your violins and how you came to collect so many. Why? I had heard other violinists play different ones depending on the music, but not you. You only play the Stradivarius."

"It's a long story. But come and sit by me. You're not afraid of me?" he asked, sitting at the end of the sofa. "I hope you'll learn to trust me."

She joined him. "All right."

He went on to detail his family history, his father's murder, and how he came to work for Leo Steinhoff at an antique musical shop after inheriting his father's Stradivarius.

"I suspected something like that," she said. "And you never found your mother?"

"I discovered where she lived, but unfortunately, she died before I could ever meet her."

"That must have been heartbreaking," she added.

"It left a permanent hole in my heart," he said.

A brief silence fell between them.

"Back to the story of the violins," he said. "The arrangement between Leo and myself was perfect for the first few years I worked for him until the day I came home from school, and my father's violin was gone. I confronted Leo, but he refused to say what he'd done with it. I was distraught for days. I demanded that he return the violin as it was all I had left from my father. Leo finally confessed to selling it and said he couldn't return the money, as he had lost it to gambling. A week later, he signed over the title of his business to me, insisting it would be safer in my hands, although still less valuable than my violin. I accepted of course. We continued to live and work together until he died. He was a good man after all, and I'm thankful as he gave me shelter and work when no one else would. Over the next years, I went to every music shop in search of my father's violin, buying one for every time I did not find his. Don't ask why because I don't have a reasonable explanation. Then finally in 1930, I found it at an auction and was able to buy it back. As you've noticed, it's now the only violin I play."

"How did you know it was your father's?"

"I never trusted Leo, so as a preventive measure I carefully carved a tiny mark with the letter E onto the scroll of the instrument. Of course, the brown color of the wood, the sound, and the case was also confirmatory."

"That's a sweet and strange story," she said. Then she removed the Stradivarius and brought it to him. "Will you please play for me the music you selected when you recovered your father's violin?"

He took his father's violin and bow from her hands, slightly brushing her hand and said, "I haven't played for months, so forgive me if I'm rusty."

"It doesn't matter. I want to hear you play again," she said.

As he serenaded her with the solo from the Violin Concerto in D Major op. 35, by Pyotr Ilyich Tchaikovsky, he thought so what if she didn't reciprocate his love. She may place an emotional distance between them, but he knew she loved him a little, and that was good enough for him. She was there in the flesh, listening to him, and trusting him like no one ever had. He was feeling high, playing on that old Stradivarius for the woman who had given him yet another chance at life. Like countless times before, the music would have to be his vehicle to express his feelings for her. And that made him sane, made him real, and made him good.

SONATA NO. 15, OP. 28

In the middle of the night, Alejandra woke up feeling agitated, with images of Nazis pillaging Jewish homes and businesses, as well as images of works of art she had seen in the stockroom the previous afternoon. Of course, it was just a nightmare, but she couldn't abandon the feeling that there was more to what Anton had told her. He was a man of many contradictions. He was ambitious yet unassuming, strong yet weak, generous yet greedy, and sometimes even a bit too sure of himself. But she believed that at his core he was a man with a noble heart and good intentions who often made bad choices as he struggled to find his compass in life. She needed to be sure, and so she must go back to the storeroom to find proof he had told her the truth about the provenance and purchase of those goods.

She put on her robe and tiptoed to the library, lit only by light emanating from an outside street lamp. She lifted the tapestry, opened the door, and stepped into the warehouse, turning on the ceiling light. She looked around thinking about what Anton had said about the frenzy of Nazi collectors who acquired works of art obsessively for their personal gratification and aggrandizement. It seemed to her they were placing more value on art objects than real people. That was ironic, since many of the paintings often portrayed images of virgins and gods in heavenly landscapes, as if by owning and viewing those works, their sins could be forgiven and forgotten.

She felt so upset at the idea of looting. She felt she must verify that nothing in the stockroom had been acquired by those repulsive means. On the far right side she spotted several metal file cabinets. When she reached them, she pulled out the top drawer containing files. She took one at random and found a record of the transactions of a Monet painting bought in 1924 and sold in 1926, then a Modigliani painting sold in 1929, a Rodin sculpture in 1929, a Beethoven bust in 1930, and so on. The records were all cataloged by dates, so she looked for the files from 1933 where she found the record of the Rembrandt painting sold to Hannah Adelman. She scanned the original acquisition date and its provenance. Anton had bought it in 1925 from a Klaus Van de Berg. Then, she saw the file for Picasso's *Girl before Mirror* sold in 1933 to a Günther Kaiser. A Raphael altar piece sold to Sacha Korsakov, his Russian friend. A Michelangelo drawing sold to Thomas Walker, Van Gogh's *Olive Trees* sold to Hans Dietrich, a Velazquez painting sold to Hermann Göring, and hundreds of more sales. Alejandra inspected dozens of other files in the various cabinets, five in all, in which all transactions had taken place to the end of 1937. She sighed with relief. Anton had told her the truth—the records proved everything he owned there was acquired prior to the Anschluss. In fact, he had stopped buying and selling by the beginning of 1938. She supposed that was around the time his health had deteriorated drastically.

She was about to leave when a painting, largely covered with a cloth but with bare feet showing, caught her eye. She made her way to the corner of the room and lifted the fabric, revealing a nude painting of a model resembling Isolde. With heightened curiosity, Alejandra uncovered other nearby paintings—all nudes of Isolde in various erotic poses with landscapes in the background. She observed each in detail, noting the woman's natural physical beauty and the painter's extraordinary skill. Then she carefully covered up the paintings, four in all, signed by Karl Schmidt, whom she assumed was also Anton's forger.

It was evident to Alejandra, at that point, that Anton and Isolde had been lovers for a long time, perhaps dating back to when she had met her in Leipzig five years earlier. Did they also love each other? So why had he kept that a secret? But why should she care? Was she feeling a hint of jealousy? She admonished herself for feeling that way, for it would be better for everyone if Anton loved Isolde.

As she came back to the library, she looked for a book to read for those nights she could not sleep when she had too much on her mind. On one of the shelves, she came across an unusual looking book—ten inches thick with a red velvet cover. She took it, opened it, and discovered a coin collection. Some of the coins dated as far back as 260 BC—a Carthage dekadrachm Goddess Tanit. Other coins of foreign currency included: an Egyptian octadrachm Arsinoe II 261 BC, a Greek tetradrachm 449-BC, a Syracuse Silver dekadrachm fifth century BC, a Russian ruble Catherine II 1762, a United States half dollar 1857, an English five pounds Queen Victoria 1887, a Mexican fifty pesos 1921, and a Nevada gold nugget from 1865. She was astonished but quickly put the book back on the shelf when she heard steps in the drawing room.

Anton met her in the library, dressed in a navy-blue robe. "Were you not able to sleep?"

"No. Is there any book you can recommend?" Alejandra asked.

"Were you in the warehouse?" he asked.

"Yes. I woke up troubled by all kinds of violent images," she said.

"What kind of images?"

"Images of people screaming, ransacking, and looting works of art."

"You still don't believe me?" he asked.

"I was frightened. And I had to go back there and look around. You understand?"

He walked to her. "I'm not upset. You're free to look everywhere. Did you find what you were looking for?"

She nodded.

"I have no secrets. You can ask me anything you want."

"Why weren't you honest about your relationship with Isolde?"

"You saw the paintings? I didn't lie. It's true that I've never admitted to being lovers. Isolde was only a distraction. I don't love her. I never have. It was a convenient arrangement. We said we weren't going to talk about this, but you must know that the only person I love and will ever love is you and nothing can change that."

"I wish you did love her. I want you to be happy. But how does she feel about you? She was very concerned when you were ill."

"She sees me as her protector, nothing more," he said.

"You mustn't abandon her. She's fragile."

"She's not that fragile! But I won't," he said, laughing. He gazed at her. "Is our relationship to remain in purgatory forever?"

"I can't do anything about that," Alejandra said. "This is awkward and uncomfortable, but as I've told you before, the only relationship I can or will ever have of that nature is with my husband. Now that everything is completely honest between us let's put our energy to the matter at hand. When will you send the gift to Göring?"

"I've never known anyone with such a strong character and will," he said.

She smiled. "It's my greatest asset, don't you know?"

"Yes, don't I know it, but to answer your question, I'll do that later this morning. I suspect we may hear from him by tomorrow or the next day," he said.

"I hope so," she said. "I am eager to know something about Hannah and her family. And I want to go home."

"Yes. Try to get some rest, will you?" he said.

Wearing a straw sun-hat, a white short-sleeve cotton blouse, and blue pants, Alejandra was in the garden pulling out weeds around a fountain when Anton came out, dressed in beige pants and a beige shirt. "Alejandra, I have news."

She took off the weathered garden gloves and tossed them on the ground, meeting him on the patio. She sat down on a rusted wrought iron chair and served herself a glass of water from the ewer. "You don't have to do that, you know," he said.

"I'm not one to sit around with nothing to do. I like being outdoors, and as you've indicated, going for walks alone is almost prohibited these days. You heard from Göring?"

"Yes. He's willing to see me on Sunday at his country estate, and I think you should come with me," Anton said. "He likes beautiful women."

"Is that remark supposed to entice me? No way. I'd rather spend the whole day pulling weeds than go there," she said.

He chuckled.

"And what are you insinuating with the beautiful women comment?" she asked.

"You really want an answer?" he asked.

"No. But what else can I expect in case I change my mind?" she asked.

"It's rumored he's addicted to narcotics."

"Is that how you became good acquaintances?"

"No," Anton replied. "I just wanted to prepare you for any possible situation. Remember, we need to be strategic like diplomats. I'm certain your previous Ambassador Dodd, and now Wilson, has had to meet with him on more than one occasion."

"Well, I'm not a diplomat. What other advantages do you see for me to go?"

"I think you could be more persuasive than me, considering you're American, they're your good friends, and that's the reason you came to Berlin. You could also tell him about Ben's distinguished career as an opera conductor."

She paused to consider his suggestions. She'd be walking into a lion's den. But her friend's lives were at stake. She had to try mostly anything.

"You're not even curious?" he asked.

"No! But your request has merit. So I'll go with you. Where is this place anyway?"

"Just north of here, right in the middle of German woodland and near Lake Großdöllner. He built a hunting lodge a few years ago, known as Carinhall. More recently he expanded it for his summer residence."

"Have you been there before?" she asked.

"No, so I must admit that I'm intrigued," Anton said. "I hear the drive there is stunning. Oh, and did I mention he owns a lioness?"

Recalling her thoughts just now, she shook her head. "So, we're going into the lion's den, or should I say the pit of hell."

"So dramatic. Ále, trust me when I say you don't know what the pit of hell is, and I hope you never do."

A few days later, driving through Schorfheide Forest in a black Mercedes, Alejandra looked out the window thinking that with different conditions, she would enjoy the beautiful springtime countryside, just as Anton had said. But the idea of exchanging pleasantries with the Nazi's second in command was revolting. He had a list of titles—Aviation Hero, Hunting Master of Germany, Chief of the Luftwaffe, and Reichsmarschall. She wondered how accomplished men could be so corrupted. Was that what unlimited power did to men? She was not a psychiatrist, but if ever there was a description for their kind of flawed thinking and behavior, it was collective immorality or insanity.

Upon arriving at Carinhall, they were stopped at the gate, and a uniformed guard asked for their documents. Anton identified himself and his guest, showing the guard their passports. They were allowed to drive ahead until they came to a stop at the courtyard. After exiting the vehicle, she took in the large structures extending over several blocks. Then, walking on a stone pathway, they came to the entrance built with a stucco front. They met a stunning, tall red-haired woman with a flawless complexion, her hair pulled tightly into a bun. She led them to the spacious *Jagdhalle* through a long hallway lined with large Belgian tapestries, sculptures of Greek gods and goddesses, and an enormous collection of paintings and other decorative arts that would be better suited displayed in a public museum.

"The riechsmarschall will be with you in a few minutes," the red-headed woman said in a surprisingly friendly tone.

Anxious because of the impending encounter, Alejandra paced back and forth in the hall, noting the high ceilings, wood beams, stag antlers, chandeliers, and a stone fireplace. She stopped in front of a floor to ceiling window, choosing to enjoy the beauty of the landscape beyond the gaudy estate. It was all so surreal, except that it wasn't another one of her dreams.

Suddenly, the gravelly voice of Hermann Göring echoed, "Welcome to my estate."

"Thank you," Anton replied, standing to greet him. "This is my friend Alejandra Stanford Morrison who's visiting from America."

She took a few steps toward Göring.

He extended his hand, obviously noting her elegant all-white attire. *"Freude, Ihre Bekanntschaft Zu Machen."*

With reserve, she shook his hand as he stood tall in his garish hunting attire. She was expected to also reply by saying a pleasure to meet you, but instead, she said in German… "What beautiful gardens you have."

"Yes, and as you can see by my outfit, I was in the midst of archery drills. Please sit down. I'm glad to see you're in fine form, Anton. I had heard you were deathly ill," Göring said.

They sat in the oversized furniture, upholstered in emerald-green velvet fabric.

"Fortunately, I've shaken off those demons, if you know what I mean," Anton said.

"That's good to hear. I much prefer to work with you than Frederick. He's such a bore."

"But he's efficient, is he not?" Anton replied.

"I'm quite busy so let's get right to business. I enjoyed your gift, so what can I do for you?" Göring asked.

"Dear friends of Mrs. Morrison are missing. They're American, which makes it even more of a puzzle," Anton said. "They were in Vienna as recently as March of this year, and they were planning on returning home to New York. Unfortunately, we haven't heard from them."

"You've gone to the American embassy?" he asked.

"Yes, and they had no information, although now they're listed as missing persons."

"So you think they may have been inadvertently detained?" he asked. "What were they doing in Vienna?"

"Benjamin Adelman is a conductor who was employed as the musical director of the Mozart Staatsoper at the time of his disappearance," Alejandra said.

"Mrs. Morrison also happens to be a conductor. She and Mr. Adelman studied here in Berlin and Vienna only a few years ago," Anton said.

"That explains why you speak such good German with only a slight accent. I take it that it was you who chose my signed manuscript?"

Anton interjected, "Yes, it was her suggestion. Ever since I've known her, she's been a Beethoven enthusiast."

"We all are. With so many German opera manuscripts to choose from, why did you select *Fidelio* and not *Die Walküre*, or *Parsifal*, or *Siegfried?*" Göring questioned.

"Isn't it obvious? There are thirteen Wagner operas, but only one Beethoven opera," Alejandra answered.

He turned to her and said, "To own a first edition vocal score of *Fidelio* is priceless, but to have you, an American woman conduct it, would be provocative and something worth considering. Would I be correct in assuming you're exceptionally good? With everyone deserting, we're in short supply and always on the hunt for guest conductors."

She wanted to laugh at the irony. Göring was known to be ostentatious but was even more so than she imagined. It was as though he was straight out of a Shakespearean tragicomedy—a bombastic, corpulent man, dressed in medieval attire blurting out half-truths and believing his every word.

"You have two highly celebrated conductors of your own, who I'm sure the public would rather see at the podium," Alejandra replied, hoping his earlier intimation was nothing more than a stunt. So where was he going with it?

"Furtwängler and Karajan. Have you met them?" he asked.

"Only Furtwängler a few years ago," Alejandra replied. "He's an exceptional conductor."

"He hasn't been too happy with recent policies that he claims interfere with artistic freedom, and Karajan is a rising star who will be directing at the Berlin opera house later this year. All of which brings me back to the idea of having you conduct *Fidelio* for one night only here in Berlin at the State

Opera House. It's rare to have a female conductor, but there's precedence as I'm sure you know."

She had no interest and considered how to decline his invitation. Before she could say anything, however, Anton interceded, "That's an extraordinary offer. And I assure you she's up to the job. But at the moment, our priority is to locate the Adelmans. We hope you can help us."

Göring, undeterred, turned back to Alejandra. "If your friends are, by some mistake, under our custody, I'll have them released with the expectation that you'll agree with my terms to conduct *Fidelio* at my opera house."

Maintaining her usual grace, she asked, "And what are the terms?"

"Don't look at this as an unwanted imposition, but as something mutually beneficial," Göring said. "We find your friends and have them released, and you'll get to conduct one of the great operas with a premiere orchestra, making history in the process. And we'll both do it while enjoying the music of one of our musical heroes."

She knew she was in no position to negotiate or to decline his offer under such precarious circumstances. "I accept, but not until after our friends are located and released," she said firmly.

"I like a woman who knows what she wants. I'll have the manager of the opera house contact you with the details should our plans come to pass. Or better yet, I will send a car for you tomorrow morning so you can meet our musicians. Do we have an agreement?"

At this point, she had no choice but to accept. Was it only an innocent meeting with the musicians as he said? Or did he have a sinister idea in mind? "I'd like Anton to join us," she said.

"No. We don't need him. It's nothing personal, Anton," Göring said.

"I'll be waiting for your driver," she said.

"We don't want to take more of your time," Anton said.

"Before you go, why don't I show you my private hunting grounds," he said.

"All right," Anton said. "I hear you have quite a selection of deer and wild boar."

"And much more," he said.

Göring then led them through the hall, taking his double rifle with scopes, which was hanging from a hook on the wall, and strapping it over his shoulder. He put on his brown hat with a feather sticking out and asked, "Mrs. Morrison, did Anton tell you I was appointed Protector of the German Hunt by the Führer?"

"No, he did not, but he did say you have a lioness," she said, thinking how she now had to put on a cordial performance for this Nazi when all she wanted to do was to get the hell out of there and never have to deal with him again.

"You want to see it too?"

"Some other time," she said.

As they walked beyond the house and into a wooded area, he pointed to several elevated platforms overlooking woodlands. It was a cloudy and windy day.

"Mrs. Morrison, may I call you Alejandra?"

"Yes," she said.

"Have you ever held a rifle?" he asked.

"I have not," she replied. From the corner of her eye, she could see that Anton was getting anxious by the way he moved back and forth, but he remained silent. She could see he was perspiring more than usual.

"I love first timers," Göring said. "Let me show you how to handle one and how to shoot at that pine tree you see straight across the pond. Depending on what method you want to hunt for Hochwild or Rehwild, you may be Ansitz or Pirsch. So what do you want to do?" Her options were sitting or stalking. She replied, "Keiner."

"Keiner. Nein! None?" Göring then walked to her, standing so close she could smell alcohol on his breath as he spoke, and showed her the details on the rifle—the over-under side lock, the engraving on the rib, and the double triggers. He then handed her the rifle. "Now you hold it, but be careful, it is loaded." Alejandra stared back at him for a moment, then she took it, holding it with both her hands. It was heavy. He then stretched her left arm toward the barrel and lifted it with his fleshy hand and fingers.

She wanted to slam him across the face with the rifle, but just carried on, placing her right index finger on the upper trigger and her right eye on the scope.

"Now, shoot," he ordered.

Her heart was beating hard. "Are you sure there's no one out there?" she asked, feeling pushed by him and distressed by the entire situation.

"I don't think so," he said.

She hesitated. "You don't think so? What if I shoot at an innocent person?"

"It would be his fault, wouldn't it? For walking about my private hunting grounds uninvited." Göring laughed. "Shooting has got to be easier than standing at the podium conducting Beethoven's Fifth. Watch your target."

"And if I refuse?" she asked.

"You wouldn't, would you? Nobody refuses me, ever!" he said, looking straight at her.

She steadied herself, bending her knees slightly, then rather than targeting the evergreen tree, she lowered the rifle down slightly, targeting instead a swastika flag at the top of a fountain in the pond. Then she pulled the trigger, and the bullet went through the bottom of the swastika, then landed in the pond, making ripples. "Oops." She laughed, releasing all the tension. "I'll never be a hunter!"

He burst into a hearty laugh and said, "Maybe better if you stick to conducting." She handed the rifle back to Göring. "Next time, I'll have you over for dinner to enjoy a large cut of Polish bison," he said. "Then you might want to reconsider."

There won't be a next time, she thought.

Anton finally spoke. "Thanks for seeing us. I know you're a busy man."

"Alejandra, I'll have my driver pick you up at nine tomorrow. It might be advantageous for you to become acquainted with the orchestra. You might have to hunt down a few opponents if you want to put on a good show." He laughed again.

"And I hope you'll be able to chase down the exact location of where my friends are. I'd like to see them again very soon," Alejandra said.

"And what did you say their names were?" Göring asked, shaking her hand.

"Benjamin, Hannah, and Joseph Adelman."

"I'll see what I can do," he said. Anton shook his hand, and they left.

Driving back to Berlin, Alejandra was feeling tense about what had just happened. Far away enough from Göring's lodge, she spotted a wooded area on the side of the road. "Can you please stop? I need fresh air."

"Sure," Anton said.

After parking the vehicle, they went to a secluded spot under the shade of a linden lime tree, near wetlands. They sat on an elevated rock outcropping.

Alejandra took a deep breath.

"You must be upset by Göring's scheme to conduct. I'm sorry for getting you into this, but did we have any other options?" Anton said.

"I'm worried, anxious, hopeful, and yes, angry at that son of a... Is this a game?"

"I was as astounded as you were. But I suppose it was predictable," Anton added.

"Why?" she asked.

"Everyone knows Göring and Goebbels are in a battle of their own. Each as the head of an opera company, they're often in competition for the best conductors and performers."

"A problem of their own making," she said. "The good news is he's at least willing to work with us on finding the Adelman's whereabouts."

"So you could say that being a conductor has given you an unexpected edge in the negotiations," Anton said.

"That's not something I ever expected. But it may be true," Alejandra said.

"So what's the bad news?" Anton questioned.

"That I'll need to stay here longer than I promised my family. I might have to work with serious opposition, as he alluded to. There will be people back home who'll judge me harshly for conducting here. Do you recall when you asked me if I'd ever do that a few years ago? And I said to myself that I'd never! And now it's a complex dilemma."

"Well, there's still a chance you might not have to do it," he said.

"I can't consider that as it would mean our friends are still missing. I feel trapped, and I hate it!" Alejandra said.

"I need to warn you about something else. Karajan is also debuting *Fidelio* at the Berlin Opera House in late September. Some say Göring is his biggest fan."

"So I'm a pawn, and he's setting me up to fail?" she concluded.

"He wouldn't have asked you to conduct at his prized opera house if he thought you couldn't pull it off," Anton said. "What could be more enticing for opera fans than to see two young conductors, a man and a woman, German and American rivals, performing the same opera at the same opera house?"

"I don't like it, but I don't think we're rivals. I don't even know him. I wouldn't want it to be seen as a competition. I've heard Karajan is extraordinary. I would much rather meet him and discuss his work as a conductor," she said. "But, I do find all this very odd. If I do this, let me be perfectly clear it's only for Hannah, Ben, and their son. I may compromise my work, but I'll not compromise my person in the way you insinuated a few days ago."

"Of course not. But be careful tomorrow. Can I do something to make you feel better?"

"I'm in an impossible situation," she said.

"Courage, *mein Liebling*, if anyone can do it, it's you," Anton said. "Remember, you're doing this concert for a greater good."

The next day late in the afternoon, Alejandra had just returned from visiting the opera house. She went to the drawing room, sat, and took off her pumps. Wearing a gray suit, she straightened her skirt as she leaned her head back on the sofa. The experience of meeting Ivan Ziegler, the artistic director, as well as most of the musicians in the orchestra, had left her second guessing whether she would be conducting or not. Ziegler had been gracious and welcoming, but several players voiced their strong opposition to Alejandra as a guest conductor.

Then Anton joined her, dressed in his too familiar black slacks and gray pullover. "Well, how was it? Was Göring there?" he asked, sitting in the wing chair.

"No, but his driver gave me a note inviting me for dinner tomorrow tonight," she said. "But I'm not going."

"And you told that to the driver?"

"No. I wrote Göring a note and gave it to the driver this afternoon, saying that I'd accept his dinner invitation at a later date when we could toast the release of my friends and the success of the concert. Although, after today, I doubt if either one will come to pass."

"Why do you say that?" he asked.

"It was clearly an audition, as I had expected. The artistic director asked many questions about my background, experience, music theory, conducting proficiency, if I had been on an apprenticeship, and if I played other instruments. Then Ziegler asked me to conduct on the spot Beethoven's Symphony no. 2, final movement, and then Puccini's *La Boheme*, Act 1, Rodolfo's aria "Che Gelida Manina." And I didn't mind that at all. For there was no way I'd be hired to conduct in Göring's opera house until he could confirm my expertise in the field."

"How did you do?" Anton asked.

"There's always a danger in being too confident, but I think I did fine. You know Beethoven's music is sacred to me, and I know most of it as though it's permanently etched in me. As for Puccini, I'm not as well versed, but I had studied *La Boheme* in detail with Ben. The problem was that there was one musician, the concertmaster of all people, who refused to play as I conducted. A few others followed his lead, but then most of those who had originally declined accepted to play after I directed Beethoven to their satisfaction, except for that same gentleman by the name of Herbert Wolf, who was adamant that he'd never play if I were allowed to conduct in a future concert. If there is one thing I've learned it's that there must be a consensus among the musicians, otherwise one person can influence others, and you run the risk of mutiny. So I wonder, maybe I didn't do as well as I thought, and maybe this person who opposed me and is concertmaster has considerable weight within the orchestra. So then why would Göring cooperate with our request if I'm not even going to conduct?"

"Knowing you as well as I do, I'm sure you were great," Anton said. "And if Göring wants you to conduct, no one in their right mind would refuse. You heard what he said to you yesterday that no one opposes him. I'm more worried about your rejection of his dinner invitation. Göring might just decide to call the whole thing off because of that. Now we'll have to wait and see what happens."

She shrugged. "Let's then hope it comes to pass if it will bring our friends back to us."

"May I ask you something? Now that you've been conducting for some time, what is the most important thing or things between a conductor and his orchestra?"

"Last year a woman in an orchestra, a bassist, told me that she considered the conductor's competency during rehearsals and whether there was chemistry between the conductor and his players. And another, a violist, said that she considered whether the conductor was a kind human being who treated all musicians with respect. There are of course other traits ascribed to good conductors, but those observations have stayed with me."

"Well then, let's hope it happens," Anton said. "How about a glass of wine with a bowl of stew? It's pretty damned tasty if I say so myself."

"Anton, a chef? I'll give it a try," she said.

Five days later, they received the news they had been eagerly awaiting. There was, in fact, an undocumented man, who claimed to be Benjamin Adelman, in Gestapo custody. According to the report, he was at a camp northwest of Munich. The detainee's release was contingent on identification by Anton Everhardt, who was summoned by the camp's commanding officer, Horst Müller.

That afternoon, as Anton left for Munich, Alejandra stayed behind in Berlin. A courier arrived at the residence and delivered a sealed envelope. He would return at the end of the day after Alejandra had time to read and sign the documents. She leafed through five pages of an agreement that stipulated she would perform in the capacity of guest conductor on August 27, 1938.

As musical director, she would have a significant say in decisions governing staging, music performance, and music selection. The final program, to be submitted by June first, would be subject to review by the artistic director of the opera house, Ivan Zeigler. The terms further specified she would have access to the orchestra and choir for rehearsals, one week prior. As musical director, she would receive a compensation of three thousand reichsmarks paid upon completion of the performance. The only cause for cancellation would be incapacitating illness. The contract was in effect from May 23, 1938, to August 28, 1938.

She realized she was being tested in numerous ways. In the past, she had thought that political implications had no place in artistic expression. But now she was confronted with a serious dilemma—whether or not to perform under the auspices of a fascist banner. Artists with such a predicament fell into three categories. The first group was those artists whose moral code superseded their dedication to their art. The second group included those who were guided by moral considerations but had an equally overriding devotion to the art itself or other unknown personal reasons. And the third group were those whose ambition surpassed any moral consideration. It was crystal clear to her that under normal circumstances, she fell into the first group, but that the current extraordinary circumstances pushed her into the second group. She simply had no choice but to succumb to what was tantamount to extortion. With that, she wondered how many times she had been quick to criticize other artists without knowing all the facts or circumstances of their actions—something she swore never to do again.

She took the pen, briefly closed her eyes, and signed the contract. Would this act be considered for a greater purpose? It was.

In the evening, the messenger returned to pick up the contract. It was done.

She would question for some time to come whether she had made the right choice, as there was still no news on the whereabouts of Hannah and her son. As part of her attempt to keep the glass half full, and to distract herself, she began outlining the musical program.

As a student at the Vienna Conservatory, she had described her ideal concert program—Vienna con Brio. The program included her favorite concertos and symphonies of the Austrian-German repertoire. But now, she wanted to communicate something uplifting to the public, and she needed to distinguish her program and for sure did not want to conduct the complete two-act opera *Fidelio*.

In the end, she decided to do an all-Beethoven program. For if ever there was a German artist and composer who understood human suffering and redemption, who loved his fellow men and valued the principles of freedom, it was Ludwig van Beethoven. Inspired by his spirit and courage, she sat down at the pianoforte to play the composer's favorite composition, Sonata no. 15 op. 28, "Andante," the very same sonata he had often played when he found himself downhearted and in search of repose.

40

ABSCHEULICHER ARIA

Awakened the next day by the sound of footsteps, Alejandra got dressed and rushed to the foyer. There, in the faint light of dawn, she teared up upon seeing Ben's wretched appearance. She hardly recognized him. His hair was gone, his face pallid and bruised, and his sunken brown eyes revealed profound grief. She embraced him. "Ben. I'm so relieved you're here. You must be exhausted. Can I get you anything?"

"Yes. Where's my wife and son?" Ben whispered, shivering.

"I don't know," she said.

"We'll find them," Anton said. "Get some rest, you've been through hell."

Alejandra led him to a bedroom down the hall and across from her own. As they entered, she turned on the floor lamp and proceeded to close the paisley patterned drapes, until he cried, "No! I want to see daylight."

She had made up the room the previous day. The bed was covered with a white, feather-filled comforter. There was a small crystal vase filled with yellow tulips, and a glass of water was by the bedside. Ben took off his overcoat, revealing tattered clothes that hung loosely on his emaciated frame. He tossed the coat on a bench at the foot of the bed. He then touched the flowers. "Ále, I'm so grateful to you, but as you can imagine, I haven't eaten or slept much for weeks. I feel numbed and alive only by the grace of God, as well as you and Anton."

"I understand. Can I do anything?"

"I'd like to clean up first. I must look and smell awful," he said in a subdued voice.

"Try to get some sleep. Everything will be better, you'll see," she said and left.

Just before two o'clock in the afternoon, the three friends sat in the dining room, eating their meal quietly. No tablecloth or fancy dinnerware was on the table. White ceramic dishes and plain glassware and silverware served its purpose. Alejandra looked out the window. It was cloudy. She had a recollection of the night when everyone had gathered there in high spirits after the auction many years before. She envisioned Hannah's beautiful face and felt a knot in her throat.

Placing her hand on Benjamin's arm, she said, "You hardly ate anything. Would you like a little piece of Kaiserschmarr'n and a cup of tea?"

"I've become accustomed to eating one meal a day, if I was lucky, so I assure you I'm quite full," Ben said. "A cup of tea, I'll take."

"I'll get it," Anton said and left.

"You seem a bit more rested," she said.

"I can't remember the last time I slept properly," Ben said.

Then Anton returned with tea and another cup for Alejandra.

She took Ben's hand in hers and asked, "Do you want to talk about it?"

He took a deep breath. "I don't even know where to start."

"You don't have to do it now, but I'm hoping it will help us figure out where Hannah and Joseph might be," she said.

He took the cup with his two hands, taking a sip of the cinnamon tea. "It was the night of March ninth, and after meeting friends at a café for the last time, Hannah, Joseph, and I took a taxi to our apartment. We were to leave the next day. As we approached the flat, we knew something was wrong. The door was slightly ajar, and when we went inside, we saw the apartment ransacked. Anything of value was gone. But worse, our legal papers and passports had been stolen from a locked drawer in the desk, which was smashed open with a hammer left behind. We immediately left for our friend's house, and they insisted we stay that night, and so we did. The following day we had planned to go to the American embassy and report what had happened. However, with the shock and commotion of the previous night, Hannah had forgotten a box containing family pictures and her personal jewelry that she had hidden under floorboards in the kitchen. Under the circumstances, we should have left it, but the items held significant sentimental value. The next morning around eight, I returned to the apartment and found the box, just where she said it would be. I opened it, confirming its contents—her parent's photos and a few pieces of jewelry including her pearl and cameo necklace, a bracelet, and Joseph's Star of David."

He paused briefly, putting his cup on the table. "I had no idea that when I exited the building there would be several SS men brandishing revolvers, waiting for me. They asked for my legal papers, which I obviously did not have. One of them violently grabbed the bag I was holding. Upon seeing the jewelry, he said, 'Another filthy thief. They're like cockroaches multiplying by the day.' I tried to explain what had happened and that the jewelry belonged to my wife. I told them I was an American citizen but to no avail. 'Everyone seems to be an American citizen these days,' one of them said. Then they directed me with their bayonets toward their vehicle. I knew that if I resisted they would likely kill me on the spot, so I went along, hoping that their superiors would believe me and eventually let me go."

Ben's voice had been breaking, and he started sobbing uncontrollably.

Seeing he was too distraught to continue the conversation, Alejandra said, "Maybe you want to tell us the rest some other time."

He took a handkerchief and wiped his face. "No. I want you to know everything if it's going to bring back my family."

Ben went on to describe the horrific events of the next days and weeks after he was transferred to the Dachau concentration camp in northeastern Bavaria. Between insults, frequent blows to the head, and forced labor in an old munitions factory, as well as pathetic screams of other prisoners, he remembered only bits and pieces. There were thousands of prisoners, including Jews, communists, and anyone else deemed to be an enemy of the state.

When he finished his painful recounting, he turned to Anton angrily, as if he alone was to blame for his suffering. "Why? Why such cruelty?"

Anton replied, "Ben, no words can express my sorrow for what they've done to you. I cannot even allow myself to think of what might come next. But I swear to you we're not all devoid of compassion. We're not all fascists. There are many of us who have the courage to resist, but we're all living in fear. One word, real or imagined, against the regime could lead to lethal consequences against ourselves and our families. They're too powerful and have no conscience or soul. This is what tyranny looks like. And to make matters worse, what did world leaders do after the Anschluss? Nothing. I suspect they will also stand by idly after they invade Poland and the rest of Europe as well. I ask myself every single day how bad it has to get before other leaders finally do something. I'm so sorry for all of us."

"I know what you say to be true, and I'm sorry too," Ben said. "I didn't mean to put the burden on you. This is just beyond comprehension. I'm afraid that if Hannah and Joseph were taken, they won't survive. This is all my fault. For months Hannah begged me to return home. She only came because I had refused. I'll never forgive myself if anything happens to them."

"And that son of a bitch Müller wouldn't give me any information about them, and he refused to confirm or deny whether they were in their custody. They're stalling," Anton said.

"I'll go the embassy here in Berlin, as we still have one, and demand they negotiate for their release," Ben said.

"They can replace your papers, but I doubt they can do anything else," Anton said. "They probably don't know where your family is, and any inquiry will take months."

"Perhaps our only option for their release is that I fulfill my contract. That was the agreement we made with Göring," Alejandra said.

"It pains me for you to go through with it, but maybe it's our only hope. Richard must be beyond worry, and I do understand how risky this is for you too," Ben said.

"You could go with the embassy, but that's a long shot. For now, we need to stick with my engagement. They did release you," she said. "I couldn't live with myself if I left now."

"Well, I need my papers, so I'll go to the embassy and hope for a miracle," Ben said.

"Could she have gone with your relatives, Sarah and Joshua, in Melk?" Alejandra asked.

"Yes! That would be a hopeful possibility," Ben said. "I'll have the embassy check that."

That night after retiring to her bedroom, Alejandra finished a letter to her husband, to be sent the next day through the American embassy.

May 25, 1938. My dearest Richard: How calming it was to hear your voice a few days ago, and to know you and the children are well. I comfort myself by seeing your pictures by my bedside, and soon I hope to be with you. I'm sorry I could not be more specific about events here, as our telephone conversations are being monitored. This letter will be sent through the embassy to avoid being intercepted. I didn't want to write you until I had good news. First of course is that Anton's health has improved considerably. Your advice for his recovery proved to be exactly what he needed, and I would have not been able to do it without the assistance of the Augustine canon, Nicholas, who met me at the sta-

tion. He was extremely helpful during my stay in Vienna. Thank you for having the foresight to make all the arrangements.

My time in Berlin has also proven beneficial, and our efforts have not been in vain. With Anton's unholy connections, we succeeded in finding Ben. He was released just this morning after being detained for more than two months by the Gestapo in a detention camp. It's a long story that will have to wait until my return.

To guarantee Ben's release, and hopefully Hannah and Joseph, I agreed to something I still question to this day, but I had no good alternative. It's all very complicated, as most regrettably the arts and politics are increasingly connected, something I thought I'd never see, much less be a participant. I will be a guest conductor for a program at the end of August. Now, I see the reality, that the arts have always been used for the benefit and manipulation of the powerful. Machiavellian politics has a whole new meaning.

Sadly, we still have no information on Hannah and Joseph, but we hope to have news soon. And if by a miracle we do find them, we can all return home. Please forgive me for not coming back as promised. I hope you understand. Be patient and pray for us. Love, Alejandra.

With two days left to submit the musical program, Alejandra considered her selections for the last time. She did not have the time to put on a full opera production, and while she had the experience of conducting for orchestras and choral ensembles, she wanted to challenge herself further. For despite the unusual situation, there was a sense of pride in conducting with such a fine orchestra and in a country with family roots and historical musical prominence. These factors she must separate from current events. Ironically, the concert would mark a high point of her professional career. And there was always the hope that music could be the catalyst for change. After a week of reviewing dozens of Beethoven's works, she chose the program, which she appropriately titled "An Ode to Joy":

Symphony no. 5 in C Minor op. 67 - Beethoven
Fidelio Overture - Beethoven

Fidelio - Leonore's aria "Abscheulicher" - Beethoven
Intermission
Symphony no. 9 "Ode to Joy" Choral - Beethoven

She was pleased to have chosen two of the most demanding symphonies, including the composer's work combining vocal and symphonic writing. If she was going to give everything she had, she was grateful to be able to finish with Beethoven's choral symphony—his ultimate expression of brotherhood and universal love.

There was still, however, one more decision to make—who would sing *Fidelio's* Leonore's aria "Abscheulicher"? Ben had suggested that Alejandra consider the internationally renowned German soprano, Lotte Lehmann, who had performed with the Minneapolis Symphony Orchestra back in March of 1934 when Lehmann toured the United States. But like many other musicians of her caliber, most if not all were not willing to perform in Germany at this time. So Alejandra came up with a bold but risky idea—to have Isolde Beckman perform the aria. Anton had insisted she was not up to the task, but Alejandra disagreed, recalling her magnificent soprano voice when she had sung for her back in 1933. Isolde was expected to arrive at any moment. It was three o'clock in the afternoon.

Alejandra, wearing a beige laced dress and sandals, joined Ben in the parlor. She noted the room's neutral colors, and like years before, a fresh bouquet of bleeding-heart flowers adorned the piano. Anton had brought them that morning, noting their arching stems and variety of colors from pink and fuchsia to amethyst. But he also had alluded to unrequited love. Her thoughts were interrupted upon hearing Ben tuning one of Anton's violins. A dozen violins rested on the cocktail table. By the sound of his voice, he still seemed very demoralized. "I haven't seen you all day."

"The concert program is keeping me busy," she said, sitting next to him. "I need to decide who'll sing *Fidelio's* Leonore. I'll appreciate all the assistance you can give me in this matter. Perhaps you can agree with me or not if Isolde is the right person for the job."

"I'll be happy to do so," Ben said.

"Are you almost done?"

"I have three to go," Ben replied. "I need to keep myself engaged in something. Hannah and Joseph are constantly on my mind. And I can't just sit and wait to hear from the embassy. I wish we could go elsewhere for the next two months. But I'm afraid that if we leave, we'll not be allowed to return. Well, it's me who would not be allowed to return."

"Have you chosen a violin for yourself?" she asked.

"No. It was generous of Anton to insist that I take one," Ben said. "I'll borrow one for the time being, but I don't feel comfortable in keeping one."

"So which one are you considering?"

"The Amati. It seems to have the best sound thus far, made by a Luthier from Cremona. It was the first brand ever to be produced. It would be Amati's students, Stradivari and Guarneri, who are known today as having created the world's best violins. I hope that whoever stole mine and Hannah's cello has some appreciation for them."

Just then, they heard voices, and moments later, Anton and Isolde made their way into the drawing room.

Alejandra immediately noticed Isolde looked healthier, but her floral-print flare dress still seemed a little too big on her petite frame. While relieved by her rosy cheeks and improved physical condition, Alejandra thought Isolde would need to add more pounds, for opera singers required physical stamina, a strong diaphragm, and lungs.

"*Schön dich zu sehen. Ich danke Ihnen für Ihr Kommen.*" Ben also greeted her.

Alejandra poured Isolde a glass of water. "Can I get you something to eat?"

"No, thanks," Isolde said, sitting next to her on the sofa. She took the glass of water and emptied it. "We stopped to eat just before coming."

"Did Anton explain to you why you're here?" Alejandra asked.

Anton leaned against the piano with his arms folded, dressed very casually in black trousers and a pullover. "I told her."

"I don't think I can do it," Isolde added.

"Please be honest with me. Is it that you don't want to do it? Or you don't think you have the voice for that?"

"I'd like to do it, but I've never sung for people of the upper class," she replied.

"Anton told me you'd sung this aria before."

"Yes. Many times, but just for fun."

"Everyone can appreciate true talent. Can you sing it for us? I'll be honest. Agreed?"

Isolde nodded.

They went to the piano, and Alejandra handed her the score to the aria "*Abscheulicher, wo eilst du hin*" from *Fidelio*.

Isolde cleared her throat several times, took a deep breath, and then on Alejandra's signal began to sing. At first, she was hesitant and awkward in her performance, but as she relaxed, her voice improved considerably, exuding warmth and brilliance. Alejandra was convinced that with intense practice and training over the next two months, Isolde could perform the aria splendidly for she, in fact, had a superb talent. The only question would be if she could commit to the intensive work ahead.

When she finished, Anton remarked, "I've never heard you sing like that before. I'm very impressed, Isolde."

Isolde smiled, clearly pleased with herself.

"Will you then agree to sing at my concert?" Alejandra asked. "You'll need to practice five times a week for several hours each day. We'll work on your breathing, posture, diction, and your emotion. When we finish with the training, you'll be perfect."

"Yes, I'd like that," Isolde said. "But…"

"What is it?" Alejandra asked.

"I don't want to use my real name," Isolde said.

"You can choose any name you like. Many singers have stage names."

"I want mine to be Carla Braun, like my grandmother who raised me and taught me how to read music."

"That's a beautiful name. Where will you be staying in Berlin?"

"With her," Isolde responded. "My mother died, and I never knew my father."

"I'm glad you have someone like that. Come back tomorrow around ten, and we can begin. Will that work for you?" Alejandra asked.

"Yes. I'm so grateful for this opportunity, and I won't let you down."

Alejandra smiled. "I have every confidence in you."

"This could be the start of a new life for you. Let's get you home," Anton said.

After they both had left, Ben joined Alejandra at the piano as she was making notes on the score where she thought Isolde would need extra work.

"Can I ask you something?" Ben asked. "And what happens if for some reason you don't go through with the concert? The poor girl will be disappointed to the point she never recovers."

"I thought about that. Tomorrow I'll tell her there's a chance the concert may not happen, but either way she needs to find a way to use her talent. You heard her. She was excellent and could be great. I don't know if it's for lack of opportunity or confidence why she has not taken her ability seriously. She's still young, and I want her to realize she's capable of pursuing this as a profession. Besides she's a perfect companion for Anton."

"Ah-ha, now I understand," Ben said with a nod and wink. "I thought there was something going on between them. She was very flirtatious with Anton before they left, inviting him for the night."

Alejandra sighed. "I hope he accepts. Then I've accomplished something good today. But on the topic of Isolde's training, will you help us?"

"Yes," Ben said. "I must believe I can make a difference in someone's life." He paused. "Last night I dreamed about Hannah and Joseph. My boy was laughing with that contagious giggle, and I picked him up on my shoulders, and Hannah said, 'I love you.' I must have hope, otherwise the guilt will kill me. They're missing because of my pride and stubbornness."

"No," Alejandra said. "They are missing because of the brutal actions of others. You can't blame yourself for any of this. You'll see, we'll get through this."

FIDELIO

The Grand Opera House, a beacon of architectural and musical inspiration since the eighteenth century, was filled on August 27, 1938. With thirteen hundred seats and not one to spare, the orchestra and the audience sat noisily awaiting Alejandra Stanford Morrison, who was the first American-born female guest conductor to ever step on the stage.

While waiting in the dressing room, appointed with two upholstered arm chairs in blue velvet, a vanity with mirror, a bright crystal chandelier, and beige carpet, she reviewed the program titled *Ein Ode an die Freude* with growing apprehension. She had chosen to begin the concert with one of the most challenging and best-known symphonies ever to be interpreted by a conductor—the Fifth Symphony in C Minor, Opus 67 by Ludwig van Beethoven. Was she making a mistake? Was it courage or merely an obsession for the composer that had been present all her life? It took years, if not decades, to properly interpret such a grand symphony to perfection. She scanned, for what seemed the hundredth time, the first page of the score of the first movement, titled "Allegro con Brio." It was, like all symphonies, comprised of four movements—opening sonata, an andante, a fast scherzo, and grand finale.

She placed the marked score back into her leather portfolio upon hearing the raspy voice of the concertmaster, Herbert Wolf, a man with a husky physique, blond hair, and elongated face, who was in his early fifties. In an authoritarian tone, he said, "Are you prepared to do this, Frau Morrison? We begin in five minutes." Wolf, like Ivan Ziegler, the artistic director, had shown from the first time she met him, a few months earlier, a strong opposition to her being there. He had expressed his refusal to play if she were allowed to conduct. So, even though she was feeling intense emotion—a combination of excitement, nervousness, and fear—she replied with a firm voice looking at Wolf, "I am as ready as I'll ever be, and I'm glad you've decided to join us."

"Not by my choice," he said.

"We all have crosses to bear," she said, smiling. "And I'm sure you will all be splendid."

"We will see," he said, and left.

It was her first time conducting the prestigious orchestra. She had rehearsed with the musicians for several days, many of whom she had met before when they auditioned. During rehearsal, most of the musicians had been welcoming and kind, but a few others seemed put off by her presence. Wolf, an arrogant man, was thought to be intimidating by his fellow musicians. With a fierce rivalry toward her during rehearsals, Wolf had questioned many of her decisions, her tempo and her style of delineating the musical line with her baton during soft passages or broader strokes in vigorous passages, putting them at odds before the musicians. But because of her knowledge, command, in-depth understanding of the scores, and her ability to challenge him when necessary, she had obtained the respect of most.

Yet, all that seemed trivial at the moment. For Alejandra knew she was in a dangerous situation, putting her reputation and even her physical well-being at risk by exposing herself publicly, but she had a contract and a mission to fulfill, one that she believed would soon bring the return of her most beloved friend and her son.

Alejandra acknowledged the gravity of the situation on so many levels. For without a doubt, she was living in perilous times where the boundaries between art and politics had vanished, and music had become a political instrument.

It would be a symphony of rivals.

Taking a deep breath, Alejandra proceeded through the corridor leading to the stage, playing the notes in her mind. She donned a pearl satin, ankle-length dress with box pleats and long sleeves, which could be mistaken for a wedding gown if not for its distinguishing detail of ruby red stones sewn into the collar. Her chestnut hair was pulled into a chignon with free strands framing the sides of her face. With little makeup, except for pink lips and rouge on her cheeks, she displayed a natural look. She entered the Rococo style venue with an air that was distinctly her own, and it had often been described by others in her profession as graceful aplomb.

On the stage, she had a momentary flashback to the day she had attended Mozart's the *Magic Flute*, five years earlier. Who would have ever thought then that she would be here now ready to conduct Beethoven. She might have imagined it as a dream, but it had come true. When a welcoming applause ensued, she bowed, hoping the magnificent music to come would fill the soul of everyone in attendance with pure enjoyment. She briefly looked to the most distant points of the grand venue, as if trying to make eye contact with every member of the audience. She thought of Mahler, Grieg, Strauss, and Walter, and for a second or two, she felt distressed and even inadequate trying to stand in their shoes.

In the fifth row, she spotted a handsomely bearded man holding a single white rose, who even from a distance was familiar. The man's presence held her gaze until he suddenly stood and shouted out *"Fidelio, Fidelio, Fidelio,"* referring to Beethoven's only opera written as a symphony with four large-scale overtures. It was a libretto based on actual events of the French Revolution—"a story of love, politics, and an ode to freedom." *Fidelio* would be performed right after the Fifth Symphony. Was he trying to signal something or was he simply eager to hear the piece?

In that fleeting instant, she recalled Beethoven's words—"Of all my spiritual children, this is the one that cost me the worst birth pangs." *Fidelio* had been the most heart wrenching composition he had ever written, for it took the composer over ten years to complete with ongoing revisions as he reconstructed the entire opera.

Then in an attempt to escape her own birth pangs, she turned her back to the public and focused on conducting, by memory, the first movement of Beethoven's Fifth Symphony. Facing the orchestra, composed of eighty-five musicians dressed in black tuxedos, she smiled at them, believing that they were dedicated to the task at hand and would perform their best to honor Beethoven's legacy. They would be one, and together they would resurrect Beethoven's spirit through the harmonious joining of string, woodwind, and percussion. She breathed in and raised her white baton to mark the downbeat. Then the first four notes of the "motif molto ritardando," a pronounced slowing of the melody of the first movement, rang out like fireworks. Those four notes were recognized around the world—a symbol to mean s*o pocht das Schicksal an die Pforte,* thus fate knocks at the door. Did Beethoven believe in the concept of fate as she did?

For the next forty-three minutes, she moved her baton to the beat and in horizontal motions when requiring a more emotional expression. She was filled with passion and energy while *Symphony no. 5 in C Minor op. 67* and the "Fidelio Overture" unfolded.

Throughout that period of exaltation, she felt Beethoven and God's hand were guiding her and lifting her spirit to the heavens.

Then came *Fidelio*, Leonore's aria "Abscheulicher." And Isolde Beckman, now known to the world as Carla Braun, appeared on stage, dressed as a man, in the role of Fidelio. She sang the aria as if she had been preparing for that moment her whole life. With her emotive and powerful voice, she enraptured the audience and not only looked every bit the part of an opera singer but a star. Alejandra could not have been more delighted by her superb performance.

At the conclusion of the first part of the program, Alejandra's heart was pumping hard with overwhelming emotion. She knew it had been the height of her musical career, that moment of spiritual and musical ecstasy where Beethoven's melodies spoke to the hearts of everyone there.

She extended her hand toward Carla Braun and the orchestra, joining in the applause. For Alejandra was also thrilled by the performance of the musicians who seemed to have put their heart and soul into every note; they had come together as one. Then Alejandra and Carla bowed one last time as the public gave them a standing ovation.

Music had transcended politics, and for that Alejandra felt immense joy and gratitude.

During intermission, a few moments later, in her dressing room, still on a musical high she had never felt before, Alejandra wished Richard could have been there to share her experience. Despite the circumstances and uncertainties, this had been the most unforgettable concert of her life. Music had been an entity in itself bringing everyone together in complete harmony.

With only fifteen more minutes left before the next performance, she proceeded to freshen up her lipstick. Standing before an oval mirror under a bright light, she saw her blushed cheeks. Her anticipation and emotion of conducting Beethoven's Ninth Symphony, "Ode to Joy," was so intense she had to sit down for a moment to steady herself. This was an exercise often required before a concert. Tapping into the solitude of her dressing room, and notwithstanding the distant commotion outside her room, she closed her eyes and envisioned the second part of the program unfolding. She would conduct Beethoven's last symphony with the greatest fidelity and surrender mentally and physically to his creation. She still could not believe that in only a few minutes she would be conducting the orchestra and the ninety-six-voice chorus. She began to recite Schiller's words that took Beethoven thirty years to set to music:

"Freude, Schöner Götterfunken, Tochter aus Elysium, Wir betreten feuer-trunken, Himmlische, dein Heiligtum! Deine Zauber binden wieder... Joy, fair spark of the gods, Daughter of Elysium, Drunk with fiery rapture, Goddess, We approach thy shrine! Thy magic reunites those whom stern custom has parted. All men will become brothers, under the gentle wing."

She remained in absolute concentration, nothing distracting her until the harsh sound of heavy boots and someone abruptly entering the room startled her. Before she could turn and know their identity, she felt her mouth and nose covered with a pungent smelling damp rag that rendered her unconscious.

Amid the darkness and coldness of the black night, Alejandra slowly recovered from the effects of the anesthetics. Feeling light-headed, with nausea and short of breath, she was in the back seat of a car moving at high speed. In panic, she realized that two men had abducted her. Why would they have done such an outrageous thing in the middle of her concert? Her scalp felt electrified, and her stomach twisted. She couldn't breathe. A strong smell of benzene and cigarette smoke made her turn to the other end of the seat where a man with a pointed chin and a Bollman hat had dozed off. With a broad nose and large nostrils, his breathing was heavy. The driver, with spiked hair, was wearing a cracked leather jacket. She straightened herself and leaned forward to speak to the driver. "*Wer bist du, und wo Sie mich nehmen.* "

She wanted to know who they were, and where they were taking her.

The driver did not respond.

"I demand you take me back to the opera house," she continued, now angry. As she raised her voice, the man next to her woke up. She asked, "Who's behind this?"

"You'll find out soon," the man with the Bollman hat said.

As her mind cleared, she was trembling and couldn't reconcile that just minutes or perhaps hours before she was on top of the world but was now terrified. Was this the price for leaving her family? Would she ever see them again? She had risked everything. Was it all for nothing? No, at least Ben was free. She felt a wild terror and thought of escaping by opening the door, but the man next to her would prevent her from doing so.

What possible reasons could explain her abduction? Perhaps it was some stupid prank in which she was made to play the role of a female version of Florestan in Fidelio's opera—abducted unjustly, waiting to die, or waiting to be saved by a courageous Fidelio, not a woman in disguise, but a man deeply in love. Or was this the action of a vengeful man with scores to settle with someone else? Or worse yet, was this the deed of a perverse mind? None of the three scenarios made any sense. She knew she would need to keep her wits about her for the truth would soon be revealed.

VIOLIN SONATA IN G MINOR

Anton slammed the door behind him as he entered his house. He rushed to the drawing room where Ben was playing Bach's Sonata in G Minor on the Amati violin.

"She's been kidnapped," he said, enraged. "I'm going to fucking kill whoever is behind this vile act."

Ben put the violin on the table. "What are you talking about?"

"Alejandra was taken from the opera house," Anton said. "Before the beginning of the concert, a man with a Bollman hat approached me, his face partly concealed as he handed me a folded piece of paper. And before I could read it, he vanished. The note said that the conductor would disappear before our very eyes during *Fidelio's* overture." At first, I thought it was a sick joke, and I went to my seat thinking the man was crazy, for who in his right mind would do such a preposterous thing in front of hundreds of people. But then I remembered that crazy is in these days and attempted to warn her from my seat by shouting Fidelio three times. I wasn't sure if she could hear, but I'd hope that by standing and shouting she would realize that something was wrong. But how could she possibly know what I was trying to say? During intermission, I immediately went backstage, but two guards were standing at the door and prevented me from seeing her. I tried to push my way through, but they warned me that if I tried again, they would escort me outside and send for the police. I thought that I would be more useful if I didn't get arrested again. From the open door, I could see it was hectic as members of the chorus and the orchestra organized themselves. I gave the note to one

315

of the guards and pleaded he give it to Alejandra as soon as possible. He agreed, and I convinced myself that soon she would reappear on stage to conduct Beethoven's Ninth."

"And then what?" Ben asked.

"I returned to my seat," Anton said. "Ivan Ziegler appeared on stage and introduced the concertmaster, Herbert Wolf, who would be conducting the second part of the program. He gave no other explanation, and I knew something was wrong. I could hear people in the audience questioning what had happened to the woman conductor. I ran out of the auditorium and went to the backstage door again, demanding to speak with Ziegler, who after several minutes came and met me. Together, we went to her dressing room located at the end of a long corridor. I could still smell a lingering odor that I can only assume was chloroform. Her handbag, briefcase, and coat were all there. So it was almost as the note had warned. Alejandra was kidnapped not during the program but in the intermission when she was alone in her dressing room."

"What did Ziegler say?" Ben asked.

"He was as stunned as I was and could not comprehend how it had been possible with so many people around. Neither of us had any explanation or idea who could have done this or why. He said he would report it, and I wish I could have seen the face of the man who warned me."

"Was Göring there?"

"No, he wasn't, now that you mention it," Anton said.

"I have to believe he's behind it. Maybe that was their plan, one life for another," Ben said. "I'm terribly sorry for all this. What can we do?"

"It seems absurd," Anton said. "What would be his possible motive or anyone else's for that matter? I'm calling Göring and demand she's released. I'll do whatever it takes."

Anton excused himself and left to make the call from the library. He dialed Göring's private number, but he wasn't available, apparently out of town. After the telephone conversation with his assistant, Johann, Anton was certain that Göring wasn't the culprit, but then who? He returned to the drawing room where Ben was pacing back and forth, smoking a cigarette.

"Well?"

"He wasn't there, but Johann said we'd have information on Hannah and Joseph soon."

"What did he say about my family?"

"Nothing more," Anton replied. "Regarding Alejandra's abduction,

Göring is not one of the good guys, but I don't think he'd do something like this. The last thing he wants is to be involved in the disappearance of an American woman who was last seen conducting at his precious opera house. This crime would make front page news, and he doesn't need that kind of publicity. I get a sense this may be the work of someone inside the Gestapo."

"But isn't he the one in charge?" Ben asked.

"He was in the beginning, but that post was taken over by Himmler in 1934, and I have reason to believe there's no love lost between them," Anton said. "The Gestapo has carte blanche to do anything they want. It's above the law."

"How can you possibly deal with them?" Ben asked.

"I have a lot of calls to make. I promise you, I'll find the fucking bastard who did this," Anton bellowed.

The next morning, Anton and Ben were in the library, drinking a cup of coffee, when the telephone rang, and Anton answered it. The American embassy's secretary, Margaret Edison, requested to speak to Ben who then took the receiver. For most of the conversation, Ben listened attentively, and by his expression, Anton assumed there was good news. "Yes. We'll be there shortly," Ben said, hanging up. "Ms. Edison has crucial information on my wife and son."

"Are Hannah and Joseph at the embassy?" Anton asked.

"She would not confirm nor deny. What else could it be?" Ben said. "I'm a nervous wreck and stayed up all night. I want nothing more than to hold them both in my arms and to tell Hannah how sorry I am and what an idiot I've been for not listening to her reasons. She never wanted to come back to Europe. You know they're everything to me."

"I'll make arrangements for you and your family to leave as soon as you've replaced your traveling documents."

"We can't go until Ále is safe and we've found her," Ben said.

"Ben, that could take some time and some doing. I hate to say it, but you being here may only complicate things. Let's wait a week, but I think you may be able to do more back home."

"If we don't hear anything soon, I'll have to notify Richard. I assure you he'll be at your doorstep in a week," Ben said.

"I would expect nothing less," Anton said. "Perhaps he can put pressure on both the American and German Embassies."

"I can report her missing to the media, although I'll leave that up to

Richard," Ben said.

"I'm afraid whoever has abducted Alejandra couldn't care less about any embassy or what the American press writes," Anton said. "Whoever is behind it will only release her by pressure from internal sources. It's all very odd, and I can't understand who would do this, or his motive."

"Odd is too mild of a word to describe what's happening here. It's utterly despicable," Ben said. "Ále is as strong as anyone I've ever known, and I hope that will be enough. But now we need to go."

FANTASIA FOR PIANO IN G MINOR, OP. 77

At daybreak, it was foggy, they had driven for hours, and Alejandra didn't know where they were headed. She opened the window just as the vehicle made a turn and caught a glimpse of a dilapidated street sign pointing to the village of Benediktbeuern. She recognized the name of the city for it was linked to a well-known musical work. The town in the southwest region of Bavaria was at the foothills of the Bavarian Alps. As they approached their destination, driving through an ordinary neighborhood but with extraordinarily lush surroundings, the vehicle finally stopped in front of a modest brown brick house flanked by pine trees.

The driver, the first to step out onto the curb, opened the back-seat door. "*Sie wird Sie zu Ihrem Quartier zeigen,*" he said. As she stepped out into the street, she noticed his sullied black boots, dark pants, and heavily-worn leather coat. Then the man with the Bollman hat also got out of the burgundy 540 K Spezial Coupe, and said, "*Es tut uns leid.*" They're sorry, he had said. Sorry for abducting her, sorry for following orders, or sorry for what was to come? Upset and tired, she turned away and met, at the entrance of the residence, a plump grandmotherly figure who said, "*Bitte folgen Sie mir.*"

Inside the house, Alejandra followed the woman with short wavy hair, who wore a black skirt, beige long-sleeve blouse, apron, and flat shoes. As they climbed a creaking stairway, she noticed the house was far from ordinary—walls covered in tapestries, and the overall space was cluttered with paintings and decorative arts.

On the second floor, through a dimly lit corridor, they reached a bedroom. The housekeeper said, "You'll find everything you need in the armoire. Your meals will be brought to you, and at eight o'clock tonight I'll take you to the grand salon to meet the master of house."

"And who would that be? And what's your name?" Alejandra asked.

"You'll find out tonight. My name is Greta," she said, before closing the door.

As if in a daze, she walked about the bedroom noting the opulent furniture—a tulipwood bed with gilt bronze mounts, a matching secretary's desk, a Louis XV gondola upholstered armchair, and a wooden armoire that nearly covered an entire wall. Above the bed, a Vermeer painting of a woman playing a harpsichord was softly illuminated with the natural light that funneled through a window. Her eyes soon turned to the outside view as the fog seemed to have lifted, and she could now see with more clarity the snow-covered mountains in the distance. Below her window, in a garden, she saw two guards talking to each other. Although her initial fears had subsided, she was desperate to face her abductor, bizarre or insane as he may be. For at least then she would know who she was dealing with and what he wanted.

She pulled open the carved oak armoire and found a complete woman's wardrobe for all occasions in dated fashion from the late twenties. Were these clothes meant for her to wear? Or did they belong to someone else? It was absurd for her captor to think she would agree to wear them, as if she was an actress in a play. Whatever his foolish fantasies were, she would not participate. She slammed the cabinet closed.

Greta returned a few moments later, tapped on the door, and placed a breakfast tray on a side table outside her door. Alejandra rushed to see her, but she was already walking away down the corridor. Thirsty, she drank the entire glass of orange juice. For a split second, she considered escaping again, but where to? And how far could she go with no documents and money? She had no choice but to wait until nightfall.

In the evening, after having dinner in the bedroom, the woman returned at five minutes before eight o'clock. Alejandra, still wearing her white gown, met her at the door. "He's ready to see you," Greta said.

"And who's he? Can't you tell me now?" Alejandra asked.

"You'll know soon," she said.

Greta escorted Alejandra down the stairway and into a grand salon with wood floors covered with oriental rugs, eighteenth century furniture, and a Graf pianoforte at the center. Alone, she turned her gaze toward the walls filled with oil paintings in various styles from Renaissance and baroque to

Impressionism, but one painting in particular caught her attention for she recognized it immediately—Picasso's *Girl before a Mirror,* the very same painting that had been auctioned off at the Steinhoff Auction House in Berlin when she had met Anton five years prior. What was that painting doing here? Then she heard the voice of a man who came into the salon. "You like it?" He had a thick German accent.

She felt her stomach churning upon seeing the man with hair slicked back, gaunt face, empty dark eyes, whose face she had never forgotten. He was the same Nazi who was at the Adlon Hotel the night of her arrival in Berlin in February in 1933, and who swore at the musicians demanding they play their anthem. He was at the Wagner festival, seated behind Hitler at the opera house, looking identical to him except without a mustache.

He motioned toward a seating area in front the grand piano. "Do you remember me?"

Hesitantly she followed, sitting across from him on one of two brown leather chairs.

"Wasn't the wardrobe to your liking?" he asked.

"I'd rather wear my own clothes, but who are you and why am I here?" she asked.

"Let's start with the first question. To your circle of friends, I'm known as Anonymous. Are you familiar with this designation?"

It can't be, she thought, but said nothing.

"Think hard. I know you've heard it before," he said.

"And how do you know that?" she asked.

"We're not going to get far if you reply with more questions. This is not a game of wits."

"Yes, I've heard it. So you obviously know more about me than I about you. What is it that you want?" she asked.

"First, you might like to know that I'm Anton's principal patron. He's my buyer of Renaissance and modern paintings, antiquities, and original musical manuscripts."

She paused, feeling sick to her stomach again. "Is Anton part of this bizarre game you're playing with me?"

He laughed as if enjoying his reply. "That's something you'll never know."

She didn't know what to believe but could not accept that Anton was behind her abduction.

"Did you think I was going to turn over a priceless original Beethoven manuscript like *Fidelio* so you could save your cherished Jewish friends? Just like that! Nothing is that easy. Although your Beethoven signed "Moonlight Sonata" was helpful in the negotiations."

She remained silent.

"You have nothing to say. I had heard from Anton you were the most emotionally controlled person he had ever met. I see he was right."

"Then you should know that provoking me is not going to scare me."

"I have to admit, I do find rather appealing that dismissive, even aloof quality you possess," he said. "There's a fearlessness about you."

"I'm bored with this conversation. What do you want?" she asked.

"I've been called a lot of things, but never boring. Wasn't your dream to live in the time of Beethoven? And didn't you also say you'd like to meet me and to see my art collection? Weren't those wishes that you expressed to Anton on more than one occasion?"

She looked away, evading his perverse smile. One phrase after another, the man was revealing things that she had shared in private conversations with Anton.

He continued. "That's why you're here. It's your destiny to play for me every single composition Beethoven ever wrote. And I want you to organize his entire body of work."

"So, that's your fantasy," she said.

"No. I don't believe in fantasies. It's our reality. The idea came to me when you played Beethoven so passionately at the home of Wagner. Do you recall that?"

"How could I forget?" she said. "You were there?"

"You were too preoccupied with saving Anton to notice anyone else. Then I thought I'd never see you again. But there you were a few years later conducting at the State Opera House of all places. And how could I not take that opportunity when Herbert Wolf, your strongest rival, wanted nothing more than to see you fail and to be your replacement. He loathed the idea of having a woman at the podium, and a foreigner at that. At my order, he arranged to have you abducted, and as if nothing had happened, Wolf went on to conduct the second part of your program. I was there too! And I have to admit you were awfully good. It's a shame you couldn't finish the program."

She looked at him with disdain. "And Ziegler, was he in it too?"

"No. He was just the perfect cover with his anti-Semitic rants but would have never gone that far. He's too loyal to Göring to create problems for him. He's a terrible liar. Wolf distracted Ziegler away from your stateroom while my two men carried you out of the opera house."

"And back in Bayreuth, was it you who had Anton arrested?"

He laughed perversely once again. "No. That was providence, and neither did I have anything to do with his release. That was all your doing. But it got my attention. I wished to keep my connection to Anton a secret. I did not intervene."

"And after I'm done with Beethoven's catalogue. Then what?" she asked.

"You'll either live or die," he said coldly.

"Is this another one of your perversions?"

"It's no joke. I assure you," he replied.

"And why Beethoven?" she asked.

"Because like you, I'm also obsessed with his music. I'm a man who values the arts."

"No. You use the arts as a shield to hide your immorality," she said. "And Beethoven would also be appalled. Perhaps you might consider learning from his noble ideals."

"No, that was his only weakness."

"I refuse to go along with this ploy!" she said, now standing up and preparing to leave.

"I'm not done!" he said, raising his voice several decibels. "You wish to die of boredom? It's not like you, is it? I won't force you to do anything you don't want to do. I'm not a savage."

"But you are," she said.

"By the end of your time here, you'll know who's right and who's wrong," he said.

"And how is all this to take place?" she asked.

"You'll have access to my library where you'll find hundreds of Beethoven's manuscripts, some copies and some originals," he said. "I want you to organize every single manuscript in chronological order. The originals, however, are in a locked safe, and you'll have to copy edit those. Oh, and you'll have to figure out the combination too. The safe is hidden behind a rather provocative painting."

She remained silent.

"I expect you to play for me every evening at eight o'clock from Beethoven's first to his last composition, although, you may choose the order. That will give me an element of surprise every night. Isn't that what Beethoven did, play privately for his benefactors? I might not have been Beethoven's benefactor, but I'm perhaps the largest collector of his manuscripts. I think he'd be pleased, don't you?"

"He was never abducted by any of his patrons."

"He still had to please them to go on working. Just look at all the dedications he made."

"You're mad. An incredibly twisted mind," she said.

"I could send you elsewhere, and I guarantee that those places and their surroundings would not be as comfortable. We have special designs, you might say, for all the musicians who will be imprisoned."

"What design?"

"The world will know soon enough. Music will be their refuge. In fact, you may find out sooner rather than later if you refuse or if your work is not done to my satisfaction."

"They'll find me," she said. "I know they will."

"No they won't! And if you try to escape, believe me you won't get far. You're free to walk about the garden, but my property is guarded at all times. Your work begins tomorrow."

She remained there, immobile, trying to digest what he had said. The gestures and words of this madman whirled in her mind, like a tornado about to destroy everything in its path. She was filled with doubt. Could she have been such a poor judge of character regarding Anton? Could he be part of this sinister plot? Or was he also a pawn in this web of deceptions that seemed to be the currency of the day? Speculating was worthless at the moment, for nothing mattered except getting out of there sane and in one piece.

"Do you have any questions?" he asked.

"Why not just give me the combination to your safe? It's a silly game."

"I have to entertain myself in more ways than one, silly as it might be. I have no intention of letting you go that easily for the moment, and I doubt that you can figure out the combination. But I'm a generous man, and if by some remote chance you succeed, then I would let you go."

She wanted nothing more than to spit in the man's face. But for the time being, she must believe he would keep his word. "Do I have your assurance?"

He looked at her. "Men need incentives to survive. I'll set you free if you fulfill those tasks. But if you fail, you'll never see your family again. I'm letting you choose."

You nasty bastard, she wanted to say. "I'll play along for now, but I may soon grow tired and you'll have nothing! How many numbers are in the combination, and are they connected to Beethoven's life?" He raised his head, looking up at her with surprise. "How quickly you seemed to have grasped a clue to the combination. Yes, and there are four numbers."

Later that night, from the window of her bedroom, she looked out at the shadowy forest before her, wishing she could be instantly transported back home to her family. Gloom and doom overcame her previous composure, and tears of anguish began running down her face, providing a catharsis for the restrained emotions she had suppressed since her abduction. She then thought of writing a letter to Richard that would record her sentiments. She felt, more than ever, doubtful about her future, but her faith had not diminished.

Sitting before the eighteenth-century desk, she dipped the pen into the inkwell, took a piece of parchment paper from a drawer and wrote:

August 28, 1938 "My darling Richard: I write to you not knowing whether I will ever see your face again, kiss your lips, or hold our children in my arms. I find myself imprisoned in a strange world of someone else's making, but there is light amidst the darkness as music will accompany me each day.

I blame myself for leaving you, for putting others before you, and now all is lost. I don't regret my choice and hope my dear Hannah and her son are alive, and that they and Ben will return home safely. But I fear about how it might end for me.

I'm living in a world where nothing makes sense, where right and wrong are footnotes to be simply read in secret by a few, and evil permeates every word and action as it spreads in the hearts and minds of those who have turned away from reason and God.

For the moment, there is no misery of the body, nor will I be left to die, like others will. I'm still free to enjoy God's creations of the land with its soaring mountains, and the sky with a shimmering moon. I'm surrounded by beautiful art and vestiges of things from centuries past, but now they only serve to hide the cruel truth of my current plight.

My heart is filled with love for you, Leidy, Richie, Del, Mother, and the rest of our family who enriched my life. Until my last breath, I will fall asleep thinking of you and listening to the sweet sounds and melodies of my dreams, hopes, and to the music of "Ode to Joy." My prayers are for the living and the dead, for the weak and for the strong, and for the forsaken and the blessed. May God's mercy be upon us all today and forever. Yours always, Alejandra.

The next morning, after much reflection, Alejandra was determined not to allow uncertainty about her future. With steadfastness and focus, she proceeded to the library to commence the task of organizing Beethoven's works.

The twenty-foot room was a replica of an eighteenth-century library, similar in décor to the grand salon, with plank flooring, gilt wood, velvet burgundy draperies, crystal chandeliers, and more paintings. Turning to her left, an upright piano was housed in the corner, surrounded by Klimt's *Beethoven Frieze*—a three-panel painting, resting on wooden stilts, which depicted exquisite and hideous figures representing sickness, madness, ambition, evil, and compassion—all searching for salvation through the arts and a mythical savior, a work of art that had been described by Anton years earlier. She looked closer at the visual journey of allegories rendered in bold colors of blue, brown and sparkling gold, ending with a chorus that sang Beethoven's triumphant choral symphony. And she conceded that the prospect of spending her days, perhaps even her last days, immersed in Beethoven's music would bring her own salvation.

It was behind one of these panels, her abductor had said, where the safe was hidden and where Beethoven's original hand-written manuscripts were kept. She assumed the safe was behind the panel that depicted the chorus. For the moment, she would leave the task of deciphering the combination for another day.

She made her way to the opposite side of the room where floor to ceiling bookcases stored hundreds of folders and books. From one bookcase at the center she picked several folders at random and carried them to a desk that was behind a burgundy sofa. She began the work of sorting out Beethoven's manuscripts with and without opus numbers. The first folder contained scores for piano trios and sonatas that were dedicated to musicians, princes, and kings, including Franz Joseph Haydn, Prince Karl Lichnowsky, and King Friedrich Wilhelm II of Prussia. Soon she came across a manuscript dedicated to Count Anatol Brunsvik. Written in 1809, the piece was titled

Fantasia for Piano in G Minor, Opus 77. Liking the title, she scanned the score, noting the lively, dynamic, and melancholic intonations that played against one another—a piece that mirrored her current emotions. She took the manuscript to the piano. The idea of having to play nightly for her abductor was repellent. So, she decided to approach it as though she was playing for Ludwig van Beethoven himself.

That would be her fantasy.

While playing, unexpectedly, she spotted a five or six-year-old girl, with blond tousled hair, who was standing by the entryway. "Hello," Alejandra said. The girl lifted her head slightly but did not reply and hid her face partially behind the door.

"*Komst du herein*," Alejandra said, resuming the piece to draw her in. She repeated two descending scalar passages, and the girl came into room, sitting timidly on a chair against a wall. For the next minutes, she listened to the nine-minute piece. Then Alejandra approached the child, but she ran out of the library. "Wait," Alejandra said to no effect, and the girl vanished.

For the rest of the morning she thought of the child with the unusual demeanor. So when Greta brought her lunch, she asked, "Who is the girl, and what's her name?"

She placed the tray on a round table by a window and said, "No one you need to know about." Alejandra sensed Greta's agitation as though she had made a mistake by letting the girl out of her sight. "It's all right. But since I'll be staying here for some time, I thought we could be friends and maybe even gain your trust. Please, will you join me for a few minutes?"

Greta agreed, taking a seat. From a distance, the housekeeper gave the appearance of someone stern, but from up close, her almond shaped eyes and curved mouth displayed a friendlier look. "I don't know anything about you," she said.

"You can ask me anything," Alejandra said.

"Why didn't you bring any suitcases?" Greta asked.

Alejandra thought that for the moment she mustn't contradict Anonymous. And it was necessary to keep Greta as an ally if possible. "That's a good question. I'm not sure where they are," Alejandra said. "But I can tell you that back home, I have a family that I miss very much."

"And what is the work that you're expected to do while you're here?" Greta asked.

"Create a catalogue of Beethoven's music. You see, I've spent my whole life studying his works," Alejandra said. She wished she could tell Greta the truth at some point. But her gut instincts told her it wasn't the right time yet. "May I ask you a few questions of my own?"

"Perhaps another day," Greta said.

"Of course," Alejandra said.

She left the room.

Later that evening, Alejandra entered the salon at four minutes past eight, dressed in her white gown, which she had washed by hand, and as expected the silk fibers were damaged, giving the dress a lackluster appearance. The man in a dark suit was smoking a cigar and pacing about the room. He said, "You're late, and I don't wait for anyone except for the Führer and other top commanders. Don't ever let that happen again."

She proceeded to the piano without saying a word, but as she prepared to play Fantasia for Piano in G Minor, he walked to her. "I think tonight, before you play for me, I want to discuss something."

She tilted her head upward. "What is there to talk about?"

"Oh! Music, art, family. I'm sure you have questions, and I'm in the mood to answer them," he replied, taking another drag of his cigar.

"I prefer to stay where I am." From her vantage point, she had a clear view of Picasso's *Girl Before a Mirror*. And she remembered just then having seen the invoice of the sale back at Anton's house only a couple of months earlier. There was a name that was listed as the purchaser, but she could not remember it—something starting with a G. What was it?

"Well! Don't you want to know anything?" he asked.

"Yes. Your name," she said.

"Günther," he replied.

That's it, Günther Kaiser. She remembered his last name but said nothing. "Were you at the auction house that winter of 1933? I don't recall seeing you there," she said. "Though, I clearly remember the Picasso painting."

"I was," he replied. "You came in only a few minutes before the start of the auction. I recognized you promptly and watched your every move from my seat in the last row across the aisle, although I left during the intermission. That's the day I met Anton. Do you remember when he was called elsewhere while you were talking to each other? It was me who summoned him as the buyer of the painting."

"Is he involved in all this?" she asked for a second time.

"The answer to that question is the same. Perhaps."

"What about the *Beethoven Frieze*? Did Anton sell it to you?"

"Maybe. Would that change how you feel about him?" he asked.

She remained silent thinking that it would. Anton had told her he had never participated in the selling or exchanges of stolen works of art that belonged to Jewish art collectors. And she knew this piece had belonged to a well-known Jewish businessman.

"What, no more questions?" he said.

"What's the point if you won't give me straight answers? It's all a game to you and not interesting to me."

He laughed. "Weren't the Beethoven manuscripts of interest?"

"The only thing," she said. "But there's something I want you to do."

"Oh?" he asked, exposing his yellowish teeth, too big for his mouth.

She gave him an envelope, addressed to Richard Morrison. "It's a letter to my family, and I hope that after reading it, you'll find the content vague enough, and you'll agree to mail it."

"And what do I get in return?" he asked, taking it from her hand.

"What do you want?" she asked.

He stared at her with a lustful leer. "Things you would decline to do, but for now wearing something different will suffice. The clothes in the armoire should fit you well."

She nodded agreement. "Whom did they belong to?" she asked.

"No one you need to know about," he replied.

"Then perhaps you'll answer this question. Do you have a daughter?"

Upset, he looked away. "You were never supposed to see her."

"I'd like to see her again," Alejandra said. "She was drawn to the music this morning."

"She reminds you of your daughters, I suppose," he said. "Unfortunately, you'll never get a word out of her as she's mute. I'm done with our conversation."

"Didn't you say you wanted to talk about family?" Alejandra asked.

He glared at her and walked away. "Just play," he said.

A t nine o'clock, in the library, Greta brought Alejandra breakfast. "Thank you. We didn't finish our conversation yesterday. I just have a couple of questions, please," she said.

With her hands folded on the table, Greta sat across from Alejandra.

"The house is very beautiful. So is Mr. Kaiser a high-ranking officer in the Führer's administration?" Alejandra asked.

"Oh, yes, madam, he's the second most powerful official in the Gestapo," she said.

Then Greta went on to detail his military career. After fighting in the Great War, he realized that the path to a better life was in seeking a high military rank. He became an early member of the Nazi Party and joined the Militant League for German Culture in 1929—a national organization dedicated to making a supreme imprint on cultural life in Germany based on Nazi principles. He was introduced to Adolf Hitler by Alfred Rosenberg, who founded the NGDK—National Socialist Society for German Culture—and who was also one of the principal authors of Nazi ideology. Hitler, Rosenberg, and others from the party embraced the arts to enhance their political agenda. And Kaiser's first major assignment was as commandant of Dachau, the first Nazi concentration camp.

"Greta. You're well informed in politics. Can you tell me something about his personal life? How did you become acquainted with him?"

"I have known him for a long, long time. But I think I've said too much already. I hope you'll be as candid with me in the future as I've been with you. I have to go now," Greta said.

"Yes," Alejandra said.

When Greta left, Alejandra was pleased with what she had learned about Kaiser. It was evident to her that there was more to their relationship than simply boss and employee; for Greta was an unusually knowledgeable and educated housekeeper. As the second most powerful in the Gestapo, and with unlimited access, he had obviously seized many works of art over the past years that were now kept in his residence. Did he keep this endeavor a secret? It dawned on Alejandra with sadness that many of the art and antiquities adorning the house had likely been pillaged by the Nazis from the art collections of Jews.

MUSIC, MAESTRO, PLEASE

September 4, 1938 – Minneapolis, Minnesota

Trying his best to not think of the last few days, Richard Morrison was reading Hemingway's newest novel—*To Have and Have Not*. He thought he would much prefer to be, for a day, Harry Morgan, a man trying to keep his family together by running contraband between Cuba and Key West. He too felt as though his family, or at least his marriage, was crumbling apart, and no amount of money in the world could fix that.

The doorbell rang.

Moments later, Richard welcomed his friend, Stephen Johnson, who was an Irish-looking man with wavy red hair, freckled face, and a robust physique—a likeness to his Irish mother. Wearing Shetland trousers and a light-yellow shirt, he looked as though he was the poster boy for a sports magazine, Richard thought, compared to his lounging attire. "What are you doing here on a Sunday afternoon?" They shook hands warmly.

"I just finished a round of golf, and I thought I'd stop by to chat," Stephen said, "You've been a bit of a recluse all summer, and perhaps I can get you to agree to go out tonight. Olga told me your kids and the rest of the family are at your lake cottage until tomorrow."

"It's so damn quiet in here," Richard said, closing the door. "How about a drink first?"

"Sure," Stephen said. They walked into the porch, furnished with wicker chairs.

Once there, from a portable Bauhaus era bar-cart, Richard took a bottle of whiskey and two glasses. Then he placed them on a glass table. After filling both glasses, they took their seats across from each other.

Stephen took his drink. "How have you been?"

"Surviving," Richard replied. "Too much work since my partner moved to the west coast. And you? Has business picked up at all?"

"Fair. We're building two office buildings in St. Paul around the capital and are trying to finish them before winter sets in. But tell me, any news from Ále?"

"Not for several days. She was expected to conduct at the opera house on the 27th of August, and I spoke with her the day before. I tried calling a few times after that, but no one answered the phone," he said. "I did receive a telegram from Ben who said he was on his way back to the States, and he would contact me then but nothing else. I also contacted Ben's family in New York, but they had no additional information, nor if Hannah and Joseph were found. So, I can't figure out for the life of me why she won't call or write me."

"I'm sure you'll hear from her soon. Maybe a little distraction might do you some good."

"What I need is my wife! Sometimes I don't know how much more of this I can take. How the hell did we end up like this? Why isn't her family enough for her?"

"I can understand your frustration. And, of course, having a family is good enough for her," Stephen replied. "But you also know she's strong willed. She has always been of the mind that women can be as capable as men in most endeavors, and that's why you fell in love with her. Don't try to deny it now. You were accustomed to having your way in everything, and women fawned all over you, until she came along. She challenged you."

"I suppose you're right. Although, part of me thought she wouldn't accomplish as much as she has done," Richard said. "I have come to terms with it."

"Is her success a threat to you?" Stephen asked.

"No, but I'm afraid I'm losing her. I thought our lives were perfect before she left. These last years were some of the happiest in our marriage, but everything seemed to have changed when Hannah and her family disappeared. I understand that."

"I don't believe that you're losing her at all. This time she's not away for professional reasons. She just wants to do what's right for her friends. You know how much she cares about them. I'm sure of it. I talked to her at length before she left. Remember, Ben did get released, so something good happened from her efforts. But seeing you're down in the dumps, all the more reason to join us tonight."

"A little distraction might help. Where are you inviting me this time?"

"Do you remember Sally Stuart from our high school days?" Stephen asked.

"Sally, the sugar plum?" Richard said with a sardonic smile.

Stephen laughed. "Yes, that Sally. She moved to the Tudor house down our street after her husband died a couple of years ago. He left her very wealthy, and she's having a Labor Day party. She suggested we bring you along since many of our friends will be there. How about it?"

"What for? So I can be asked where my wife is a dozen times?"

"Just say she's off conducting someplace glamorous, and they'll leave you alone."

For a moment Richard looked away, noticing the trees had begun to change color. Fall was Alejandra's favorite time of the year, but he did not want to think about her. It was too painful. "Why the hell not. I'm tired of worrying, and I hate the silence here. What time?"

"Seven? You can't miss her house. It's the only one of its kind in the vicinity," Stephen said. He then finished his drink and got to his feet. "I can see myself out."

"I'll see you later," Richard said.

Stephen had always been his most loyal friend since childhood, and they were still best of friends, having shared a long history together. He thought about everything Stephen had said, but he was not convinced, for Richard had started to wonder if Alejandra had abandoned her family. He felt a pang in his stomach.

With reluctance, Richard arrived at the Tudor mansion later that night. Wearing a beige jacket, light-green shirt, and cream trousers, he was in the smoky formal entry. Sally Stuart, a strawberry-blond socialite known for her garish laughter, heavy makeup, and flamboyant taste, said, "Richard, look at you. You haven't changed a bit." She kissed Richard on the cheek, barely missing his lips.

"You haven't changed much either," he said, noticing her voluptuous figure, sequined black dress, and flashy jewelry on her fingers, arms, and neck.

"Everyone is in the ballroom, and the band is about to play," she said.

Just then a waiter walked by holding a tray filled with a variety of drinks.

She took a martini and gave it to Richard. "It's still your favorite, isn't it?"

"Some things never change. You still remember?"

"That's all we drank together until you fell for sweet, innocent Alejandra." She laughed. "And, by the way, is she still abroad?"

"Yes, but I'd rather not talk about it," he said, taking a drink.

He then followed her down a paneled hall and into the ballroom with vaulted ceilings and appointed with dark wood beams, Gothic chandeliers, and heavy furniture. The place was packed, but he soon spotted Stephen and his wife, Olga. They were standing near the bar.

"Excuse me," he said to Sally.

"Now don't go too far," she said.

He finished his martini and made his way over to his friends.

"Rich. I'm so glad that you came," Olga said, hugging him.

Stephen introduced Richard to Leslie and Robert Eastman.

They shook hands.

"You're Alejandra's husband?" Leslie asked.

"You know my wife?"

"I know about her, though I've never met her. My cousin is in her chorus. When will she be back? I hear the group is not too keen on her temporary replacement."

"That's an understatement," Olga said. "Maybe she isn't planning on coming back."

Richard turned to Olga. "What a ridiculous thing to say. Of course, she's coming back."

"You know Olga's sense of humor, always a little hyperbolic," Stephen said.

Richard thought it might have been a joke, but deep down inside he was thinking the same thing. He had no interest in pursuing the conversation, and as he had predicted, he felt out of place. Since his wife's departure in the spring, he had avoided social gatherings except for family functions. "I think I need another drink." He then left for the bar, a few steps away. "A straight up Martini please, with two olives."

A young bartender, dressed in a striped black and white suit, replied, "Yes, sir."

Just then Sally stepped up to the stage and formally greeted all her guests. "Thank you all for coming to this evening of celebration, and it's with great pleasure that I introduce to you the Moonlight Swing Orchestra."

Richard glanced at the eight-piece band as a young black man stepped in front of the microphone. The orchestra followed his cue, giving him a brief instrumental preamble. Then he began to sing. "Maestro, music, please. *I could use a chaser for my blues. Tonight I mustn't think of her, music, maestro, please! I must forget how much I need her. Play your lilting melodies ragtime, jazz time, swing, any old thing to help me ease the pain that solitude can bring...*"

Richard wished he could be like that fellow singing and chasing away those blues.

Moments later, the bartender placed his martini on the bar, and Richard drank all its contents. He had only come to the party to escape the growing loneliness he had felt since Alejandra's departure, but being there without her only served to deepen it. Long separations between married couples were never a good thing, and as far as he was concerned he had already experienced more than his share. Perhaps he should have gone to be with her despite her objections. Over the last weeks, he had questioned her absence and now feared she had also stopped loving him.

He was on his third martini when the singer finished the song, and the band started playing the upbeat swing piece, "Sing, Sing, Sing." Sally joined him at the bar. "Care to dance with an old friend?" She took the glass from his hand, setting it down on the bar. Already a little intoxicated, Richard allowed Sally to lead him onto the dance floor. "Let's see if you can still twirl me around like old times." She laughed.

He placed his hand around her waist and grabbed her hand. Then along with the rest of the couples, they went into a dance craze, tapping their feet, bouncing, and spinning like wildcats. For the next twenty minutes, one upbeat song after another followed, and they continued to dance until the band turned out a slow tempo piece. Wiping his sweaty forehead with his handkerchief and feeling a bit woozy, he said with slurred speech, "I'm so wooorn out. I think I need some air."

"Yes, you do that. I'll meet you outside. I need to freshen up first," Sally said.

Richard then went outside to the courtyard where Stephen was seated on a swinging bench, flanked by dozens of potted plants of purple and orange mums. It was a warm fall night. He stumbled and nearly fell before taking a seat next to him.

"Looks like you were enjoying yourself out there," Stephen said, taking a puff of his cigarette. "I haven't seen you dance like that since high school."

Richard lit a cigarette with some difficulty and then took several puffs. "She's still as suuugary as ever."

"Be careful, she might still have a crush on you," Stephen said jokingly.

"You don't have to worry about me," he said, speaking in slow motion. "I'm a saint, don't you know?"

"What I see is that you're drunk. I think I better take you home," Stephen said.

"I don't want to go home. To fucking what?"

"Rich, this is not like you at all. You're out of character. I think it's the alcohol talking."

Richard burped. "Yeah. I'm a character all right, in one of Ále's damn tragic operettas."

Just then Olga came into the courtyard and said, "I'm ready to go home."

"Give me a few minutes. I'll be right in," Stephen said.

"Don't delay," she said, leaving the garden.

He then stood and leaned over toward Richard. "Let's go home, my friend."

Richard dismissed him with a wave of his hand. "No. I can manage just fucking fine on my own. Get out of here."

Stephen shook his head. "Have it your way. I'll call you tomorrow."

The following day, Richard woke up naked on the bed of Sally Stuart. His mouth was dry, his whole body ached, and the smell of vomit was in the air. But whose? He turned over and Sally, also naked, was spread out like a butterfly, with one of her arms dangling off the mattress. Her hair was messy, her upper eyelids were smudged with mascara, and she was lightly snoring. Images of her undressing and climbing on top of him flashed before him. How the hell did he end up here? Was he so drunk that he fell for Sally Stuart's limited charms? Unfortunately, the answer was obvious. In a night of debauchery, he had done the unthinkable. He was overwhelmed with shame and guilt for betraying his wife. That was something he never thought capable of doing.

Sickened by his actions, he sat up on the bed looking for his clothes, which were strewn about the floor next to a dresser covered with makeup. The room, decorated in floral pink wallpaper, was cluttered with cheap statuettes everywhere. He quickly got dressed and glimpsed at his haggard appearance in a mirror. Then as he tiptoed out of the bedroom, catching one last glance of the vulgar woman on the bed, he knew he would never want to see her again. How many others had been in his position since her husband died? He hoped he had not picked up a venereal disease from her, but even worse was how to explain this terrible misstep to Alejandra—breaking their wedding vows. Would she forgive him, and could he ever forgive himself? He shook his head, disgusted by what he had done, and walked away.

45

15 VARIATIONS AND FUGUE OP. 35

Nearly a week had transpired, and from early in the morning to late afternoon, Alejandra worked in the library organizing Beethoven's manuscripts. For an hour every evening, she had performed the composer's first six opus compositions written for trios and sonatas, which she arranged for piano. Günther was a moody and strange man who had given her the silent treatment. And while she would prefer not having to converse with the man, she was concerned about the child who seemed to have completely disappeared. His behavior reinforced Alejandra's notion that he was determined to raise the girl in confinement, and this troubled her immensely.

Alejandra decided that as long as she was a captive herself, she'd do whatever was necessary on behalf of the young girl. How to engage Günther in a discussion about the matter would require a compelling argument that could convince him to reconsider his position. After a couple of days of mulling it over, she conceived a plan, fortuitously triggered, when she came across one of Beethoven's letters, from June 29 of 1802, written to his longtime trusted friend, Franz Gerhard Wegeler from Bonn. In it Beethoven revealed sentiments regarding his physical impairment and mounting hardships. And more significant to her was the composer's poignant communiqué demonstrating an inner fortitude and unbreakable spirit.

At night, Alejandra, dressed in a lilac silk gown, came into the salon and sat at the pianoforte, glancing at the score of Sonata no. 5 for Piano in F Major, op. 24. Before playing, she turned to Günther, who was seated, smoking his cigar.

"The sonata I'm about to play was composed at a time when Beethoven was already struggling with his hearing. What do you suppose might have happened if Beethoven had given up composing after losing his hearing?"

His eyes narrowed. "Why do you ask such a question?"

"Curious about your thoughts on the subject."

"You care about my opinion? I see the silent treatment worked," he said.

Alejandra smiled to herself. She had found his Achilles heel—challenging his ego was a sure way to rile him up and get him to engage.

"I assure you it has nothing to do with your silent treatment," she said. "But if you can't think of an answer, then forget about it."

"Isn't it obvious? It would have been a great loss," he said.

"So you too may find yourself at a terrible loss."

"Me? What do I have to do with it?"

"Yes, you! When Beethoven was suffering from growing health problems and hearing loss, he confided in a letter to his friend. 'I will defy my fate,' she said, quoting the composer.

With his ever-present tortuous smile, he replied, "Oh. I see. Is that what you propose to do? To defy your fate?"

"Maybe, but the person I'm speaking of is not me… it's your daughter. She too might defy fate if allowed," Alejandra said.

Showing agitation, he walked to her. "And how do you know she's my daughter?"

She stood, taking a few steps toward the opposite side of the piano, using it as a shield.

"I don't know with certainty, but by the expression of disappointment on your face the last time we spoke, it was the only conclusion I could make."

"She must never be seen in public. You must know that people who are physically impaired are useless in our society," he said.

"A threat to your Aryan purity? Is that it? And you believe that nonsense too? And do you realize that there are probably thousands of people who have lost their sight or hearing for one reason or another? So if Beethoven lived now, would he too be victim to your inhuman practices?"

He looked away briefly. "I did believe that until my daughter was born five years ago."

"When in 1933?"

"January 21. Her mother died in childbirth," he said.

"Has your daughter ever been seen by a doctor?" she asked.

"Yes. I took her to Switzerland, but the doctor couldn't give me a definite diagnosis," he said with a bitter expression. "She needed testing. No one must ever know of her condition. Understand!"

"Would her mother approve of keeping her isolated?" she asked.

"Probably not," he replied.

"Well then, as long I'm being kept against my will, leave your daughter free to join me in the library whenever she wants," she said. "You have nothing to lose."

He stared at her for a few seconds. "I'll do it for her mother," he said.

"What's your daughter's name?" she asked.

"Sophia," he replied. "Enough of this conversation."

Alejandra then played the sonata.

In the morning, she was in the library, confident that Sophia would make an appearance. The room was spacious, but dark and uninviting. Alejandra drew open the velvet drapes, allowing light to funnel in through a large window, which had a view of the Benedictine monastery of Benediktbeuern. From her studies, she recalled it was in that monastery that a collection of poems, known as *Carmina Burana*, were discovered. The verses, written in Medieval Latin by students of the clergy, represented fanciful and tragic stories beyond their life of seclusion. Words that spoke of "Fortune, like the moon, changeable and ever waxing and waning; hateful life first oppressed and then soothes as fancy takes it; poverty and poser it melts them like ice…" She thought that if a life of seclusion could have led to such inspiration, then she could teach Sophia to think of a life beyond the walls of her physical existence and her impairment, a life where she could communicate despite her inability to speak, and a life where she could dream and create a world of her making.

Just as those verses had inspired Carl Orff to write a scenic cantata—twenty-four poems set to magnificent choral music in the Renaissance style of Claudio Monteverdi—Alejandra, too, could be inspired to make a difference in Sophia's life. And she imagined further a time beyond her confinement when Alejandra would conduct a concert where her loved ones heard the magnificent work of words and music, a future so idyllic that the voices in her chorus would heal barren hearts, spread peace among men, and where life and death would stand still.

With the hope of catching Sophia's interest, Alejandra played Beethoven's spirited piece, 15 Variations and Fugue op. 35. Soon, she spotted the girl, with a ponytail, in the corridor. She looked like a playful little elf, wearing a green cotton dress and hiding her face behind the door.

"Guten Morgen, Sophia," Alejandra said, as she diminished the volume of her playing.

The little girl came into the room, walking toward Alejandra who moved to make room. "Sit next to me," she said. With an oval face and blue eyes, the color of the sky, she sat as directed and placed her hands on her lap. Alejandra played random notes. "Now you try." Then Sophia placed her small fingers on the keys, moving them awkwardly.

"Excellent. Just remember the more you play, the easier it gets. Would you like me to teach you how to play?" she asked. "I've done this before with my two daughters. Their names are Leidy and Del, and my name is Alejandra."

Sophia looked up and smiled, nodding slightly.

"I'm here every day, and you can come anytime you want," she said. "And even if you don't feel like playing, you can still visit with me. I can read you magical stories from one of the many books here. Some of these stories were read to me as a child."

Sophia nodded.

"Then let's start our first lesson with how to place your fingers on the piano. There are eighty-eight keys, and their names begin with middle C."

Late that night, for the first time since her abduction, Alejandra felt more hopeful about her own prospects and those of Sophia, as well as Hannah and her son, thinking that everything would be all right for everyone. Now at the desk, she would finish the letter to Hannah. Upon reading it again, she realized it was rather gloomy and crumpled up the paper, tossing it in the wastebasket. Then she started a new one.

September 9, 1938. My dearest Hannah: My friend and my sister, every day I think of you and wonder where you are. I pray to God He keeps you in his care, and that soon we'll see each other once again. Today, I imagined a world filled with love and happiness; a world where we could escape from all the madness; a world where we're back together and see the same blue skies; a world where time stands still.

I think of the time, all those years ago, as I heard your laughter that summer day in 1920 when we were aboard a ship crossing the Atlantic Ocean. Barely seventeen, we were both filled with hopes and dreams. It was our love of music that bound us together...

Then, she wondered whether this letter would get to its destination, or would it be lost like the one she had written to Richard? Alejandra was certain Günther never followed through with his commitment to send it. Perhaps she could give this letter to Greta. She placed the letter on her nightstand with the intention of finishing it the next morning and went to bed. It had been a good day.

At dawn, however, she woke up feeling chilled by a disturbing nightmare in which Hannah pleaded for mercy from an abandoned place in the wilderness. Anxious because of the images in her dream, Alejandra turned on the bedside lamp. Were her dreams a premonition? Not wanting to believe it, she took the letter and continued to write it, as if by doing so she could prevent something horrible from happening.

Tonight, I dreamed you spoke to me from the depths of your despair, and I wish you know how much you are loved and can only hope those images are but a nightmare—a manifestation of unconscious fears. So much has happened in our lives, yet throughout the years, it was our friendship that was our anchor through life's sweet and bitter moments. Please know how grateful I am you are in my life. Know that your faith will keep you in God's glory, and He will keep you and Joseph safe wherever you may be.

Tears filled Alejandra's eyes, and whatever hopeful feelings she had last night had evaporated under the harsh reality before her. For the truth was that she might never again behold the faces of Hannah or Richard or her own children. And for the first time in her life a great void opened in her, cold, lonely, terrifying, and she felt as though her own faith was beginning to dwindle.

JEWISH PRAYER

In the countryside, an hour away from Vienna, Hannah was in a farmhouse having supper with Joseph and their two relatives, Joshua and Sarah Oldenburg. Owned by Joshua's family since the turn of the century, the cottage held a table and four chairs next to a small kitchen. On the opposite side, a faded upholstered sofa was set against a window, and two rocking chairs lay in front of a brick fireplace. A stairway to the right led to the upstairs where two rooms served as their sleeping quarters. Hannah and Joseph had been living there since their abrupt departure from Vienna in the spring after the Anschluss.

In May, Hannah had gone to the American embassy to inquire about Ben who had gone missing. With no information as to his whereabouts, the embassy staff assured her they would investigate and keep her informed. She had requested new documents that would allow her and her son to return to America. And while Sarah was an American citizen, her husband, Joshua, was a German native who had requested asylum in the United States. But like many Jews in a similar situation, it would take time for an exit visa to be approved. With the violence spreading across the country, Hannah had decided to join her relatives at their lodge. She concluded it would be safer for everyone involved, and it would also give the embassy time to investigate Ben's disappearance. In August, Hannah had obtained her documents from the American embassy in Vienna. She had gone twice to Anton's residence in Vienna—one time in July and another in August, but both times no one was home.

She often wondered whether Anton had recovered from his addiction or if he had fled Europe at some point, or was he dead? As for news of Ben, she had lost all hope. She felt she could no longer wait for Joshua's documents, as the situation was increasingly dangerous for Jews across Austria. Her plans to leave that country by the end of September had been finalized. She had written to her parents, notifying them of both her current situation and of her future travel plans. However, to this date, she had not received any correspondence from them.

After supper, Hannah cleared the table and brought a pot of coffee. "I wish you were both coming with us."

Sarah, dressed in a pleated skirt and tucked-in floral blouse, was an elegant woman, with red hair and green eyes. "I wish it too, but the truth is you can't wait any longer, and we understand," she said.

"Of course, we understand," Joshua said, pouring himself a cup of coffee.

Still at the table, Hannah turned to Joshua, who was soft-spoken and an intellectual. A slender man with a broad forehead and large brown eyes, he was forty-two years old. He had been a professor of theology at Humboldt University of Berlin until he was dismissed from his post in the fall of 1935 after the passing of the Nuremberg Laws, which deprived all Jews of their German citizenship and other rights. Joshua and Sarah moved to Vienna where he worked for the University of Vienna but was also discharged, two years later, due to anti-Semitic policies.

She was very fond of Joshua, for he was kind, especially to Joseph, and he often read passages from the Torah and taught her son German. He frequently reminisced about his work while at Humboldt University where some of Germany's greatest scholars had studied. He was a proud German who always hoped to return to his country when Hitler and his government were ousted from power. He believed that Germany would return to its former democratic glory.

"I'm sorry that all this time has not produced any information on Ben," he said, drinking from his cup.

"What if he's dead?" Hannah asked.

"Don't think that way," Joshua said. "Somehow, we've got to keep on going. You'll see. Everything will resolve itself one way or the other."

"You're always so reassuring," Hannah said. "That's what I've been doing for the last three months. The only person that keeps me going is that little boy upstairs who inherited his father's curiosity and intellect."

"And your energy," Joshua said. "I'm going to miss him very much."

Hannah placed her fingers over her eyelids, trying her best to hide the sadness she was feeling. Sadness for not knowing anything about Ben; sadness for having to leave without Joshua and Sarah, and for the state of the world. She felt at the lowest point in her life.

"You must be strong," Joshua said.

"You know, I always knew things would get this bad for all of us. This is why I never wanted to come back while Hitler was in power," Hannah said.

"My dear, you know us Jews have survived for many centuries. One man will not change that no matter how powerful he may be, and no matter how many followers he has. You must always keep your faith. That's our principle source of strength."

"I want to," she said. "But why would God allow all this to happen?"

"Believe me, I've done a lot of soul searching on this topic, and I have discussed it at length with others. God has nothing to do with it. He gave us all a spiritual guide and free will to act upon this world. And each one of us must choose either love or hate for one another."

"Yes, I do agree with that," Hannah said. "Even if it seems such a simplistic concept. That's something my father would often say."

Just then, Joseph came down the stairs and ran to the window. "Mommy, it's Bertha," he said, pointing to a woman who was fast approaching the house.

Hannah looked at their neighbor in the distance. With no children of her own and widowed, she had taken to Joseph. The little boy, too, had bonded with Bertha who was an older German woman in her seventies. Pudgy, short and very friendly, she visited them daily, often bringing loaves of homemade bread and apple strudel—Joseph's favorite pastry.

Moments later, impatiently, she knocked on the door.

Joshua greeted her. She was short of breath. "Bertha, are you all right?"

"No. You must leave here at once. I just got word from my sister that a group of SS men is going to nearby towns hunting for Jews and workers for a labor camp. Rumors are that they are taking people to Mauthausen."

"I knew this would happen eventually," Joshua said. "We should pack immediately and leave for Vienna."

"We won't be safe there either," Sarah said.

"We won't be safe anywhere, but that's our best option for now," he insisted.

"There's no time for anyone to go now," Bertha said, looking out. "They're already driving past my house. Let me take the child, and then you can pick him up later. He'll be safer with me. I'll say that he's mine if they question me."

Hannah sighed. "Yes, I suppose that's true. Please be careful. He's all I've got now."

"We've got no choice but to hide in the barn," Joshua said.

He took a pistol from a closet in the kitchen. "This is just a precaution."

"Maybe you should leave it behind," Sarah said.

"It's only for self-defense."

Bertha picked up the boy. "I will. Now, go through the back door. Hurry," she said.

Hannah kissed her son, feeling a lump in her throat. "My little Joseph, I'll see you very soon. I promise. Bertha will take care of you," she said. "Mommy loves you very much."

"Yes, Mommy," he said, putting his arm around the old woman's wrinkled neck, as though he was just visiting with her as on many occasions in the past.

Then Hannah, Sarah, and Joshua left through the back door and rushed down a dirt road that led to the barn about one hundred feet away from the house. The barn looked abandoned, and as it no longer served its purpose it was mostly vacant, except for several tall stacks of hay and rusted tools scattered around the floor. Other rusted farm and lawn equipment lay on the side of the space. They hid behind the haystacks and waited silently for some time until Hannah heard gunshots in the distance. Shortly after, a vehicle approached and stopped outside the farmhouse.

As car doors opened, she heard the voices of several men. One said, "I'll look in the barn, and you two go to the house."

Moments later, the SS man was inside the barn. "I know someone's here. You left fresh tracks outside, you idiots," he said.

From a little gap in the stacks of hay, she could see a man, red-faced and husky, wearing a uniform with a swastika armband. He held a rifle.

Joshua slowly came out from his hiding place with his hands up. "I'm the only one here. Take me if that's what you want, but I'm a German citizen," he said.

"You're sure about that? If you were, you wouldn't be hiding like a Jew."

He then pushed Joshua with the rifle pointing to his back toward the door until Sarah gasped, giving their location away.

"You fucking liar!" he said, returning to the same spot from where Joshua had surfaced.

"Are you coming out, or do I have to get you?"

Hannah and Sarah both came out from their hiding place.

Now pointing the rifle at Sarah, the man said. "Go there with him, now!"

"Let them go," Joshua said. "They're both American."

"You don't tell me what to do," the man said.

Hannah stepped forward. "As far as I know, our countries are not at war," she said.

"Not for long, I'm sure. And what about this Jew here?"

"We're expecting his visa anytime soon," Hannah replied. "We're all going back to America. So, you have no reason to detain him. He's my cousin."

"Let me see all your documents."

"They're back in the house," Hannah said.

"Bring them to me," he said. "But only one of you go."

"I'll do it," Hannah said. She then ran back to the house, and upon arriving there, two other SS men were seated at the table eating as though they lived there, drinking and laughing.

"And who the hell are you?" one asked.

"An American, and I'm here to get my documents from upstairs," she said.

"Let's see what you've got," he said. Then he took another bite of the meatloaf, chewing with his mouth open.

Hannah glared at them and ran upstairs. Upon seeing Joseph's papers on top of the dresser, she decided it would be best to leave those behind for the moment. She hid them underneath the mattress. The last thing she wanted was for them to hunt down her son. She then went to the other room and took Sarah's documents, which were in the top drawer of her nightstand. A few minutes later she came down the steps and showed her passport to one of the SS men who was blond-haired and neatly groomed. He inspected each of the documents. "You better go. We don't want your kind here," he said. Then she heard him say as she walked out, "I think this little hut will serve us pretty darn good."

When Hannah returned to the barn, Joshua and Sarah were outside next to a rusted lawn mower. The SS man grabbed the papers from her hand and looked at them carefully. Joshua took the opportunity to pull out a pistol from the back of his pants, concealing it behind his waist.

The SS man gave the papers back to Hannah and turned to Joshua. "The women can stay, but you come with me."

"What do you want with him?" Sarah asked.

"None of your business. You'll never see him again." He laughed. "Just be glad I'm letting you both go."

"Do as he says," Joshua said. "Don't worry about me."

"No," Sarah said. "Then take me too."

"All right. Have it your way. Now move," the man said.

As they started to walk away, the other two Nazis who were in the house came out. "He's got a pistol," one yelled out.

Joshua was about to raise his hands to surrender, but before he could do that the blond-haired SS man shot him in the back.

When Joshua fell to the floor, Sarah screamed, "You bastards," taking her husband's pistol and shooting at the aggressor. The bullet hit the Nazi's leg.

"You fucking bitch!" he yelled.

Then the man with the rifle, in execution style, shot Sarah in the head. Blood gushed out, and she collapsed to the ground next to Joshua.

Hannah, who was seeing all this as if in slow motion, screamed in shock, just as the husky man turned the rifle toward her and shot her through the chest. She fell to the dirt floor and looked at the injured SS man who got up but was limping. She was still holding on to the documents. He snatched them from her hand. Then he joined the other two men. All three got into their vehicle and drove away as if they had just killed wild game. Dead bodies and pools of blood lay around Hannah. It had all only taken minutes. Hannah felt numb.

She felt a sharp pain in her heart and gently pressed the wound with the palm of her hand in an attempt to contain the burning ache as blood slowly trickled out of her body and spread across the dusty ground, dampening the dry earth beneath her. She was trembling, left to die in a remote land far from home and everyone she loved. She now watched, from a distance, as Bertha, holding her three-year-old son, approached and suddenly stopped—as though she was afraid to let the boy see his mother die before his eyes. She only hoped that her son would remain in Bertha's care, for she would love Joshua like her own son. Would she ever tell her son the truth? Probably not, but she hoped.

Hannah felt such sorrow as Joseph's big brown eyes stared at her. He had brought so much joy to her life and would grow up not ever knowing his real parents or that he had Jewish blood. She turned her gaze to the heavens where little sunlight remained. Moments of happiness and grief flashed before her, like the clouds now drifting across the rapidly darkening skies.

Gasping for air, Hannah thought of everyone she loved, but even as she drew her last breath, her faith in God did not diminish despite all the evil around her. In her mind, she heard the exalted melody of Bloch's Jewish Prayer. Then she turned to her son who had pushed himself down to the ground and was now running toward her with that high-spirited force that would serve him well in his life. He was crying, "Mommy, Mommy." When he reached her, his face was wet with tears, and he fell on his knees beside her, touching her face with his warm little fingers.

Hannah whispered to Joseph her last words and her father's most repeated saying, echoing sweetly in her dimming consciousness, "I love you! Be a mensch. Be a mensch."

CLAIR DE LUNE

October 22, 1938 – Minneapolis

Richard raked leaves in the backyard. It was windy, and the maples were now bare and devoid of the colors of two weeks prior when the neighborhood had been a kaleidoscope of orange, yellow, red, and green. It was long past the time when Alejandra should have returned home. For nearly two months, he had not been able to communicate with her. He had made many failed attempts by telephone, and telegrams had all gone unanswered. Rightly or wrongly, he now believed that he and his children had been abandoned. It was not, however, a reality he was prepared to discuss with them.

His thoughts were interrupted by the distant sound of his daughter, Leidy, who was in the house playing Debussy's "Clair de Lune." The music resonated perfectly with what he was feeling—desolate. But then, near him, a burst of laughter made him turn toward his two youngest children, Richie and Del, who, accustomed to their mother's absence, were playing in a sea of leaves, throwing them up in the air. That playfulness between them gave him a little spark of hope… hope that he would soon hear news about Alejandra and that she would return any day now. And that by the next season they would all be a family again.

Then suddenly, the piano music stopped, and Leidy came running into the backyard. "Daddy, there's a man at the door asking for you."

He dropped the rake on the ground and hurried into the house. Standing in the foyer by the door, he saw Ben who looked much aged. His clothes, brown slacks, beige shirt, and pullover sweater, were loose on him.

"Am I glad to see you! I've been trying for weeks to reach Ále. Where is she?"

"Oh, Richard, I don't even know where to start."

"Let's go into my office," Richard said, leading him into the room only a few steps away. He closed the door behind him.

"Is she alive?" Richard blurted out.

Ben sighed, closing his eyes momentarily. "She's dead."

Richard, overcome with emotion, covered his face. "No. It can't be."

Then Ben grabbed Richard's arm. "It's not Ále... it's my Hannah who was killed."

Confused, Richard turned to Ben, who started to sob. "How? And where's my wife?"

"It's all so despicable," Ben said. "I've been dealing with my grief for some time, hoping against all odds that by some miracle Hannah was not dead as I had been told. Her body was never found. My son Joseph is missing too. I stayed in Berlin waiting to hear news about him, but that never happened. I sent you a telegram and a letter explaining everything. I was also hoping to bring you better news about Ále."

"I received your telegram, but it didn't say anything about this, and I never got a letter from you or Alejandra, except for the one she sent through the embassy when you were released. And what do you mean by better news?" Richard asked.

For the next twenty minutes, Ben told Richard about the events of the last several months, his capture in Vienna by the Nazis during the Anschluss, his time at Dachau, Alejandra's efforts and negotiations that led to his subsequent release, and her abduction on the day of the concert. He described at length going to the American embassy in Berlin with the anticipation of reuniting with his family, but instead, Ben was told that Hannah was dead. The only information they had regarding his son, was that he, like Hannah, had been to the American embassy in Vienna, and they were given documents to return to the United States.

"And how do they know it was Hannah?" Richard asked.

"According to the embassy's records, Hannah was staying with my relatives, Sarah and Joshua Oldenburg at their farmhouse in Austria," Ben replied. "A report from SS offices alleged that Joshua attacked and almost killed one of their officers and Sarah shot another in cold blood, and that Hannah was in the crossfire. The SS officer collected their papers and reported that there was no child when they searched the premises. I don't believe that Joshua or Sarah would have tried to kill anyone in cold blood. That's preposterous. Whatever they did had to be in self-defense. What I believe happened was that after I was arrested in Vienna, my family decided to flee to Melk, thinking it would be safer in the countryside. As far as my son goes, I don't know anything at all. In mid-September, Anton returned to Austria to my cousin's cottage but found it occupied by a local couple who knew nothing about my family."

"This is unbelievable!" Richard said. "Does anyone know who's behind Ále's abduction? And what, if any, attempts have been made to locate her? Someone must know where she is. Why wasn't I notified immediately?"

"As I've said, I sent you a letter from the embassy. We had some leads, but nothing in the end. I wanted to tell you in person."

"For the better part of this month, I was convinced she'd abandoned us," Richard said.

"We've reported what happened to the American embassy, and I've been there many times, always getting the same answer—'we're still investigating.' Anton thinks she was taken by someone higher up within the Gestapo."

Richard got up, almost bursting with anger. "Why would anyone want to do this? What possible motive could they have? It doesn't make sense, and time is not on our side. Nobody seems accountable for what goes on there. I can't just sit here and wait, or I'll go insane. I'll telegram Anton today and leave for Berlin as soon I can make arrangements."

"You can try, but we're certain that by now all correspondence is monitored. I think he was planning on disconnecting the phone line. Things are awful there. I wish I could have done more."

"Ben, you need to go home. You've dealt with enough. Please give Hannah's parents my deepest sympathy. They'll be shattered."

"I don't know if I'm ready to face them yet, but I'll have to," Ben said. "As for Joseph, somehow I feel he's alive, but where?"

"Again, I'm awfully sorry for your loss," Richard said. "Perhaps, if he is, someone will take him to the embassy."

"I won't give up. I'll return to New York for a week, and I'll find a way to go back to Austria and bring someone along with me who can help me search for him," Ben said. "I was told that Joseph is like thousands who have gone missing. As for Hannah, I've tried to convince myself that she died bravely defending other Jews. She'd never have been afraid to intervene."

"I'm grateful that you came to see me. I wish I'd known all this sooner."

"I feel responsible for pushing Alejandra to go through with the concert," Ben said.

"Don't blame yourself. Nobody can convince Ále into anything she doesn't want to do. I'm stunned by all of this, and I'm sure I'll have more questions," Richard said.

"I was planning on staying here for the night and catch a train tomorrow morning."

"Of course. You can stay here for as many days as you wish." Richard turned his gaze toward the window as dusk set in. "But I've got to go to Berlin very soon. I should have been there with her. I can only hope she's alive."

"We can go together, if you wish," Ben said.

"I appreciate that, but we're going to different places, and I don't want to wait any longer," Richard said. "I'll probably stay with Anton if I can reach him. If not, I'll end up at the Adlon again. It won't be safe for you to go back. You know that, don't you?"

"What does it matter now? Life is not worth living if my son is gone too," Ben said.

"You'll find him," Richard said.

Later that night when Richard retired to his bedroom, in the dark, he collapsed on a chair, sobbing as never before. Faced with the prospect he might never see Alejandra again, he felt inconsolable. He didn't tell the children she had been abducted. He was burdened with regret for letting her go, doubting her, betraying her, and not being a stronger man. He wondered how his once idyllic life had unpredictably gone so devastatingly wrong. He wished he had gone with her despite all her objections. He felt that had he been there on the day of the concert, she would never have been taken. Now he must go and find her to make things right between them and bring her back home. His love for her had not lessened, and if he was fortunate enough to see her again, he would ask her for her forgiveness.

A week later, Ben had gone to New York, and with all arrangements complete, including contacting the American embassy in Berlin where Richard planned to meet with the American ambassador, he was ready for the long journey ahead of him. The staff at the state department in Washington had been helpful in assisting him with all his requests, and he felt more optimistic about the investigation of his wife's disappearance.

As he said goodbye to each of his children, Richard, standing at the door, tried to put on a brave face and sound reassuring, for they had no knowledge about what had happened to their mother. "We'll be back in no time."

"And Mommy too?" Del asked.

"Of course, sweetie."

"Will you be back by Christmas?" Leidy asked, handing him an envelope. "It's a letter for Mommy."

"Oh, sure," he said, embracing her. "I'll do my best." He put the letter in his coat pocket.

Lydia, holding Del's hand, said, "Please take care of yourself and be careful. Bring her back to us."

"Call me at the hotel if you need anything. Stephen has agreed to help you with whatever you or the children need," Richard said.

"We'll manage just fine. It's you and Ále we'll be worried about," Lydia said.

"Watch over your sisters," Richard said to his son. "I love you all, and remember your grandmother is in charge. I promise you, we'll soon be together." He felt a huge sense of dread because he could not assure them their mother was safe, much less alive.

The children nodded in agreement, but Leidy's eyes teared up, as though she understood it was a promise he might not be able to keep.

"I have to go now, the cab's waiting," Richard said. Then he took his coat and picked up his suitcase. As he got into the taxi, he waved goodbye to his children who were now outside in the courtyard. "They are far too young to lose their mother," he said under his breath.

LA CAMPANELLA

November 9, 1938

It took nearly a week on the *Queen Mary* from New York to Southampton, and two more days to Bremerhaven. Richard then took the train to Berlin's Lehrter Bahnhof. Before his arrival, he had sent Anton two telegrams, but like before, they went unanswered. The absence of communication served to increase Richard's concern that Anton was either deliberately avoiding him, incapacitated, or dead. Whatever the reason, he found his behavior inexplicable. Desperate for news about his wife, he decided to go directly to Anton's house that night.

It was twenty minutes past nine when he exited the station. It was cold, noisy, and busy with a long line of people waiting for cabs. He cringed, recalling his last visit to Berlin more than five years ago. He thought he would never return, especially now with the circumstances even more dire. All through the trip his stomach churned at the thought of never seeing Alejandra again.

He waited in line until a cab stopped in front of him. He placed his suitcase in the trunk and gave the driver a note with Anton's address. The taxi drove him through the city and into the borough of Charlottenburg, west of Tiergarten Park. When the taxi stopped in front of Anton's house, he noticed that the once regal structure now seemed abandoned, and an atmosphere of decay was evident in the neighborhood. He asked the driver to wait until he could ascertain whether anyone was home.

He rang the doorbell several times, but no one responded. Then, to his left, he noticed a dim light emanating from a room. He peeked through the dirty glass and was encouraged by what he saw at the kitchen table—a fruit basket, a pitcher filled with water, and a dirty plate and silverware as if someone had supper but had left suddenly.

He saw no point in waiting, but he would leave Anton a note and return early the next morning. From his coat pocket, he took a pen and a piece of paper and wrote:

> Anton. I'm at the Adlon Hotel. Please call me tonight or as soon as possible. I'm desperate to find my wife. Richard Morrison.

He considered putting the note in the letterbox, but it was open for anyone to take it, and so he decided instead to slide the folded note thru a narrow gap below the door.

He checked into the hotel. To calm his nerves, he decided to have a drink or two before retiring to the room. On the way to the restaurant and bar, he picked up an English newspaper—*The Daily Telegraph*. When he went into the crowded and noisy bar, he had a flashback and recalled the night Alejandra was at a table near the musicians. This night only a young male pianist was playing a familiar tune—"La Campanella" by Liszt. For a moment he stood at the doorway deciding whether he wanted to go in or not, but somehow listening to the music he had heard Alejandra playing on many occasions was enough to persuade him to stay, if only for a drink. What he would give to go back in time and be there with his wife enjoying the simple pleasure of each other's company. He spotted one empty stool on the far right side of the bar area. The walls were covered with wood paneling and shelves with dozens of liquor bottles. As he made his way there, he remembered the Nazi officer he had seen five years earlier, but now the place was crammed with dozens of them, as though they owned the hotel, and for that matter the country, and soon perhaps the whole of Europe. He despised them all.

"Scotch on the rocks and the check please," he said to the bartender.

The young bartender, with a friendly attitude, replied, "Yes, and welcome. I have a few orders ahead of you, so it will be a few minutes."

While he waited, he placed the newspaper on the counter and noticed his hands were shaking. He took a cigarette from his coat pocket, put it in his mouth, and lit it. Taking several quick draws, he felt more at ease as the nicotine coursed through his system. He then unfolded the front cover of the newspaper and read the headline: "On November 7, 1938, Hirshil Grynzspan, a seventeen-year-old Polish Jew, walked into the German embassy in Paris and shot the first diplomat he saw – Ernst von Rath."

"Oh, fuck," he said to himself, realizing what this could mean for Jews and that this may be the worst time to be there. He quickly folded the newspaper and dropped it under his stool. Just then the bartender placed his drink and the check on the counter. He didn't want to bother with charging the bill to his room, so he paid cash, drank the contents in one gulp, and left.

W hen the alarm clock rang at seven the next morning, he was already awake. In fact, he had been awake for more than an hour after hearing sirens and other loud sounds of angry mobs disrupting the peace in the streets. He called the front desk clerk to inquire what was happening and was told that there were people protesting the assassination of a German diplomat by a Polish Jew. There was no cause for alarm. After hanging up the phone, he walked to the window and saw it was more than a mere protest as buildings were being set on fire. He suspected the demonstrations were only a pretext that would lead to even more violent campaigns against the Jews.

He got dressed in a suit and wool overcoat. And despite admonitions from the hotel staff to stay indoors due to the ongoing protests, he proceeded with his plans to return to Anton's residence. At eight he left the hotel and took a cab. Suspicious of everyone and worried about tipping his final destination, he had the driver take him to the affluent and commercial section of Charlottenburg. On the way there, he saw dozens of Jewish business establishments and random houses torched and vandalized.

When he exited the cab, he noticed the Byzantine Synagogue on Fasanenstrasse, with three large cupolas burning. The acrid smell of smoke lingered in the air, and his eyes burned. The synagogue was the same one where Ben and Hannah Adelman went for services when they lived in Berlin. It was the largest synagogue in Germany, which ironically had been dedicated to German Jews by Emperor Wilhelm II, only two decades before. Crowds of people and police barricades surrounded the once magnificent structure as firefighters tried to prevent the fire from spreading to nearby buildings.

Doing his best to avoid the Brownshirts and other civilians who roamed the streets unrestrained, he turned right at the next intersection. But it was all to no avail, for no matter which direction he turned, violence and lawlessness were spreading like wildfire. As he advanced down the sidewalk, blanketed in shards of broken glass, he also witnessed several SA men who directed their incoherent rage at Jewish civilians and arrested them at random. He saw an elderly man being pulled from his house, beaten, and shoved inside a waiting vehicle. All this was happening while the police stood by idly doing nothing to stop the vigilantes.

A few more blocks down, he finally reached Anton's residence, but could only watch helplessly as dozens of thugs were vandalizing his house. From across the street, he witnessed as a gang of men, dressed in civilian clothes, looted dozens of objects that he had seen when he had received Anton's hospitality, years before. Anton's was not a Jewish house. The city had gone mad. Although, he wondered whether his past confrontations with Nazi officials and his willingness to assist Jewish citizens were the reasons. He now feared that Anton may have been arrested or killed. Richard thought of going to the Steinhoff Auction House to inquire whether anyone had heard from him. However, a visit to the auction house would have to wait for later in the day, as his next stop was the embassy where he was expected to meet with Hugh R. Wilson, the American ambassador. He hoped that there he would receive more encouraging information.

The American embassy had been temporarily located in the Tiergarten, near Stauffenbergstraße, and he arrived there fifteen minutes before his appointment. After showing his documents to the guard, who was standing by an iron gate, he walked to the building and then stepped inside the lobby, which was filled with long lines of asylum seekers. He was pleased that he had made all the arrangements prior to leaving the States as most of the staff seemed overwhelmed with the large crowds. He was directed to the ambassador's office at the end of a hallway. There he approached the ambassador's secretary, Margaret Edison, a brunette in her forties who was behind a desk, typing a document. A framed black and white photograph of President Franklin D. Roosevelt hung on the wall.

"Are you Ms. Edison? I have an appointment to meet with Mr. Wilson," Richard said.

Because of chatter in the background, she raised her voice slightly. "You must be Dr. Richard Morrison. The ambassador is not here yet. Please wait over there." She motioned to a seating area equally packed with people.

"I'll do that," he said.

He took a few steps and noticed a bench set against a wall that was close to the secretary's desk, preferring to wait there. He stood next to a middle-aged couple seated there, speaking with agitation. The woman pointed to a picture of a young man. Richard assumed the boy in the picture was also missing.

He waited for what seemed like an eternity until the secretary finally called his name. "Dr. Morrison, I have some news."

"Thank God," he said, rushing back to her desk.

"I'm afraid the news is not good," she said. "Due to the increasing violence in Berlin, the ambassador will not be available all day as he has pressing matters to attend to. We hope we can reschedule the meeting for tomorrow. I'll call you with an update in the morning."

"Is there anyone else I can see?"

"I'm afraid not. As you can see, we have our hands full," she said.

"I understand, but please, if the ambassador cannot meet with me at all, I implore you to schedule a meeting with whoever is second in charge. I have my own urgency. For God's sake, my wife has been missing since the end of August, and we still have absolutely nothing. This is unacceptable."

"Yes, sir. I'm aware of your situation, and I'll do everything I can. Give us one more day," she said. "Just look around you. They all have similar stories."

He nodded, momentarily closing his eyes. "I'll be expecting your call," he said.

Outside the embassy, feeling powerless, he lit a cigarette and took several puffs, looking at the people who walked by and whose faces, angry and gloomy, hid God knows what. There was a sensation of mistrust everywhere. He had yet to go to the Steinhoff Auction House. Perhaps there, he would have better news.

Walking briskly along the river Spree, Richard felt as though he was walking an obstacle course. With every step forward, he seemed confronted with one impediment after another, and wondered if his luck had finally run out. When he arrived at the Steinhoff Auction House, he entered through the open door. But like Anton's house, the atrium and gallery too seemed to have seen better days. The once regal gallery had been scarcely furnished, with all the antiquities, plants, and chandeliers gone. Even the wallpaper was ripped off in places. The only glimmer of hope, Richard noticed, was that the auction hall still housed dozens of chairs neatly arranged in front of the stage. The podium and several easels were set to the side.

An older woman, with short gray hair and a tattered dress, was sweeping the stage. *"Darf ich Ihnen helfen?"*

He spoke no German, and he was reasonably sure she spoke no English, so using his English-German phrasebook, he was able to say. *"Wo ist Anton Everhardt?"*

"Ich weiß nicht," she replied.

She doesn't know where Anton is. Now what? He searched for other words. *"Sie ihn gesehen haben?"*

She nodded yes.

"Wann?"

The woman took a few moments to recall. *"Gestern Morgen."*

Feeling more hopeful knowing that Anton had been there yesterday, Richard scanned his dictionary for other words. *"Wird er kommen hier?"*

She shrugged.

Not certain what to do next, he wrote another note. He was sure the first one he had left at Anton's house had been trampled on.

Anton, I'm in Berlin at the Adlon Hotel. Please come and see me now!!! I am desperate to find Ále. Richard Morrison.

He then gave the note to the woman. *"Sie geben ihm diese, danke."*

"Gerne," the woman said, taking the note from his hand, smiling, and placing it inside the pocket of her apron. She resumed her work.

Richard left the auction house certain that the kindly woman would give Anton the note if he were to stop there later today or tomorrow. So if he was in town, why had he not replied to any of his messages? Could he have been arrested the previous night?

The anti-Jewish pogrom continued into the next day and night, so he did not sleep at all. Expecting a call from the embassy, or a visit from Anton sometime the morning of November 11, 1938, Richard decided to remain at the hotel. But as the hours passed, and he didn't hear anything, he became impatient and frantic. At two in the afternoon, he ordered a bottle of gin and was on the bed, with his back against the wall, drinking his third glass, when the telephone finally rang. As he answered it, he clumsily spilled a bit of gin on his shirt and pants. "Hello."

It was Wilson's secretary, Margaret Edison, who informed him that as a protest over the attacks on German Jewry, President Roosevelt had recalled Ambassador Wilson back to the United States. She did not know if or when he would return, but that she did have a file containing the ongoing investigation into the disappearance of his wife. They had a few leads, and he could meet with the Chargés d'affaires at ten the next day. He thanked the secretary for her efforts, but he slammed down the receiver—without the ambassador the search would go nowhere. At least, he would meet with someone of authority and demand that they do everything in their power to follow the leads and pursue a vigorous investigation.

He gulped one more glass of gin, and not even changing his clothes, he left for the Steinhoff Auction House, hoping to have news about Anton.

While walking on Leipziger Strasse, near the platz and a busy area of town, it was late in the afternoon, and he noticed two tall Brownshirts approaching him from the opposite direction. He considered crossing the street to avoid them but knew that would likely only raise their suspicions. As they passed him by, he avoided eye contact, but one of the men came to a halt and asked, *"Haben Sie ein Feuerzeug?"*

"I don't speak German," Richard replied.

With moderate English, the man asked, "Do you have a lighter? You're American?"

"Yes. But I don't have a lighter with me." He had forgotten it back at the hotel.

"Not too many Americans here lately. Where are you going?"

"I'm here on business," he said.

He laughed. "Business at this hour? What type of business, smelling like a drunk?"

He paused to consider his reply knowing that in his haste he had been negligent by not changing his clothes, but that had seemed unimportant at the time. "I spilled a glass of wine at lunch, but as you can see I'm perfectly fine. I'm here to meet with an art dealer."

"Oh? You're a collector?"

"I'm looking into it," Richard lied.

"A Jew no doubt?" the man said.

"No. Look I'm late, and I have to go," Richard said, attempting to walk away.

"What's the name of the art dealer?" he asked.

"He owns the Steinhoff Auction House."

"His name I said!"

Refusing to give up Anton's identity, he replied, "Obviously, Steinhoff."

"I don't recognize that name," the English speaker said. "Maybe our superiors will know him. You're coming with us."

The brown-shirted man aggressively grabbed Richard's arm. Under other circumstances, he would have fought to free himself but realized these were extraordinary times, and no reasoning or demanding of his rights would likely change the outcome.

"Wait. You're wasting your time, don't you think? Don't you have more important things to do than to arrest an American businessman?"

Relaxing his grip on Richard's arm, the man laughed and asked, "What kind of art are you interested in?"

He paused, uncertain what to answer. "Modern," Richard replied.

"Anyone in particular?" the man asked.

Wishing that he had paid attention to art in the past, he blurted out the first name that came to his mind, a name he had seen splashed on the front page of a newspaper back at the hotel. "Kirchner."

The storm trooper asked his partner, in German, if he'd heard that name before. He told him what he knew, and then he turned back to Richard with a nasty tone. "Ernst Ludwig Kirchner. We remember that name. Weren't his paintings at the degenerate art exhibition last year? He killed himself, probably on account of we destroyed dozens of his paintings."

Richard, clearly flustered, ran his fingers through his hair, and trying to sound unconcerned, replied, "I don't know anything about that." He assumed that what they meant by degenerate art had something to do with purification of the arts. "I really have to go."

"You're not going anywhere now but with us. You can explain to my boss your interest in degenerate art, and who's selling it to you," he said.

From his coat pocket, he took out his American passport. "I'd prefer you take me to the American embassy. You have no reason to take me in for questioning," Richard said.

"Whatever for? You don't even have an ambassador anymore. Don't you know he's gone? Stupid Americans. You think you're so much better than us and that you can just walk here and go unnoticed? You're coming with us!"

"Fuck," Richard whispered.

Then the two men escorted him to their vehicle. He loathed everything about them and what they stood for, and he was determined not to appear intimidated, although inside he was scared... scared that he would end up like Ben or dead like Hannah, and his children would become orphans. There would be no justice. His good fortune had definitely run out.

"What did you say?"

You fucking beasts, Richard wanted to say to them, but, instead replied, "Jackasses."

QUASI UNA FANTASIA OP. 27 IN C SHARP MINOR

Alejandra and Sophia had become inseparable, although, as dictated by the girl's father, by five in the afternoon they went their separate ways. Having established a daily routine, she devoted her mornings to reading and teaching the five-year-old girl how to write, read music, and play the piano. In the afternoons, Alejandra occupied herself with the organization of the library and arranging Beethoven's scores, and even then, her young apprentice remained there by her side, drawing and coloring in notebooks.

It was an ideal place to raise a child, surrounded by the beauty of nature, making it easy to teach a child to love and develop free of prejudice. Perhaps it was a blessing that Günther had little influence on his daughter, especially given his negative beliefs and attitudes. She had no idea if Sophia saw her father in the evenings or if Günther's interest had changed upon seeing the child's progress, notwithstanding her inability to speak. Twice or three times a week they took walks together in a fenced-in garden.

It was also a way for Alejandra to see if there was a way to escape and if the two guards remained there, which they always did, stationed at the front door or walking about the premises of the house. She noticed that the guard, whom she had seen on occasion wearing a Bollman hat, did not always wear a uniform. She had started to befriend him with the hope that he would help her, but then toward the end of September he was gone and had been replaced by someone far more sinister looking with a gruffer physique and brandishing a pistol at all times. He rarely spoke and was the type of man who would not think twice about shooting someone on the spot. He had threatened her when she attempted, on one occasion, to walk away from the house early in her captivity.

She had become fond of Sophia, who was a sensitive child with a gift that needed to be preserved and encouraged. Caring for the girl gave Alejandra a sense of purpose. And while she wanted nothing more than to reclaim her freedom, she also wanted to prepare and teach Sophia the necessary skills for when it came time to part ways or for what she may face in the future. The best person to continue with her instruction would be Greta, who in the past had been reluctant to discuss the topic, but Alejandra was determined to prevail.

At midmorning on November 14, Sophia was at the piano practicing her scales. Alejandra was pleased that the last two months had proven to be of definite benefit to the child. She seemed to have a good ear for music and the dedication to study without being persuaded to do so. Sophia had made considerable progress in learning how to read notes and showed innate curiosity. Although, from time to time she would interrupt her studies and request that Alejandra read from one of the volumes of the Brothers Grimm fairytales. Thus far, those included the better-known tales such as "Cinderella," "Rapunzel," and "Sleeping Beauty." Sophia also liked Alejandra's own stories based on places she had traveled to, detailing the country's scenery, history, customs, language, and musical traditions.

When Sophia finished her piano exercises, she pulled out a thick book from the bookcase and carried it in her arms, placing it on the desk. The child leafed through the pages and pointed to her favorite story, "The Goose Girl," about a princess who had a magical horse that could speak. Alejandra smiled, for Sophia not only seemed more confident in herself but expressed what she wanted, showing a strong character. "It's nearly lunch, but we have time." Alejandra read:

> "The king of a great land died and left his queen to
> take care of their only child. This child was a daughter,
> who was very beautiful; and her mother loved her dear-
> ly, and was very kind to her. And there was a good fairy
> too, who was fond of the princess, and helped her moth-
> er to watch over her. Now the princess's horse was the
> fairy gift, and it was called Falada, and could speak…"

They were interrupted by Greta, who brought platters of potato salad and schnitzel sandwiches. As was now customary, they ate lunch viewing the monastery. Alejandra often read Sophia poems, and on this day, it was those of *Carmina Burana*.

When they were done, Sophia remained at the table, sketching in her notebook, and Alejandra resumed her work, but not for long. For soon the child placed a note before her. While the letters of the words were clumsily shaped, they were now legible, and more importantly, Sophia wrote her thoughts on paper and was inventing a world beyond her borders, making pictures of flowers, castles, and everything she imagined. "Play piano," she wrote.

"And what would you like us to play?" Alejandra asked, wiping a breadcrumb from the girl's mouth. Sophia tilted her head upward, and with her pencil drew a half moon and scribbled the word sonata.

"You want to play 'Moonlight Sonata,'" Alejandra said, smiling.

The girl nodded.

For some time now, they had been playing together the first movement of "Moonlight Sonata," also known as Quasi una Fantasi op. 27. It had become the child's favorite piece of music. The piano sonata was written in three movements—Adagio, Allegretto, and Presto, but it was the Adagio part they played together. Alejandra would play the piece but allow Sophia to play the motif, upon her cue, in the lower register of the keyboard.

"As you wish," Alejandra said. They proceeded to the pianoforte, sat down, and played the composition. Touched by that bond between them, Alejandra was finding it harder to hide her emotions as she thought of her children, especially her youngest daughter, and life with her family, but also about the fate of Sophia if and when she was given her freedom.

The next day, as she was arranging a score for piano, Greta came in with a lunch tray. "I'd like to speak with you, please," Alejandra said.

"Only for a moment," Greta said. Like most days, she wore her lime-green uniform and a white apron. At times, she could be chatty, even gossipy, but occasionally distant.

"Where's Sophia?" Alejandra asked.

"She's ill with a cold," Greta replied.

"May I see her?"

"No. She's sleeping right now."

"I'd like to speak to you about her," Alejandra said. "Please sit down."

"Oh! madam, I'm just the housekeeper," she said, sitting.

"You're much more than a housekeeper. I'm sure you're like a mother or grandmother to her. You know, I'm not always going to be here. In fact,

I've completed most of the work assigned to me, and perhaps it's wishful thinking on my part, but my days here may be numbered. As I've come to know Sophia, I can tell you she's an intelligent child. I hope you'll take the time to continue reading to her as I've done every morning, to encourage her natural talents of drawing and playing the piano, and to take her out for walks."

"You don't know her father," Greta said.

"He's gone most of the day, and he can't prevent you from doing so, knowing how much progress she's made."

"I can't teach her music like you."

"But you can follow instructions," Alejandra said. "I've written detailed weekly lesson plans to last her for a long time. They're very simple and may not be perfect, but it will require consistency on your part. She has learned to read notes, and I've written easy arrangements of known classical music compositions. Every day, at least five times a week, she must dedicate thirty minutes to practicing and rehearsing the scales and new pieces. And if she wants to play longer, let her. This will help her to develop a good ear and maybe even give her the opportunity to teach herself. Many musicians play only by ear. The goal is that music serves to entertain her, soothe her, and to be an outlet for her creativity and emotions. I wish we knew whether her speech impairment was physical or psychological. But either way, we won't know. You can find those manuscripts and lesson plans in the armoire in the bedroom. The files, titled with the name *Sophia,* are arranged from one to fifty. Can you do this?"

Greta nodded. "When have you done all this?" she asked.

"In the evenings after I perform for Günther," she said. "What's important to me is that you follow my instructions for Sophia's musical education. I'll begin to prepare her for my eventual departure."

"I'll try, but where will you go?" Greta asked.

"Home. I have three children who I miss terribly, and I hope you can help me."

"Help you? How?" Greta asked.

"You said before, you've known Günther for a long time?"

"Yes. I was Sophia's mother's nursemaid," she said. "I was like a mother to Theresa, that was her name, and she confided everything in me. She was forced to marry Günther when she was only eighteen years old, and she detested him."

"She died in childbirth, right?" Alejandra asked.

Greta paused, looking sad. She sighed. "No. She cut her wrists when Sophia was two years old. Günther confirmed that she had a speech impairment after they returned from Switzerland. He had plans to send the child away. He wanted only healthy children. He had said that to Theresa one night after he raped her."

"Oh, my God. I'm so sorry. I can't imagine the anguish she must have felt in order to commit suicide, and how dreadful for you. So what stopped him from sending Sophia away?"

"I've got something on him," Greta said. "After Theresa died, he sold his apartment in Berlin, bought this house, and put it in my name so he could keep all his holdings secret and have a clandestine existence here. He works in Munich and maintains a small flat for appearances. I've stayed around because of Sophia, and if not for me, he'd send her away. So, you see, even if I could and wanted to reveal his secrets, it would mean Sophia would suffer the consequences, and I can never let that happen."

Alejandra now felt she could trust Greta and tell her the truth. "I appreciate your honesty about all this. You're so courageous. Where I may need your help is in escaping. I'm not here freely. Günther had me kidnapped. He agreed to let me go when I completed my work, but now hearing all this makes me doubtful of his word. Compared to the hardship that Theresa had endured, my situation may seem bearable for the moment, but I fear it will deteriorate into something terrible soon. And I now feel that Theresa's fate could be my own. As I've said, I have children and a husband who must be sickened by my disappearance." Then Alejandra noticed Greta seemed flustered with the conversation as she was fidgeting. "What's wrong?"

"I'm sorry. I knew you didn't come here as you've said. But I can't help you to escape. He'd kill me as he did Luther, the man with the Bollman hat, who threatened to expose that he had kidnapped you."

"This is all so crazy." Alejandra extended her hand to Greta's. "It's all right. I understand. All that I ask is that if I'm successful in escaping or he lets me go, that you continue to care for Sophia as well as you've done and follow the plans we've discussed. Her well-being is what's important to both of us."

"Her mother would be grateful for what you're doing," Greta said.

"I wish I could do more. Always remember that you're making a difference in Sophia's life, and I'm glad she has you. When she wakes up, please tell her I hope she feels better."

"Yes, madam. She's very fond of you. But, please don't leave before Christmas."

"Why not?" Alejandra asked.

"Because she hasn't had one. Günther forbids it, but you've been able to make him do things on her behalf that I thought I'd never see. Maybe you can make that happen for her."

When Greta left, Alejandra thought about their conversation. She felt depressed by what she had learned and was newly afraid of Günther. The revelations proved he was an evil man. It would only be a matter of time before he displayed his true intentions to her. As for Sophia, she wouldn't talk to her about the fantasy of Santa Claus. It was ridiculous during such times. She did not feel it her place to discuss religious beliefs of any kind either, so what was the point? But maybe some evening she could open a discussion with Günther regarding his future plans for his daughter. Perhaps, seeing how she had changed, he might reconsider his position of sending her away. Was he capable of feeling something for his child?

"Oh, God, please make it so," she whispered.

THE CONSECRATION OF THE HOUSE

December 17, 1938

It was a sunny winter morning and the birthday of Beethoven, born in 1770, and Alejandra had completed most of the cataloging of the compositions. With a sense of accomplishment, she recalled perhaps what might have been some of his last words: "All that is called life shall be sacrificed to sublime art, a sacrament of art." In the end, he had dedicated his entire life to music.

In front of a bookcase, she scanned the dozens of files containing the majority of the composer's work. To perform all his music would take several more months. Up to now, she had played about a third of Beethoven's compositions, many of which she had arranged for piano. But she had not yet been able to open the safe, which contained his original manuscripts that must be copyedited and incorporated into the inventory. She had tried all the obvious combinations of numbers connected to Beethoven—his birth and death date, his various addresses, and premiere dates of all his symphonies. For the last three months, she had attempted to open the safe without success. She thought that the combination must be not only related to the composer but also to Günther's life—something of a more personal nature, and so she must glean additional clues.

She was prepared to perform that night. But with each day that went by, she was more afraid. With his moody disposition, she never knew what to expect, even when he chose to engage in conversation. It was difficult to comprehend how he could so completely compartmentalize his wicked behavior. He apparently enjoyed fine art and music, but on the other hand, he rationalized to a flawless degree his immorality and perversion in other contexts of his life. She had come to believe that his obsession with art, like the rest of his ilk, was a reflection of their futile obsession with a perfect race. Perfection could only be found in the essence of static art, but humans were not static beings. Ironically, their search for perfection failed miserably, given their aberrant ideology, and negated all traces of their humanity.

With this in mind, a little before eight o'clock she was in the salon, briefly looking into a mirror. Her hair had grown to below her shoulders. She donned a purple, laced blouse, long black skirt, and flat shoes. These clothes, she thought, were worn by another woman who once felt the same revulsion as she did for the man across the room. Ignoring Günther's presence, she went to the pianoforte and was about to play when he said, "I hope you've chosen well tonight. We're commemorating our favorite composer's 168th birthday."

"I did, and from reading another of his letters, I think he believed in God, a benign, intelligent power, and as such had a genuine interest in church music."

"Is it your wish to discuss religion tonight?" he asked.

She shrugged.

"Don't give me that dismissive attitude. I've watched you long enough to discern when something interests you," he said.

"I suppose that's a topic that never enters your mind," she said. "How could it?"

"I don't believe in any of it," he said.

"Then what do you believe in?" she asked.

"The only thing that matters in this world," he said. "Power. I'm sure you've read Nietzsche's *Will to Power*."

"Yes. But I think your interpretation of his philosophy may not be entirely accurate. You fool yourself," she said.

He put his cigar down in the ashtray and walked over to her, leaning on the piano. "I fool myself? How so?"

"You may control things, situations, and people at your whim, but it's of a superficial nature. There's no love or respect."

"Well, it's good enough for me. Why should I care what anyone thinks or feels about me, or morality, so long as I can do and have what I want? I could do as I please with you, but I don't. I've told you before that I'm not a savage."

She paused. "How long do you think you and your leaders can get away with it?"

"For as long as it takes to conquer the world. That's what men have done for centuries. Conquer and enjoy the spoils of war," he said. "You know that. We have dramatically improved our economy, and we had our most successful military year to date, and no other country can stop us now. We shall reign for a thousand years."

"So what is it? An endless pursuit of power, a belief that you're better than any other race, or a futile pursuit of perfection?"

"All three. One supports the others. After we manipulate people's minds with good propaganda, information, and the right language and tactics, we can enforce any policy we want."

"Once again you're fooling yourself. You lead only by fear and intimidation. All cultures since the beginning of time have had their share of strength and contributions to mankind. No one civilization can claim all the credit. Is your ego so great that you're blind to that?" she asked.

"Most citizens don't know much beyond their next meal or their front door. It's easy to control people's views if they don't have access to the truth," he said. "Once you categorize anyone else as being inferior, you can rationalize any violence or demeaning actions against them no matter how evil it may seem. Wasn't that what was done for centuries with the crusades and slave ownership?"

"Is this what you intend to teach your daughter and to contaminate her mind with?"

"I won't bother with her. She's incapable of forming or voicing her thoughts."

"And even with the improvements she's made, would you ever send Sophia away?"

He paused. "Not for the moment!"

"Is she like other millions of people who don't have a voice to speak against your government's brutal policies?"

"Surely, no one will dare voice any objection because they know what the consequences are for doing so," Günther said.

"You do realize, though, that governments and civilizations come and go, but their art is the only thing that lives on for all eternity. And someday your power will cease to exist," she said. "And what will your legacy be?"

"What do I care about that? That's a worthless humanistic construct invented by academics and dreamers from the past," he said.

Alejandra remained silent, realizing there was no point in taking the conversation any further. "Perhaps we should just stay on the subject of Beethoven's birthday," she said.

"You're finally learning what it takes to please me," he said.

She had no desire to please him, as he put it. She wanted to get him to talk about Beethoven's music. "I'm almost finished with the catalog, except for the originals in the safe. Wouldn't it be easier for you to give me the combination? It seems a rather ridiculous request for me to figure it out, frankly."

"Yes, I agree, but as I've said, it's entertaining. You've tried opening it?"

"Many times, with every combination possible of significant dates in Beethoven's life," she said. "It's like trying to find a needle in a haystack, maybe worse. I find it hard to believe your entertainment comes from such pettiness."

"The truth is I have no intention of letting you go," he said.

"A red herring. The only reason I've cooperated in doing this catalog and performing for you was with the goal of having my freedom at some point," she said.

His mood then suddenly changed to his usual morose one. "Exactly. It worked, didn't it? So just get on with it and play."

"No! That won't do. Will you or won't you release me?" she asked again.

"And if I refuse, what you will do?" he asked.

"I don't see the point of going on with this charade if your word means nothing," she said, taking the score from the ledge as she prepared to leave. "I'm not afraid of you."

"You women are so tedious when you want something. Fine, I will," he said. "Besides, knowing how much you love Beethoven's work, you mean to tell me you're not interested in seeing his original manuscripts?"

"And I'm finding all this also very tedious. Of course I would, but that's not the point. To be clear, if and when I open the safe and finish the work, you'll let me go, without any other exception."

"Yes!" he said.

Alejandra sighed, thinking he was probably lying, but she had nothing else but hope. She played the piece that Beethoven had composed in the style of Handel, "The Consecration of the House," Opus 124. From the corner of her eye, she saw Günther take another cigar from a box on the piano. Then slowly he lit it while fixing his stare on her. "That's just marvelous. You chose well tonight, and may I also add you play the piano with exceptional feeling."

Then, with the arrogance of someone in total control, he returned to his chair.

Upon finishing, Alejandra did something she had not done before—rather than leaving the salon immediately following her performance, she went to sit across from Günther.

He spread his arm over the back of the chair and said, "Oh? You'd like to keep me company? You know that you're a beautiful woman, don't you?"

She ignored the remark. "Was your affinity for Beethoven's music acquired from someone, like your father or mother?"

"You want to know about me?" he asked, leaning toward her.

Not even a little, she thought. *I just want a clue to that damn combination.* "Everyone has a story, so why not? Tell me about your mother. Was she a musician?"

"She was not, but she worked for Königliche Bayerrische Musikschule," he said.

"And what did she do at the music conservatory?" Alejandra asked.

"She was the secretary to the librarian. As a music aficionado, she often took me to concerts and always reminded me of my privileged birth in a country of musical dominance. She died when I was very young."

"It must have been difficult for a young child. And your father?" Alejandra asked.

"He was nothing but a coarse man lacking in aspirations. And as you can see, he had little influence on me. I always knew I would overpass his station in life. He's dead too. But that's all you need to know about me."

As she prepared to leave, he said, "So long as we're discussing personal matters, you should be aware I want more children, and I have my eyes on you." He laughed.

She felt a shiver down her spine. While he had not attempted to force himself on her, she was beginning to think he would do so. She would prefer to die rather than to allow that to happen.

She laughed too, pretending it was a joke, although inside she was afraid and disgusted with his insinuation. "I didn't realize you had a sense of humor. But you may want to find the perfect woman elsewhere who shares your beliefs and live happily ever after. Besides, I do plan on opening that safe, and you gave me your word!"

Then she quickly left the room, wondering if she could believe Günther's word meant something. She had no other choice but to try. It was true that seeing and holding Beethoven's original manuscripts was definitely worth her every effort.

Several hours later, Alejandra woke up in the middle of the night feeling anguish about Günther's menacing comments. Her only hope was that she could complete the work and that he would follow through with their agreement. As she recalled their earlier discussion, she had an idea that might lead to figuring out the safe's combination—now that she had new information. As assistant to the librarian, Günther's mother had access to hundreds of musical manuscripts. Alejandra went to the desk and took a piece of paper from the drawer, writing down other possible clues. But she needed to be in the library where Beethoven's manuscripts were kept. It was five o'clock in the morning, and she had never been there at that hour, knowing he was often up at that time. However, she was suddenly eager to decipher the safe's combination.

After dressing, she went down the stairs, and when she got to the bottom she saw a light coming from Günther's office, which was across from the library. The door was ajar, and she could hear him speaking on the phone. She went to the library and hid behind the door from where she could see and hear everything. He was discussing that Germany had recently signed a non-aggression accord with France and that he had a new assignment. What did that mean? Might he be transferred somewhere else? Could her captivity be finally over regardless of whether she completed the work or not? She couldn't count on that.

He hung up the phone, turned off the lights, and locked his office. He was dressed in a gray-green uniform with a swastika armband and an SS eagle-pin cap. Holding an envelope in his hand, he stormed out of the house, got in the car, and drove away.

She turned on the lights and noticed that one of the panels of *Beethoven's Frieze*, had been removed to the side, revealing the safe. Then from a bookcase, she took a folder with Beethoven's earliest manuscripts. The file contained a series of piano variations and the composer's first manuscript—printed in the year 1783. She reasoned that, as a Beethoven collector,

Günther might have chosen this date for the combination, especially considering that she had already tried dozens of other obvious numbers over three months, all of which had failed.

She went to the one-meter-tall black Peltz safe. As on other occasions, she turned the knob several times and proceeded to the first number—1. Twice to the right, 7, twice to the left, 8, once to the right, and 3, once to the left. The safe did not open. She tried again. No luck. Then she tried other combinations of those four numbers. Still nothing. She was feeling desperate by now.

"It has to be this number," she whispered. Then came the last attempt—1, one turn to the right, 7, seven turns to the left, 8, eight turns to the right, and 3, three turns to the left. She then heard a most beautiful sound—a click when she pulled on the knob, and the safe opened.

Her heart was racing, and, smiling to herself, she looked at the stack of Beethoven's precious body of work. With the utmost care, she took the original manuscripts from the safe's shelf and carried the treasure trove to the desk. Her eyes glistened upon looking at the original of Symphony no. 3, op. 55, "Eroica," where Beethoven's own hand had scratched off Napoleon's name and replaced it with Prince Lobkowicz. She then scanned each page, hearing the music in her mind, lyrical and exhilarating. Next was the original manuscript of the Violin Concerto in C Major, but it was only the exposition. She turned to the next score, a signed copy of the String Quartet in F Major, op. 18, and an original edition of the Serenade in D Major, op. 8, for violin, viola, and cello.

Then she found an original letter from Beethoven to his brothers:

> *"O you men who consider, or describe me as*
> *quarrelsome, peevish, or misanthropic, how greatly*
> *you wrong me! You do not know the secret reason why*
> *I seem to you to be so. From my childhood onward my*
> *heart and soul have been filled with tender feelings of*
> *goodwill, and I have always been willing to perform*
> *great and magnanimous deeds... Oh God, you look*
> *down on my inner soul, and know that it is filled with*
> *love of humanity and the desire to do good..."*

She wept to know so intimately Beethoven's sentiments. An image of Beethoven's face surfaced in her mind. She didn't need to go back in time to know that everything she had thought about him was true. Despite his deafness and other physical burdens, he had maintained a life-long love for humanity. She placed the letter apart from the manuscripts.

"Oh, my God," she said upon seeing the original manuscript of *Symphony no. 5, in C Minor, op. 67*, a symphony that Beethoven had altered at least five times. She was in utter awe as she took in the entire score again hearing the music in her mind, humming it, and feeling her soul filled with abundant joy. The recollection of having conducted this very symphony at the opera house only months ago brought a flood of emotions and memories. She placed the manuscript over her chest as she turned to the window just as the first rays of sunlight revealed the snowcapped mountains. In the end, she was grateful to be alive to see all those handwritten musical notes on paper. She carefully and devotedly paged through the rest of the original manuscripts, a total of eighteen, including her own signed copy of "Moonlight Sonata." How could she ever regret this night of touching and beholding Beethoven's master works. Would she ever be free again to conduct the composer's glorious music? "Oh. God. Make it so," she said.

In that instant, invisible and sublime, she felt connected to Beethoven as though his spirit stood beside her, and he would protect and save her from harm. So then, very gently, she took his letter and placed it on her lips, imagining she was kissing him. She loved him for the kind-hearted man he was, for all his creations, and for those emotions his music evoked in her—adoration, agitation, courage, curiosity, elation, gratitude, melancholy, and peace.

She now had at her fingertips his complete body of work that included copies and original manuscripts—138 compositions with opus numbers including piano sonatas, bagatelles, marches, rondos, overtures, string quartets, concertos, and symphonies... and 205 works without opus numbers, including minuets, dances, and contredanses, as well as dozens of other unfinished works. The composer's legacy and better-known masterpieces included seventeen string quartets, thirty-two piano sonatas, twelve violin sonatas, nine symphonies, and one opera.

With a sense of reverence, she would dedicate the rest of the days and nights to copy editing the original manuscripts in order to include them in Beethoven's catalog.

It was her pathway to freedom.

MOONLIGHT SONATA OP. 27 THIRD MOVEMNT

December 22, 1938

Beethoven's catalog was now complete. Alejandra now believed that having accomplished Günther's commissions, he would finally release her. He had given her his word.

Dressed in a long, apricot-tone dress with ruffled collar, she entered the music salon, carrying a twelve-inch folder, feeling confident, and even cheerful. She placed the folder on the piano, hoping this would be the last piano performance for Günther Kaiser. He was seated in his chair, wearing a dark brown suit. "I'm done arranging all of Beethoven's works as you requested. Beethoven's originals have been copyedited and incorporated into the collection, and this folder contains the last compositions he wrote."

"You figured out the code, did you? I realized I said too much a few days ago about my mother," he said. "Very impressive."

"The complete catalogue is in your library, arranged in chronological order, and the originals are back in the safe."

"Aren't you curious to know why I picked 1783 as the numbers in the combination?"

"I know. It was the date of Beethoven's first printed manuscript. It must have something to do with your mother."

"You're a very intuitive woman," he said. "She gave me a copy of that manuscript for my tenth birthday and told me that I should become a collector of as many of his manuscripts as possible. For Beethoven was and would always be considered the premiere composer of all time. Or at least she thought so. She died only one month later, but I never forgot her counsel."

"You obviously cared for her. Have you considered that perhaps your own daughter might have inherited from your mother that appreciation for music?"

He remained silent.

"I'd like to see my own children. You must understand how powerful the love of a mother is," Alejandra said, almost pleading. "Now that I've fulfilled your assignments, I'm planning on leaving after Christmas, as I want to spend that day with Sophia."

She hoped that perhaps she had broken into his steely exterior. But then with a sinister expression, he laughed, giving her chills.

"First, you haven't finished performing all his works. But when you do, why would I ever let you go?" Günther said, walking to her and standing too close. "I have everything just the way I want it! During the day I do what I have to do to keep my position, my house, and my power. For those restless times, I have any woman I want at my disposal away from here. In the evening, I come home to my sacred place where I answer to no one."

He paused as if waiting for her to react. Then he continued. "Oh! And to top it off, I have a refined woman and a very fine musician playing Beethoven for me every night. And lest I forget, she also seems to be doing wonders for my daughter. So you see, you've made yourself indispensable. And as I've said before, you would make a perfect mother to my children. I don't need to look anywhere else. What is it that you're playing for me tonight?"

"But you gave me your word!" she exclaimed.

"Yes. But words and promises only mean something to men of honor. And for me, having honor is weakness. And you now know, I don't care about that."

She turned away from him, closing her eyes, saying, "And if I refuse to go on playing?"

He ran his bony fingers down her arm and replied, "If that's what you want to do, fine with me. But now, I finally have something you care about under my roof. If you want to continue to see Sophia, then you'll go on playing for me and do as I say. Did you think I would let you get close to her just for altruistic reasons? It's not a bad arrangement, don't you agree? So you see, we're the only family you've got."

"How does someone get to be like you?"

"By ridding myself of worthless morals and false promises of redemption. It's only the survival of the fittest in the end. There's no salvation after we die. It's here and now that counts."

"How long will this go on?" she asked.

He stared at her with peering eyes. "Until I say so," he said. "Now, just play before I do something else." He stretched his hand and placed his index finger over her clavicle.

She removed it with disdain.

"You know I could take you by force if I wanted to this very moment. And I might just do that very soon if you don't cooperate," he said.

She longed to escape. Her hopes had been dashed in an instant, and her eyes filled with tears, but she would not allow him to see her defeated. She moved away and didn't care anymore whether or not she provoked his rage, so she replied, with her back to him, "Never! I'd rather die first," she said, running out of the salon.

She went into the library and shut the door. Sobbing, she went to the safe, opened it, and took the Beethoven signed Moonlight Sonata manuscript, which once had belonged to her, and placed it on the piano's ledge, turning the pages to the third movement—Presto agitato. As she stared at the music, she could not believe this could be her destiny; she would never accept it. Her only hope was a miracle and that Richard would intervene and rescue her before Günther carried out his more despicable fantasies about her.

For the next seven minutes and ten seconds, she poured all her emotions into playing the last movement of the sonata, stormy and implacable, yet filled with ache and ecstasy in passing passages, intensifying her heartache, each sharp piercing through her heart as the music diffused through her soul. Alejandra cried profusely, and her tears dropped onto the piano keys wetting and cleansing them at the same time. Her fingers slipped and trembled on the keys with the ferocity her emotions dictated.

Still devastated by the exchange with Günther, the next day she stayed in her room hoping to make one more attempt to summon his better angels. She doubted he had any, but the alternative of ending her life by her own hand, a plan she now considered a real possibility, was against all her principles. That was an abominable thought, and it would be an abominable act. It was against God.

Seated at the desk, she wrote:

Günther: What do you say to a man devoid of all humanity? What do you say to a man that holds power above all things? Who calculates his every word and his every deed? Who shuns the noble-hearted and the very God who created him? I don't believe that such a man exists! Nor do I think our beloved Beethoven did, for he poured his very soul into the music of his last symphony, "Ode to Joy." With his ethical and religious beliefs, he hoped to bring mankind together and to demonstrate that pure joy and love comes from the divine. By putting music to Schiller's poetry, Beethoven summoned our better angels. And in the words of Berlioz, who upon hearing the ninth symphony, once wrote: 'Who can say that God himself did not wall up the doorways through which the noise of the world would have penetrated into him, so as to purify and spiritualize his ideas'... I implore you to release me! Alejandra.

She placed the letter in an envelope. When Greta brought her dinner, Alejandra said, "Please give this letter to Günther, and tell him I will not be playing for him tonight."

"Madam, he'll be very angry," she said.

"I'll never play for him again," Alejandra said. "But, I do want to see Sophia tomorrow."

"Yes, madam," Greta said.

The next afternoon, Alejandra and Sophia were for the first time having refreshments in the baroque style dining room. Greta, wanting to cheer her up, had decorated the room with white and gold Christmas adornments on top of a headboard. The table was set with a red tablecloth, an angel centerpiece, and the finest china with laurel leafs. All morning she had baked favorite German and Austrian pastries, including Sophia's favorite, Dominostein. From a large platter, Sophia took as many of the pastries that could fit on her plate.

Alejandra was drinking tea when, suddenly, Greta came into the room. "Madam, madam, a Christmas tree and a set of candles has just been delivered. Come, I told the delivery man to install it in the library." Alejandra saw Sophia, who seldom showed much facial expression, smile enthusiastically and jump from her chair, waiting for a response. "Let's take a look, shall we?" Alejandra said, taking the girl's hand.

The scent of pine hung in the air. Sophia ran toward the six-foot tree, next to the window, touching the prickly needles with the same wonder she had showed when touching the trees in the garden. Immediately, Alejandra visualized her children who probably thought she had forgotten about them. Her daughter, Del, like Sophia, always marveled at the beauty and simplicity of an evergreen placed in a house, beautifully decorated with sparkling and colorful ornaments. Remembering the previous Christmas with her family brought a deep heaviness in her heart, and she felt a knot in her throat at the realization she would never see or hold them again. For this would be her last holiday, as she had decided to carry out her sacrilegious plan the day after Christmas.

Alejandra gazed at Sophia's joyful face, trying her best to suppress her own growing desperation. She had to put on a good face for the child's sake and pretend everything was all right when inside she was falling apart. "Come, let me tell you a story." They sat on the divan, and she cleared her throat.

"My grandmother, who was born not far from here, told me that long ago, in the sixteenth century, Germans began a tradition of bringing evergreen trees into their homes and lighting them with candles. We will do this later. On December 25, many people around the world celebrate the birth of a man named Jesus who believed we should all be kind to one another. We call this tradition Christmas. Other cultures have their own special celebration with special meanings. Someday you'll learn about them too. But for the next days, we shall celebrate Christmas. And you, my precious Sophia, get to make a wish. So tonight, think carefully what you want most, and tomorrow write it down for me, so maybe it might just come true."

Sophia, for the first time, placed her head against Alejandra's shoulder with unspoken affection, and she gently put her arm around her. "Now, let's place those candles on the tree."

Greta brought a standing ladder and distributed several candles at the top, lighting them. Alejandra and Sophia put the rest of them about the tree in pyramidal shape. Carefully, they lit them, and together they watched the glowing tree. In complete awe, Sophia ran to the desk to fetch her notebook, then kneeling before the tree, she began drawing in earnest. Alejandra was pleased to see her so happy and industrious, and she watched as the young girl scribbled words on a paper and drew, with considerable skill, a woman and child in their likeness. Then, Sophia got up and proudly gave the drawing to Alejandra who was filled with tenderness upon reading the words "*Mama und mich.*"

Alejandra briefly closed her eyes, wondering how she could tell the child that she was not her mother. "Sophia, my dear, it's a beautiful drawing, and I'll treasure it forever... thank you. I want you to know that I care for you with all my heart. Remember to think about that special wish."

Later that evening, Greta came into the library to collect the supper tray.

"Please sit with me for a moment. I have something to tell you," Alejandra said. She put her hand over Greta's hand. "Don't ask me why, but soon my fate will be that of Theresa. You understand? After Christmas, when you find me in a state of permanent repose, pray for me, and don't let Sophia see me like that. Tell her I had to go, but that I love her very much."

Greta covered her mouth. "You mustn't commit..." She teared up, and before she could finish, Alejandra placed her index finger on her lips. "Hush. I can't bring myself to say it aloud, but I must, and I will."

"Is there anything I can do to help you?"

"Yes, I'll write a letter to my family, and hopefully, you'll find a way to send it."

She nodded. "I hope you won't do it. Sophia loves you." Then Greta left.

Now alone in the library, Alejandra, at the lowest point in her life and in a state of resignation, wrote:

My dearest Richard, Leidy, Rich, and Del: I write to you from a dark place in my heart. A place I have never known where I've lost all hope. You shall never see me again, but remember I've always loved you. Please forgive me...

The emotion and sadness was so intense she was unable to complete the letter. What words could explain the abominable action she planned to take? All the night before, she struggled to reconcile her feelings. She could never live this life and allow that despicable man to do the unthinkable, but how could she go against her religion and commit suicide. What did it matter now? She had lost all her faith.

As the room darkened, as the candles on the tree were melting down to the bottom, Alejandra took a silver-plated extinguisher from the top of her desk and slowly proceeded toward the tree, putting out, one by one, the candle flames until there was no more light.

O n Christmas day, when Alejandra entered the library in the morning, the curtains had been drawn open, and she found a vase on her desk filled with flowers... amaryllis and garden white roses. A folded piece of paper leaned against the tall crystal vase. She picked up Sophia's note, and while the handwriting was imperfect, it was legible enough to understand it—"*Sie, mich, Klavier spielen, zum vaten.*" Alejandra knew what the girl wanted. She felt willing to comply with her wishes, but how could she sit at the piano with Sophia to play for Günther when she felt so much repulsion toward the man?

Just then Sophia came running into the room, smiling. "*Fröhliche Weihnachten.*" How could she possibly disappoint this innocent girl, who was finally blossoming like those beautiful flowers Greta had left for her? "Sophia, I understand you'd like us to play together on the piano before your father. Is that your wish?" Sophia nodded, looking as bright and happy as she had ever seen her, wearing a ruffled pink dress. "I'll do my best to make that happen," Alejandra said. "But first, I want to show you something." She led her to the piano where dozens of folders, titled Sophia's piano lessons, laid in a stack in chronological order from December 25, 1938 to December 25, 1940. "You see, these are all for you." Sophia opened the top folder, revealing the first lesson—December 25, 1938, Ode an die Freude, Ludwig van Beethoven. The lesson plan included a piano arrangement of "Ode to Joy," for beginners, a brief description of the composer and the composition, one-page charts of music theory, and daily scale practices.

Greta came into the room, as Alejandra had requested, and sat next to the piano. "Sophia, as we have played on other occasions, please try to play this piece. Will you?" She nodded. Then Alejandra turned on the wooden metronome on top of the piano, setting the tempo to 120 bpm. Slowly, Sophia began to play the one-note arrangement with her two little hands—la, la, la, la, la, la, la, la... "You see, Greta, she's very good, and already knows her notes. But you have to practice every day, all right, Sophia? I'm going to go and sit at my desk, but Greta will stay here and help you until you play the piece as good as you can, or you may stop after fifteen minutes. Don't forget to count like we've practiced. That's very important."

As Sophia continued to practice the piece, from time to time Alejandra would say, "That's excellent, we're so proud of you."

Then after a few minutes, Alejandra quietly left the library, allowing Greta to finish the lesson plan.

J ust minutes before eight o'clock on Christmas night, Alejandra came into the salon wearing a loosely draped royal-blue gown with long sleeves, holding two manuscripts of "Moonlight Sonata," a copy and Beethoven's signed copy.

Her stomach clenched at the sight of Günther, for she had not seen him since the day of their confrontation. She assumed he had read her letter, and for now he had left her alone, but she knew he would soon follow through with his threats. Determined to do something bold on this occasion, instead of sitting on the piano bench, she approached the wood burning fireplace and threw into the blaze one of the musical manuscripts.

Günther, who was in his chair, reacted by saying, "You've decided to play for me again? And that better not have been an original."

"And what if it was? What will you do? I told you I'm not afraid of you, and your threats of not seeing Sophia won't move me this time either. I'm done," she said.

He stood, and his face was contorting angrily. He raised his hand as if to strike her, but she moved away.

"Unlike you, I'm not insane. That was a copy, and this one is the original of "Moonlight Sonata" signed by Beethoven. As you know, it once belonged to me, and it was of great sentimental value, so I want you to frame it and give it to Sophia. The first movement is her favorite piece of music. And tonight, we will play it for you. It's her Christmas wish."

"You and Sophia?" he asked.

"Yes. And if you so much as say an unkind remark or have a foul expression on your face, you'll never see me again."

Standing before Alejandra, she could smell his foul breath when he spoke, and she turned her face away. She wanted nothing more than to slap him and run away, but she must think of the young girl's wishes and maintain her composure for this last time.

Only a few inches taller than Alejandra, he moved her chin to face him once again. His touch on her face felt disgusting. "Get your hand off me!"

"You're bluffing," he said.

"I've never bluffed in my life. I've lost everything I hold most dear to me. You can't hurt me anymore. And you'll never have me."

"I read your letter. Sweet, but it didn't change my mind either. You'll be mine tonight! If I can't have you willingly, I can have you killed at the snap of my fingers."

"If that's God's will, so be it!" Alejandra said. "Go back to your chair and listen to us, as this will be my last performance."

Then she walked back to the doorway. She had previously instructed Greta to have Sophia on standby, dressed in her best attire, considering the occasion. She would be joining her at the piano. "Greta, please bring Sophia now." The housekeeper, who had been listening from the door, ran to fetch the young girl.

Günther appeared stunned by Alejandra's defiant attitude. She looked at him as he was about to go into a rage, but suddenly Sophia was standing before him looking like a princess, gracious and beautiful. With her hair in braids, she wore a red velvet dress with a white collar and puffy sleeves. Black shining shoes and white socks completed the ensemble. Sophia smiled at her father, looking proud.

Alejandra took her by the hand. "Are you ready?"

The girl nodded, and as they walked toward the pianoforte, she noticed that Günther, who was obviously caught off guard, retreated back into a corner, next to a chest of drawers. Then Alejandra and Sophia sat down side by side. She placed the signed manuscript on the piano ledge. "Sophia. You remember I told you this sonata was written by Beethoven, and you see his handwriting right here, she said, pointing to the signature. This manuscript is a Christmas gift for you, and your father will have it framed, and you may hang it wherever you can see it every day so you remember music is a gift from God and it's part of you. Would you like that?" Sophia tilted her head toward Alejandra, smiling and nodding.

Alejandra played a few notes of "Moonlight Sonata," allowing Sophia to play the motif on cue like they had practiced many times. Playing that most peaceful and melodious sonata brought her a flood of memories—memories from her childhood, from her youth and her life, as though the sonata was an entity and recalled her experiences. And the experience of playing it with Sophia for the last time was so moving that Alejandra began to cry softly. She turned to Sophia whose presence was calm as her little fingers pressed the piano keys. That brief moment of expressive tenderness intermingled with thoughts of despair marked the end of her journey; for that night she would carry out her plan, and she was saying goodbye to life.

Forgive me, God, she said to herself.

When they finished playing, Alejandra gently squeezed Sophia's hand. "That was marvelous." But the girl turned to her father, waiting for a word of praise.

"You did very well, Sophia. You see, Alejandra. We're an ideal family now," Günther said with a sneer.

But then a guard abruptly burst into the room.

"Sir, Anton Everhardt demands to see you immediately! He's threatening to blast his way into the house. He says he's got an army of men waiting for his signal."

"Don't you move," Günther said to Alejandra as he reached into the top drawer of the chest and withdrew a Luger. "How the hell did he find me? Let him in!"

Soon, Anton came into the room, dressed in a military uniform. With a long beard, he looked as rugged and fierce as Alejandra had ever seen him. She was surprised and relieved, but the chance that he had been part of this abhorrent plot in some way, made her reaction tentative.

Anton turned to Günther. "It's over, you bastard," he said as he walked toward Alejandra.

"What? Are you reneging on our deal? Wasn't this your idea all along?" he said, pointing the gun at Anton.

"Don't listen to him, Ále. He's a cunning son of a bitch who fooled me too. I swear to you, I had nothing to do with this."

Alejandra turned to Sophia who seemed frightened and confused as she started whimpering. She wasn't sure what or whom to believe, but if she had to take sides it would be with Anton. She had no choice but to trust her instinct.

"Where's this army you claim to have?" Günther asked. "I doubt you would blow up this place knowing your beloved is here. And how the hell did you find me?"

"You have enemies," he said, signaling for Alejandra to walk away. She stood, stepping away from the piano bench as Sophia remained seated.

Günther then pointed the gun at Alejandra. "If any of you take one more step I'll kill her on the spot," he said.

Then, in a quick motion, Sophia jumped from the bench and surrounded Alejandra's waist with her arms, screaming, "No, Papa!" While her words were not entirely clear, the guttural sound of her speaking voice was so compelling and disarming, it shocked Günther, and he lowered the gun.

Alejandra then embraced Sophia. "My sweet, I'm sorry. I have to go. You're the bravest girl I've ever known. You're going to be all right because you have a big heart and a strong mind. Never forget that." She tenderly kissed her on the head.

Sophia began to sob, and Alejandra attempted to comfort her, but Anton pulled her away from the child. "We have to go now!" She made her way to the doorway, and before exiting, she looked over her shoulder, heartsick at abandoning Sophia. And Gúnther, whose aggressive stand had diminished, appeared to be in a state of disbelief by his daughter's actions. He placed the gun on top of the wooden chest, and said, "Sophia! You can talk. Stop crying and come here." Still crying, the child went to her father, and he embraced her awkwardly. But then Alejandra left, and her cries faded in the distance.

As she and Anton exited the sandstone dwelling, she breathed in the cold air. Anton draped his long military coat over her shoulders. One of Kaiser's guards lay unconscious. Three black Mercedes, filled with men, were stationed outside the house. Anton rushed to speak to the driver of the nearest one, who then signaled for the rest to leave. Then Alejandra and Anton got into the back seat of the last Mercedes, and with the headlights illuminating the snow-filled streets, they drove away. Alejandra held Anton's arm tightly, astounded by the turn of events, but she also felt sadness at having left Sophia behind. *What would become of her?* "Oh, God, please keep her in your care," she said under her breath.

ADAGIO IN G MINOR

Milan, Italy

Alone in an austere bedroom, Alejandra splashed cold water from a basin situated on top of a limestone vanity. The furnishings were plain, resembling a convent with only a twin bed, nightstand, and one wooden chair. Wearing only her slip, she took a towel and dried her face, neck, arms, and hands. Then she stepped up to a small window to catch a glimpse of the rising sun. The sky, tinted in hues of pinks, blues, and yellows, was stunning and beyond anything she had ever seen, or so it seemed to her that morning of December 26, 1938 when her captivity had ended.

At dawn, she and Anton had arrived at the seventeenth century villa, a block from Piazza San Sepolcro and the Milan Cathedral. They had driven for more than six hours from Bavaria into Milan. With Italy an ally of Germany, Anton had been able to procure the necessary documents to enter that country, and in Milan they would go to the American and French embassies to obtain additional documents to travel by train to Nice, France. From there they planned to stay for a few days before Alejandra returned to the United States.

As they drove to Milan, Anton had explained to her satisfaction what his relationship was to Günther Kaiser, how he came to learn of her whereabouts, and how he planned their escape into Italy. Nothing had been easy, but good fortune had intervened at the least expected moments. Alejandra could not be more grateful that Anton had rescued her from her perilous plight. And after listening to the explanations, she had no reason to mistrust him. She knew she had not been wrong about him; he had always shown her kindness to a fault, and his actions had always proven to be that of a man in love. It was something she could no longer deny.

For his part, Anton acknowledged where he had gone wrong, having poor judgment regarding Günther Kaiser, whom he had met at the Steinhoff Auction House on February 22, 1933 when he acquired Picasso's *Girl Before a Mirror*. Since then, Kaiser had paid Anton to act on his behalf in his pursuit of a collection that included Renaissance and modern works of art, as well as a collection of original Beethoven manuscripts. All along, Kaiser had presented himself as being anti-Nazi, liberal minded, and part of the German resistance. He had convinced Anton that he and other officers in the Third Reich had chosen to stay and work within the system in order to find a way to depose Hitler and his henchmen. But as Kaiser rose within the party ranks, he turned to art collecting as an investment to boost his meager administrative income. With unlimited access to art collections of Jewish citizens, particularly after the Anschluss, he had illegally seized many works of art, keeping it a secret not only from Anton but everyone else. In past dealings, Anton and Günther always had met in public places in Berlin, and when it was necessary to ship a work of art, Anton did so to Günther's address in that city. Throughout the years of their business association, Anton had in fact, foolishly, confided in Günther his feelings and views, believing he was of the same mind. Anton never suspected Günther's treacherous ways.

In late September, Isolde Beckman, who was now known publicly as Carla Braun, became romantically involved with Herbert Wolf. Sometime in the fall, under the influence of alcohol, Wolf alluded to a kidnapping plot as he bragged about it to Isolde. Little by little Isolde had collected more information from him, until she established that Herbert Wolf was connected to Günther Kaiser. Wolf and Kaiser had plotted the kidnapping, and Kaiser's guards had carried it out. Isolde then reported the whole scheme to Anton who continued with the investigation and had Kaiser followed from Munich to Bavaria where Kaiser lived a clandestine existence. The house was registered under the name of Greta Heinrich.

It was then when Anton finally made the decision to sell the Steinhoff Auction House to Frederick Huntsman, his associate, as well as his entire inventory. He then put the majority of his assets in a bank in the principality of Monaco, twenty kilometers from Nice, France. Monaco was known for its financial secrecy, something that perfectly suited Anton's dealings. He spent the last month recruiting men from an underground anti-Nazi group to help plan and execute Alejandra's escape from Kaiser's home in Bavaria to Milan, Italy.

As she considered Anton's explanations, Alejandra had many more questions, but at that point the only factor of significance was that she was free and would soon be back home with her family. She reproached herself for having shown weakness and losing her strength and faith in the last days of her confinement. So now, the thought of reuniting with her family filled her with joy. She had a second chance at happiness. But why hadn't Richard tried to contact her? Why had he not been the one to rescue her? Had he given up on her? He did say once he would not tolerate another long separation. Had he grown weary of her absence? And how could she blame him? She had tested his patience one too many times and felt increasingly depressed at the possibility of losing his love forever. But perhaps she had lost him a long time ago when she aimed so high. Was it all worth it? And where were Hannah and Joseph? Anton had completely avoided the topic of their whereabouts.

Now, with a clear mind, Alejandra wondered if she had avoided inquiring about Hannah and her family out of fear that something was wrong, as if by not talking about it she didn't have to face the truth. For the last two months dreams and thoughts about Hannah's well-being had crept into her consciousness, but she had always rejected them, convincing herself she would see Hannah playing that favorite melody of hers—Adagio in G Minor, by Tomaso Albinoni—on her cello. For a moment, she listened to the music in her mind, and tears ran down her cheeks. A feeling of sorrow overcame her because she sensed that Hannah was gone.

She then opened her brown canvas suitcase that Anton had brought with him. Sorting through her clothes, she selected a lavender colored knitted dress. She found a small box containing her personal correspondence that Anton had kept after her disappearance. She quickly poured its contents out on the bedspread, feeling desperate to find a letter or a telegram from Richard, but she found nothing. Among the correspondence, she found a letter dated October 26, 1938 from Octavio Fuentes Medina, the chargé d'affaires of the Mexican consulate in Vienna, Austria, the same diplomat she had met in Vienna several years before. The letter now came from an address in Marseille, France, and it had come through the Mexican consulate in Berlin. She tore it open and read it:

Dear Alejandra: I hope this letter finds you in good health and every-thing is well with your family and your endeavors. Please accept my apologies for not replying earlier to your letter dated August 12, 1938. As you know, world affairs and borders are changing before our eyes, and diplomats are being discharged, replaced, or relocated to new lo-cations at an ever-faster rate as situations on the ground are constantly changing.

Hitler's forces have occupied Austria and Czechoslovakia's Sudeten-land, and European nations met to discuss the future of the European continent. Some wish to proceed through appeasement, but even that has no certainty of success. Italy is a fascist state under Mussolini, the Soviet Union under Stalin and the Red army is undergoing its own great purge of political dissidents, Spain is in the midst of a violent civil war, and China and Japan are at war once again. The rest of the world awaits the outcome while crafting policies to address these conflicts. Who will end up on the right side of history? God only knows.

I have been reassigned to the Mexican consulate in Marseille, as we await the new consul general, who I'm told will carry out our gov-ernment's policies aiding refugees from across Europe, who have been caught in the current chaos spreading throughout the region. We need all the help we can get, as vast numbers of refugees are pouring into France and Switzerland. I'm now in a position to aid your German friends by providing them visas to travel to Mexico. From there they will reach safe haven no doubt.

I hope you can accompany your friends to France, because as pleased as I am to help them, I have something to request from you. It is so delicate, it can only be discussed in person. You are the only one that can assist me with this matter of extreme consequence. Please be safe. Sincerely, Octavio Fuentes Medina – Chargé d'affaires, Mexican con-sulate, Marseille, France.

She realized there would be much more struggle ahead, maybe not for her, but for thousands of others whose suffering would be so much greater. So what did Fuentes want from her? She wasn't sure she could help any-one, since she almost didn't make it through herself. She sighed, knowing it would be possible to go to Marseille, for it was about a three-hour train ride from Nice, her next destination. But that would mean postponing her trip back home. Would she even want to do that? And what was *this matter of extreme consequence?*

At midday, Alejandra emerged from her self-imposed seclusion. When she entered the drawing room of the Italian home, the afternoon sunlight highlighted Anton's profile, and she was glad at the sight of him, as if she was seeing him through new eyes. He was hunched over a desk writing something. Anton soon noticed she was leaning against a pillar, observing him.

"How are you feeling?" he asked, walking up to her.

"You tell me," she said.

"Tell you what?" he asked, holding her hand. "Haven't I said enough? I hope you'll forgive my poor judgment. You know that I'd never do anything to hurt you."

"I believe you. I can see it in your eyes, but I still have more questions. Although, I'm not ready to face the answers, just yet," she said. "Can we take a walk? I need fresh air. I want to feel the freedom to go anywhere, and I want to go to the cathedral. You have no idea what I was planning on doing had you not rescued me." She wanted to thank God for her freedom and to pray for those who intervened in some capacity on her behalf to give her liberty—Anton, Isolde, and Sophia. But mostly she wanted to ask for God's forgiveness for having lost her faith.

"I don't need to know," he said, grabbing her coat from the closet. As he helped her, she took her white silk scarf from the pocket and wrapped it around her face, tying it below her chin. "Let's go."

At nightfall, they returned to the villa, which was now bathed in earthen shades of white, cream, and brown. Floor lamps with fringed golden shades lit the room, exuding comfort.

For the first time in a very long time she allowed herself to drink two glasses of wine over dinner, as if the effects could numb the emotions of doubt and grief she was feeling. She felt tired, weak, and vulnerable, but she was ready to face the truth no matter how painful. After taking off her shoes, she fell into the twilled-woven upholstered sofa. The room was a little cold, and she unfolded a woolen blanket and covered her legs. Then she leaned backward, resting and listening to the crackling of the fire that Anton had just started in the rustic fireplace.

"Can I get you anything?"

She shook her head.

He too slumped onto the sofa. "There's something you must know," he started to say, but she interrupted. "Wait, I have some things to ask you first, although by your silence I think I already know the answer. Where's Hannah and Joseph?"

He took her hand. "Hanna didn't make it," he said solemnly. "Her son is missing."

She knew that in her heart, but with his confirmation tears began to flow.

"I'm so sorry. I wished things would have turned out differently," he said.

She sat there sobbing softly for some time. When she was able to calm herself, she whispered, "How?"

"Unfairly. Like so many others, she was killed by the Nazis, but her body was never recovered. And there's no trace of Joseph."

"Perhaps we didn't do enough to save them," she said.

"We did everything we could. Some things are beyond our control," he said.

"I felt it," she said. "I wrote her a letter during my captivity telling her how much I missed her and how much she meant to me. That night, I saw her in a dream. We were walking together through a forest and she said, 'Don't cry for me. I'll see you again when it's your time.' I woke up shaking and sobbing uncontrollably. I knew she was dead, but I never truly permitted myself to admit it. That's why I didn't ask you yesterday, because I knew the answer. And if I didn't hear it then it wouldn't be real."

"She was a good person who loved to make us laugh," Anton added. "It's going to take some time for Ben to come to terms with it."

"And Ben?" she asked.

"Ben stayed with me, waiting to hear news of his son. I went back to Austria to the home of Ben's relatives, but no one there knew anything. Somehow, I think he might have survived, but I don't know what else to do. In October, Ben left to go back home, but I know he first went to see Richard to tell him what happened, and he had also sent him a letter about a week after you were kidnapped."

She looked away for a moment and wiped the tears from her face with her fingers. "Did Richard ever contact you? Did he go to Berlin?"

"As far as I know he did not. Ále, I'm so sorry."

She felt such heartbreak upon hearing his words. Had Richard stopped loving her? Because she had never stopped loving him. How was it possible that in so many months he had not called, or sent a telegram, or a letter? How after learning she had been abducted, he hadn't come to her aid? She could rationalize that under the circumstances it was for the best that the children had their father. On some level, she could understand his desertion, but this was one of those times she could not change how she felt—anger, sadness, regret, and an overall feeling of devastation. His abandonment was more painful than being in captivity all those months. For the only thing that had kept her going was the thought of being with Richard and her children again. She was certain she had given her best in all situations and of herself to all those she loved, but perhaps not in equal measure.

She started crying again. "Have you spoken to Ben since he left?"

"No. I left Berlin the evening of the eighth of November, a day before Kristallnacht. I was warned by an acquaintance, a German officer, that my house had been targeted by the Gestapo and would likely be vandalized and ransacked along with many others in the city. But please don't ask me to explain that now. Besides, I'm not sure there's an explanation. It's all too insane for words. To tell you the truth, since you were abducted, I haven't cared about anything else but finding you."

She remained silent.

"Not having you for all these years has been demoralizing, but the thought of you dying was unbearable," Anton said. "I lived in agony, blaming myself for putting you at risk, and I promised myself to do everything in my power to bring you back safe." He paused. "And we're not even out of the woods yet. Getting out of Milan may not be as easy as getting in."

"Why not?"

"I didn't want to tell you, but I'm certain that by now Günther has alerted the Gestapo of my escape, and has labeled me as a traitor," Anton said. "He knows everything about me, and once he has had time to come to terms with our escape, he's going to do everything to seek revenge. He's a very vindictive man who doesn't like to lose. They have strong allies here in Milan, which puts us in enemy territory. So perhaps tomorrow you should go without me to the American embassy to seek asylum. You know they won't take me."

"That might be the logical thing to do, and it would guarantee my safety," Alejandra said. "But how can I leave you to an unknown fate after what you've done for me? So, no, we're going together to Nice. I know it's safe there, as I heard Günther speaking that France had come to a peaceful agreement with Germany. And besides, don't you already have some type of visa from when you went there to open your bank accounts?"

"Yes, I did. But that was only a thirty-day visa, so it has expired," Anton said. "For all I know the Gestapo might have also contacted the French embassy here."

"If we could only get to Marseille," she said.

"Why Marseille?" he asked.

"Do you recall Octavio Fuentes from the Mexican consulate? He's now there. In a letter he sent me, he asked for my assistance in a delicate matter. But more importantly is that he offered to provide you with the necessary documents to leave Europe."

"I doubt I can even get that far. But what are you saying?" Anton asked. "What about going back home?"

"I don't know what will happen, and as you've said before, too many things are beyond our control, but I'm ready to face whatever plans God has for me," she said. "I doubted Him once before, and I won't do it again. As far as my family goes, I love my children with all my heart, and I hope to see them soon. And Richard, well, he abandoned me. Not a word from him in all this time. I know things are disruptive everywhere, but surely we should have some news from Richard by now. He did warn me once that he would not tolerate another long separation. Maybe I'm insecure with everything that's happened, but his abandonment hurts me beyond any words I can express. My heart is shattered." Her voice began to break. "I don't blame him, for it was me who failed him, and I must live with that. I've tried to do my best, and it wasn't enough."

He squeezed her hand, and she rose to her feet and walked to a window. He followed her, putting his hands on her shoulders, and she turned to him.

"You've touched so many lives. I'll love you for as long as I'm on this earth," he said.

She held his gaze knowing that nothing else mattered but the man before her who had risked everything to save her life and who had shown the kind of love that had only grown over time.

"You saved my soul, and I'm indebted to you," she said, thinking she could no longer deny she had feelings for him, but was it friendship, gratitude, or love? They had shared a wealth of experiences that had brought them together in moments of bliss but also despair. If in the future, he, or she, or they both perished in the unstable world in which they were living, they had a special bond that would carry them through their final sojourn.

Anton brushed away strands of hair from her face and drew Alejandra closer to him, kissing her damp eyelids and then her lips. She kissed him back with tenderness and love, emotions she had been holding back, and finally let go.

They looked longingly at each other until Anton broke the spell. "Do you know how many times I've dreamed about this moment? To have you in my arms and to have you be mine? I have always loved you." He surrounded her with his arms, and she trembled at his touch. At that forsaken moment of her life, she desperately needed to feel his unconditional love.

A glowing moonlight shone through the window as they made love in full surrender.

The next day, she was awakened by the sound of Anton's voice. "Ále, my angel, last night was the happiest day of my life. I did not think it was possible to be in heaven, and my heart is bursting with joy and love for you." His fingertips traced the outline of her lips. Then, she pulled the covers over her bare chest and straightened herself with her back to the headboard.

She smiled, running her fingers through his hair. He moved closer to her, and she felt his entire body lining up next to her. A mild scent of patchouli emanated from his nude body as he leaned toward her, kissing her on her neck and collar bone.

"I don't want to ever leave you. I wish we could stay here forever," he said, taking a folded note from the nightstand. "A poem from Mörike to my beloved. You remember? The poetry that delighted us on that first day we met."

"Yes. It's the poem you never had the chance to read to me. Will you now?" she asked, closing her eyes and feeling his gentle caress and the morning sun on her face. She curved her body toward him and spread her hand across his chest. In a low and rhythmic tone he read:

"An die Geliebte, To my Beloved: Veiled in your flesh, angelic life shines through, Whose gentle sighing breath I seem to hear when speechlessly, as if in sacred fear, I gaze upon your face, and ever new, such joy fulfills me. Can it be in you? My puzzle smile still wonders if a mere dream has deceived my heart, that now, that here, my boldest wish, my only wish, comes true? Oh then from deep to deep I plunge, I sense the darkness of The Godhead, where from far the streams of destiny are murmuring. Melodiously: dazed, I look up, the immense night is smiling, and from every star a music shines, I kneel to hear them sing."

And so, Alejandra fell once again into Anton's passionate enchantment that slowly pulled her toward his will, as she no longer wanted to resist.

NABUCCO

December 27, 1938

Later that morning, they went to the French embassy, and they were successful in procuring a transit visa for Alejandra, although as expected not for Anton. Yet he had made the decision to travel to Nice, France, hoping that once they were in that territory he could seek refugee status. He assured Alejandra that such a course of action would be preferable to remaining in Italy, where it would be just a matter of time before he would be captured and turned over to the Gestapo. In the American embassy, they confronted the same problem—he was denied a visa. There, she attempted to call her family in the United States with no success, so she sent them a telegram.

When they left the American embassy, after midday, the mountain air felt cold but refreshing at the same time. Alejandra's gloved hands were inside the pockets of her camel coat, and Anton, with a long overcoat and black gloves, was by her side. They walked vigorously and came upon Palazzo della Ragione, and something of note caught Alejandra's attention—a relief of Oldrado da Tresseno. She remembered this image from a book she had seen and briefly read earlier in the villa. Oldrado da Tresseno had been a prosecutor of Cathar heretics back in the Middle Ages. She sighed, for only a week ago she might have been considered a heretic herself for contemplating suicide and going against Catholic doctrine. It was something she would never understand about herself—how low she had fallen. What happened to the faithful and God-fearing woman that she was? It was only by God's intervention, she believed, that she was saved, but not entirely, for she had now broken her marriage vows.

Anton asked, "Are you all right?" How could she tell him what she was thinking? But she didn't regret that she had consumed his love; it was like drinking and bathing in fresh water after being immensely thirsty and near death in the desert.

"I'm just taking it all in. So much to process, you understand?" she said.

"Yes, I do. I know you," Anton said, placing his arm around her shoulders and kissing her on the head, protectively. It was a strange sensation for her, and everything that had happened recently came into clear focus. Her life seemed to be taking a new direction, but it felt as though the events were dictating the course, and she was not in control. But did she want to be? No, not now. Richard had abandoned her, and that fact alone was constantly on her mind. Yesterday and today she had ceased trying to be perfect, and she felt free to do as she pleased. And if that was a sin, so be it.

As they made their way toward Piazza del Duomo, she noticed a post-Christmas market. "Let's take a look," she said. Walking past several stands, she glanced at the merchandise being sold, from baked goods, like panettone, to handmade embroideries, to jewelry. She stopped at a table with religious icons and picked up a four-inch wooden statue of St. Ambrose, Milan's patron saint. She asked the young sales woman with long black hair and covered up in layers of colorful clothes, "Who was St. Ambrose?"

"He was a man of great knowledge and influence and was also the patron saint of beekeepers and beggars," the woman said.

Then a man of similar age, who was seated next to the woman, added, "He's best known for coining the phrase 'When in Rome, do as the Romans do.' He advocated for liturgical plasticity."

She laughed at his curious comment. "Now that's something I've never heard… liturgical plasticity? And that's exactly what I need. I'd like to buy it, please," Alejandra said, paying the amount noted on the figurine. The woman wrapped the object and placed it in a paper bag. "Grazie." She put it away in her handbag, turning to Anton. "Something of faith to carry with me should I come across more trying times. Perhaps it is now I who's lost my moral compass."

"Not you," he said. "You've gone through extraordinary circumstances that would change anyone and make you question everything. But I do like, even more, who you are when you're with me."

"You do have a strong pull on me now, don't you know?" she said.

In a playful tone, he said, "It was about time. So, I was thinking of taking you this afternoon to one of the greatest opera venues. Is that something you would like to do?"

With a reserved smile, she said, "Teatro alla Scala. All that seems so inconsequential now. How I once dreamed to be at the podium conducting *La Traviata* or *Madame Butterfly*, but today I only want to be a spectator from a back row. The music is the only thing that remains constant in my life, so yes."

"And how about lunch first at Caffé Motta?" he asked. "It's just across the street."

"I'm not very hungry these days, but a cup of hot chocolate sounds good."

Later that afternoon, they went inside the neoclassical building of Teatro alla Scala. Anton convinced the guard, a young man by the name of Francesco, to let them in by telling him Alejandra was a conductor who had studied under Arturo Toscanini, and she would be in Milan for only that day. The guard led them through opulent halls filled with paintings and Christmas decorations to the first tier of boxes from where she had a direct view of a rehearsal in progress. Alejandra scanned the theater that, while it was inaugurated on August 3, 1778, had changed considerably since its renovation in 1907 according to Francesco. Beautifully lit with electric lights that replaced oil lamps, the theater was as spectacular as she had imagined it with almost two thousand red velvet seats and gold leaf accents everywhere.

She examined the stage where the conductor, the orchestra composed of sixty musicians, and a fifty-two-voice chorus rehearsed for a New Year's performance. The chorus was singing *Nabucco* by Giuseppe Verdi—one of Ben's favorites, as she recalled with sadness. It was the opera that established the composer firmly in the genre, and it debuted in this very theater in 1842. This opera was not simply an opera telling the biblical story of the plight and persecution of the Jews and their subsequent exile by the Babylonian King Nabucco from their homeland. It was also a story relevant to current times. How distressing that something that had been written many years ago, based on an ancient story, could be repeating itself in the twentieth century. She thought of Hannah and Joseph and teared up again. Was humankind destined to repeat the same mistakes indefinitely?

Then the chorus began to sing *"Va pensiero, sull'ali dorate."* Of course, it was a coincidence that she would be hearing that particular opera at that particular time in her life. Was this a sign that there was something she could do to assist Ben in finding Joseph? Hadn't music always spoken to her? Melodies and words had come forth in the most unforeseen and mysterious ways. She listened carefully to the words echoing in the hall: *"Hasten thoughts on golden wings. Hasten and rest on the densely wooded hills, where warm and fragrant and soft are the gentle breezes of our native land! O, my homeland, so beautiful and lost! O memories, so dear and yet so deadly! Rekindle the memories of our hearts, and speak of the times gone by! Or, like the fateful Solomon, draw a lament of raw sound; or permit the Lord to inspire us."*

When they left Teatro alla Scala, she was in a state of renewed inspiration. It was now dusk, and the sky above had a slight tint of purple. As they walked back into town, near their villa, Piazza del Duomo was radiantly lit with post lamps and a twenty-foot Christmas tree. Street performers, mimes, and harlequins, danced as they played a scene of the Quattro Moschettieri—a comedy series of the time. She liked the sound of laughter and the music of mandolins and high-pitched voices, adding a carnival ambience.

"Let's watch for a moment. This is like a beautiful dream."

"Anything you want," Anton said. "It is me who, now, wishes that time would stand still like it is at this very moment."

It was six o'clock at night on the next day when Alejandra, in a navy-blue suit, waited in the parlor of the villa for Anton who, wanting to avoid any potential setbacks, had gone to the Milan train station to purchase their tickets in advance to travel to Nice.

Shortly after, he returned, dressed in woolen trousers, a white shirt, leather jacket, overcoat, and a wool blend newsboy cap. He was trying to look like anyone other than someone hunted by the Nazis, he had told her. "A taxi is waiting." He gave her a letter-sized sealed envelope. "This is just a precaution, should anything happen to me. The documents in here will give you power of attorney to dispose of my bank accounts as you see fit. I've also included the hotel accommodations, and I've written a letter explaining everything."

"Nothing is going to happen," she said with a hopeful smile, wanting to reassure Anton. But inside, she felt afraid and wished they didn't have to go. It was all so risky.

The reality had now set in.

"Please, take it. I need to know I did something right," Anton said.

She took the envelope and put it away inside her travel handbag.

He placed the key to his black Mercedes on the cocktail table. "The car I leave to my friend, Giovanni Scarlatti, an art dealer, who so generously let us stay here at much risk to himself. We must go."

Alejandra put on her overcoat and wrapped her white silk scarf over her head, tying it loosely. Before leaving the villa, Anton held Alejandra in his arms for a long embrace and kissed her passionately. The taste of his lips lingered in her mouth. She felt as though they were one.

"I am so completely in love with you, and letting you go will be the hardest thing I'll ever have to do," Anton said.

"You won't have to," she said.

"Whatever happens, no one will ever be able to take away from me what you've given me these three days. I never knew what infinite love was until now," Anton said. Then he picked up his violin case and two suitcases and carried them outside where the taxi driver loaded them into the vehicle. And they left.

After the taxi dropped them off in front of the Stazione Centrale di Milano, a classical two-storied building with pillars and three large arched entrances, Alejandra took her suitcase, and Anton picked up his suitcase and violin. They made their way through the crowded and noisy station and onto the second floor where their train was to depart to Nice at seven o'clock. The station was huge, but soon she spotted their train. Entering through the nearest door, they stepped inside it, finding their private compartment in first class. He placed all the luggage on metal shelves above their seats and sat next to Alejandra who was by the window.

He sighed. "I think we're safe now."

She forced a smile thinking they were not safe at all. In fact, ever since her abduction, she was suspicious of everything and everyone and obsessively aware of every sound around her. She would never be the same.

Ten minutes before departure, a young man dressed in a dark-gray uniform tapped on their door. *"Biglietti por favore."*

Anton, with his hands shaking nervously, handed him the tickets.

The Italian man stared at both of them.

"Your documents, please."

Anton handed their passports to the man, who then looked at each of their pictures and said, "You're German, and what business do you have in Nice? You're not fleeing, are you?"

Anton grinned uneasily. "Of course not, I'm accompanying my friend. She's returning home to the United States, and it's not safe for women to travel alone these days."

"Excuse me for a moment," the man said.

When he left, Alejandra watched Anton's face go pale.

"They must have already been alerted." He took Alejandra's quivering hand. "You knew this was something that could happen. You mustn't say a word on my behalf. There's nothing you can do. You must save yourself."

"No. I can't," she said.

"Ále, don't be afraid for me. If we're meant to be together we will. You have your own destiny to follow, and as you have told me many times, life begins and ends with God's will."

"I might have said that, but of late, I'm not sure anymore. Why do you believe that now?"

"I often took the wrong path devoid of faith. I've been saved more than once. After you went missing, I held on to that prayer book you gave me in the hospital. So why not believe in miracles and something greater than ourselves. It's all we've got, isn't it?" He kissed her hand.

The officer returned with two policemen by his side. He handed Alejandra her passport.

"Mr. Everhardt, you'll not be able to accompany your friend after all. You're wanted for treason by the Gestapo. Come with us and don't resist. We don't want to hurt you," he said.

Alejandra covered her mouth, but Anton was right, what could she do other than to also put her own life in danger.

Anton, with a gentle smile and an expression of resignation stood, and mouthed, "I'll always love you." Then he left with the Italian police.

From the window, Alejandra saw Anton being turned over into the custody of two men who wore civilian clothes. One of the men was about to handcuff him, but Anton struck him in the face and turned to run away. But after running only a short distance, the other man took out his pistol and shot him in the back. Anton collapsed to the ground.

From her compartment, Alejandra screamed, "No! No! Anton," just as she heard the whistle of the train as it started to move forward in slow motion. She stood up, yelling with her hand pressed to the window as she looked at Anton's motionless body, surrounded by several men. Soon, the scene disappeared from her view as the train pulled away from the platform. Feeling cold, dizzy, and unable to breathe, she finally let out a loud shriek. "Ah. You can't be dead!" With unbearable heartbreak, she started crying so loudly she caught the attention of the woman in the next compartment, who came running to her, "*Stai bene, signora.*"

"No," she replied.

"*Per favore siediti.*" The woman tried to help her to sit down. "*Calmati, calmati.*" But Alejandra now felt numbed and weak as if all the blood in her body had suddenly been drained from her, and she fainted, falling to the floor.

When Alejandra regained consciousness, several hours later, the train was stopped in Genoa. Her throat was dry, and she felt a sharp pain and a bump on the right side of her head. The man who had asked for her documents earlier that night came into her compartment. "Signora. Would you like to get off here? There's a hospital nearby," he said. "You hurt yourself badly."

"No. I need to get to Nice. Water please," she said.

"*Un momento per favore,*" he said.

As she waited, she turned to the window. It was dark, except for scattered flashing lights. Several people, holding suitcases, were stepping onto the train. Then the Italian man returned with a glass of water, which she drank in its entirety. "If you need anything, there's always someone attending in the restaurant at the other end." She nodded.

Images of Anton being shot and collapsing surfaced in her mind, and she remembered everything that had happened. She whispered, "Where are you, my love?" She was now in a calmer state, but the pain in her head was too intense. The train moved slowly at first, then as it gained speed it settled into a steady pattern, and the city lights vanished in the distance.

From her travel bag, she took the envelope Anton had given her and tore it open. There were several documents. She took the letter first, hoping his words would bring meaning and succor.

December 28, 1938 - Åle my star, the most courageous woman I have ever known. If you're reading this letter it is because we shall never see each other again, and I may not live to see another sunrise or sunset. But know my love for you kept me living, dreaming, and believing until my last breath.

She was crying so intensely that her eyes became blurred, and she had to stop momentarily.

Don't weep for me or have any regrets, and don't look back for a second. From this moment on, remember me in the form of the wind caressing your face, and in the morning's sunlight awakening you each day. I shall kiss you with raindrops and embrace you with the fullness of willow branches. May canopies of lilac and golden blossoms brighten your days, and skies of sparkling blue and magenta bring peace to your nightly dreams. I've made many mistakes along the way, for which I must now pay, but I hope the wealth I once possessed can serve to give hope and happiness to those who deserve a gentler life away from the wretchedness spreading across these lands. Trust your instincts. You will know what to do. As I've said before, providence will be on your side. I have understood too late that a man's high moral character defines his legacy and not what he amasses in treasures or accolades.

Someday amidst the heavenly clouds, we shall be together again to play the music of angels for all eternity. Let these be my final words, bis wir uns wieder treffen meine Geliebte, Anton Everhardt."

Until we meet again she repeated to herself as she put away Anton's letter, replaying his words over and over in her mind, words so deeply felt but that could not mend her broken heart.

W ith her eyes fixed on the Mediterranean Sea, powerful, desolate, but strikingly beautiful, Alejandra felt as though her life could slip away at any moment. Slip away without warning and in one last breath, or in her sleep with no one by her side to give her last rights. Since Milan, she had been crying intermittently throughout the journey to Nice when she thought of never seeing Anton again. She felt another loss. She thought of Richard, and if it was a sin to have loved two men... so be it. Everything was now out in the open just like that implacable sea before her. How did she get to this point? Life was unpredictable, but it always was, except before she thought she was in control. But no more.

In the early hours of December 29, she heard a soft tap on the door of her two-room suite at the Belle-Époque Hotel Hermitage in Monaco. She had taken a taxi from the Nice train station to that principality. With her hair down, dressed in a laced silk robe, the color of the sea, and barefooted, she let in the physician who had been summoned on her behalf.

"Dr. Gustave Moreau at your service, madam," he said, at the door.

She greeted a thin man in a suit, short in height with light brown hair and holding a doctor's bag. "Thank you for coming." She led him to the seating area of the suite and pointed for him to sit on a teal velvet sofa.

"I was told you fainted and suffered severe trauma to the head. Is that correct?" he asked.

"Yes. And since then my head is spinning, and it hurts badly," she said.

"May I examine you?"

She nodded.

Dr. Moreau first took her pulse and blood pressure. Then he examined her head, feeling a swelling on the right side of her skull. "You have a concussion, and it's going to take some time for those cells in your brain to heal." From his bag, he gave her Nyalgesic, a bottle of liquid analgesic for the headaches. "The medicine should help with the pain and to sleep. However, call me immediately if you develop other symptoms like blurred vision and more severe headaches. For that might signal hemorrhaging in the brain, and that could be fatal. I'm sorry to warn you of those potential complications. The next forty-eight hours are crucial."

"Yes. This is what I was afraid of. My husband, you see, is a physician too." She paused, feeling strange in saying it as if she didn't have a right to. "I've heard from him too many similar cases to count. But I do appreciate your honesty."

"Then you also know you must take it easy and avoid unnecessary stress and travel," the doctor said. "And most importantly, get some rest."

"You're asking something impossible for me to do. But I'll do my best," she said.

When he left, she took a spoonful of the analgesic, hoping the headache would subside and allow her to make a telephone call to contact her family. It would be midnight back home, but if she waited, she might not be in a condition to call her family later. Of course, they would want to know where she was, no matter what the hour. She had been missing for four months.

A few minutes later, she was in the lobby of the hotel, which was nearly empty except for two men who were drinking coffee and reading the newspaper. She approached a middle-aged man who was standing behind a counter in the reception area wearing a black suit. "How may I help you, Mrs. Morrison?"

She handed him a piece of paper. "I'd like you to connect me to this number in the United States, please."

"Right away, madam. I'll put the call through, and for your privacy there are two telephone booths around the corner. Your call will be in the one next to the elevator."

"I appreciate it," she said, before making her way to the booth.

Once there, she waited a few minutes until the telephone rang. She picked it up, and at the other end of the receiver was her mother, Lydia. "Oh? Mother!" she exclaimed. "At last, I hear your voice. I'm at the Hotel Hermitage in Monaco, and not well. I've been through hell. There's so much to tell you, but it will have to wait. How are the children?"

As she listened, her mother said they were not in the best of spirits because both their parents had not returned for Christmas as Richard had promised them. They were ignorant about their mother's abduction, but the oldest daughter, Leidy, sensed there was more to the story and was very worried to the point of often being sick and missing school.

"What do you mean both parents gone?" Alejandra's heart almost stopped beating when Lydia told her Richard had left at the end of October for Berlin, as soon as he found out she had been abducted. He attempted to contact Anton, and had been to the American embassy there, without success. Lydia spoke with Richard on November ninth. Then, after not hearing from him in days, Lydia contacted Ben, who later contacted someone in the government. In early December, staff from that embassy reported that Dr. Richard Morrison had been detained at a prison in Berlin, awaiting trial. He was charged with being an American spy who was working with Anton Everhardt, and who was wanted for treason for being a member of the Resistance.

Overwhelmed by the news, she felt as though her knees would buckle, and with her head spinning again, Alejandra said, "Mother, I feel terrible for everything that's happened, and Anton may be dead. It's all very complicated, and the report about Richard is untrue. I can't explain it now, but please tell the children I love them and hope to be home soon. I must call Ben, take care of other matters, and find a way to return to Berlin to see Richard. We both know he doesn't have a chance if false evidence is presented without any kind of legal defense. There's no justice. Please, pray for us. I'll call you tomorrow." Her mother tried to continue the conversation, but Alejandra said, "I'm sorry, but I do have to go. I love you."

She managed to get back to her room. There were too many complications that must be dealt with, and she was not sure of the outcome. She envisioned her three children. Would they be orphaned? Richard was now fighting for his life because of her choices, right or wrong, and the injustice of others. Her family was suffering, and she begged for their clemency. She must have hope, for if she had survived until now, with so much misery around her, it had to be for some divine reason. It was easy to have faith when everything was perfect in life. Was she being tested again? She took the little statue of St. Ambrose from a side table, spread the palm of her right hand against her broken heart, and prayed for the safety of her children and all those she loved.

Another journey was just beginning in a dangerous world. This time, she would have to confront it alone. Alejandra summoned all her inner strength, pleading to the Almighty for guidance, grace, and for the chance to live another day.

THE END

APPENDIX

A SYMPHONY OF RIVALS
Links to various chapter title's musical selections are available at
www.RomaStocks.com/music/

Part I

Part II

Chant, Ruth Crawford Seeger
The Lord's my Shepherd, Jessie Seymour Irvine
Two Sacred Works for Treble Voices, Maria Francesca Nascinbeni
Drei Gemischten ch ö re, Clara Schumann
In Dulci Jubilo, In Sweet Rejoicing, Heinrich Seuse
Chapter 35 – Concerto for Piano and Orchestra No. 4, Ludwig van Beethoven
Chapter 36 – Thine Be the Glory, Edmond Budry and George Frideric Handel
Chapter 37 – Toccata and Fugue in D Minor, Johann Sebastian Bach
Chapter 38 – Violin Concerto in D Major, Pyotr Ilyich Tchaikovsky
Chapter 39 – Sonata No. 15, Ludwig van Beethoven
Chapter 40 – Abscheulicher Aria, From Fidelio, Ludwig van Beethoven
Chapter 41 – Fidelio Overture, Ludwig van Beethoven
Symphony No. 9, Ode to Joy, Ludwig van Beethoven and Friedrich Schiller (Lyrics)
Chapter 42 – Violin Sonata in G Minor, John Sebastian Bach
Chapter 43 – Fantasia for Piano in G Minor, Ludwig van Beethoven
Chapter 44 – Music, Maestro, Please, Herb Magidson and Allie Wrubel A.
Sing, Sing, Sing, Louis Prima
Chapter 45 – 15 Variations and Fugue, Ludwig van Beethoven
Sonata No. 5 for Piano in F major, Ludwig van Beethoven
Carmina Burana, Carl Orff (Music) Students of the Clergy (Verses)
Chapter 46 – Jewish Prayer, Ernest Bloch
Chapter 47 – Clair de Lune, Claude Debussy
Chapter 48 – La Campanella, Franz Liszt
Chapter 49 – Quasi una Fantasia, First Movement, Ludwig van Beethoven
Chapter 50 – The Consecration of the House, Ludwig van Beethoven
Chapter 51 – Moonlight Sonata, Third Movement, Ludwig van Beethoven
Chapter 52 – Adagio in G Minor, Tomas Albinoni
Chapter 53 – Nabucco, Giuseppe Verdi
Va pensiero, sull'ali dorate, Giuseppe Verdi

ACKNOWLEDGEMENTS

Beyond Beethoven's musical genius was his love of humanity, expressed through his music, but also in his words. Beethoven's contribution is so compelling worldwide that I decided to make it an integral part of *A Symphony of Rivals* as a way to distinguish opposing ideologies during a devastating period in history. Is music transcendental? I believe so.

Like *A Song in My Heart*, my first novel, *A Symphony of Rivals* manifests my commitment to bring forth the contributions of all cultures through the arts, especially music, as a bridge to better understanding and appreciation.

I would like to express my appreciation to Dr. Alexander B. White, whom I had the opportunity to interview in person. As a Holocaust survivor, on the Oskar Schindler list, White wrote the book, Be a Mensch, and his story and perspective inspired me. I also wish to acknowledge other authors whose non-fiction works were useful in my research for this novel including, Alejandro Anreus, Adèle Greeley, Robin Folgarait, Misha Aster, András Batta, Leonard Bernstein, Helmut Brenner, John Wiffen Burrows, Barry Cooper, Christina Williamson Elkins, Norman Lebrecht, Eduard Mörike, Ernest Newman, Lynn H. Nicholas, Karen Painter, Roppel S. Pinson, Joseph Schmidt-Görg, Harold Schonberg, John K. Sherman, Frederic Spotts, Barbara Steffen, Anna Suh, Giorgio Vasari, and Bruno Walter.

I'm grateful to have served over the past twenty years in various roles for organizations, including Film Society Minneapolis St. Paul, Friends of the Minnesota Orchestra, Intermedia Arts, MacPhail Center for Music, Minneapolis Institute of Art, Vocal Essence, and Walker Art Center. I am inspired by their missions, and the work they do to enrich our lives through art.

My gratitude to Philip Brunelle, Samuel Pascoe, and William Schrickel, and other notable conductors and musicians for sharing their experiences in the art of conducting. I'm forever thankful to those individuals who read early drafts of *A Symphony of Rivals* or provided me with vital feedback. Special thanks to Beatrice, Tom, Anissa, and Chris. My appreciation to family, friends, and all the readers who have supported the launching of *A Song in My Heart* and *A Symphony of Rivals*.

Thank you to Ian Graham Leask for his literary acumen, generous time in the craft of writing, and editing guidance. To John Currie, for his suggestions for the cover. And especially to Gary Lindberg, Rick Polad, Rachel Anderson, and the entire staff of Calumet Editions for their editing, design work, public relations, and bringing this historical novel into the world.

My deepest gratitude to God who makes all things possible.

ABOUT THE AUTHOR

Award-winning novelist and composer Roma Calatayud-Stocks holds degrees in Music and Psychology from the University of Minnesota, and she has studied creative writing at the University of St. Thomas.

Roma is the author of two historical novels *A Song in My Heart*, and *A Symphony of Rivals* and is currently working on the trilogy's third installment, *An Ode to Joy*. And in line with her life passion and commitment to bring forth the contributions of all cultures through the arts, Roma's narratives, set to music, provide a window to locations across the world while also addressing poignant issues, politics of the era, and history.

Roma has released two albums: "A Song in My Heart" and "Carnival of Life." With classical, jazz, and Latin musical influences, the albums showcase her original songs and instrumental compositions. She has toured the United States to present her work to universities, libraries, corporations, women's clubs and book fairs. A native of Mexico City, Roma now lives in Minneapolis with her husband, Tom.

For detailed book synopses, awards, reviews, media, music, upcoming events, or to contact Roma, please visit her website at www.RomaStocks.com or www.CalumetEditions.com.